# The Artifact of Foex

**James L. Wolf**

**ForbiddenFiction**
www.forbiddenfiction.com

an imprint of

**Fantastic Fiction Publishing**
www.fantasticfictionpublishing.com

**THE ARTIFACT OF FOEX**
A Forbidden Fiction book

Fantastic Fiction Publishing
Hayward, California



**CREDITS**
Editor: Lon Sarver, Derrick N. Davidson
Cover Design: Siolnatine
Cover Art: Original art by Natalya Nesterova
Production Editor: Erika L Firanc
Proofreading: Elizabeth A. Tanner, D.M. Atkins

SKU: JLW-000183-02 FFP
ISBN: 978-1-62234-281-5

Published in the United States of America

**"Knife sent me!" Chet choked out.**

The blade was reluctantly removed from his throat. Fenimore settled back onto the gurney, his snarl transformed into a wary frown. "Knife sent you?"

"He did." It was the truth, after all.

"He?" Fenimore raised the blade once again, his eyes so intent they seemed to burn.

*Oh, shit.* Anytime a Flame was not in visible sight, they were always assumed to be female. Chet couldn't remember where he'd learned the rule; he'd never needed to know it before. It was just one of those cultural things you learned by osmosis, like *never tease a doedicu*, which Chet knew even though he'd never seen one of the enormous, hump-backed animals outside a zoo.

"She, she!" he said hastily. The blade did not retreat. "Um, Knife said you were a rake and a scoundrel, and a, a libertine, and a liar, and a cheater, and not to trust anything you said!"

Fenimore lowered the blade with a snort. "She *would* say that," he murmured. "It's true, you know."

# Also recommended...

You may also enjoy these other ForbiddenFiction works:

**Counsel of the Wicked by Elizabeth A. Schechter**
Matthias has spent his whole life on the edge of a very small world. The bastard child of a fallen woman, his magical talents as still unseen, he's known nothing but judgment and hatred from the harsh, religious people of his enclave—except for Balthazar. The son and heir of the High Elder, Balthazar shows Matthias kindness, and love...and desire. When the High Elder discovers what his son has been doing, Matthias is arrested and sent to an isolated prison known simply as "The School". There, and in the wastelands beyond, Matthias learns the secrets behind the hypocrisies of the Council of Elders, and discovers his true heritage, true power, and true love. (M/M, F/M)
http://forbiddenfiction.com/story/es1-1-000222/

**Spidermilk by Konrad Hartmann**
Eddie Stover, private eye, lives in a future where artificial humans called LifeMates serve consumers as a purchasable commodity. When Stover takes a wandering daughter case, the search for the missing woman plunges him into a world of hijacked LifeMates, psychadellic milk, and a bizarre spider-worshiping cult. As the thrall of his old addictions and the enticements of the woman he promised to protect threaten to consume him, Stover is faced with the realization that he cannot escape the choice love forces him to make. (M/F, F/F)
http://forbiddenfiction.com/story/es1-1-000222/

# DISCLAIMER

This book is a work of fiction which contains explicit erotic content; it is intended for mature readers. Do not read this if it's not legal for you.

All the characters, locations and events herein are fictional. While elements of existing locations or historical characters or events may be used fictitiously, any resemblance to actual people, places or events is coincidental.

This story is not intended to be used as an instruction manual. It may contain descriptions of erotic acts that are immoral, illegal, or unsafe. Do not take the events in this story as proof of the plausibility or safety of any particular practice.

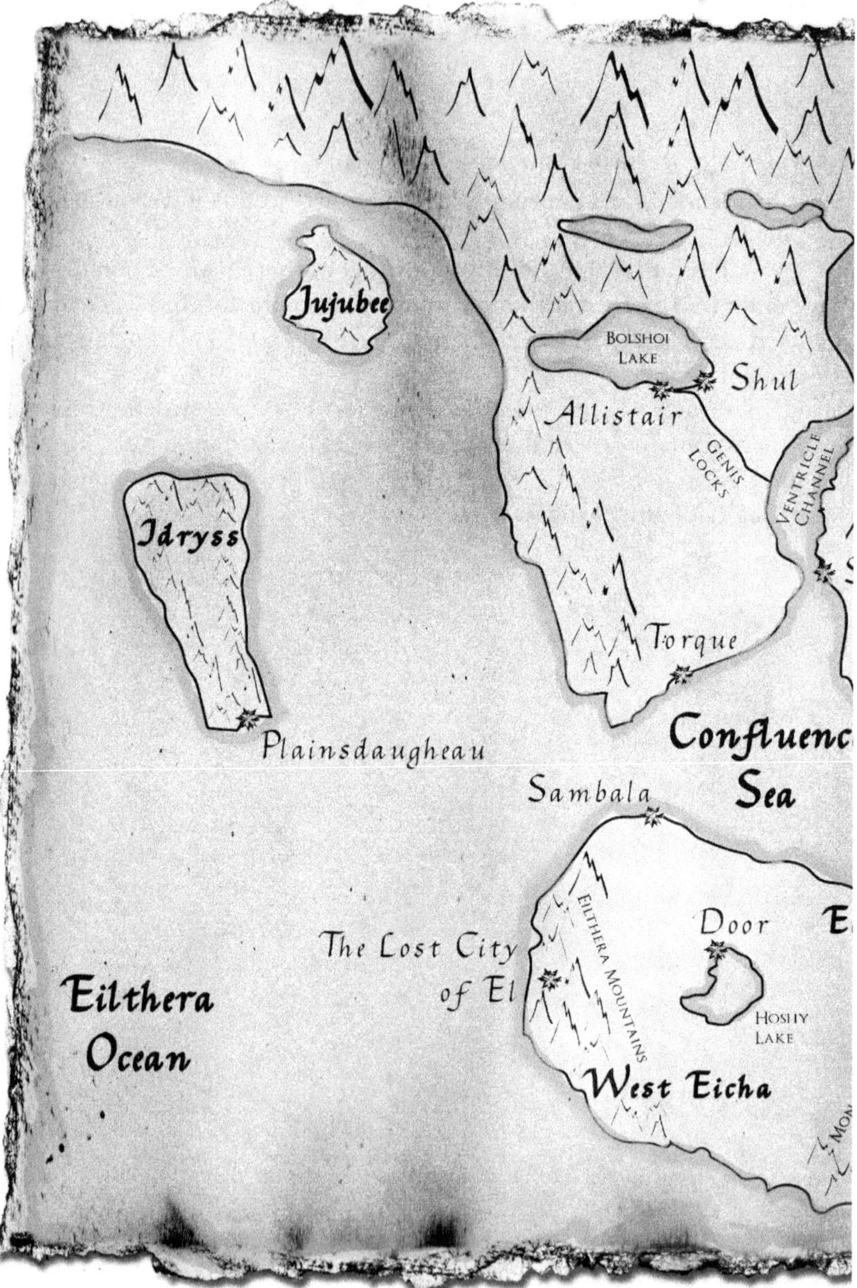
Jujubee
Bolshoi Lake
Shul
Allistair
Genis Locks
Ventricle Channel
Idryss
Torque
Plainsdaugheau
Confluence Sea
Sambala
Door
The Lost City of El
Eilthera Mountains
Hoshy Lake
Eilthera Ocean
West Eicha

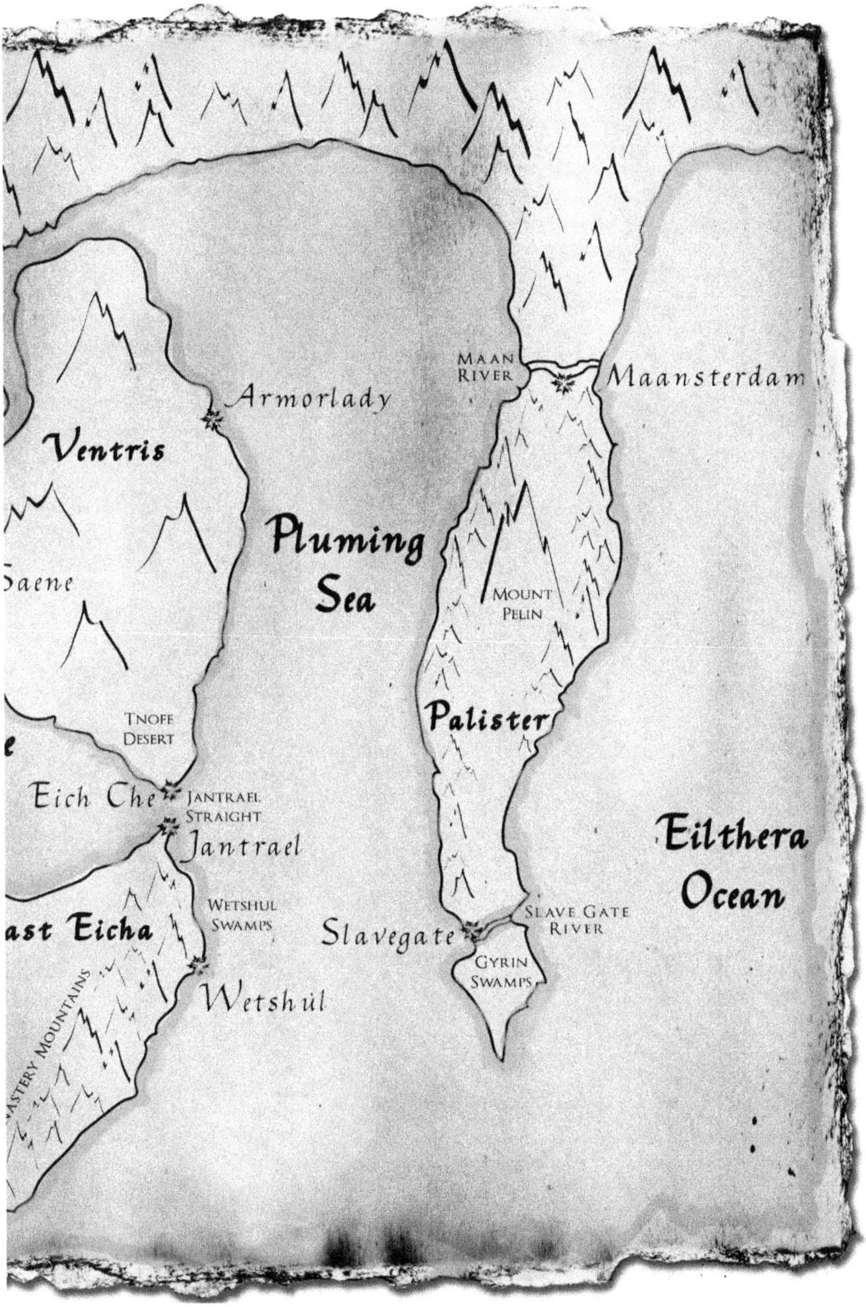

Maan River

Maansterdam

Armorlady

Ventris

Pluming Sea

Saene

Mount Pelin

Tnofe Desert

Palister

Eich Che

Jantrael Straight

Jantrael

Eilthera Ocean

Wetshul Swamps

ast Eicha

Slavegate

Slave Gate River

Gyrin Swamps

Wetshül

NASTERY MOUNTAINS

# Contents

# Chapter 1
# Lusting After the Past

Chet concentrated on pit 214, his miniature mattock grimy from sweat and dust. He was glad that the equipment was the same shape—if not size and composition—of the ancient farming tool. He loved the way the mattock's form and name connected him with the past.

Chet was less enamored with their current work site. It was dusty, both hot and humid, under direct sunlight of the poppy-colored sky. Also, it was far too close to a rumbling construction zone. Every single one of Professor Veyaon Tibbet's graduate students had accompanied him to the Lucid Mud dig site, and Chet was no exception. He coughed and lifted the kerchief covering his mouth to spit, aiming away from where he was digging. The last thing he wanted was actual mud in his dirt.

"Oh, brother. Take a look at that piece of work," Von Sampson murmured from pit 216. From his tone, Chet knew that his feckless colleague was not referring to a find. Chet followed his gaze and nearly dropped the miniature mattock.

Professor Tibbets, wearing his usual tweed suit—completely inappropriate for the Wetshul summer—was leading a lady onto the dig site. The woman was serene and elegant, her lines flawless. She was of the flaxen race—a citrus-yellow skin tone—with the usual red hair and almond-shaped eyes. Flaxen was the most prolific race on the Eicha continent, including Chet himself and most of his peers.

Pantheon, she was gorgeous.

Chet immediately decided that she'd be at home in any historical time period. His mind's eye dressed her: perhaps she would shine in the garb of ancient Tache, with its elaborate skirts and wigs. Maybe she would be splendid in Crimson Era leathers and fur. His groin tightened at the thought. Despite his meandering fancy, she was plainly a modern-day woman. She wore white gloves, and her purse matched her high-heeled shoes. Her dress was ample with crinoline petticoats peeking out just below her knees. A real lady. Her hair was cropped in the most modern of fashions, and her cat's eye glasses were tinted in respect to the sun.

Of course, Von Sampson wasn't interested in her clothing. "Nice stems. And those *tits*."

"Quite the bone structure," Wiggler said from pit 239. He should know, being the resident osteology expert.

"Put your eyes back in your head, boys," Rory growled from pit 224. "You especially, Chet Baikson."

The graduate students around him were making noises and comments more like primary-school students, all along the lines of, "*Oooo*, you're bustedddd."

Chet dropped his gaze back to the dust. It wasn't as if he and Rory were still dating, not since their amicable break up last week, but he still valued her opinion. Dating Rory had made Chet feel very uncomfortable, and he'd been relieved after breaking up with her. It wasn't that he didn't like her—he did!—but he'd felt so self-conscious. Rory's status as a Shadow Dancer made him cringe. Then again, every one of Professor Tibbet's graduate students was a god affiliate... save himself.

Few people on Uos doubted the existence of the Pantheon of gods. There was no question of belief or faith when it came to powerful, long-lived beings that radiated energy like a nuclear-hot zone. Few in numbers, they tended to stay on the God Plain. Ancient humans had thought it an ethereal place, but these days rational people considered it a different dimension. Close to the physical reality of Uos but not of it. Distance was a good thing. Personally, Chet hated the idea of beings that could crush you with a look; he wanted no truck with the Pantheon. Nor their political system, family squabbles, incest, back stabbing or dynastic power struggles. Nothing.

Well... maybe a few of the gods were okay. But the one Chet really liked was dead, alas.

"Hey, want to get some water at the pavilion?" Rory said as she wandered over to his pit, wiping her grimy face with a handkerchief. It didn't make much difference. Rory was of the bistre race, a brown skin tone so dark she almost looked purple.

As usual, Chet was awed by her beauty. He always wondered what a girl like her had ever seen in a guy like him. "Maybe later."

"Suit yourself." She looked like she wanted to say more, her mouth tight as she walked away.

This was ridiculous. He wanted her so much, and by all signs she liked him right back, but he always felt crushed by her intense superiority, both racial and affiliate wise. Rory was something by birth that Chet had chosen never to become: a god affiliate. It was a symbiotic relationship. The god granted their chosen humans powers, and thus gained numerous allies on Uos. Freakish, terrifying, dangerous, powerful, and politically savvy, it could be said that affiliates ruled Uos like monarchical regents of ancient times. Not quite god, not quite human. Chet knew that Shadow Dancers—the type of god affiliate Rory was—were often portrayed as devious spies who could become invisible, but he'd never seen her fade from view. Never asked her to demonstrate.

Maybe he was a coward at heart.

It was a good theory. Rory was out of his league in every way possible, and even if she'd never acknowledged it out loud, it was true. Everyone knew it. Chet had nothing to offer her; he was just a guy. The worst part was that she hadn't deserved his self doubts or fear cast upon her. Strict friendship was less fraught.

"Chet, come here please," Professor Tibbets called from his spot by the mystery woman.

Chet grinned, instantly heartened by the professor's choice and confidence. "Looks like I'm nominated," he said in Von Sampson's direction as he vaulted out of the pit. That was the nice thing about Professor Tibbets. He chose Chet for duties regardless of the fact that he was unaffiliated, not like *some* professors.

Upon closer inspection, the mystery woman was just as breathtaking. Chet felt his groin rise to half mast as he drew close. Hopefully, no one would notice.

Professor Tibbets was speaking to her *sotto voce*. "Perhaps male would have been the better choice to avoid attention."

"Now that I'm here, I think you're right. I haven't been to Wetshul in over a century. Didn't realize it was still this bad," she said, her perfectly formed lips frowning.

*A century?* Chet blinked. He arrived beside them and smiled expectantly.

Professor Tibbets turned to him. "Chet, this is Journey. She is my honored guest and a historical expert with practical experience in the time periods we've been studying. I'm putting you in charge of Journey's needs while she's with us. For now, please give her an overview of the site."

"Certainly, Professor. Ma'am, this way?"

Chet caught a whiff of her scent as she turned his way. To his horror, his groin tightened further, not quite fully erect but close to it. He could have sworn she wasn't wearing perfume. Not the sort that most women wore, anyway. He coughed—his throat dusty—and made a sweeping gesture of the dig.

"This site is the first of its kind this century and certainly the first in Eastern Eicha. It's very exciting. The only reason we haven't gotten much press yet is we just started. You know Professor Tibbets—have you read his papers? Do you know of his theories about this kind of dirt? It's what they used to call lucid mud..."

"Of course I know what it is. Lucid mud in liquid form used to churn throughout Uos, rising and falling through the inner layers of the planet. It's a preservative. Sometimes people used lucid mud as a dump but not often. In the old days, we always believed it churned everything down to the center of the Abyss, where the mother of gods herself resided. No one wanted to throw garbage onto Aerora. We were a superstitious lot, eh?"

He shot her a surprised look. She didn't *look* like she was smart, but Journey had hit the nail on the head. Professor Tibbets had said she had "practical experience"—meaning she wasn't an academic? "We always believed" seemed bizarre, though it matched the "centuries" comment. Journey seemed to think she was hundreds of years old.

Well, that would be practical experience, wouldn't it? With a name like that, she was probably a god affiliate of some stripe, but he couldn't tell which one. Her normal—if glamorous—appearance didn't match any god affiliate he could think of off the top of his head. Was she dangerous, like some affiliates? Would she hurt him? Tibbets seemed to trust her, anyway.

Chet decided to stick with strict academic fact. "As you say, lucid mud is a preservative. A find of this kind is an archaeologist's dream. This site seemed to have solidified more than two-hundred years ago—around 7390—to judge by the top layer of finds. The cut-off date is unsurprising, given evidence in the literature. It is estimated that most lucid mud dried or disappeared around that time period. It is believed the mud trap was here before Wetshul was founded during Resoan's millennia, 5262, which gives us a historical cross-section of over two-thousand years."

"Mmm, lucid mud isn't all gone. There's still an active system beneath Allistair, you know. Quite the churning river of lucid mud."

"What?" Chet stopped cold and stared at her. "You're kidding!"

"Not at all. You just have to know where to find it. They lost quite a few workers when they built the sewage system beneath the city-state. They're still down there somewhere, I'm sure. Sleeping—we can only hope they're unconscious rather than awake—and completely unchanged."

"Oh." Chet realized that his foot was hovering in air; he set it down on solid ground. The idea of people falling into lucid mud was well established in historic literature. However, the idea that victims didn't die—that they were in some kind of hibernation mode and could be reanimated—was viewed by most academics as little more than superstition. Journey seemed to fall into the superstition camp. "Um, in any case, let me show you some of what we've found."

Journey took in the processing pavilion with serene confidence. Chet soon learned that Professor Tibbets hadn't been exaggerating: her grasp of history was excellent. She was able to positively identify every object, whole or broken, laid out on the folding tables, including a few that hadn't been cleaned yet. She instantly identified the broken fragment of a chew stick—precursor to the toothbrush—that had given Rory such difficulty last week. Listening to her speak was an education in itself. Chet was growing more impressed by the minute. He couldn't help but wish she'd teach a class at the university. He would have fallen deeply in love with her as an undergraduate or even now.

And yet... was it a trick of some sort? Was she really a genius, the way she seemed, or was his head just foggy with lust for her?

As they exited the pavilion and headed toward the active dig site, he said, "Have you ever given thought to teaching at Semaphore University, ma'am?"

Journey chuckled low in her throat. "Even if I were inclined to do so, I'm afraid they wouldn't have me."

"What? Why not?" That seemed outrageous. Women could be associate professors in the Philapo University System. They weren't as prestigious or well paid as the regular professors, but they could still *teach*.

"For the same reason I haven't been back to Wetshul in ages." Her perfect lips tightened. "The Literati are quite specific as to their methods and structures. Professor Tibbets is a rarity among Literati, you know. I've always found him a kind and understanding soul."

"Yes, I know," Chet said automatically. The Literati—affiliates of the god Philapo—dominated the academic world.

As they passed among the pits, Journey stopped to inspect an upside-down pair of boots that were still half buried in the ground. "Tache-style stitching," she said, her voice suddenly hesitant. "Why hasn't someone pulled them out of the ground, yet? Are they... still attached to something?"

Chet shrugged—the boots were unexceptional—and instead pointed out some of the larger objects they were in the process of extracting. Case in point was the artisanal grandfather clock with heavenly bodies etched in copper. It was three-quarters extracted, the lower part still lodged in dust. Chet knew the university would probably sell it after cataloguing. It was beautifully preserved and not historically important. The same went for the complete carriage, the back end of which was sticking out of the ground at a forty-five degree angle.

Journey eyed the carriage door with amusement. "Ah, a Cerémente-style window latch, named after the inventor. The part must have been imported from Maansterdam around 7310 or so. Was the door open when you uncovered it?"

"I believe so." There was something about the carriage that gave

Chet the creeps. A strange reaction for such a mundane item. When he'd first helped uncover it, he could have sworn he'd seen it before.

"No bodies found inside, right? They must have jumped out before the whole carriage went down in mud. Have you found the ceros or ceroses, yet?"

"We haven't gotten that far." Chet knew his colleagues were looking forward to inspecting the remains of any horned beasts-of-burden that may have been hitched to the carriage. The angle at which the carriage had gone down indicated *something* heavy had dragged it down, anyway.

"You may want to get their heads unearthed sooner rather than later. They'll still be alive."

Chet couldn't help but roll his eyes. To his embarrassment, Journey caught the gesture; instead of looking angry, she smirked. As if she knew better? Abysmal god affiliates. So full of themselves.

Journey poked her head inside the carriage with an air of mild curiosity. "The individual who owned this had slaves. See the specialized ring screwed in here, to clip a slave collar to? Another Ceremente patented invention. The original owner may have been from Maansterdam, was affiliated as a Merchant, or both."

"Hey, Chet, look at this!" Rory called out, running toward him with something cradled in her hand. "Linley just found it in pit 198."

Journey climbed out of the carriage, and they both inspected tiny object in Rory's hand. It was an anuro, a flying reptile with a blunt beak. A common enough animal, completely unremarkable, except the preserving power of lucid mud seemed to have saved it from decomposition. The anuro was still covered in dust, but Chet thought it would be of the red-tipped variety once clean. He touched it and nearly jumped. He'd expected the anuro to be mummified and leathery, but instead it was soft and—warm? Chet stared at it, then looked up at Journey.

Naw. Couldn't be. Could it?

Journey chuckled at his reaction. "Want to see a trick? Miss, I notice that you have a canteen. Pour water over the anuro—especially in its mouth—and watch what happens."

Rory gave Journey a strange look, but handed the anuro corpse to Chet and unslung her canteen. Journey took a step back when Rory popped the cork. Chet frowned at Journey. Was she expecting this experiment to be dangerous? Rory poured a trickle of sun-warmed water on the body. Sure enough, the anuro turned out to be of the red-tipped variety once the dust washed away.

"Tip some water into its mouth," Journey said again.

Rory did so, and the anuro stirred in his hands. Chet jerked, repressing the desire to drop the moving creature.

"So it's true," Rory whispered, covering her mouth. "My ancestors were right."

Journey shot her a sharp look. "Ah, a Shadow Dancer. Great, more complications," she muttered under her breath.

Chet glanced at her, startled, then staring at the reptile stirring in his hand. It blinked and meeped softly, struggled upright, its tiny claws pinching his palm.

Rory laughed and stroked the anuro with her fingertip. "I can't believe it. I just can't believe it. The current layer of that pit dates back to 7280. Which means this little fellow's been asleep exactly three-hundred twenty six years."

The anuro spread its wings and swiftly launched into the air. Chet yelped, closing his hand too late. "Shit!"

"Relax," Journey said. "Let it go."

"But—but..."

"There's more where that came from." She nodded at the dig site. For some reason, she looked grim at the implication of finding more living things under the lucid mud.

Chet rubbed his treacherous hands together, hating how he'd accidentally let the living relic go. Journey was probably right, but still. Inexplicable longing filled him. History had literally slipped through his fingers; he couldn't hold onto it, couldn't cage it. But then he often felt that way about the past.

Dinner was a lively affair at the house where Professor Tibbets and his graduate students had taken up residence for the summer. The house's owner, Associate-Professor Clementina Golub, was due to show up tomorrow. She and Professor Tibbets were co-sponsors of this dig; occupation of her Wetshul house had been part of the bargain. Though her home was palatial, Chet wasn't looking forward to Professor Clementina's arrival.

He'd first encountered Clementina as an undergraduate. It had been his first semester, and he'd admittedly been a strutting, cocksure, self-absorbed guy with more book knowledge than common sense, but Clementina hadn't needed to be so *mean*. Her introductory class had been the only course he'd failed in his life. She'd ripped up Chet's term paper to his face, smiling all the while. He'd been so proud of that paper. When he'd switched graduate studies from law to archeology, Clementina had been the only reason he'd hesitated.

It was a shame, too. She taught some of the most intriguing classes at Semaphore. A world-renown scholar, she was widely published and praised. Well, he'd never really wanted to know much about Tache history. Really. Even though he spoke the language and loved the culture.

Journey supped with them. Von Sampson topped off her wineglass and tried to engage her in what he probably thought was cunning wit. His dirty jokes about the mobile brothels, a veritable fleet of specially marked vans throughout Wetshul, were anything but subtle. Von Sampson even had the audacity to hint how many prostitution vans he himself had visited since their arrival in the city. Journey did not encourage this train of thought and—to Chet's relief—Professor Tibbets snagged hold of the conversation, bringing it back to more classical matters. Journey's knowledge base was once again trotted out and, predictably, stunned the table. Chet watched his fellow graduate students grow engaged at her detailed grasp of everything from the roots of words to Pantheon political struggles. Just as he, himself, was thoroughly engrossed.

Only Rory held back as others debated and questioned, her eyes narrow. She studied Journey with the air of a skeptic at a stage-magic show. Chet raised his eyebrows at her, curious what his girlfriend—his, um, former girlfriend—was thinking, but Rory didn't meet his gaze.

She finally leaned forward during dessert. "Excuse me, Journey. May I ask what you do for a living?"

"I act on the stage in Eich Che."

"Ah. You know, I'm from Eich Che. I understand that competition for acting jobs is really tough at home. Are you any good at it?"

Journey quirked an ironic smile, though her eyes were wary. "I make a decent living. I'm currently scheduled to play Julian in a modern version of *Syche Twins* for the Basalt Stage House. Production begins next week. When Veyaon—your professor, here—asked me to fly down to observe this remarkable dig site, I knew I had a little time, which is why I'm here."

"Julian is a man's role," Rory observed, her voice tight. She acted like she didn't believe Journey, somehow, as if Journey was pulling a fast one, scamming them. Rory didn't like deception—she'd made that perfectly clear to Chet when they'd been going out together.

"It is," Journey confirmed readily. She was watching Rory closely. In fact, the two women seemed to be having a staring contest across the table.

"Are you Flame?"

Dead silence. The whole table seemed to hold its breath. Chet felt his eyes bulge out of his head at the thought. He glanced around and found the other graduate students were having similar reactions. They looked like men stuffed by a taxidermist. Flame were god affiliates, shapeshifters notorious for their sexual peccadilloes and dastardly ways. They could be any gender they chose, any race. Chet could, off the top of his head, think of at least three classical epics that featured Flame villains.

Journey sighed and glanced at Professor Tibbets, who spread his hands as if to say, *It's up to you.* Journey reached up and swept off her... her wig. She removed the holding cap, too. She was completely bald beneath it. The mark of a Flame.

# Chapter 2
# Flame and Find

Chet felt the blood drain from his face. Reactions up and down the table varied, but most people leaned away, as if being Flame was something they could catch. Von Sampson even scooted his chair back from the table. Though shocked, Chet was surprised at his colleague's disgust. He'd thought Von Sampson would love to pursue a Flame, not run from the possibility. It seemed not. Perhaps the fact that Flame could—and did, if rumors were true—change sex made a difference to Von Sampson. Chet didn't blame him.

Professor Tibbets gestured amicably. "Come now, come now. We're all friends here. Most of us are affiliated to Philapo, and of course Rory is bound to the goddess Aiena. Our gods are members of the Tutelary Party; by the gods' grace, all of us at this table are political allies. The goddess Pelin and her Flame affiliates are on our side. Why should the opinion of unaffiliated idiots matter to us? No offense, Chet."

"None taken, sir." In the company of god affiliates, someone *always* made a comment like that once a day. At least Professor Tibbets didn't mean it.

Chet tried to figure out how he felt about Journey being Flame. He'd never met a Flame before and certainly hadn't expected to find one here. Wetshul had been a primary hub of slavery back in the old days, when the nearby continent Palister had been emptied of native coteries and their Flame leaders. No one would want to live where their forerunners had been boxed, masked, and chained.

Her affiliation might hold the answer to one of his most pressing questions, though. Chet eyed Journey with new curiosity, swallowing his knee-jerk prejudice in favor of a more scholarly attitude. "Pardon me, but in *An Epic of Eicha* and *The Foex Chronicles*, there are claims that Flame reincarnate over and over again at the behest of Pelin. Are you—I mean, have you..."

Journey shot him a grateful, amused glance. Lack of hair did not change her femininity one bit, he noted, though it still felt shocking to be confronted by an intensely feminine woman with a bald head. She really could be an actress—or, um, an actor. "Yes, I'm one of Pelin's older souls. Not the oldest, though, not by far."

"You're being modest, my dear. Journey is a member of the Flame Council, also known as the Council of Six," Professor Tibbets put in, his habitual after-supper glass of aran in hand. Chet eyed it longingly. He loved the popular, licorice-flavored alcohol, but he dared not tap Professor Clementina's supply. He didn't want to draw her negative attention—or attention at all—in any way.

Tibbets continued, "Tell them what that means, Journey."

Chet noticed that Rory had stiffened, her nostrils flared. Journey, however, rubbed her face with tips of her fingers. "Oh, Veyaon. Must I?"

"Of course you don't. But it might help them understand why I asked you here."

"The Flame Council is the internal regulatory body among the Flame. We do not have a hierarchy, but we do need to order ourselves. Anarchy is not a helpful system when you want consensus-based decision making."

"No, no," Professor Tibbets interrupted, waving his free hand. "Not the deadly dull parts. Tell them about when you were first initiated to Pelin."

"Ah, I see what you're driving at. Very well. The Council of Six is by definition comprised of some of the oldest reincarnating souls that Pelin keeps in her stable, so to speak. My colleague Doyen Quor is nearly the oldest of us, originally born in Foex 980, as the Pantheon count the millennia. I'm a youngster by comparison: my first life began in Resoan 198."

Murmurs rose up and down the table; people whispered to one another, their eyes wide. Chet sat back and did the math. It wasn't easy unless one had the Pantheon calendar memorized, which he did, though he hated how egotistical the thing was. At the end of each millennium, the Pantheon voted on which one of them had made the biggest impact during those thousand years. Whichever god won had the millennium named after them. Chet couldn't help but feel it was a pissing contest, and resented having to acknowledge Pantheon members while studying historic facts that had nothing to do with them. His opinion wasn't shared by many: popular culture mavens loved contesting which god would own the current millennia, the 7000s. Personally, Chet didn't care. But he did care that Journey could remember over 2400 years of history. More than two thousand years!

He tucked his chin, feeling vulnerable for no reason he could discern. "That's why you know so much about what we're digging up at the site. You lived during those times."

"That's right." The nod she gave him was a shade more respectful.

Chet wasn't sure he wanted her respect, but... she'd originally been born in Resoan 198. Maybe should could tell him what it had been like back then. During the days he wished he'd been alive.

People were rising from their seats. The student on dishes duty was gathering the used plates and spoons, signaling the end of the meal. Usually they lingered in the large living room and well-appointed library. Tonight, however, people drifted back to their rooms. It was an unorganized, unofficial retreat.

Chet followed Journey and Professor Tibbets into the living room, hoping to learn more, but Rory beat him to the punch. As everyone maneuvered through the hallway, she leaned close to Journey and muttered, "Why are you *really* here?"

"You heard the professor," Journey said brightly.

Rory scowled, but she refrained from saying more—more of what?—as Tibbets turned to say, "Please forgive my students, Journey. They'll come around. Eventually."

"Not a problem. You could say I'm used to it."

"Nevertheless, it's a shame that..." Tibbets paused as the doorbell rang.

Chet, who was closest to the front hall, ducked out to answer it. A tall, rail-thin man stood there. He was bistre colored, like Rory, and wore a neat suit. The sort of man who looked like he'd be at home with a mixed drink on the rocks, though the only item in his hand was a small suitcase. His pressed suit trousers were tucked into wicked-looking boots: knee-high leather, brown with decorative stitching. Alert to the possibilities, Chet studied his head. Beneath his tweed cap there were no sideburns or stubble. He was bald. Just like Journey.

"Knife!" Journey cried out from behind him. She leapt into his arms, and he swung her around, laughing. They giggled like school children and kissed. It was a friendly, warm, intimate kiss.

Chet looked away, his face hot. His groin tightened again.

"You came," Journey continued. "I didn't know if you would come."

"Yes, well, I got your message." The new Flame looked sober and didn't say more.

Journey ushered him inside and introduced him around. Knife was well named, Chet decided—he looked like a weapon, all sharp edges and keen glances. Nothing wasted in that spare figure. He was clearly unconcerned about local views. Though his head was covered, he wore no wig.

Journey was bubbling on, her whole face animated. "Knife is another member of the Council of Six, professor. He also knows something about what's buried under all that dust."

"Splendid, splendid," Tibbets said, warm and welcoming as always.

Rory, however, looked sullen, even murderous. Chet had only seen her look that way once, when a fellow graduate student had edged her out on a pet project. Why did she seem to feel the Flame were infringing on her territory? She excused herself curtly and went upstairs.

Some hours later, Chet was coming out of the hall bathroom and was about to go upstairs himself when he noticed the two Flame whispering to one another near the staircase. They were speaking the language of Tache. Chet, who had learned the language at his father's insistence, eavesdropped shamelessly.

"... I figured he's your meat, or I'd leave them to it," Journey was saying.

"No, you were right to call me out. It *is* heartening that the Shadow Dancers are keeping an eye on the proceedings; a very good thing for us, all things considered. Have they found anything?"

"They're getting close. Tomorrow, I think, if we both pitch in. I wonder if that young woman will give us trouble. I hate not trusting our allies, but their failure was pretty spectacular last time."

The whispering stopped; they were both staring in his direction. Chet smiled blankly, as if he hadn't understood a word, and ascended the stairs. Whatever Knife meant, *something* was down in the dust. Something important to both the Flame and Rory's people. It seemed tomorrow would be interesting.

Chet woke with the salient question, *Which one?* Which pit would Journey and Knife volunteer to help dig? The carriage with its buried ceroses? The gaudy grandfather clock? More pertinent, however, was the tension between Journey and Rory. Chet trusted that Rory had good reason to be suspicious, and indeed, the Flame did seem to be up to something nefarious, or at least clandestine.

Alas, it was Rory's turn to drive their collective finds back up to the university. It was an hour's drive each way, with unloading and documenting to do besides. Chet regretted not seeing more fireworks between Rory and the Flame, or at least finding out more about her issue with them.

Rory cornered him after breakfast with a put-upon expression. "Could I trade shuttling duty with you? I should be at the dig site this morning."

"Why?"

"No reason."

"Then no thanks."

"Look, just trade with me! It matters."

Chet frowned. "If it really mattered, you'd tell me why. I just did it three days ago. Besides, Tibbets put *me* in charge of looking after Journey." He was afraid he sounded whiny, but he didn't want to miss out on the action. This was just too exciting. He felt like he'd fallen into a pulp novel filled with affiliate intrigue. Working on the find of the century was fun, sure, but it was also dull and monotonous. "Why were you were making scary eyes at the Flame last night, anyway? What do you think they're up to?"

"I can't tell you that." Rory crossed her arms tight, her expression thunderous. "It's none of your business. Besides, you wouldn't understand."

"Thanks a lot."

"Come on. You have to trade with me, Chet."

"Hey, we're not going out anymore. You can't lean on me for favors."

"I was asking as a friend," she hissed.

"You don't sound very friendly."

"Fine! You're nothing but a snotty, dull-witted ass."

He glared. "And you're a stuck-up affiliate who doesn't care about anything but your little political games."

"Screw you, Chet Baikson." Rory wasn't the kind of woman who flounced. Instead, she stalked away with the air of a predator denied a kill.

At the dig site, Chet hung back, hands behind his back, watching the two Flame intently. No one else was looking in their direction. The other students had avoided looking at or speaking to either Flame at breakfast. *Their loss,* Chet thought.

Journey was dressed more sensibly today, her makeup toned down. She had donned khakis and a broad-brimmed hat, though she still wore the wig. She smelled fantastic. Well, both Flame did, really. Chet had noticed the scent again this morning at breakfast, especially since the intensity was double what it had been before. Chet's involuntary, half-formed erections were becoming embarrassing. Somehow—he didn't know why—he was vaguely reminded of his friend and former roommate, Steve. Which was funny, because Steve was the exact opposite of sensual in every way.

Knife, too, was kitted out in heavy canvas clothing. His still looked dapper, though. Chet had a feeling he would look dapper while naked and covered with blood. He didn't know what Knife did for a living, but he couldn't quite see the Flame riding the train every morning to a desk job, then coming home to pot roast. Anyway, who would cook Knife a pot roast? He was *Flame*, a pervert and sexual deviant.

Idly, Chet wondered why both Flame had decided to keep the same faces as they'd had yesterday. Didn't shapeshifters shift their shape more often?

Both Flame chose flat-edged trowels from the tool table and wandered with seeming purposeless between dig areas. Chet grabbed a trowel and followed. To his surprise, they stopped at the upside-down pair of boots that Journey had commented on yesterday.

Knife stood beside the boots with a funny look on his face. In fact, he looked like a person who'd been kicked in the gut but was unwilling to show pain or cry. "It seems like yesterday."

"What seems like yesterday?" Chet asked, sidling up to the Flame, his trowel held loosely in hand. "May I join you two?"

The Flame met each others' eyes, and Journey shrugged. Chet could almost see her thinking, *He's harmless, might as well.* Knife nodded, and they all knelt down to get to work unearthing the rest of the boots.

After a minute of digging, Knife said, "So you'd like to hear the story, eh?"

"I would." Chet eyed him curiously. "This must be important or you wouldn't be here. Right?"

"Smart boy. Well..." Knife paused, then kept digging. "It started in Tache around 7305. Slavery had not yet come to the continent, and it was still good to be Flame. At the time, I was a courtier of then-Prince Konstantine."

"I've heard of him," Chet said. Professor Clementina taught a class each year on that period of Tache history. She was an internationally recognized expert on the Tache royal family. Chet hadn't taken it, of course, though he wished he had.

Knife shot him an impressed, respectful look. "We got word that an, ah, object of vast power had been found. I should say it had been found *again.* It was being pursued by a faction of powerful royal cousins who were set to oppose Konstantine's rule. I was dispatched along with a... colleague of mine, named Fenimore LaDaven, to track down the object and bring it to court."

Chet frowned in confusion. "I thought a courtier was like a fop. Someone who hung around royal courts while instigating intrigue and, um, having affairs."

Journey chuckled. "Knife does—or rather, did—those things too, but just to blend in."

"The same way I wear suits in these days. And play gentlemanly sports and read the newspaper on the train. To blend in." Knife paused in his digging and brushed dirt from their goal.

Chet was unsurprised to see that a pair of legs were attached to the boots. Whole, solid legs dressed in dusty trousers. Not skeletal legs.

Knife cleared his throat and spat into the dust behind him. "In any case, we tracked the royal cousins to the Jantrael Straight, where we lost them. By that point, we knew they had more in mind than just ruling Tache; in the tradition of insane Tache royalty throughout history, they wanted to rule the world. LaDaven and I split up. He and his most trusted servant headed for Wetshul, where the rainy season was in full swing, while I headed to Door. Needless to say, the object wasn't in Door. I returned home to Konstantine and was promptly collared into slavery. That was unpleasant but doesn't come into this story. However, it means I was never able to properly follow up."

Journey shot Knife a sharp look, but held her peace. Chet had the feeling she understood what Knife was really saying. Their relationship seemed odd: on the one hand, they clearly shared personal history. On the other, they'd probably experienced the same time periods, too. It was like they were a generational cohort, affected in different ways by the same events.

Knife continued, "It was only much later that I had the full tale from the servant. The royal cousins were near this lucid mud pit when LaDaven accosted them. He managed to kill them, but in the process he fell into the mud, going after the object which had apparently been tossed in first. LaDaven's servant said he couldn't save him."

There was something odd about the story, but Chet couldn't put his finger on it. As if he'd heard a different version years ago and forgotten it. Chet blinked and gazed at the legs; they'd now reached the thighs. "Wait. Are you telling me... is this... is *this* Fenimore LaDaven?"

"I believe so. If not, there's no harm in rescuing some poor fool trapped by mud."

Journey pursed her perfect lips. "I knew the story, and all of us on the Flame Council know about the object. We've been informed of its nature for some time. That's why I sent for Knife when the good professor invited me to Wetshul." She articulated the knees of the body. They swung readily, fully intact and working.

"Um. Okay. But does that mean..."

A ruckus from the edge of the dig site caught his attention, and Chet stopped digging. A sharp, two-packs-a-day kind of voice seemed to be raised in anger, booming across the dig site. He knew that voice. "Abyss," Chet groaned.

"What is it?" Journey said.

"Associate-Professor Clementina Golub. We call her Professor Clementina when we aren't calling her—other things."

Sure enough, Professor Clementina was striding down the grade, kicking up dust. She had a distinct presence. Though she was always dressed in the latest fashions, her face done up in heavy makeup, she always seemed to be bigger and taller than everyone else, even when she wasn't. Chet wasn't sure how she did it. Her shoulders were too broad, her voice too low. She seemed almost manly, though Professor Clementina herself would probably be appalled at the suggestion.

As if Chet would make suggestions to her.

Professor Tibbets followed her lead, his hands fluttering. "Journey is my honored guest, whom I invited to the dig site as a consultant. Her friend is welcome, too!"

"They are not welcome in any way. I will not have fire perverts degrading my dig." Clementina's voice resonated across the site.

Chet glanced down at the body, then removed his canvas outer shirt and draped it over the still form, still half buried in dust. He wasn't sure why he did it—it wasn't like he owed the Flame anything, let alone protection. And yet... he remembered that moment when Clementina had ripped his paper. She'd done it in front of the class, almost as a demonstration. Taking him down in the most humiliating way possible.

"Your father's money won't help you here," she had told him. "Get serious or go home."

He'd chosen to get serious. In a sense, she'd done him a favor, in a backwards way. But it still hurt. He didn't want to get caught by her again—especially not with a body.

What would the Flame do, anyway? Chet looked at them and did a double take. Both Flame were now of the fallow race, a light brown normally found in Tache. To match Clementina? Knife removed his hat, tossed it aside and drew himself to his full height—and then some. Journey seemed taller, too, her chest suddenly flatter. *Wait.* They really *were* growing taller. Shapeshifting in preparation to take on the striding, manly figure headed in their direction.

Clementina arrived at the pit with Tibbets, the other graduate students flitting over with the air of kids anticipating a fight in the school cafeteria. Clementina gave the Flame a long, slow, once-over look. Roasting them. To Chet's surprise, they both stood up to the treatment. Neither broke eye contact or tried to get a first word in. Masterful. Chet took a step back, holding his breath.

"You have no right to be here, invited guests or not. This is private property, and I own it outright. You are trespassing. Leave now." Clementina seemed obstinate and dangerous as a doedicu: a large, foul-tempered beast with armor and spikes.

"I'm so terribly sorry!" Professor Tibbets said. He was the most flustered of everyone, wringing his hands. Chet actually felt more sorry for him than he did the Flame, and they'd each flown across Uos to get here. Tibbets continued, "Perhaps I can make it up to you somehow..."

"It's all right, Professor," Journey said softly, but her eyes were on Clementina.

"We are simple observers." Knife's manner was more than calm, it was casual. Taking her measure? Chet noticed he'd suddenly acquired a subtle but pronounced Tache accent—same as Clementina herself. "What harm is there in letting us watch the dig of the century unfold?"

Clementina's face grew suffused. "Leave, or I'll call the police. Maybe I won't bother. There's a fire hose back at the pavilion, hooked up to the metropolitan water supply. What say I turn it on full blast and hose you both down? Like that, would you?"

Chet frowned, uncertain why it was a threat. It took him a beat to remember that Flame purportedly burned in water. On the outside, he assumed; Journey had drunk ice tea with supper last night. Indeed, Journey looked grim, and though Knife was still calm, he no longer seemed casual.

"What threat do you think we pose to the extent that you threaten us with deadly force?" Knife asked softly. Still feeling her out, trying to make her react? He had a sparkle in his eye as if he were enjoying himself.

Clementina reached into her dainty purse and withdrew a small, snub-nosed pistol with a mother-of-pearl inlaid handle, then pointed it at the Flame. "Get off my property. Now."

# Chapter 3
# Resurrection

The graduate students drew back, and even Tibbets took a step away from his colleague. Chet, too, shuffled backwards, trying to get out of the line of fire without being too obvious about it. He honestly didn't know whether Clementina would shoot the Flame. She was smiling, but that didn't mean anything.

To Chet's surprise, neither Flame moved. Knife slowly extracted a brown cigarette from his jacket pocket. It was odd, because Chet hadn't seen him smoke before. Knife lit it with a bronze lighter, then took a long, theatrical drag. "I wouldn't advise that," he said in a tone so low it was almost a whisper. Yet it carried. It locked the attention.

"Who would stop me? This is Wetshul, doedicu. No one cares whether Flame live or die here."

"Shoot us, and I pass on the favor. Surely you must realize that killing a Flame does not eliminate us entirely. Give me twenty or so years to reincarnate and grow up, and I'll come after you. And your kin. I know your family even now, Golub. I know your family like I know the back of my hand."

"It's true, you know. I've seen him do it," Journey put in with a shrug.

Chet stared. It had to be a bluff. Everyone—from Clementina and Tibbets on down—seemed befuddled by his statement. Some were probably skeptical because they didn't believe in reincarnation. The Flame had powers, sure, but they were also known as crafty tricksters. Tibbets, at least, understood Journey to be a practical authority on history, and he seemed as confused as the rest. Wondering how far Knife would take his bluff?

"I do not believe you know anything about me," Clementina said. "Prove it."

"Clementina Khal Golub, citizen identification number 392-9442e. You are the third daughter of Cyril and Vera. Cyril is balding man with a large belly, and your mother died last year of cancer." Knife blew out smoke, his whole body relaxed yet watchful. "You have three grown children. One is married, and I expect a grandchild will be on the way soon."

She looked genuinely shocked, and the students began whispering among themselves. Her grip on the gun wavered, and she put it away abruptly. "This is untoward."

Journey said, "Professor Clementina, I'm sure we can come to some reasonable agreement. We came here to help."

"Screw you. I'm still calling the police."

Clementina strode away, clearly shaken. Professor Tibbets gave the Flame a wild look before trotting after his colleague. Graduate students began drifting back to their assigned pits with many a backward glance in their direction. Knife quietly snubbed out the cigarette and pocketed the stub. At the same time, Journey uncovered the body, handing Chet his jacket back. Knife and Journey knelt and began digging again in earnest.

Their movements were so frantic that it took Chet a moment to realize they'd both returned to their original races, bistre for Knife and flaxen for Journey. Chet rubbed his eyes, his head hurting. Flame took some getting used to.

"We'd better hurry," Knife murmured to Journey in the Tache language, the same as they'd spoken last night. "Pantheon knows how deep the Raptus is buried."

How deep *what* was buried? Chet sat and began helping again. "How could you possibly know her family?" he asked in the same tongue.

"You understand?" Journey shot him a curious glance. "Funny, I had you pegged as a rich kid from Door."

Chet barked an ironic laugh, then covered his mouth, glancing around to see whether anyone was looking their way. Several were within clear earshot, even if no one was looking directly at them—probably the reason for the language shift. "I *am* a rich kid from Door.

But my father is a Merchant with international clients. He was also a collaborator during the war."

"I see." Journey wiped her brow with a handkerchief. The humidity was getting worse, Chet realized; it would thunder soon. Both Flame looked very uncomfortable.

"*Will* she call the police?" Journey asked Knife.

Knife shot her a dirty look. "Abyss if I know. I'm no Syche affiliate."

"How on Uos *did* you know all that stuff about her?" Chet said.

"I've been around. When I'm a guest in someone's house, I like to know a little about them. So, I snoop. Call it a habit. She has photo albums on the lower library shelves. Opened bills and letters in her study, and there's all sorts of other documentation in the house, too. My bedtime reading last night."

Chet stared at him, impressed. "That's not very ethical, you know."

"I notice that both Journey and I are still here, digging and not dead. Whether she calls the police is another story. Oh, *shit*," he added in an entirely different tone. "My suitcase is still in the house. I liked that suit, Pantheon curse it. Journey, your luggage is there, too, right?"

Journey nodded. She was crying, Chet noticed. Just a tear or two, no noise. She sniffed and wiped her eyes. "What just happened reminds me so much of the bad old days."

"Don't know if you've noticed, lovely one, but it's still the bad old days around here. Chet, can you get our stuff later?"

Chet nodded. "She'll destroy your things if she finds them. She's vengeful like that."

"Is it true that she owns this dig site?"

"Outright. She bought it from the city for a huge lump sum of money. They closed this spring, which is why we just started."

The Flame exchanged a significant look, then dug faster. They'd long ago reached the body's torso. Chet didn't want to accidentally hit—and damage—the hands, still covered in dust. There was movement from the corner of his eye, and he glanced up.

One of the younger graduate students was stepping between the pits and headed in their direction. He called, "Chet, do you mind if

I—oh, Pantheon. Oh, *Pantheon!* Look, everyone! A body! They're uncovering a human *body!*"

Journey rolled her eyes and sat back on her heels. "That's done it."

Knife shot Chet an exasperated look. "You've been digging here how long, and you haven't even found a body, yet?"

Chet shrugged, nonplussed.

Journey put in, "They haven't even found a live ceros yet. Told you they were going slow. Archaeologists, huh."

It became a mob scene. Graduate students gently tugged at the legs and discussed the style of clothing. Lively debate and more digging determined that the hands had to be above the body's head, like those of a diver. Fenimore LaDaven, Chet realized, hadn't fallen into the lucid mud—he'd dived. From the angle of the body, it hadn't been a shallow dive, either. Had it been a scramble, sheets of monsoon rain coming down and engulfing everything, even rational thought? He could imagine the scene so clearly... the dive was not the act of a timid man.

There were silences behind Knife's words, so many significant gaps. Chet wondered how many details had been left out for the sake of the story, and how many had been left out because of delicate information.

*Knife is a spy,* he thought abruptly. *And he's been a spy since forever.*

The graduate students uncovered the head, replete with lots of hair. The arms were still missing, shoulders clearly articulated above his head. A dive, indeed. The body still refused to be removed from the soil, as if it were stuck. Graduate students who normally spent hours—days, even weeks—uncovering artifacts, scrambled into action. Rope was found and tied to the body's ankles, then people formed a line as if they were in a contest at a country fair. Caught in the moment, no one pointed out how illogical their actions were. They tugged once, twice. Tthe body shot out of the ground as if pulled by the roots. Fenimore's arms were whole, Chet noticed thankfully. He had long, bony fingers, beautifully articulated.

"Get his mouth and nose clear," Journey called out.

No one was listening. Knife put two fingers in his mouth and whistled; Chet covered his ears reflexively. Silence followed. Knife opened his hand to Journey, who repeated herself and added, "He'll need to breathe."

"Breathe? *Breathe?* But he's *dead*," people murmured to one another, momentarily stunned.

Chet had to do something. "Someone get me water."

Water was found. Chet held his breath, eyes wide, as he washed LaDaven's exposed skin, then began trickling water into his open mouth. The moment stretched. In the breathless silence, Chet studied the man's face. Beneath the dust, Fenimore LaDaven was... Chet gulped. Beneath the dust, LaDaven was a romantic dream. His closed eyes were set wide apart with lashes a girl would envy. His mouth was full and sensual. An arrow-straight, aristocratic nose. He, too, was fallow skinned: the race of superiority and colonialism on Uos. Chet imagined his long hair, once clean, might be golden brown and puffy, like a cloud. Holding his limp body was extraordinary—though not precisely alive, it wasn't corpse-like either. Chet had never realized how beautiful a man could be.

No, that wasn't true. Chet had always admired men from ancient etchings, painted vases, marble statues and oil paintings. LaDaven *looked* like an oil painting. His bone structure was not of this century.

The body—twitched. Fenimore LaDaven coughed. Chet caught his breath, his eyes round.

He wasn't the only one. Everyone surrounding the twitching body was *reacting*. It was pandemonium. "He's alive!" people yelled. Students were running around in circles, bumping into one another and babbling nonsense, while others sat on the ground and hyperventilated, apparently overtaken by shock. Chet didn't move. He cradled LaDaven in his arms, overcome by emotion.

Professors Tibbets and Clementina arrived, along with the promised policeman. The officer had a bored, acerbic expression and seemed unimpressed with the dusty man in Chet's arms, but Tibbets and Clementina were immediately enveloped by the chaos. Fenimore LaDaven groaned, his eyes still closed. Chet almost forgot to breathe.

"Call an ambulance!" Tibbets said to the officer, his spindly arms flailing with enthusiasm.

Even Clementina seemed to have forgotten why the authorities had originally been summoned. She hovered right beside Chet, poking at LaDaven with a proprietary air. She probably felt that—this being the dig of the century taking place on her private property and all—the excitement should belong to her. Chet didn't want to be the one standing between Clementina and her, um, target. Despite a twinge of regret, Chet awkwardly handed off LaDaven's body to her and backed away. He joined the Flame at the back of the crowd, feeling glum as he brushed himself off.

"Medical intervention is entirely unnecessary," Journey said, arms crossed. The only reason Chet heard was because he was standing right beside her. "People have been surviving lucid mud for thousands of years."

She was ignored. In fact, both Flame were ignored, standing apart from the action. Curious, he studied their reactions. Journey was calm and watchful. But Knife... Chet thought he'd be cool as a cucumber, but the Flame was jittery, agitated. Knife nearly danced in place and jumped to see over heads, though he was currently over six feet tall.

Chet touched his arm, and Knife jerked around, startled. "Sorry," he said, shooting Chet a rueful grin. "I haven't seen Fenimore in three hundred years. I never got a proper chance to say goodbye."

When Knife had been telling his story, he'd referred to the man as *LaDaven*. Now he was *Fenimore?* It was as if... Chet frowned. Normally, he wouldn't have even thought they could be, um, involved. Two men and all. But Knife was *Flame,* a god affiliate known for being homophiles with bizarre sexual perversions beyond the knowledge of normal folk. Knife could become female, too, Chet realized abruptly. Neither Flame had changed sex yet, but it was what they were known for. Maybe Chet was seeing things where there were none. Maybe they'd just been friends.

The ambulance arrived just as the police left. More chaos ensued, spreading outwards like ripples in a pond. Fenimore's unconscious body was strapped down to a gurney and hauled up the dusty grade by ambulance techs. Chet's shoulders slumped, and he gazed at the ground. They were taking Fenimore away. He turned to find Knife watching him closely.

"You want to go with him, don't you?"

Chet nodded, ashamed for no reason he could discern. Of *course* he was fascinated by this potential glimpse into the past. The man was three hundred years old!

Knife assessed him with a measured look. "I would be there by Fenimore's side, but everyone at the hospital, from the secretaries to the chief physician, would bar my way. I'm Flame; I might as well be leper in their sterile ward. But *you* can go."

"But—"

"*Someone* has to ride with him in the ambulance. If you ask first, Tibbets might let you. Besides us, you're the only one here who knows anything about him. Ride with Fenimore. Answer his questions about this century. Don't leave him alone! And Chet... be careful. I'm only going to say this once, so listen closely. I'm fond of Fenimore LaDaven, but he is a scoundrel and a rake. He is a libertine who will lie, cheat and steal to meet his ends. He will swallow you whole if you let him. Do you understand?"

"No, not really." Chet felt bewildered.

Knife patted his shoulder. "Just remember, okay? Now run. *Run!*"

Chet *ran*. He reached the top of the grade and scrambled around other students to Professor Tibbet's side. Professor Tibbets seemed utterly bowled over by this course of events.

"Professor, it occurs to me that the man will be disoriented when he wakes up. He won't know what century he's in, so someone should ride with him. I'd love to help out the team with our new... find."

Graduate students began volunteering loudly to accompany the unconscious man. Although their words were more sophisticated, they sounded like children yelling, *Pick me, pick me!*

Professor Tibbets took off his wire-frame glasses, rubbed them on an embroidered pocket square and focused on Chet, ignoring the others. "You found him, didn't you, Chet? You and Journey, along with her friend."

"Yes, Professor."

"I see. Seems to me you have the right. Quiet down, you lot! Chet found him first, Chet gets dibs. Clementina and I will follow in her automobile to meet you at the hospital. Though it seems to me, my boy..."

"Thank you, sir!" Chet didn't wait around to hear what Tibbets had to say.

The ambulance technicians had loaded Fenimore into their double-tall, station-wagon like vehicle, the tiny light on top twirling around and around. A sour-faced nurse stood to one side, supervising her patient's transfer.

"Excuse me, but I'm to ride alongside him," Chet told them, expecting another argument.

The techs barely shrugged. "Don't get in my way," the nurse grumbled at him.

"Yes, ma'am." Chet scrambled inside, and the door was slammed behind him.

The station wagon was roomier than it looked on the outside. Chet hovered anxiously while the nurse checked Fenimore's pulse and blood pressure, but she seemed bored. In fact, after hooking up an IV, she climbed up to the front seat to smoke and gossip with the techs. Someone turned on the radio; the top-hits station had a crackle of underlying static. Chet hated that kind of music. Of course, he didn't like any cultural artifact under a hundred years old, and even that was pushing it.

The medical personnel weren't looking back at all. Chet swallowed. He was very nearly alone with the unconscious man. He studied Fenimore's gear with a historian's eye, anxiously trying to ignore the breathtaking beauty of his face and hands. Fenimore was dressed in what had once been a white cotton shirt, puffy and romantic as Abyss, with a wide crocheted collar. It was half unlaced, revealing dusty chest hair. He had a sword scabbard at his side. Empty, Chet noticed. He did have a long hunting blade strapped to his chest, filthy as the rest of him. Chet wished he had a magnifying glass so he could inspect the piece more thoroughly. Instead, he leaned over it, squinting, trying to ascertain its origins. The scabbard was intricately woven leather, the pattern of the most artisanal, skilled Tache craftsmanship...

There was a flurry of movement. Chet was grabbed and dragged downward by a powerful grip. Cold steel touched his throat. A pair of feral, bloodshot eyes bore into him. "Tell me why I shouldn't cut your throat, yellow-skinned pumpion."

Chet froze, the blade at his throat—the very one he'd been admiring a second ago—sharp and real. Very, very sharp. He gazed directly into the snarling face of Fenimore LaDaven.

# Chapter 4
# Wet Flight

What plea, what reasoning, would Fenimore understand? "Knife sent me!" Chet choked out.

The blade was reluctantly removed from his throat. Fenimore settled back onto the gurney, his snarl transformed into a wary frown. "Knife sent you?"

"He did." It was the truth, after all.

"He?" Fenimore raised the blade once again, his eyes so intent they seemed to burn.

*Oh, shit.* Anytime a Flame was not in visible sight, they were always assumed to be female. Chet couldn't remember where he'd learned the rule; he'd never needed to know it before. It was just one of those cultural things you learned by osmosis, like *never tease a doedicu,* which Chet knew even though he'd never seen one of the enormous, hump-backed animals outside a zoo.

"She, she!" he said hastily. The blade did not retreat. "Um, Knife said you were a rake and a scoundrel, and a, a libertine, and a liar, and a cheater, and not to trust anything you said!"

Fenimore lowered the blade with a snort. "She *would* say that," he murmured. "It's true, you know."

Chet dared to breathe. He looked at the driver's seat, but no one had even glanced back. They were still smoking and talking, the radio belting out a contemporary song with lots of silly "do-wap do-wap" harmonies. While the attack had seemed all-encompassing to Chet, he realized belatedly that Fenimore had kept his voice down. Chet reached up and touched his throat. His hand came away with a thin trail of blood. Fenimore had *cut* him. This was real. The man was a killer. *Well, of course he is*. The century he came from was a bloody one, even within one of the most cultured civilizations on Uos. Even now Fenimore's eyes took in his surroundings, darting this way and that, as if... as if he were a prisoner.

Fenimore's free hand instinctively tried to scratch at the IV needle the nurse had taped to his forearm. He jerked in surprise, then eyeballed it. "What slow torture on Uos or the God Plain is this?"

*Answer his questions about this century,* Knife had said. Chet licked his lips. "It's a needle designed to put liquid into your body," he began.

"I *know* that, you slit-eyed, red haired bastard. Are you poisoning me with poppy vapors? You fail. I do not feel... weakened." Fenimore's roving eyes had now caught sight of passing traffic out the windows. "Where are the ceroses for those carriages? Are they... they're holy contraptions, aren't they? I'm *surrounded* by holy contraptions. Is this the God Plain? Are you the servant of some god?"

Chet found himself bristling at both the racial epithets and Fenimore's assumption that he was a mere servant. Just about everyone in Wetshul was flaxen. His race was no longer so despised and poor as they had once been. Well... it made sense, too, given the time period in question. Fenimore was from a Tache high court, for Pantheon's sake. He'd assume almost every other race was beneath him, except perhaps the bistre-colored people of the Jantrael Straight.

Chet decided it was time to assert himself. "We're in Wetshul. You fell into lucid mud, Fenimore LaDaven. Don't you remember?"

"I..." Fenimore gulped, suddenly less fierce. "It's a blur. I remember rain, and a fight. I was being... hounded down. My servant betrayed me; he was following me in a stolen carriage. He couldn't shoot me because of the dark and wet powder. But I don't remember *why*."

"The lucid mud is just dust now. I'm a, a scholar, a student with a Literati university. We were digging for artifacts and found you."

Fenimore grunted and eyed Chet with rather more curiosity than before. Then his expression grew horrified, as if Chet had sprouted a second head. "Oh, Pantheon. *You* again. I thought... but no."

"What?" Chet blinked, totally lost.

Fenimore's expression grew reserved, almost pleasant. "So, you are a student up the mountain at Semaphore this time around?"

This time what? Chet nodded, grateful Fenimore was making sense—if only a little bit—and that there were *some* cultural commonalities between them. Belatedly, he realized they'd both been speaking in the Tache language. He hadn't noticed when his life had been threatened. "It's been a long time since you were enveloped by lucid mud."

"How long?" Fenimore seemed to hold his breath, his whole being focused on Chet.

"Three hundred years."

Fenimore sank back in the gurney, letting it take his whole weight. "...Oh."

"Rather a lot has changed since your time."

"*My* time?" Fenimore gave him a wild eyed look. "My *time?* Pantheon. Everyone's dead or they've forgotten, haven't they? Except... except Knife. Reincarnating bastard." He shook his head, his sensuous lips turning up at the corner. "Where is Knife, anyway?"

"Back at the dig site," Chet took a deep breath and was about to go on when Fenimore sat bolt upright.

"Where is the—oh, Pantheon." Fenimore clawed at the IV and clumsily withdrew the needle. He clearly didn't care about blood, his expression grim, eyes filled with intent will.

Chet hissed, "What are you doing?"

"Hey! What's going on?" The nurse twisted around to see them.

*Now* she noticed something amiss. Chet ignored her, focusing on Fenimore. The man was frantically clawing at the closed windows like a trapped animal, but he couldn't escape, not unless he figured out the window or door latches. Chet's smugness faded as Fenimore drew back his knife pommel and shattered the glass of the nearest window.

Chet yelped, arms raised to protect against flying glass. Fenimore began grimly punching away the remaining shards with the pommel. The techs and nurse were yelling and cursing. Chet suddenly realized that Fenimore was about to climb through the small window with its remaining glass shards poking out like teeth.

"No, not that way," Chet cried out.

He scrambled to the backdoor and pulled on the latch. The door swung outwards, then slammed shut again as the ambulance came to a screeching halt, catching Chet's fingers. He swore and cradled his hand. Fenimore pushed through the hanging door like a panicked animal, not even looking for traffic. Chet followed reluctantly.

It was rush hour in Wetshul, and they were blocks away from downtown.

*Oh, shit.*

They were surrounded by vehicles of every description, stopping for the light. At least, they *had* been stopped for the light. Drivers were inching forward and leaning on their horns to clear the traffic snarl of two men in the street. Chet scrambled over to grab Fenimore—who seemed to be frozen with shock—but his hands met air. Fenimore had lightly jumped onto the hood of a car. Chet watched, horrified, as Fenimore raced up the curved frame to the top. The metal buckled under Fenimore's weight. Apparently reacting to the sinking feeling, Fenimore leapt from the top of the car to another. Then another. He left dents—even holes in convertibles—wherever he landed. Drivers came boiling out of their vehicles, yelling and swearing, fists shaking. Behind Chet, the nurse and medical techs were arguing loudly with one another. One was complaining that he didn't have a *tranquilizer* gun, for Pantheon's sake.

"Fenimore, what are you *doing?*" Chet said, zipping around the stalled traffic to follow him.

"It's just like wrangling a herd of doedicus," Fenimore replied in a cheerful tone, "only without the spiked tails!"

Chet stifled hysterical laughter. He could see the connection: the stylish, curved tops of the cars certainly *did* look like the hump-backed creatures that had once roamed most of rural Uos. Fenimore, apparently spotting the sidewalk, took a running leap. Pedestrians—mostly men wearing suits and carrying briefcases—dove out of his way. Fenimore didn't stop but began plowing through the crowded sidewalk like a, well, like the razor-sharp blade he still held in hand.

Chet raced after Fenimore, as if sucked into the void left in his wake. He was the only one. Most people ran—or careened, or waddled—*out* of the armed man's way. Fenimore seemed like a wild-eyed madman with his reams of puffy hair and old fashioned clothes. He *was* a wild-eyed madman. Fenimore even took to yelling at the top of his lungs, brandishing his weapon to clear the path in front of him.

The crazy act—if it was an act—didn't account for his sheer speed. After a time, Chet stopped trying to offer calming words or apologies in Fenimore's wake. He simply put his head down and ran, determined to keep up.

They broke through the crowd at the edge of the Shining Futures District, with its industrial warehouses and gritty, potholed streets. Rush-hour traffic thinned and died as Fenimore sprinted on. Chet gulped for air like a fish, a stitch at his side. He'd *thought* he was in shape. Apparently not.

"Fenimore! Fen!" he called futilely, gasping for breath as he finally gave up the chase, bending over his knees.

To Chet's surprise, Fenimore slowed, then stopped. He strutted back to where Chet was crumpled over. Fenimore wasn't even breathing hard.

"You're a moist little cream puff, aren't you? What has become of men these days? You're more fit for an embroidery circle of dotardly ladies."

Chet shot him a horrified look but couldn't reply, beset by the need to breathe. His hand was throbbing: no broken fingers, but his knuckle was starting to swell. *Wonderful, just what I need,* he thought. Digging would be so much fun now. The sky overhead had thickened with bruised-looking clouds, the air hotter and more humid than ever. At least the street was quiet.

Chet leaned against a large van parked against the curb. Then he jerked back; the van was gently rocking. It had been moving before, he realized, but he hadn't noticed until he'd touched it. Blue and nondescript, it blended into the dour industrial surroundings. Except that it was bouncing up and down on its shocks. Chet realized with a start that it was a prostitution van, one of the mobile brothels.

Fenimore blinked. He walked around the van, then pressed his face against the windows, covered by sheer curtains from the inside. Though he couldn't have seen much, he grinned. It was a saucy, knowing grin.

"Ah, yes. Things have not changed *too* much in these distant times. I wonder what her rates are."

Chet felt his face growing hot. "Come on, let's keep going?" Why had his words twisted into a question? He really was a cream puff compared to Fenimore, who was lean, whip sinewy and filled with the vitality of ancient men. Or did he just exhibit more testosterone? Chet didn't know and abruptly didn't care.

Fenimore ignored him. He sheathed his knife and hummed tunelessly under his breath, face pressed against the window far longer than Chet felt comfortable with. In fact, Chet felt humiliated, lingering here like this, so near the undeniable intercourse taking place only feet away. The look in Fenimore's eye was willful and lusty, as if he were imagining exactly what he wanted to do to the prostitute within.

Turning away from the window, Fenimore glanced at Chet, about to make some comment. Then Fenimore studied him more closely. "Ah, your virginal cheeks betray you, my flaxen cherry pie. You are like a girl before her wedding night."

Chet jerked away from him, angry and confused. Fenimore's racial taunting, hard as it was to take, was nothing compared to this—baiting. Hadn't Knife warned him? Hadn't...

Chet was brought short by Fenimore's hands on his lapels. What was Fenimore *doing?*

Fenimore seemed to know exactly what he was doing. Chet fought, mumbling inarticulate uncertainties, eyes wide. Fenimore drew him in as if reeling a particularly feisty fish. He slammed Chet against the van and kissed him on the mouth. Chet froze, bewildered and targeted. Fenimore penetrated his lips and thrust his tongue inside Chet's mouth, his leverage excellent. *Oh. But... oh.* Chet's cock rose like a flag, his muscles contracting and releasing. He should, he should... *what?* The kiss continued unabated as Chet struggled weakly.

Fenimore released him slowly—ever so slowly—and stepped away, grinning. His control was appalling. "Oh, how sweet your bum will be; I look forward to its sundering. But I'm afraid there is business at hand first. Come, my virginal catamite, let us be off."

Chet noticed the dig site was less populated than before, mostly because graduate students were milling inside the processing pavilion. The students were apparently taking a break with the professors gone. A refreshing breeze cut through the stifling humidity as ugly, bruised clouds roiled overhead. A few graduate students were covering half-unearthed items up with tarps. Chet wasn't worried. The dust had the tendency of only absorbing half an inch of water—if that—before the rest rolled off. Lucid dust did not soak through like soil because it was not a water-based medium. Complex chemical reactions of lucid mud, so important for his last final, flitted through Chet's brain as he followed Fenimore down the steep grade.

"What *is* this barren wasteland? The work of your university?" Fenimore seemed taken aback. "This was all swamp. Trees and swamp, nothing more."

"Oh, that's long gone. They're building a new highway nearby," Chet said absently, wiping his sweating forehead.

Ah, there were the Flame. He'd been expecting them to seek shelter, but they were still out on the dig site, same pit as before. Both were digging frantically. Chet saw Journey glance upwards at the coming thunderstorm with panicked eyes, her expression terrified.

"Knife!" Fenimore cried out as they drew closer. "You old cynodict, you look exactly the same. Why am I not surprised?"

Chet blinked at Fenimore's words, and it wasn't because he had just compared Knife to a skinny, hairless canine with a whip-like tail. Chet hadn't realized that a shapeshifter would use their infinite flexibility to remain the *same* for three-hundred years. Or more.

Knife glanced up with a grin but didn't stop digging. "Hello, Fenimore. I had a feeling those misguided doedicus couldn't hold you long."

"Why aren't you two in the pavilion?" Chet said. Didn't they realize rain would burn them? It was a stupid question, of course they knew. They must know. Lightning arced overhead.

"We won't get another chance thanks to Clementina. We're so close. It's almost—" Journey gasped as the object they'd been unearthing popped free. She toppled backwards, the relic in her hands.

They all froze, staring at the dusty thing. It was about ten inches in diameter, a spherical shape with spikes coming out, like an archaic morningstar, or a doedicu's tail. Under the dust, Chet realized the object was wrought of copper and glass, set with jewels. It was unabashedly gaudy. Chet knelt for a closer look, not yet touching the piece. There were Magician's symbols etched around the spiky parameter.

He knew some of those symbols from years of study.

"Oh, *Pantheon*," Chet whispered.

This was fantastic! What a find. The god Foex had encouraged his honey-eyed affiliate Magicians to delve into dark, blood-bound magic. Real magic, not the fake stage stuff. Every affiliate had powers of one sort or another, gifted by their chosen god. Even Literati, like Professor Tibbets, had their mysteries and tricks. But no one—not even Flame with their showy shapeshifting—could hold a candle to Magicians. Foex had gifted his followers with astonishing power: the ability to draw energy from spilled blood, a power which ancient peoples had called magic. It hadn't mattered if the blood had been animal or human. Chet had always been taught that magic had vanished from the world since Foex's death, yet here was something that *looked* like a magical relic.

Thunder echoed throughout the dig site.

"*That* would be mine," Fenimore growled, making a grab for it. Journey pulled it away as he scrambled after her. "I lost three hundred years of my life because of the Raptus."

*So* this *is the Raptus.* Chet stared as Knife placing a restraining hand on Fenimore's shoulders. "Absolutely not, Fenimore," Knife said soberly. "We're taking the Raptus to the nearest Shadow-Dancer Cluster. It won't be hard; their representative is nearby."

"What? You want to give it away? Knife, we both know it was the Shadow Dancers who failed in their vigilance, letting the Raptus fall into the wrong hands. Why give it back to them when they're clearly not the correct guardians for it?"

"It's their god-given responsibility. Better than that professor woman, anyway. Petitioning a Pantheon member to destroy it would be best, but first we'd need to unlock it. Too risky. Not a task I was planning on taking on this week."

"*Destroy* it?" Fenimore was obviously enraged.

He grabbed the object—the Raptus—and tried to pull it away from Journey. Knife grabbed it as well, and the two Flame united to keep it from Fenimore's possession. A fierce tug-of-war ensued.

Chet was growing angry, too. "Stop it! That's a valuable relic! Anyway, you can't remove something from the site before it's been catalogued." Who did these Flame think they were? Give away or destroy a cultural artifact? The idea was repulsive. Horrifying. Instinct rallied against his training, and Chet grabbed the object, too.

An enormous pressure hit him, slamming him into unconsciousness.

He awoke to dust. Chet coughed and raised his head. He was lying on the ground, his hand still grasping the Raptus. Chet glanced around and realized Journey, Knife and Fenimore were all lying on the ground, unconscious. They formed a human cross around the object, each positioned at right angles with regard to each other. To Chet's relief, the others stirred as a flash of lightning split the sky. No one was dead apparently.

"What was that?" Journey whispered.

Fenimore groaned, still face down in the dust. "Were we hit by lightning?"

Knife was frowning at own hand, still grasping the Raptus. "I can't... can't seem to let go."

Chet tried and found that the ancient relic was stuck to his palm as if it had been superglued. "I can't, either."

"We must have triggered some reaction in the Raptus, asleep as it is," Fenimore said as he looked up, his face plastered with dust.

"*Locked* as it is," Journey correctly sharply. "Neither of you two are god affiliates. This should not have happened."

Chet stared at the Raptus. Journey's condescending attitude was like a slap in the face, but it was a familiar feeling. Not like a magical relic which shouldn't still work. Foex was dead, and nothing would ever bring him or his Magicians back. So why did this object still hold power?

Thunder cracked overhead, loud and immediate. "About fifteen miles away now," Knife whispered under his breath. Had he been counting the pause between lightning and thunder? "We don't have much time."

Chet grabbed his own hand and attempted to lever it off, using all his upper body strength. Fenimore was doing the same. They locked eyes. Fenimore's pupils were enormous. No one had to say it aloud: they were trapped, and the Flame were about to burn. Chet wondered what that would look like and immediately decided he didn't want to know. Journey and Knife didn't deserve to suffer and die.

Chet licked his lips. "We'll all run together. But where to?"

"Not the processing pavilion," Journey said. He could see the whites around her eyes. "Clementina will be coming back."

Reminded, Chet glanced over his shoulder. A few graduate students had spilled out of the pavilion and were headed straight for them. They must have seen the Raptus... Chet was suddenly possessed with an unfathomable urge to get away from them, to protect the relic stuck to his hand.

"We'd best run *now,*" Knife growled, as if echoing Chet's instinctive urge.

Chet scrambled to his feet, dreading another marathon. His body was already aching. The alternative, however, was to witness Journey and Knife—do what? Melt or bubble away, hissing and sputtering like pure sodium dropped in a bucket? Not much of a choice.

Journey and Knife murmured, conferring as everyone scrambled up the grade, but this time, Chet didn't understand the language. Journey glanced over her shoulder at him. "Chet, when you and Fenimore traveled here, did you see any of those prostitution vans?"

"Yes!" Chet cried out. "In the Shining Futures District."

"Lead us there."

"But... the prostitute had a customer," he said, gasping with exertion. Was that a drop on his cheek just now?

"Unless men are made of stauncher elements than they once were, he should be done by now," Fenimore put in. He loped along at a steady pace, his expression grim.

Chet counted blocks and watched for landmarks. Yes, they'd passed that bank, that laundrette. Right, left, another left. People jumped out of the way as they ran. Chet saw a mother with her daughter, both of them wearing white gloves, neat and clean. The mother issued a short scream and grabbed her daughter, clutching her in fear as they passed. Chet blinked. *Why is she afraid of us?* Then he glanced at the Flame and *got* it. Knife had lost his cap somewhere along the way; his bald head was exposed for all of Wetshul to see.

The random drops resolved into a light pattering rain as they crossed over into the Shining Futures District. Three blocks or four? Knife and Journey were sprinting, and Fenimore's loping had resolved into an all-out run. Perforce, Chet raced as fast as he could, yet he was slowing the others down. He could not breathe. The stitch at his side was agony, but the Flame must be in worse pain in this light rainfall. He could hear their labored, gasping breaths, their small whimpers. They should really duck into one of these buildings. *Any* of these buildings. It was stupid to keep going, but the Flame did not stop. Knife's jaw was set, Journey's eyes half closed to slits. Chet realized he could see the answer in the expressions of just about everyone they passed. This was Wetshul. Knife and Journey did not know what their reception would be in random locales, only that it would be unpleasant, possibly lethal if one or both of them were thrown out again. Who knew how long the rain would last?

They rounded a corner and Chet spotted the blue van. "There!"

The last hundred feet were the fastest he'd ever done in his life. Against all bets, the door was open. It was the usual sign of a prostitute waiting for a customer as Chet understood the process but still. They slammed inside the vehicle with the force and speed of stampeding doedicus, collapsing into a pile inside. Chet was buried beneath someone, but he didn't care. Just so long as he could hold still and *breathe*.

"Hey, hey, this ain't a playground. There's no crack-the-whip games here. And I don't *do* group rates!" a female voice complained. Chet groaned into the vinyl pressing into his face. He hadn't considered that a prostitute van meant a resident *prostitute*.

Journey's voice growled, "I will give you two-hundred gilt to let us stay here through the storm, and afterwards to drive us to the location of our choice in the city."

"I ain't fucking all of you. Well, maybe the two men, but not you, lady, or the Flame."

"*You* will not be fucking anyone," Journey said. Chet heard Fenimore protest wordlessly somewhere above him, and Journey added, "Or rather, if *someone* wants to have you, he can negotiate from his own belt purse. I'm not paying for it. Three-hundred gilt and that's final. Best offer you'll get in this rain."

There was a sound like popping chewing gum, then, "What, I'm just supposed to sit here with you four, playing card games while it rains... for three-*hundred* gilt? Are you crazy?"

"Actually, we'd prefer if you stayed in the front seat and didn't say anything," Knife put in. Chet realized the small whimpering noises filling the van emerged from Knife's direction.

The prostitute snorted. "You've got a deal. Give me the money, and I'll shut up."

By the shuffling taking place above him, Chet assumed money exchanged hands. There was a slamming of van doors, and the space suddenly seemed darker. *Of course,* Chet thought. The windows were covered by gauzy curtains. Curious of his surroundings, he untangled from Fenimore—who had been draped over him—to looked around. Unsurprisingly, a majority of the space was taken up by a bed, built right into the van frame. It was covered by a demure, flowery comforter. The inside walls of the van were wallpapered with a print of sunshine and wildflowers. Chet hadn't imagined a prostitute's van would be so... homey.

Now that negotiations were out of the way, both Flame were hastily removing damp clothing. Sure enough, their skin was reddened and bubbled in places, as if from a very hot fire. Journey's head had been mostly protected by her wig and hat, but Knife had been exposed. His bald scalp was covered in bubbling burns, some of them as large as a cherry. Water drops sizzled his skin as they dripped down his face; he swiftly wiped them off as he discarded clothing. Knife was crying, Chet realized. Journey murmured soothingly in some other language, perhaps the same tongue they'd conferred in earlier. Both Flame were down to their skivvies now. Journey's bra was bright fuchsia and satiny—her tits filled it magnificently.

Chet looked away, his face hot. Then he gasped. "Knife, Journey, look! You're not touching the object. The, um, Raptus."

They appeared startled. "I still *feel* it, though," Journey said as she retrieved Knife's lighter from his discarded trouser pocket.

Chet tried to let go of it, and found that he could. Barely, but he could. He could feel an invisible cord running between the relic and his navel, as if it were physically tied to him. What a bizarre sensation. Journey was running the lighter over the worst of Knife's head and face burns, which—depending on their size—smoothed out or burst under the tiny fire. Knife sighed in relief, his eyes shut tight as she ministered to him. Chet noticed that she ignored her own burns, which were admittedly lesser. Knife tended to his own hands, then gave her the lighter as he looked her over critically. Apparently satisfied with what he found, he turned to Fenimore, who was picking himself off the floor.

Knife took hold of Fenimore by his crocheted lapels, hauled him upright... and socked him full in the face. "You *asshole.*"

# Chapter 5
# Deflowered

Fenimore spat blood and grabbed Knife, grappling with him. "How—dare—you!"

"How dare *you!*" Knife said through set teeth. "You know what's at stake! You *know* what destruction the Raptus could cause should it fall into the wrong hands. In this century, the danger is greater than ever before; it's far easier to communicate and travel these days. The power of the Raptus would be a disaster."

"I fought and nearly *died* for it."

"You and I were charged with bringing it back to Konstantine. Well, he's dead. Who are you going to bring it back to now, LaDaven? Who?" Knife let go of Fenimore, hissing under his breath. Fenimore must still be wet. "You weren't even thinking, were you? You were just *reacting*."

"So what? I— " Fenimore stopped, as if struck by a thought. "Oh. Prince Konstantine *is* dead. Isn't he."

"He is." Knife sank to the bed where Journey was tending to herself. "He died in 7314 of a bleeding ulcer and treachery. Not that he didn't deserve treachery at that point, the cunning bastard. While he might have had something to offer us as a prince, *Emperor* Konstantine would not have been a good guardian for the Raptus. I know that now."

Chet had pressed into a corner to avoid the fight. As it seemed to be over, he reluctantly perched at the edge of the bed. They were going to be here for a while: Wetshul summer storms usually lasted an hour or two. They had time... which meant he might be able to find out what was going on.

"What is the Raptus? Is it *holy?*" he asked. Meaning, had a god created it?

Knife glanced toward the front seat of the van, which was cut off from the back only by a flimsy curtain. Chet could hear gum popping on the other side. The prostitute was clearly listening—they must be better than a radio soap opera. Though the rain on the roof had become a heavier drumming and thunder grumbled outside, the storm wasn't covering their words. Knife switched languages to the tongue of Tache.

"No, it's not a holy object. The gods never had anything to do with it. Directly, anyway. It was created by the Magicians Tene and Zang around 3900, Foex's millennium. The Raptus's purpose is simple and direct: it's a mind-control device. The person with full control of the Raptus can control every human within earshot."

Chet had books by both Tene and Zang, respectively, in his bookcase back home. Also, admittedly, a few condensed volumes by each of them in his suitcase at Clementina's house. He loved reading those two. Such different men with wholly divergent philosophies, yet similar in tone and style. But this was new information; how could these men have done something Chet had never heard of?

He scowled. "I don't believe it. Why did they create something like a mind-control device? I would have expected more from the Magicians Tene and Zang than something a *stage* magician would use. In any case, I don't understand why it works at all. All the Magicians are gone. Their god is dead. How did this thing just catch us like bugs on fly paper?"

Knife and Journey looked at one another, their expressions reserved. "We're not entirely sure why it still works, either," Journey said. "Let alone why it just caught us. Aureate would know more."

Who? Chet frowned at them and crossed his arms. "The Raptus sounds like nothing but a cheap, showy trick."

Knife snorted. "Oh, sure. Imagine being forced to kill your own parents, or to slaughter thousands of children, or to launch a nuclear assault, all against your own will. Some trick."

Journey put in, as if to console him, "It does other things, too. I recall there was some sort of shielding power when it's mostly unlocked. Don't know how well it would work, though, with something like modern bullets."

Her wording piqued Chet's interest. He glanced at the morning-star-shaped object, currently in Fenimore's lap. Fenimore's mouth was closed tight and he cradled the device as if it were his child. Chet felt a protective twinge, too. The Raptus was an ancient tool of the Magicians, out of circulation for three-hundred years. This was his milk and meat as an archeologist.

"Still, I've never heard of this thing," he said at last.

Journey leaned back and stretched; even in the dim light of the storm, Chet could see her muscles flex. And, um, other parts of her body move, too. "I'm not surprised. The Raptus was lost and forgotten, save by us and the Shadow Dancers."

"You keep mentioning the Shadow Dancers." Chet was trying not to look at her breasts, as he wanted to keep his mind clear. Clearer. What had the Flame said yesterday about Rory's people? And Rory herself had acted affronted by their presence, which wasn't in character for her at all.

"Aiena was the goddess in charge of cataloguing Foex's things after he drank himself to death. Some of Foex's creations she used or taught to other gods, like Pelin's barrier that has such prominence in the history of Palister. Other creations were more difficult. Some she buried, and some she destroyed."

Chet swallowed as a wave of self consciousness washed over him. Journey wasn't including herself in this litany of historic events—and interactions with Pantheon members—but surely she had been around for some of it. Knife, too. Weren't they among the oldest reincarnating people on Uos? They *remembered.* And here they were trapped together in a van, talking like normal people. Not like historic celebrities, quiet though they were.

*Wait.* Chet frowned, trying to remember. What had Journey said about the Shadow Dancers messing up? And Fenimore had just said something similar, hadn't he? Perhaps that was how the Raptus had ended up in the hands of ambitious royal cousins, which had caused Knife and Fenimore to be dispatched by their prince.

Along the same lines, why did the Shadow Dancers need it back? "Did Aiena give the Raptus to her affiliates because she wanted them to have this mind-control power, too? Did one of them try to steal it?"

Knife said, "Just the opposite. Aiena was swamped while dealing with Foex's things—let alone the Magicians' things—after their deaths. She had too much to do before dealing with something so piddly that just impacts humanity. She realized that not just any human should be put in charge, so she gave it to her Shadow Dancers for safe keeping, and she took an extra step, too. You see, the Magicians had explicitly locked the Raptus by linking it to six of their own kind. It was the ultimate security measure. Magicians, of course, reincarnated like Flame."

"They reincarnated *before* the existence of Flame," Fenimore said.

Knife frowned at him, apparently perturbed at being interrupted. "Yes, yes. I cannot fault your classical education, Fen. In any case, Aiena decided it would be prudent to lock the Raptus for safety's sake. Being that she is Pelin's foster mother and that Flame were the only reincarnating god affiliates left on the planet, she asked the Council of Six to stand in as guardians. We're even the right number."

"We took on the responsibility knowing full well what might happen if we did not. We weren't happy about it, though." Journey lay down on her back and tucked her arms behind her head. Chet was vividly reminded she wore nothing but a fuchsia bra and satin panties. Oh, Pantheon, those tits were magnificent lying down, too... Chet wished she'd put on clothes, but they were still wet and would be for a while.

"Well, this sort of charge isn't our specialty, is it? Not even mine."

Chet frowned. "So why are *we* bound to it now? The four of us?"

Journey sat up. The movement didn't help, and Chet tried to look elsewhere, failing miserably. Her breasts were too full and exciting, wrapped in those fuchsia shells. "We don't know. It's a problem."

"Has it ever done anything like this before? In your experience."

Both Flame shook their heads. Their eyes were round, expressions equally disturbed.

"The Raptus wants masters, I think. It wanted masters three-hundred years ago, and it doesn't seem to have noticed the time gap," Fenimore said. "My understanding is the Raptus can still be partially used, locked as it is, but not fully."

Journey frowned. "Yet this seems very odd, what with you two being unaffiliated. I cannot believe that the makers of this object would wish to endow it upon random, unaffiliated people."

Chet nearly groaned at this attitude. Of *course*, unaffiliated people were so *random*, the un-chosen and all. He turned to Fenimore. "Were the, um, royal cousins you were pursuing god affiliates?"

"Of *course* they were," Fenimore sighed, making the same lemon-eating face.

Chet smiled at him. Fenimore *understood*. He was unaffiliated, too—just another guy. Just a guy from the 73rd century with an incredible will and sinewy musculature, but hey, Chet had to take them as he found them.

The rain grew more intense overhead. Lightning flashed and thunder boomed at the same time, incredibly loud. The inside of the van had grown even darker, Chet realized. No one could possibly see anything if they looked in the covered, steaming windows now, as Fenimore had done—less than an hour ago? It seemed longer.

Chet glanced around at the others. Knife and Fenimore were looking at one another with the same intense, hungry expression. Chet frowned, uncertain what they were thinking. Then Fenimore slowly stretched. Every movement languid, Fenimore began removing his shirt. His chest still had dust clinging to it. Chet noticed curiously that Fenimore's torso wasn't like those of bodybuilders: he was hairy and covered with imperfections, the most prominent of which were smallpox scars and healed knife wounds. Nevertheless, when he moved Chet could see his muscles ripple in the shadows. Then Fenimore *leaned* into Knife, his whole body arching over him like a bridge. Fenimore took hold of Knife's shoulders and tried to push him down.

Knife was smiling, his eyes knowing. He reached up and grabbed Fenimore in turn, tossing Fenimore lightly to the bed beside him. "If you think you're to be on top, you are surely mistaken."

"I think you should throw yourself upon your back and stick your feet in the air, Flame, and be grateful about it," Fenimore growled, fighting for leverage.

"Is that what you think?" Despite his satisfied purr, Knife didn't quite have Fenimore pinned. Fenimore was smaller, but his reach was sufficient, his will just as intense.

Chet froze as he watched them play, not sure what he was seeing.

Their movements were like a wrestling match in secondary school—only the guys in secondary school didn't fight nearly so dirty. Maybe it was more like watching mating animals, except there was no male or female here, no obvious conclusions based on anatomy. They were writhing intently, each trying to gain ascendency over the other. Sometimes a moan emerged, sometimes a growl. Knife lost ground by getting Fenimore's pants off; he immediately went under. Fenimore's uncircumcised dick was hard, ready to go, his hips already bucking. Yet Knife wasn't giving up without a fight.

Chet wanted to shield Journey from this, then realized she was no lady, she was Flame. Her eyes were shining as she stared, and her right hand... Chet's inhaled in shallow bursts. Her right hand was inside her panties, touching herself with slow, circular movements. Her left hand, in turn, was stroking her satiny bra. The smell he'd noticed in Journey and Knife's presence before had filled the van full force. Again, he was reminded of his former roommate Steve, though the connection felt inappropriate. Especially because Chet's cock responded readily, rising to full mast.

"Hah!" Fenimore had Knife's boxers down, but an instant later he lost leverage as Knife grabbed him from beneath, flipping him onto his back. Chet gulped at the sight of a naked Flame. There was nothing obviously wrong with him, though. Knife's penis was long and unusually thin—on purpose?

Knife threw himself on Fenimore and crooned in his ear, "That's right, boy. You're mine."

"You can't perforate me dry!" Fenimore snarled. He seemed genuinely outraged, and they both paused, as if the game were in timeout. Then they turned to look at the curtain separating the driver's seat.

"Excuse me, miss?" Knife called out. "Do you happen to have any oil-based lotion or cream on hand?"

The prostitute stuck her head though the curtain. Chet, who hadn't seen her before, blinked in surprise. Flaxen skinned, she was chubby cheeked and amazingly young; she actually looked like one of his sisters. She didn't seem at all shocked at the position Fenimore and Knife were in. The idea of two men—or a man and a Flame, rather—in such a compromised position didn't seem to faze her. Did she often harbor homophiles in her van?

The prostitute pointed helpfully. "Look in the second wire rack from the top, behind the magazines. See it?"

"Thank you," Knife said.

Chet craned his head. He hadn't noticed the organization racks screwed into the back of the seat. They held all sorts of items, the bulkiest of which were clean towels. He was vaguely reminded of the tools table at the dig site in that everything necessary was at hand, carefully prepared and organized.

Knife squirted a generous dollop into his hand. Chet held his breath until he realized that oil-based anything won't hurt the Flame. Then he frowned. What about spit? Or semen? Or whatever fluid women had?

He glanced at Journey. "Won't he be burned by, um, bodily fluids?"

"Hardly." She grinned up at him. Her hand rested outside her panties, to his relief. "We wouldn't be very well designed if that happened. No, by Pelin's grace, we can interact with bodily fluids without burning."

"But that... makes very little sense, when you think about it."

"Pelin is a *goddess*. She doesn't have to bow to the laws of nature nearly as often as you and I."

Fenimore waited patiently on his back, legs upright and spread. The timeout was apparently in full effect. Knife massaged the thick liquid into Fenimore's ass without further comment.

Feeling like an anthropologist in the field, Chet whispered to Journey, "Won't Knife need some, too?" Or was it now assumed by everyone that Knife was going to, er, penetrate Fenimore? Was the ritual mating fight over?

Journey rolled her eyes, as if she wished he'd just let her watch the live show, but she said, "As I've mentioned before, Pelin is thoughtful in many ways. *Our* asses never require lubrication, or even stretching in advance, since we're fully capable of shaping ourselves to match whatever comes our way."

"Oh." Chet hunched, feeling vulnerable.

Journey smiled up at him, her expression more hungry than friendly, her body turned his way. Chet felt himself straighten automatically at her attention. It was funny how she seemed no less feminine with a bald head. Really, one got used to that feature quickly. Especially because Journey was otherwise physically breathtaking. The smell in the van now filled him completely, making him feel heady with longing. With, with *lust.*

"You'll have to forgive me," Journey murmured as she reached over and touched Chet, stroking her fingers up his arms. "I feel the need to take something for myself here."

Chet mewled as she pulled him onto the other side of the hefty bed. Luckily, Knife and Fenimore were standing up as they did their—business. Journey stripped Chet with a thoroughness and efficiency usually reserved for the armed forces. She brushed his cock with her hand and he gasped, trying not to come.

Journey frowned. "I think I'd best be on top. We don't want you spent too soon, do we? You are not to move without permission, and that means no thrusting up into me. Do you understand?"

He nodded frantically. She pulled off her panties—her cunt was hairless, too—and mounted him as if she were riding a ceros with one critical difference. Chet gasped as she reached down and slipped him inside her. Oh, she was wet, and warm, and tight, and... and perfect. *So* perfect. Chet began moving instinctively, and she slapped his chest, a playful swat rather than a real blow.

"I said hold *still,* boy. You are inside me, and I'm in charge here. Do you copy?"

"Y-yes, ma'am," he whispered, then put a hand over his mouth, regretting the rude slip. Journey was not a ma'am, she was Flame. But Journey didn't withdraw. Indeed, she barely seemed to have heard him at all.

Chet couldn't believe his luck. He was inside her, warm and wet as a tropical ocean. Journey rocked above him, breathing in time with each scintillating movement. She threw back her head and moaned. He wished he could touch her breasts, still enclosed by the satin bra; they were the central focus of his world. Chet bit his lip, hands outstretched without touching.

Journey seemed to have noticed, for she reached back and unclasped the bra, tossing it away apparently without a second thought. "There you go. Please, feel free."

Oh, Pantheon, her breasts were huge. Chet had never touched human breasts except through clothing. He couldn't believe he'd waited so long. They were soft, marvelous, the nipples and areolas profoundly exciting. Journey's bouncing movements accentuated the luminosity and impact of her breasts. Even the snug encompassing of his cock dimmed compared to this treat.

It occurred to him, somewhere in the back of his head where he was still rational, that Journey had shaped her breasts large on purpose. Like distracting a baby with a pretty mobile? Journey had what she wanted, and she was willing to give him something in exchange. The thought made him crumple inside. He thrust up into her, blatantly disobeying her command.

Journey groaned and slapped his thighs. "Bad boy," she moaned. "Bad, bad boy."

Her movement, her words, her tits—everything—filled him as he came, arching up into her.

Journey sighed and rolled off. "Shit. There goes my fun, for the moment."

Chet glanced past her and realized that Fenimore and Knife were still in full coitus. Knife was on top, Fenimore was on the bottom, writhing and giving Knife trouble. Knife had him by the hair—such long hair—and was using it for leverage. Knife was taking Fenimore almost violently. The sound of their fucking filled the van.

Chet grabbed his own cock; he was getting hard again. Journey stroked his shoulders absently but made no move to mount him again. Was she angry? But no, she was smirking at Knife, who was clearly on the verge of coming. Chet, seeking a closer look, noticed that the base of Knife's penis was now very thick. Huge, in fact. Knife let loose a wild howl as he climaxed, Fenimore snarling beneath him.

Knife and Fenimore parted. A thoughtful silence followed as people cleaned up. The towels in the organization rack were put to good use while Knife and Journey took turns with the lighter. Chet looked once, then had to look away. Even knowing that fire was their natural element, it still *seemed* painful. *Fire to genitals, ick.* Chet found himself facing Fenimore, who shot him a sly smile.

Fenimore's smile took on a predatory glint as he studied Chet's dick. "Ah, such a resoundingly fit model of the flaxen race. I'm honored."

Chet scowled. "Great good Pantheon, I wish you'd knock that off. I've never met anyone so racist in all my life."

"He doesn't know that word, Chet," Knife said from the other side of the van.

Chet glanced over at Knife. He and Journey were cuddling together, spooning—Knife in the back, Journey in front. They didn't seem to be having intercourse. It looked... comfortable, like old friends enjoying one another's company. Her tits were smaller now, Chet noticed regretfully.

Fenimore stepped closer, grabbed Chet's shoulders and reeled him in. Chet froze, all thought of the Flame evaporating from his mind. Fenimore's penis touched Chet's, like two swords crossing. Chet gasped, overtaken by the sublime sensation. Then Fenimore threw him to the bed. Chet instinctively rolled over and tried to scramble away. He was stopped, locked down by rock-hard arms. With languid movements, Fenimore sank on top of him, pinning him to the mattress. It wasn't even a contest. Knife could play these games, but Chet was nothing in comparison. He was soft, a rag doll for Fenimore's pleasure.

Fenimore licked his ear. "Now, my little friend, I am going to explore your sweet arse and take you hard."

# Chapter 6
# Taking One for the Team

Chet couldn't breathe. He couldn't think. He didn't know how to react, or indeed, whether there was any reaction he should be having. It was so strange to be lying face down and naked under a forceful man, about to be penetrated, trapped inside a prostitute's van with Flame looking on. Let alone bound to a lost magical object of vast power. If someone had told Chet that he would be doing this a week ago, he'd have never believed it. He would have laughed.

He wasn't laughing now.

"For Pantheon's sake, LaDaven, ask for Chet's consent first," Journey said. Chet looked up. Though she was only a foot away, it might as well have been miles across the mattress. "He's not a servant for you to plunder."

"Don't dare judge me, Flame. I notice *you* didn't ask the boy's consent before you took him. You had your pleasure as he whimpered beneath you, demolishing his virginity without a second thought. Now I seek to do the same, and you speak out on his behalf?"

Journey reddened and looked away. Chet blinked, utterly shocked at the insinuation that Journey had raped him. After all, she was a woma—no. She was Flame. Was Fenimore right? She'd certainly ordered him around, but he'd *enjoyed* it. She'd given him something in return. Would Fenimore?

Chet cleared his throat. "Could I, um, please sit up, Fenimore? I can't see you at all like this."

Chet felt Fenimore sigh as he rolled off. Chet sat up and folded his legs beneath him. He looked at Fenimore. He had the same bottle in hand that Knife had used and was squirting out the thick contents into his palm, giving it an extra squeeze as if marveling at the bottle's construction. Chet gasped as Fenimore wrapped one hand around Chet's waist, his wet hand disappearing under him. The oily fingers found Chet's ass and penetrated him. Chet gasped, his eyes shut tight. The pain was worse than he'd imagined. Oooh, that was a tender spot. How could Fenimore's entire dick possibly fit inside him?

"There you are," Fenimore whispered in his ear. "Such a beautiful virgin boy."

"I—I'm not a boy. I'm twenty-four years old!" He'd just turned twenty-four a few weeks ago, a fact he didn't point out.

Fenimore grinned. "I'm three hundred and thirty two, and you just serviced a god affiliate a few thousand years old, minus a century or two while she was dead. Brings this into perspective, doesn't it?"

Chet stilled at the thought. All his life he'd longed for the past with an obsessive persistence that had baffled his family. Now the past was all around him. The past was about to penetrate him. Would Fenimore back off if Chet asked? It seemed unlikely. Chet didn't doubt that Knife and Journey could stop Fenimore, but at what cost? They were all bound together by the Raptus. Even now Chet could feel the invisible cord binding them together to the relic. Though he could endure rainfall—unlike the Flame—he still couldn't go anywhere without these people, and who knew how long this condition would last? If the Raptus had never done anything like this before, there was no precedent. They *had* to work together. It was like being a... a team. Chet knew all about taking one for the team; he'd been doing it all his life.

He bowed his head and, ever so slowly, sank to his hands and knees. Then he lowered his elbows to the mattress so that his ass was sticking out. Waiting for Fenimore's ministrations, tender or otherwise.

Chet didn't need to see Fenimore's grin to know it existed. A second finger wiggled its way into Chet's ass, then a third. Chet writhed, facing the pain with deep breaths. Sodomy was something he'd always sort of dreamed about in the back of his mind, but had never actually considered trying. He envied the Flame with their gift of being able to *relax* those muscles at will.

Knife said, "Fenimore, you *will* wrap your penis in the modern equivalent of a glans bladder. Pantheon knows what diseases you carry. Miss," he called to the front, "where do you keep your condoms?"

"In one of the little drawers under the bed. Third from the left. See it?"

Fenimore scowled as Knife knelt to riffle through her drawers. "Lucid mud should have killed off anything I—"

"Lucid mud is a preservative," Journey interrupted, eyes narrow.

"I don't have the clap!"

"Didn't say you did," Knife said steadily as he tossed a few rubber condoms onto the bed. "Yet you had intercourse ten times a week with six different people, back in Konstantine's court. Chet doesn't need to share anything you do have."

Fenimore swore at him. Knife simply looked at him, and Journey had the same expression on her face. Chet wondered why Knife hadn't brought this up earlier... neither had Journey, for that matter.

Chet looked at her; she seemed to take in his bewilderment. Journey leaned closer and murmured, "You couldn't possibly catch anything from me, Chet. Flame are sterile in more ways than one. We do not contract or spread disease, including venereal disease. Nor could you get me pregnant," she added, as if an afterthought.

Pregnancy had been the last thing on his mind. Apparently, it had been the last thing on her mind as well, with reason. Chet glanced back at Fenimore, who was rolling on a rubber condom with the expression of a heckled husband nagged by his wife into taking out the trash.

Fenimore slopped more of the oil solution atop the rubber and slapped Chet on the ass. "Down, boy."

Chet complied, lying upon his belly. He spread himself and waited. *Now for it.* Yet... nothing happened. He wondered whether Fenimore was standing behind him, stroking himself and enjoying the view of Chet's unencumbered rear. Chet was about to look over his shoulder when Fenimore settled on top of him. Chet cried out as his ass was forced open. Oh, Pantheon, it hurt, it *hurt*. Fenimore began thrusting gently, belying his earlier violence. After a while, Chet remembered to breathe. It felt—oh. When the pain had faded a bit, it...

actually felt fantastic. Chet had never even guessed his anus could be so sensitive. Chet's pleasure grew as Fenimore caressed him.

"There you are—you have me now. Such a good boy, taking my sausage without a sound. I love that you aren't even whimpering."

Chet couldn't help but be pleased. He *was* taking Fen's cock. He *was.* Only minutes ago he'd thought it impossible, yet he was doing it. Chet began moving beneath him, writhing. In response, Fenimore quickened his pace, thrusting with more intensity. What had been bearable swiftly devolved into more sensation than Chet had been prepared to deal with. Chet shuddered and gasped. He couldn't think. He couldn't understand anything but the dick inside of him, splitting him thoroughly. It was messy and scary, yet terribly important, the most important thing on Uos. He was crying and laughing at the same time.

Then Fenimore reached around and grabbed Chet's cock. Chet arched upwards, bucking. He came in a flurry of internal lightning and thunder, semen poured into Fenimore's hand. Fenimore grabbed his hips and increased his pounding to a staccato tempo. Oh, *Pantheon.* Chet moaned, yelled, screamed. Fenimore's frantic intensity was torturous, and Chet could only take it.

Fenimore thrust one final time and came deep inside him.

Chet's body felt lighter than air, a balloon filled with helium. Only Fenimore's weight pinned him to the mattress. Then Fenimore pulled away, grumbling as he took off the condom. Chet flopped onto his back—a sensual being set free upon the prostitute's bed. He laughed, delighted at his body. Delighted at the whole *world.*

"Rain's just about stopped," Knife said after a while.

Chet opened his eyes. The others had begun putting themselves back together. Journey winced as she shook out damp clothing, Knife was again grooming himself with the lighter, and Fenimore—half dressed—handled the Raptus with a studious frown.

"I don't feel the invisible tether as strongly, now. I wonder how far apart we can stretch ourselves."

"There's one way to find out. Get your trousers and boots on, Fen." Knife held out his hands for the Raptus and Fenimore tossed it to him—gently, Chet noticed.

Was the relic robust or fragile? Despite its delicate appearance and materials, it seemed to have survived almost four thousand years without so much as a scratch. By magic? Even the idea of magic—missing so long from the world—was exciting. Chet wished he could have lived during the millennia when Foex was alive if only to witness blood magic. Why on Uos did this thing still work? Even the Flame, who'd locked it centuries ago, didn't know. The mystery was absorbing, fascinating, almost more vivid to Chet than his first sexual encounters.

Fenimore opened the van door, and a delicious scent of wet gravel and pavement wafted through the van. Chet breathed in greedily, but both Flame winced. The rain hadn't quite stopped, the air alive with humidity. Topless and sweaty, Fenimore traipsed down the street, looking back every few seconds. He slowed near the corner.

"Is it stopping you?" Knife called.

"Indeed, yes. But... it also feels like there will be more give to come. Like whatever binds us is stretching even now, like gut string," Fenimore said, walking back to the van.

"Mmm. About a hundred feet, give or take." Knife turned to address the front seat. "Miss, we have an address for you to drive us to, so we can pick up our luggage."

"Right-oh," came the cheerful reply.

The curtain swished aside and the prostitute smiled at them. Her smile became a grin when she looked at Chet; he dropped his gaze, ashamed. His face was cherry red, he was sure. He'd just been deflowered—both ways!—and she'd witnessed the whole thing.

Chet gazed up at Clementina's palatial residence with misgivings. He noticed the university van was parked outside; was Rory back from the shuttle errand?

Journey studied him with an anxious expression. "You will go in, won't you? We do very much need our luggage. Knife and I can't even get dressed as our clothes will be damp for some time, and I'm afraid this wig is done for until I get a chance to work on it."

"Right." It was time to take one for the team, again. Chet sighed. At least most of the graduate students should still be at the dig site this time of the day. Was it only early afternoon? Chet's sense of time had vanished in the van. With all the strange events and disruptions, who knew where people would be?

Chet's key worked just fine. No one seemed to be around. The invisible cord binding him to the Raptus stretched like a rubber band as he poked through the living room door into the library. It was a bit like being attached to an umbilical cord; it physically hurt to stretch too far.

Journey's bulky suitcases were mostly still packed. He stuffed loose items recklessly, though his fear of being caught decreased as time passed. There were no footsteps in the house. Knife's small suitcase was easier, already packed. Chet humped everything downstairs to the porch for Fenimore to take to the van. Emboldened, he decided he wanted his own things. Who knew how long he'd be gone in this cascading stream of events? He hopped upstairs again and slipped into the room he shared with several of the other guys...

Rory was waiting for him, sitting motionless on his cot. Chet froze. Her brown eyes were murderous. "You're a doedicu, Chet Baikson."

He frowned at her, his shock giving way to an awkward uncertainty, off balance. Had she been in the house all this time? He knew Shadow Dancers could reputedly turn invisible, but she'd never done it around him. "Um, I don't think name calling is necessary, Rory."

She waved this aside. "You're in serious trouble. Among other things, Clementina is threatening to have you expelled from the program."

"I—you're kidding." Chet was conscious that he was feeling—of all things—his aching anus. He'd never realized that sex with a man meant a sore ass afterwards. He'd never needed to know, and now was the *worst possible* time to realize the fact. "Surely Tibbets won't let them expel me. He's my senior advisor."

"Just watch her." Rory turned away, her arms crossed. She gazed through the window at the prostitute's van, visible from the street. "That's... rather clever of the Flame. I'll give them that much. Considering they just won the arms race, they're certainly ready to run with their prize."

"Arms race?"

She shook her head. "You wouldn't understand. I think. I *hope* you don't understand. Oh, Pantheon, Chet. I pegged you as a normal guy. When you refused to trade places with me on the university run, I thought you were just being obstinate. Have I misjudged you so badly? Are you really one of us?"

One of who? Or maybe he should ask, one of what? For a woman who hated deception, she'd certainly deceived *him*. "I *am* a normal guy," Chet said, clinging to the only truth he knew in this floating conversation.

"If that's true, you're caught in the riptide. Tell the Flame the others will be here at dark, and we expect them to fully justify their actions."

"Yeah, I gather there's something going on between them and your people, but I don't think it's about you personally."

She glared at him. "Of *course* it involves me. I'm leaving the university. My doctorate isn't nearly as important as what the Flame—and you—are holding right now. This matter impacts my Cluster on both personal and political levels. My *family*, Chet. Not to mention the world at large. So, if you'll excuse me..."

She didn't move, despite her words. Chet realized he could see the window frame right through her. Right through her body. His ex-girlfriend was fading before his eyes, fading into thin air, except she was still a wavering shape. Ghost like. He took another step toward her just as the faint outline of Rory raced at him, toward the door.

He was knocked to the ground. She—whatever she had become—was like touching an electrical current. Chet gasped, the breath knocked out of him. When he was finally able to struggle upright, Rory was gone.

# Chapter 7
# Shift of Plans

There was no sign of Rory. Chet looked at his strewn clothing and books. He packed mechanically, leaving dirty clothes under the cot. He did make sure to take his books. He'd need them, he thought, for comfort if nothing else. His compact array of classics with tiny print would keep him going as he traversed unknown territory.

The rain had stopped, sun peeking through clouds. Knife and the prostitute were chatting amicably in the front seat of the van, sharing a cigarette like comrades in arms. Journey was swiftly unpacking a suitcase, half dressed in sensible, casual clothing. Fenimore seemed to be napping on the bed. All was apparently under control. Only Chet was undone.

"Look, I have to tell you guys something," Chet said. He recounted Rory's words and actions as they were driven to—where? Chet didn't know what came next.

Journey and Knife shared a significant glance. "I'll talk to them," Knife promised. Journey nodded and kept riffling through her suitcase.

Chet hugged his knees. They didn't see surprised or even mildly curious. Of course, they were god affiliates, too. God affiliates' inborn or granted powers had been a point of contention his whole life. Chet's family *still* expected him to choose a god or goddess, like all eight of his siblings had. He had carefully chosen not to do so. His unaffiliated status and field of study had been the only times he'd ever disappointed his family. Chet had never been able to fully answer their persistent questions of why he didn't want to become a god affiliate; none of the Pantheon appealed to him. He didn't want them.

He didn't want to be bound, entrapped, to surrender his humanity to a god's political goals and agenda.

Well, Foex had always appealed to him, bloodthirsty as he'd been. But Foex was dead.

The Raptus was on the bed next to Fenimore, who lay snoozing. Chet picked it up and turned it over his hands. The etched writing caught his attention, and he studied the markings intently. The ancient language was one he'd studied about two years ago when he'd transferred programs from law to archaeology: it was a variation of a Door dialect used by Magicians. Zang and Tene had been clever to create something like this—perhaps a little too clever. Chet recognized the symbols for "control," "force," and "stifle," but couldn't make out anything else. He licked his lips, feeling nauseous. What a... one-track device. And he was constrained by it now, along with the others.

The van slowed to a stop. "You're here," the prostitute said from the front seat.

"Where?" Chet asked, bewildered as Journey and Knife opened the door and began decamping.

By the painted bricks and blocky architecture outside, they had to be in a historic district, one that harkened all the way back to Wetshul's days as a camp for the First Conversion Army. Fittingly enough, it was called the Training Grounds for United Victorious Equality District. Chet really had to wonder at the church fanatics and poor squatters who would choose such a mouthful to describe their patch of swamp.

"We're at a hotel that will hopefully take us," Journey replied shortly. Knife was heartily thanking the prostitute as he shook her hand; by Knife's words, Chet realized she'd recommended the place.

It turned out to be a hole-in-the-wall, not in a bad way. It smelled intensely of the past: lead paint, musty curtains and a certain fragrant mold beneath it all. Chet breathed deeply. The proprietor seemed about eighty years old and was going blind, though he addressed Journey and Knife readily as, "My good Flame." He personally rode up with them in the rickety, old-fashioned elevator to a room. Unlike the lobby, the room was bright and airy. There were two double beds and mullioned glass doors leading out to a wrought-iron balcony. The view was spectacular. Chet even caught a glimpse of the university, an hour's drive up the Monastery Mountains.

"... I'll have your meal sent directly up," the proprietor noted congenially.

Chet's head snapped around, alert at the possibility. "What meal?"

"They have a kitchen downstairs, run by that gentleman's wife. Traditional Wetshul cuisine," Journey promised.

Fenimore sat on a bed to remove his boots. "Mmph. Prepare yourself for sand and false teeth in the dirty rice." He curled on a bed in the same position he'd taken in the van.

"Pessimist," Journey laughed at him. She seemed far more at ease now that they were settled.

Despite Fenimore's low opinion, Chet's own spirits were decidedly repaired by fish stuffed with sweet potatoes and crawdads, doedicu in white garlic sauce, and spongy flatbread that was the local custom. A shower after the meal was also welcome. Chet had never before appreciated clean underwear in quite the same way.

When Chet emerged, he found Journey, Knife, and Fenimore had gathered on one of the beds, gazing at the Raptus. It lay nestled atop the white comforter, innocent and inert as Abyss. He joined them self consciously; as always, Chet felt the odd man out. Nevertheless, there was a place for him on the bed. As if echoing the ancient magic that had brought them together, they'd automatically formed a cross-like shape around the Raptus... even Chet had done so, he realized with a start.

Knife looked like a man—a Flame—laboring under a heavier load than he'd anticipated. "We must decide how to proceed."

*Proceed?* "I thought you were going to give the Raptus to the Shadow Dancers," Chet said.

"We were," Journey said. "But it has us, now. We're trapped. We don't know what it wants with us, and I'm afraid we're going to find out."

"Is our course not obvious? It wants to be used. It *should* be used," Fenimore said. Though he seemed to be trying to look relaxed, he was failing miserably. His pinched nostrils and the tension in his shoulders gave him away.

Both Journey and Knife shook their heads. "I want to consult with

Aureate and Doyen," Journey muttered. "We shouldn't be the only ones making this decision."

"It's ours to make." Knife raised an eyebrow. For the first time, Chet noticed that both Flame actually had eyebrows—and eyelashes, for that matter. How bizarre that they were bald, yet Pelin allowed this. It seemed to fall into the same category as distinguishing between bodily fluids and water: an irrelevant, subjective distinction, completely illogical.

Knife continued, "Everything's changed, yet nothing has changed. The Raptus is as big a pain in the ass as it's ever been, and it's high time to be done with the thing. *I* say we strive to destroy it. Barring other methods, all members of the Flame Council are currently alive and have been initiated to Pelin. This sort of confluence doesn't happen often."

Before Chet could ask what he meant, Fenimore jumped in. "Is this a democratic vote, the way independent city-states do it? Because there may be no clear majority, here."

"Flame have always operated via consensus," Journey said, her voice as gently corrective as that of a primary-school teacher.

The message was clear. The Flame clearly felt the Raptus was their territory, that their rules applied. Journey and Knife seemed comfortable in their ownership—dominance?—regarding the Raptus. Chet vaguely wondered how long it had been since their council had been made guardians of the Raptus. Foex had died over five-hundred years ago. It was a measure of Chet's acclimation to his new companions that five-hundred years seemed like a brief window of time. Though, to be honest, he'd always possessed a long-term sense of history, even before he'd become an archeologist. A mindset, it seemed, shared by everyone on the bed.

"You don't have the majority or authority to arbitrarily settle upon a mode of decision-making," Fenimore countered.

Knife gave him a mild look. "You object to destruction, I take it?"

"By the Abyss sundering Uos, of course I oppose destruction. It chose us, don't you see? *It* chose *us*. That tells me we need to explore what we have, not mindlessly discard it."

Journey snorted. "Explore how, exactly? We know too much as it is. The Raptus was created for complete control over people. The more you try to use it, the more you slide downhill into a bloody mess. The worst case scenario is an all-mighty autocracy instigated upon Uos. I assume Magicians had some form of checks and balances to keep this from occurring. We do not. The gods might eventually step in, but only after much human blood had already been spilt. They are not generally known for their mercy in such matters."

Fenimore turned to Chet. "What say you, scholar?"

Chet reached out and touched the Raptus with his index finger. "I want more information..."

"I shouldn't have asked. Scholars always want more information."

"LaDaven," Journey rebuked, her eyes glittering a subtle warning. "Yes, Chet?"

"Why can't we study it to find out how it works? A find of this magnitude is amazing. Even you don't know how it works, right? Aren't you curious?"

"Not really," Knife said. "We're more concerned with how ancient and recent technologies will mix."

"Apart from these cord things, that's why we're so jumpy," Journey said. "Modern technology definitely ups the ante. Imagine one person having control of every nuclear weapon and arsenal on the planet. Such power would be absurdly simple through this device."

"But I thought you said getting rid of it wasn't something you wanted to take on," Chet said, feeling lost. "How do we destroy it, anyway?"

Knife's expression was resolved. "It's too dangerous to leave lying around for another failure of vigilance. I didn't want to do this the hard way, but it's acting up in an aggressive manner. Better we go on the offensive than remain passive. As for destruction, we'll need to unlock it first—each member of the Council of Six will need to help with that—then one of us will have to order the Raptus to destroy itself. I volunteer myself for that part. I'll involve Pelin if I have to; she'd be willing."

Journey gave him a sharp look, then asked him a question in an unknown language. The same language as before? Knife replied in like. The exchange seemed significant, and Chet squirmed, hating that he was locked out of it. Fenimore, too, was scowling. Journey's eyes flickered upon Fenimore, then down at the Raptus. She shrugged, opening her hand in Knife's direction. He didn't look smug, but it was clear to Chet that he'd somehow won their—argument? Debate?

Fenimore looked like he was sucking a lemon. "How did the Flame manage to lock it, anyway? You have no magic, in the classic Magician sense."

"The goddess Aiena led us through the ritual. Each of us spilled blood upon it in turn while speaking words. To unlock it, we'll need to do the same."

"Specific words, I assume."

"Of course specific words," she said. "Each of us chose a different children's poem. I have mine memorized. Knife?"

He grinned at her. "Thespian. I did have mine memorized for a while, but I can only recall bits and pieces now."

Chet shot Knife an uncertain look. "You seemed to have an eidetic memory this morning."

"Hey, memorizing relevant data in the short term is one thing. That's just a trick I've picked up. *You* try to remember intricate, iambic-pentameter stanzas for five-hundred years. Through death, slavery, genocide and a world war, no less. In retrospect, I didn't choose my passage well—something about pretty little anuros flying in the springtime. Absolute poppycock."

Fenimore frowned critically. "This will be a futile plan if you've all forgotten your sacred charge."

"Oh, hush. Of course I have it written down at home. I re-transcribe the passage from my caches every lifetime or so, at my house in Allistair, I'm afraid. The others will undoubtedly have their own systems."

Journey turned back to Chet. "So... what *do* you think?"

He frowned. The Flame were self assured, convinced that destruction was the right thing to do. Besides, Fenimore didn't seem to have good reason—or a viable game plan—for the relic. He wasn't defending a helpless people or even bringing it home to a rightful ruler. There was too much at stake for simple curiosity to lead the day.

Chet shrugged, glancing at Fenimore. "Sorry, I'm with them."

"Very well. It seems we are set upon destroying it. Don't expect me to be happy about it, though."

Both Flame nodded, their expressions reserved, even respectful. No one tried to pat Fenimore on the arm condescendingly or invalidate his opinion.

Knife rose and stretched, then began a series of isometric exercises. Journey put the Raptus away in her large purse and got out a book. Chet stared at them. Hadn't they just made the decision to run like abyss and destroy the Raptus? Yet they seemed to take it for granted that they were done for the night. Well, it was their call. He led Fenimore to the bathroom and showed him how to use the shower. When Chet emerged, Journey eyed him speculatively, her book upturned on the bed. She was idly fingering a tit, and Chet's mouth began salivating as if he were a conditioned lab animal.

Journey smiled at him. "Come here, sweetie. Are you ready to try this new skill of yours again?"

"But I thought—aren't we getting going now? Isn't time of the essence, all that?"

"We need to wait to speak to the Shadow Dancers. Besides, we don't have a ride. We'll have to rent a car in the morning."

"I see." Chet looked away, self conscious. "Can I ask a question of a personal nature?"

"Of course."

"You and Knife both have this, um, smell." Would she take offense at the empirical observation?

Journey chuckled low in her throat. "That's ichor, Chet. It's the Flame god gift that allows us to survive fire. We are chemically altered by Pelin upon initiation. You probably didn't notice in the van, but all my bodily fluids have a slight purplish tinge to them."

"It makes me, er, responsive. More responsive than I usually am," Chet said. His cock was hard even now.

"Ichor is an aphrodisiac—best on Uos," Journey grinned at him. Her body was undulating beside him, her need apparent. "Here, you climb on top this time. Knock yourself out and just fuck me, okay?"

# Chapter 8
# New Territory

Chet scrambled to comply, shedding clothing with each step forward. Funny how he'd thought Journey was a fancy, glamorous lady only... yesterday? "Just fuck me" felt more like prostitute's language. Or the way he'd thought stereotypical Flame would speak, except Journey defied stereotypes. At least Knife had quietly slipped outside and was leaning over the balcony, Chet noticed with relief. He was grateful to have sex without an audience this time.

Journey, too, rid herself of clothing and sank on the bedspread, her knees spread outward. Her nudity was still new to Chet. The rational part of him wanted to look at her sex closer this time to see the ichor tinge for himself, but his cock was quivering, the hunger all consuming. He crawled on top of her and began bucking. Then Chet frowned. Something was wrong, different from last time. The formula oddly changed. He could feel her slippery, wet sex but didn't seem to be inside of her yet. Maybe he should buck harder for sex to happen?

Journey snickered. "Here, I'll do it."

Chet tingled with embarrassment as she took hold of him and tucked his dick inside of her. He hadn't realized he'd need to fit inside her, key-in-lock style. Last time Journey had done all the work, but now he was in charge. *Right?*

He thrust experimentally, curious how sex should be best accomplished. Her wet tightness still felt superb the second time around. Journey grinned up at him, biting her lower lip. Her hips were thrusting upwards to meet him, her tits jiggling in the most alluring manner. Chet found a tempo she seemed to enjoy and hung onto it as long as he could. Journey tilted her head back, emitting moaning noises low in her throat. Chet felt himself warm to the work. *Hey, I'm pretty good at this,* he thought with delight, increasing the tempo.

"No, go slower. *Slower.* Make it last."

But Chet found that he couldn't slow down. He was coming, coming—he threw his head back and spilled into her.

Journey sighed, gazing up at him with evident disappointment. "I really am going to have to train you, Chet. I'll have you fucking properly in no time, if you're a willing student."

Chet cleared his throat awkwardly as he rolled off. "Sorry."

A noise behind them startled him. He glanced back; the bathroom door was open, steam pouring out, and Fenimore was standing naked at the base of the bed, stroking his erect penis. "My turn, eh?" he murmured, crawling on the bed toward Journey.

She sat up abruptly, her legs audibly snapping closed. "I don't think so, LaDaven. Go jerk off or ask Knife to accept you."

"Oh, come now. You'll like me." He started fondling her breasts with both hands. "I won't spill early like your bashful swain here."

Journey growled, moving her legs under her in a crouch, then slid her hands up Fenimore's arms. She stopped just below his elbows and savagely pinched the fleshy part of his forearms. Fenimore yelped, thrusting himself away from her. He rubbed his forearms, his face mottled with confusion and anger.

Journey knelt on the bed as if ready to spring, her whole attitude fierce, almost animalistic. "You touch me again without my consent, Fenimore LaDaven, and I'll do permanent damage to your scrotum. I've castrated men before with my bare hands. Do we have an understanding?"

Fenimore opened his mouth and shut it, his expression enraged. "Yes, good Flame."

Journey slowly sat back on her heels. "You don't *get* to be as old as I am without learning where the boundaries lie. I don't like being raped."

Fenimore looked as if he'd like nothing more than to slam out the door and leave, except he was bound here through the Raptus. They all were. Chet could almost see him thinking about it as his eyes lit from Journey to the Raptus, sitting innocuously on the bedside table. Fenimore grabbed his dusty pants and stalked out to the balcony.

Chet realized Knife now faced them, watching everything through the sheer curtains, his arms resting easily on the wrought-iron balcony. Knife nodded at Fenimore and murmured something that Chet couldn't hear.

Chet regarded Journey on the bed beside him. He'd thought that she would have scrambled to get dressed like Fenimore, but she was breathing deep, her eyes closed. Regaining her composure? She glanced at Chet apologetically. "Excuse me, I don't mean to startle you."

Chet opened his mouth to reply, his confusion palpable, then froze. Journey was changing. Her body rippled as fat and musculature morphed under her skin. Her tits receded to a flat chest, and a penis and scrotum blossomed between her legs. Between *his* legs. Chet barely restrained himself from crying out, jumping out of bed and scrambling out the door. Journey was definitely male now. Even his face was different. Journey was still of the flaxen race, but he had a thicker jaw, flat cheekbones, his nose a different shape. She—he—still appeared young. A little older than Chet's age, maybe his late twenties.

Journey opened his eyes and smiled at Chet, his expression tinged with irony. "Are you freaking out?"

Chet discovered that he was frozen in a protective crouch. He deliberately forced himself to sink back to the bed. Journey seemed to take it as an invitation to cuddle up beside him. Chet paused, aghast. There was something viscerally wrong about the situation, but Journey was warm and familiar.

Chet took a deep breath and tried to relax with the man—Flame—in his arms. "A little." His voice was shaking.

They lay quietly together. Feeling calmer as each minute passed, Chet's scholarly curiosity perked up like a dium—a reptilian rodent which couldn't resist getting into everything. "Do you do this often? Change sex?"

Journey chuckled. His voice had changed too. Did he have a wider throat now? Chet leaned back and decided that Journey really had changed the external width of his throat. If he could do that, it probably meant he could change the internal larynx structure as well.

"Yes, I am most decidedly bi-sexed. Not every Flame is. Knife doesn't like being female, though he'll do it when there's need."

Chet glanced over his shoulder to the balcony where Knife and Fenimore were chatting. Though Knife was not technically in the room, he supposed Knife was still in eyesight, which was why Journey hadn't changed pronouns to the ubiquitous female. "This is why people are scared of Flame," Chet grumbled. "It's because we never know what you're going to do. Or be."

"Are *you* scared of me?"

Chet chewed it over a minute. "I'm not sure. I don't *think* I'm frightened anymore." In fact, the thought of fucking—or being fucked by—Journey in male form was rather... arousing. Chet found himself growing hard again.

Journey knew it, too. He eyed Chet speculatively, then deliberately reached over and brushed Chet's dick with the back of his hand.

"Oh, Pantheon," Chet gasped, his cock rising to fully erect at Journey's touch.

"Fenimore's forcefulness aside, it seems to me that you enjoy both men and women. Yes?"

"I—I've never..." Chet swallowed. He wanted to grab Journey's exposed cock. To, to suckle it, to have Journey come in his mouth. This was insane. He squirmed under pressure of having to produce an answer to a question he'd never considered, except... Chet *had* felt this way before.

"Yes," he finally said. Admitting the truth hurt.

Journey leaned back and took in his reaction with a practiced eye. "*This* is why people are frightened of us: so many don't know that they're flexible until we show up on their doorstep. And in their beds. Some have blamed us—even killed us—for helping them discover their own innate sexuality. Are you going to blame me, too?"

"No, mostly I plan to blame Fenimore."

"That's all right, then."

Journey curled up beside him and undulated, rubbing himself lightly against Chet. Chet hesitated. He wanted to kiss Journey, kiss him deeply, but did he have the guts to do so? *Oh, Abyss.* Chet climbed on top of Journey and kissed him. Chet felt Journey's lips smile beneath his. Journey was writhing under him, his hands stroking Chet's hair. Chet drew back to breathe and found that Journey was in the exact position under Chet he'd been in as female. His legs were spread and everything.

Yet when Journey spoke, he said, "I want to be inside of you. Think you can withstand another dick today? I'll be far more gentle than LaDaven, I swear.

Chet gulped. His ass still felt sore from Fenimore's sundering, yet that had felt so good. Journey might feel even better. "Um. Okay. Please be gentle with me!"

"I'll be better than gentle. Roll onto your stomach," Journey said as he got up to riffle through his luggage. Chet complied hesitantly as Journey plunked a familiar bottle on the bed. "That delightful young woman threw this in gratis when we were decamping. She said we'd probably need it again, the way we were going. She was right."

Despite his words, Journey did not squirt some of the oily liquid into his hands. Instead he spread Chet's buttocks and stared between them.

Chet squirmed, gazing at Journey over his shoulder. "What are you doing?" Why did it feel so alarming to have someone study his ass with such intense scrutiny?

"Fenimore really did plunder you open, didn't he?" Journey leaned in and—oh. *Oh*! Chet squealed like a girl as Journey's tongue pierced his anus. How soft and wet his tongue was, but this *couldn't* be hygienic.

"Aren't you afraid of getting sick?"

Journey chuckled, withdrawing his tongue to speak. "No. You just took a shower and I'm Flame. Like I said, we don't get sick—*any* sort of sick. Just deal with having my tongue in your ass, boy."

Chet *dealt* with it. He wondered whether this was the way women felt. The noises emerging from his mouth were womanly enough—high pitched squeaks and tiny moans—as Journey lapped him out. After a time, he drew back and slapped Chet on the ass.

The pain was sharp and palpable compared to his ethereal tongue. Chet yelped involuntarily. "Don't stop!"

"Stop? Why should I stop when you are so very sweet?" Journey said, diving back in. This time Journey suckled his balls, too.

Chet was beside himself with pleasure; spread and sundered. He didn't know how long he writhed. Minutes, hours, it was all the same.

Occasionally, Journey would draw back and slap or pinch to make him squeal. Chet could almost *feel* Journey's grin, feel his enjoyment of Chet's reactions. His skin was too small to hold him, and he came without warning, spurting onto the bedspread with vigor.

"That's better. Now you're relaxed."

Chet realized Journey had the bottle in hand again. He squirted an oily trail directly onto Chet's ass: it felt bizarre and dirty, and Chet reveled in the sensation. He really was dirty. A dirty little slut, spread before a Flame, ready to take his dick and fully intending to *enjoy* it.

Journey didn't disappoint him, but when he inserted himself, Chet frowned. Journey seemed rather too small, more like a finger than a cock. Chet didn't think he was *that* relaxed.

"Um..." he said hesitantly.

"I'll grow when you're ready for me."

As Chet had suspected, Journey's style of fucking was completely different from Fenimore's. He went slowly. He took his time. He was not afraid to stop occasionally and just lie on Chet, letting Chet take his full weight. As promised, his cock began to swell larger after a time. Chet was so absorbed, feeling the changes of weight and length inside his anus, that he barely noticed his own dick becoming erect again.

After a time, Journey nibbled his ear. "How about right there? Is that comfortable?"

"Make it bigger."

"You'll hurt afterwards, and I don't want to rupture your virginal ass."

"Bigger!" Chet insisted. "I want to feel full. Completely full."

"As you wish." Journey began fucking him harder, his penis growing by the minute.

Chet groaned; the dick felt *enormous*. "Okay. Okay. Right there."

"You're a size queen, sweetie." Journey snickered. He began thrusting in earnest; even pulling his cock all the way out before pushing—pushing!—back in. Chet came again, unable to hold back. It hardly mattered what he did. Journey was enjoying him thoroughly and would continue doing so no matter *how* many times he came. There was a certain freedom in that.

"Up on your hands and knees," Journey instructed and Chet

pulled himself upright. "Get to the edge of the bed. I want to stand and drill you like a line driver."

More oil was applied. Chet braced himself as Journey fucked him—hard. Chet yelped with each pounding, his hands closed to fists, gripping the bedcover. Journey threw back his head and whooped, slapping Chet's thigh as he came.

"Pantheon, you two are loud. It's a good thing we don't have neighbors in the next room yet," Knife commented from the other bed. Chet blinked—when had Knife and Fenimore come inside from the balcony? He and Fenimore were cuddling naked together, as if they'd just fucked, too.

"Hah." Journey threw himself onto the bed.

Chet snuggled up beside him. He gave Knife a worried glance. "Are you going to fuck me, too?" Every *else* liked his virginal ass, or his once-virginal ass.

Knife chuckled. "I like my lovers to have an edge to 'em. I especially enjoy self-righteous, cynical bastards, like certain unnamed parties." Fenimore, face down in the bed, mumbled an inarticulate protest at these words. Knife grinned and continued, "You know, the type who are used to being dominant in any relationship. I like breaking them like ceroses so that they whine and shiver under me. No offense, Chet, but you aren't my type."

"Oh. Okay." Chet yawned, curling beside the warmth of Journey's body—male, female, it didn't matter. He was so *relaxed*...

When Chet awoke, it was dark outside the mullioned balcony door. The bedside clock read 27:01. Midnight. Someone had tossed a blanket over his naked body. Fenimore was asleep on the other bed, and neither Flame seemed to be in the room. Chet saw an outline on the balcony—Journey? Too small and short to be Knife, anyway. He threw on his pants and wandered out to join... her?

Yes, Journey was back in female form. Chet gazed at her and noticed via the streetlight directly below them that she was rather more androgynous than before. Though she was dressed, he could tell her hips were long as a young man's, her tits small. No bra. Her face, too, was squarer and less pronounced female. Thin lips. She didn't acknowledge him but stared down at the street. Chet wondered whether he'd done something wrong. He was about to ask when Journey nodded downward.

"See them, a little ways from Knife? They're finally here. I take it they traveled all the way from Eich Che at your friend's insistence; you know, Zamie's daughter."

How did Journey know Rory's mom? Abysmal god affiliates with their inside connections. Chet looked down at the quiet street. There was a party with loud music a few blocks away, but this street was silent. It took him a while to pick out Knife smoking on the street corner. Knife wore his cap tipped at a rakish angle and had his arms crossed, an attitude that suggested that he could wait *forever*, if necessary. He looked like a cliché from a spy novel come to life.

"I don't see anyone but Knife," Chet said, rubbing his bare arms. The heat had broken, and he was chilled by the breeze.

"There. Right in the center of the road."

Chet rubbed his eyes, uncertain what he was seeing. It was like staring into a very small, compact black hole. Only it wasn't black—instead, it was almost entirely transparent. The thing *rippled*. "Is that... is *that* a Shadow Dancer Cluster?"

Journey nodded absently, and Chet scowled. "Why aren't they doing anything?" Was this Rory's family, here and now?

As if in reply, the Cluster suddenly split into two. The second ripple resolved itself into a human form in a flowing grey robe. The figure threw back its hood, and Chet gasped. It was Rory. He gazed down at her as he gripped the balcony with white-knuckled intensity. She didn't seem to know Chet was watching; she stepped closer to Knife and they spoke quietly.

Chet couldn't stand it. This was absurd. He needed to talk to her, to tell her things and make everything right. He opened his mouth to yell, but Journey grabbed his arm. Hard.

"Do not interrupt," she hissed in his ear.

Chet glared at her but closed his mouth. Whatever was happening was between god affiliates, which meant it was political. Rory was clearly representing her Cluster, speaking covertly to a Flame—a Flame *spy*—at midnight. Another pulp-novel cliché come to life: Shadow Dancers and Flame plotting dastardly deeds in the dark.

Suddenly, Chet felt anger broil up inside of him. *Screw all these dium eating, cynodict-humping affiliates,* he thought with a huff. His rage slammed him like a high-tide breaker. He was sick of their condescending attitudes and insider connections. Without thinking it through, Chet turned and slammed through the open balcony doors, out of the room and into the hallway beyond.

# Chapter 9
# Undercover

Journey called after him, cursing, but she kept her voice low... so she wouldn't wake Fenimore? Chet didn't stop. He could feel the cord to the Raptus grow taut, but he could also feel Knife up ahead. Such a bizarre sensation to be tied by the belly to another person, let alone a near stranger.

Stairs, lobby, street. Chet was vividly reminded he wasn't wearing either shoes or a shirt. He shivered but jogged along, little pieces of gravel making him hiss and swear, yet Knife was just ahead.

Chet slowed. Now that he was out here, he wasn't sure he wanted to interrupt Knife and Rory. He'd been pretty stupid to leave the room, but the anger inside of him still simmered, and he didn't want to go back. Chet approached slowly and stopped just within earshot, standing under the awning of a nearby building.

"... Pelin can't do it. You *know* that," Rory was saying. "The historic records are very clear. Abyss, apparently you were there, Knife."

"Indeed. Which means *you're* going to have to take all necessary steps to call Aiena, little as I envy you the task. It was your Cluster—and ancestors—who originally lost the Raptus, it's only fitting you fix this. We'll go slow, drag our feet. Shouldn't be too hard; the other Flame Council members are scattered across Uos, so we can ramble about and take our time. Just don't lose us."

"Well, don't disappear off the map."

Knife looked over his shoulder and glanced at Chet, then turned back to Rory. "We'll do our best." Knife dropped his cigarette and ground it under his foot.

Rory, too, looked at Chet. A plethora of expressions crossed her face—concern, anger, regret—within an instant. Chet surged forward, her name on his lips, but she turned away. Rory strode to the black hole and dove—*dove*—inside.

The black hole winked out.

Chet realized he was shaking. Hard as he looked, he couldn't see it anymore. Would he ever get another chance to see Rory again?

Knife sighed and sauntered back toward the hotel. He wasn't going fast enough to lose Chet, yet there was something about his body language that was chilling. Repellent. Chet followed him, rubbing his arms, cold from the inside out. He knew only one thing: Knife had lied, earlier. Rory had said Pelin couldn't do something, and Chet assumed that meant she couldn't destroy the Raptus. Why had Knife lied?

"I don't suppose you want to tell me what that was all about." Chet's tone sounded whiny even in his own ears.

"Not particularly, no," Knife said pleasantly. He opened the hotel doors for Chet, ushering him inside. "You ran out of the room without your key, didn't you?"

Chet had. He scowled, feeling like a child caught sneaking after bedtime. "I still don't see what my girlfriend has to do with any of this."

"You mean your ex?" Knife still appeared calm, but a slight sharpness had crept into his voice.

Chet hadn't told him or Journey about their relationship. Had Rory said something? Abyss, his whole life had turned upside down. He had no control over where they went next... where were they going, anyway? Knife had spoken of Flame Council members scattered across the world.

"So, where do we go now?" Chet said as they started up the stairs. "At a leisurely pace, no less."

Knife turned and, without warning, slammed Chet into the wall. Chet yelped—then his air was cut off. Knife held him by the throat in a secure manner. It felt like a practiced move. Chet's body was supported, his weight distributed evenly, yet he was unable to defend himself or breathe.

"You will say *nothing* of what you just heard. Do you understand?"

Chet nodded frantically as best he could. He was held a moment longer—long enough to understand he wasn't in control—then released. Chet crumpled over, coughing and gasping, tears running down his face.

"You may have been sheltered all your life, but this isn't a game. Time to grow up, Chet Baikson."

"Abyss! Why on *Uos...*" Chet looked up with watering eyes as he felt for bruises on his neck.

Knife turned and started up the stairs; Chet realized he had to follow. The Raptus made it so. It had changed everything. Still, Chet couldn't help bucking at the enforced order of silence. "What if I *do* say something?"

Knife paused and Chet tensed. He turned slowly and Chet scrambled away, but not too far. He couldn't go far on the invisible leash. Knife finally smiled. "I was under the impression you're a smart guy, Chet."

There was a long pause. Very long. Chet could feel his face growing hot. "Um. I like to think so."

Knife nodded. "Just so." He turned away again.

This time Chet followed without the backtalk. But he couldn't help asking while Knife was keying their way into the hotel room, "So where *are* we going?"

"We need to find Oak, the first Flame Council member on our list." Knife kept his voice down, but he was by no means whispering.

Chet glanced around the hotel room. The lights were off, but the curtains were pulled back from the glass doors, letting in the glow of streetlights. Alas, it was too cloudy for Elderbeth—the enormous gas giant which Uos followed doggedly in her orbit around the sun—to lend more light. Nevertheless, he could see Journey was awake, sitting cross legged on the bed. Fenimore still seemed to be asleep. Or at least he was snoring.

"Where would we find Oak, then? Maansterdam? Plainsdaugheau? Some Pantheon forsaken island? The arctic circle?"

"We go to Semaphore University. Your university."

Chet shot him an incredulous look. "There are no Flame at Semaphore."

Journey smiled at Chet and extended a hand. "Come to bed, sweetie. Tomorrow may be a long day."

Chet stared at her, his stomach sinking. The Flame wouldn't explain—they were definitely in on this together—and he had to go along anyway. Whether he wanted to or not.

Chet was in a dour mood as he drove everyone up the winding road to the university. His own vehicle had died eight weeks ago of a broken timing belt, and as his father had yet to replace it, they'd needed a means of transportation. Thus, Chet had rented a car with cash supplied by the Flame. It had been surprisingly easy, especially as their group was far less conspicuous today.

For one thing, Knife wore a long, messy wig bound in a ponytail. He'd changed his skin color to fallow once again; he and Fenimore looked like brothers. Fenimore's own long hair helped Knife blend in, Chet realized upon seeing them together. They wore argyle vests and penny loafers in the style of undergraduate college students everywhere, though Knife also wore a leather bomber jacket over his sweater. He hadn't carried *that* in his thin suitcase. Chet was shocked when he realized the outfits had come from Journey's extensive luggage, though he didn't know why he was so surprised that she owned male clothing. Some part of his brain had yet to catch up with events, he supposed.

Making his confusion worse, Journey was back in heavy makeup, cat's eye sunglasses and the modern-cut wig. She looked much as she had the day she visited the dig site. Chet realized with a jolt that it wasn't real makeup—she must have colored her face by shifting. It was hard to remember that she'd been a guy last night. With a penis and everything. When she was female, it was like that part of herself didn't exist and never had.

Despite their preparations, Chet felt sourness eat away at his stomach. No one would tell him who the Flame on campus was, only that her name was Oak and that she'd been initiated last summer. Maybe she was a measly undergraduate in sociology or the arts. Something benign and unassuming. After last night, he hated the idea that this, this *drama* had somehow seeped into the normalcy—the sacredness?—of his studies. Journey and Knife fascinated him, despite the fact that they were doing things in an underhanded fashion, yet Chet bristled at the idea of a Flame on campus. A Flame sharing *bathrooms* and eating in the cafeteria along with normal people. It seemed... indecent. Though he knew he was being irrational, his shoulders ached with tension.

Journey, too, was in a foul mood. "The director said that he'd never work with me again. He literally screamed over the phone line," she said to Knife in the backseat. "It's not as if I don't have an understudy. The director's vindictive, too. I might even get blacklisted from the Eich Che theater scene if he's in an especially bad mood."

"Shouldn't have slept with him, then, should you," Knife murmured. There was the sound of something—or someone—being hit, and Knife chuckled.

Chet glanced in the rearview mirror. "Do I need to come back there and separate you two? And you need to stop that, Fenimore."

Fenimore drew his head back through the window to grin naughtily, then stuck his head back out, hair whipping in the wind. Chet wouldn't have been surprised if he'd stuck his tongue out like a cynodict. Chet kept the car centered in the lane, hoping passing trucks barreling down the corkscrew mountain road wouldn't cut off Fenimore's head. Though... he supposed he should be grateful Fenimore wasn't nauseous and complaining. The three-hundred year old man had taken to automobile trips like a doedicu to water.

The university was quiet today. Well, it was summer term. Chet parked in the economy lot near the archaeology department, and they walked up the winding roads of campus. A campus security car passed them, and Chet held his breath. The vehicle didn't even slow down. *Good, the disguises are working.*

To Chet's astonishment, the two Flame headed directly toward the law library.

"Okay, I *know* there aren't any Flame in the law school," he said as they climbed the outer stairs. "I attended this graduate school for a year until I switched to archaeology. They're the most stodgy, conservative group on campus."

They were about to enter the library when, of all people, Professor Clementina emerged from inside with Professor Espies, head of the law department. Espies kept rambling on about something, though Clementina stopped dead in her tracks at the sight of them.

Espies blinked. "Is there a problem, Clementina?"

Chet didn't doubt Clementina was fully capable of making a scene. He winced as she opened her mouth... except she shut it. "Not at all," she said, linking her arm through his and leading him away. "Now, what were you saying about the censure of the Jantrael Straight Parliament?"

Espies prattled on as they strode away, arm in arm. Clementina glazed back over her shoulder, her expression hard to read.

Chet stared, shocked. "I thought for certain she'd call security."

"There're always interpersonal politics on a campus like this one. She may call them as soon as she can get away from the fellow," Knife said. "We'd best hurry."

The library was hushed, serene. Chet sometimes missed this place, though he didn't miss the law itself. His father had insisted on his becoming a lawyer to help with the family business. Chet hadn't exactly done well.

He glanced around the library and spotted a friend, his former roommate Steve. Steve had seen Chet, too. He rose from the wooden table where he'd been studying enormous reference texts and walked over.

"Steve, how've you been?" Chet began.

"Hi, Chet." Steve nodded at him before turning to Journey and Knife. "Come on, let's go somewhere more private. My dorm room is close. I'll lead you there."

"Why'd you want us meet you here, then?" Journey grumbled.

"I'm studying for my final in maritime trade with Professor Espies. I can't have you disrupt my whole day, you know," Steve said evenly.

Chet blinked. He blinked again. He gazed at Steve's head as he led them out the backdoor and across the quad to the graduate-student dorms. Steve had the same unfashionable, longish mop of messy curls he'd always had.

Steve said, "By the way, Knife, thank you for the gift last autumn. The miniature propane torch really comes in handy, since my plan to use the furnace in the basement fell through."

"You're very welcome. I know what it's like to live without a fireplace."

"Was there no privacy in the basement?" Journey asked. "Too drafty?"

"Custodians protested. Fortunately, they don't know which student I am; the administration simply calls me 'the Flame' when talking to people outside the loop. The gossip around here is something fierce among the faculty. Most think 'the Flame' is Bradrick from engineering."

Chet could see why. Bradrick was *that* kind of guy: a loose partier who dressed in drag while drunk and slept with a different woman every night. Last spring, he'd shaved his head on a bet, too.

Steve, on the other hand, was a young genius who'd studied his way to a secondary-school degree at fourteen. The gravely serious student who flossed his teeth and clipped his toenails when everyone else was out drinking. Abyss, he still *was* that guy. Chet had gotten along with Steve as a roommate because they both preferred reading over talking.

"The administration seems to be taking your initiation calmly enough," Journey said.

"Don't you believe it. I've had to attend a number of closed-door meetings regarding my status, even though I fully warned my department heads—well in advance, no less—that I was going to initiate. They can't accuse me of not preparing them. It's humiliating what they put me through, at times. Even the propane torch needed to be approved by the fire marshal before I could cleanse myself, but it's worth it for the degree."

He unlocked the door of a single-occupancy dorm room. It was tidy and swept, the bunk raised in a loft-like manner above the desk. In fact, it looked exactly like Steve's side of the room when he and Chet had been roommates. Steve hadn't even changed his classical-music conductor poster on the wall.

"At least they let you have your own room."

"Hah. They put me here so I won't seduce any potential roommate, and I get to pay for it, too. Full price," Oak sighed.

Knife snorted. "They didn't believe you on the monogamy thing, eh?"

Oak shrugged as he settled at his desk. "I don't need to tell you stereotypes are pervasive near the defunct Slave Trade Route." He dug through a drawer and came up with a folding pen knife. "Which one of you has the Raptus? Much as I enjoy seeing you, Journey, Knife, I'd like to get this over with."

Journey withdrew the relic from her roomy purse. Steve—or rather, Oak—bled a few drops on the relic. He gave them an embarrassed look and said, "I'm afraid this is going to sound a bit silly.

"There was a woman
Who ate an indricoth
As a baby she started on the tail
That took her ten years
As a girl she ate the haunches
That took her ten years
As a maiden she ate the offal
That took her ten years
As a mother she ate the forelegs
That took her ten years
As a granddam she ate the neck
That took her ten years
As an old woman she started gnawing on the skull
And realized she had no teeth left at all!"

Chet, listening to the old nursery rhyme, blinked when the Raptus flashed bright green in Oak's hands. Chet stared at it, wondering whether it would do something else. The Raptus remained silent. Oak handed it to Journey, who put it back in her purse.

"Thank you," Journey said.

"You're welcome. I want to know what happens, you hear? Don't just fall off the face of Uos as usual, Journey. You need to write, and write often."

"Yes, Oak." They kissed. It was a dry kiss on the mouth, not like the friendly, flirting kiss Journey and Knife had shared only—two days ago? It seemed to be a ritual and not from passion. Knife's kiss was no less chaste.

The others began leaving, but Chet didn't move. "I want to talk to, um, Oak. Can you please go on without me?"

# Chapter 10
# The Body

Chet handed the car keys to Journey. "I'll be down in a few minutes, okay?"

The door closed behind the others. Chet wasn't sure what to say. This was Steve. The guy who'd snored across the room every night for over a year, who'd loaned him books, let him cheat on a test. Steve currently owed him eleven gilt. Yet he was Flame.

After a moment of silence Steve folded his arms, raised his eyebrows, and said, "Yes, Chet?"

Chet felt like he was going to throw up. "Steve, are you really Flame?"

Steve removed the wig, and yes, he was bald. Otherwise, he looked exactly the same as he always had. Fallow skinned and brown eyed with a little scar on his forehead from a childhood accident. Nothing had changed... except *everything* had changed.

Chet licked his dry lips. "When?"

"Last summer. I'd had it planned for a couple of years."

"You've been Flame a whole *year?*" Oak's words caught up with him, and Chet's eyes nearly popped out of his head, cartoon style. "You had it planned? You *knew?* You knew when we were *roommates?*"

"Of course I knew. I was saving my hair even then so that it could be made into wigs." Oak frowned at him. "What, you feel betrayed because I didn't tell you?"

"Well, yeah. The way I see it, you owe me! Why did you keep all this from me? We *do* things together, man. I showed you the steam tunnels when you first arrived on campus, and you let me cheat off your test that one time. It's only been three *weeks* since we went out for aran-spiked coffee with Rory to celebrate my birthday. You're such a liar. Why didn't you tell me, Ste—Oak?"

Oak rolled his eyes upward, as if seeking patience from the God Plain. "You would have freaked out, the way you're freaking out now."

"I am *not* freaking o..." Chet stopped and took a few deep breaths.

Why was he panicking, anyway? He'd never thought of himself as anti-Flame. Was he really prejudiced? *No,* he thought defiantly, yet he couldn't apologize to Oak. It wasn't that the guy was Flame, it was because he was a sneak and deceiver. Abyss, Oak probably had orgies in here every night, while Chet had always assumed that Oak was just another student. A dull student, sure, but also normal, uncomplicated and most importantly, *unaffiliated*. Like Chet.

Oak watched Chet with irony, arms crossed. "You know, for someone who's been sleeping with Journey, you're treading a very fine line, here."

"I... uh. How did you know?"

"Please, give me some credit. I'm fond of my colleague, but Journey isn't exactly discriminating. I, on the other hand, am."

He sounded so certain—and stuck up—Chet couldn't help raising his eyebrows. "Why should I believe you? You've lied about everything else."

"I don't care if you believe me. We're friends, but I'm not going to sit here and be insulted." Oak's eyes were narrow, sharp as broken glass. "Go away, Chet. Leave me alone."

Chet started to rise... then sat back down. Part of the reason he'd liked Steve was because he valued the past as much as Chet did. If Oak was another reincarnating soul of Pelin, he hadn't lied about that part. What if he wasn't lying now? "Oak, I want to believe you. Could you explain? I mean, I'm just trying to learn."

"No, you're not. You're being a doedicu." Oak sniffed and looked away.

Chet slumped, uncomfortable as Oak grabbed a tissue to hide his face. In Chet's experience, men didn't cry, and they especially didn't cry in front of other men. He hadn't cried since he was nine, and he didn't expect to do it ever again. It was visceral proof that Oak wasn't a man anymore, or at least not the kind of person Chet recognized as male.

He cleared his throat. "Uh, sorry. I guess... I guess I'm having a hard time with this because I've discovered a new side of me, and I'm not sure I can live with it. I'm just trying to figure out what it all means." Could Oak help? Did he have a solution to Chet's newly discovered sexuality, his love of men and women... and Flame?

Oak snorted acerbically. "I'm the wrong person to talk to about this sort of thing."

"Huh?"

"Look, I'm considered the most conservative member of the Flame Council for good reason. I practice monogamy and work on long-term relationships. Abyss, over my lifetimes I've buried more common-marriage spouses who died of old age than the rest of the Council combined."

"Oh." Chet digested this. "Guess you wouldn't have tried to seduce me when we were roommates."

"Spare me. That's such a stereotype. Among other things, you're the wrong gender—I'm heterosexual."

"You're... no, you can't be. How would that even work?" Chet frowned at him. This conversation couldn't get any weirder than if Oak had sprouted a second head. Something else was distracting Chet. After a moment, he realized that the invisible cords binding him to the Raptus—and the others—was stretching farther than it ever had. It was starting to feel tight and painful, but Chet couldn't leave now.

"I like women when I'm a man, and vice versa."

"Yeah, I know what heterosexuality is. But you can change your sex..."

"No more than once or twice a lifetime, if I can help it."

"Then why are you Flame?" Chet asked plaintively. It seemed everyone had their own rules when it came to this stuff. Why couldn't the rules be consistent? It seemed each Flame tailored her own identity to match their internal comfort level, whatever that might be.

Oak looked out the window. "I like Pelin, and I enjoy being alive. Flame live a long time, did you know? We can clock up to a hundred and forty years if we're lucky and plan well. I plan well."

Chet could see that. Oak was completing a degree under punishing conditions for the sake of his future career. Chet knew all about being singled out for an affiliation, or lack thereof. Meantime, Oak had drawn his knees up to his chest and was gazing out the window. He looked so sad and depressed that Chet felt alarmed.

"What's wrong?" he said. Despite everything, it worried him to see a friend looking down.

"Just... thinking about planning. It doesn't always work out the way you'd hope. I was a teacher last time I died, during the war. Soldiers tracked me and my students down. I..." He gulped and stopped abruptly. "Some days, I regret having to remember. It gets bad on snow days; that's when I have a hard time leaving this room. Rory brought me dinner, last time."

"*Rory* knows about you?" Chet whispered. Sirens were wailing in the distance through the open window.

"She's been very understanding."

Chet opened his mouth, then shut it. Did Chet believe his ex-girlfriend had known about Steve—Oak—without saying something? Considering Rory hadn't even told him about her ability to give him *electric shocks* and *dive into nothingness,* let alone wander about at midnight dressed in a dark robe... well, yes, put it that way, and he could believe it.

Rory had said something about being, "one of us." Which meant she was—what? A spy, like Knife? Abyss, how had he overlooked that aspect of her life for so long? Chet found himself wondering what would it might be like to date Rory for real. To know her secrets, yet still love her and enjoy her company. He felt like she was a book he'd tossed over his shoulder after reading a few pages. There was so much more to Rory than he'd allowed himself to understand.

Then there was Oak himself. Tears non-withstanding, he seemed intensely vulnerable. Enemy soldiers in the snow? Chet had endured many a war story from older, boorish relatives, but he'd never spoken to someone who'd actually *died* during the war. Oak had died. He'd been dead, and here Chet was being a jerk about it. Ste—Oak was a good friend, Flame or not. Feeling awkward, Chet extended his hand and patted Oak on the knee, keeping his distance more for Oak's comfort than his own. Oak blinked at him, coming out of whatever reverie he'd fallen into.

"I'm sorry," Chet said.

Oak smiled and put the wig back on. "Didn't mean to go all deep on you, there. I hope you don't mind, but I need to get back to studying. We can talk after you get back from whatever you guys are doing with the Raptus. I hope it turns out well for you. Tell me more when it's all over, okay?"

That was the Steve Chet knew: good student from head to foot. "Yeah, okay." Chet stumbled out the door, not sure what to feel.

This was insane. Everything Chet thought he'd known about the world was a lie, yet... was it such a bad thing? Chet inhaled as he walked back to the economy parking lot; the air was redolent with the scent of pine trees and grasses warmed in the sun. There were immense aspects of the world he'd never even dreamed about. Knowledge of such things wouldn't kill him. In fact, it might even make him a better archaeologist. A better person in general.

The invisible cord—which had grown looser the farther he walked—started tightening again as soon as he turned into the economy lot. He ignored the sound of sirens and kicked a beer can up the road, concentrating on the weird feeling. Why was the tightness still there? In fact, it was getting worse.

*Oh, shit,* Chet thought as he walked up to the silent, unoccupied rental car. He frowned. Where were they? The cord was tightening even further... he blinked. A police car with the siren wailing was coming closer at top speed, headed for the archaeology quad. Chet gulped and began trotting in that direction. The invisible cord loosened—the direction was apparently correct.

Those had been real police, not campus security.

Chet raced into the archaeology quad and froze, uncertain where to turn. A group of police officers and Professor Clementina were at the center of the courtyard. No, he definitely didn't want to see her. Chet turned to go back the way he came. Maybe he could go through a backdoor, or use the underground steam tunnels?

A deep, two-packs-a-day voice rang out across the courtyard. "There! That's one of them."

Chet instinctively began to run. The policemen tackled him to the ground before he'd even cleared the quad. They were strong, and he yelped as they twisted his hands behind his back. He was cuffed, the metal harsh and cold against his skin. Shocked shivers ran through

Chet's body, making him feel stupid. The cords had stopped feeling so tight, but what would happen when Chet was driven away in a police car?

"Do you know this person, ma'am?"

Chet couldn't see the police officer who'd spoken, splayed on the ground as he was, but the guy sounded properly respectful and intimidated. Like so many people who met Clementina.

"This is Chet Baikson, an archeology student who was working on the dig site. He and the others stole a valuable relic, running away with it together. Over thirty of his fellow students witnessed the act."

The police hauled Chet to his feet and walked him around to the back of the quad, where a two squad cars and the campus security vehicle were waiting. No one else was there.

One officer muttered to the other, "Thought we were looking for couple of Flame baddies, but this one's just a kid. He's got student written all over him."

As if to confirm the observation, the other tugged at Chet's hair.

"Ow," Chet muttered, resentful and frightened. Pantheon, the cords were really beginning to hurt, again. One of their group was traveling too far away, and the link was stretching, pulling him. Surely the person would stop... unless they were being chased by police.

"Yep, just a kid, all right. Probably talked into it by the fire perverts." Despite their words, they opened the back door of a police car and made Chet climb inside. The policeman sighed. "You want to drive him back to the station, or should I?"

"I'll take him. I got paperwork to catch up on." The guy paused as yet another officer stuck his head around the quad corner.

"Both of you jokers better get back here. We found a body. It's still warm, too."

A body? A *body?* Chet craned his head over his shoulder as the police ran off, leaving him alone. He jittered, trapped in the back of the police car. His arms were starting to hurt, too. Chet absently wondered whether the Flame ever had circulation problems with their shapeshifting talents, then snorted. They could probably just shape out of handcuffs.

*Speaking of which...* Chet closed his eyes and concentrated on the invisible bonds. Now that he was properly paying attention, he could feel the movement of the others. Though they were in three different places, he was pretty certain none of them were dead. The Raptus was headed toward him, he knew that much—it was growing closer by the second.

"You thought you and your nasty friends could grab it without repercussions, didn't you?"

Chet's eyes flew open. Professor Clementina stood outside the car window. They were alone, no police in sight. The window was closed, but Clementina was pressing her face against the glass as if he were a biological specimen in a zoo. Chet scooted into the middle seat by instinct, wanting to get as far away from her as possible. She smiled and opened the door—wait, hadn't the police locked it? Chet yelped as she reached in and grabbed him by his lapels. Clementina pulled him from the car like someone cracking open an ocean crustacean for its meat.

Chet squeaked, pumping his legs. He was being held inches above the ground. "Hey, I'm in police custody! What do you think you're doing?"

"I know you and the others stole the Raptus from the dig site, so don't play games with me," she hissed, slamming him into the police car. "Where is it?"

How on Uos had she known the relic's name? Did everyone else know about this thing but him? How had he been surrounded by a conspiracy yet never twigged to it? Chet stared at her, made stupid by fear and shock. "What?"

She maneuvered him so one arm held him up, bracing him against the car. Then she wrapped her free hand around his neck and squeezed. "Listen, you little dium, the Raptus is mine. I didn't spend hundreds of thousands of gilt on the dig site for chew sticks and clocks. Where is it?"

Chet wheezed with what little air he had, struggling for breath. As his vision grew dark, he realized with the rational part of his mind that he'd felt safer with Knife's hand around his throat than with Clementina's. Knife had just wanted to make a point: she was a professional and had known precisely when to stop. Clementina didn't. He could see it in her eyes, her reddening face. Spots erupted in his vision... he was passing out...

"What are you doing?" someone yelled. "That's our suspect!"

Chet was released. He fell onto the pavement, choking. Abyss, he'd been throttled for the second time in as many days—he was going to have some spectacular bruises.

Clementina and the officer were talking above him, but he couldn't focus properly. He blinked his watering eyes as Clementina turned and walked away. *What?* Why hadn't the police officer arrested her for assault and battery? Chet's indignation broiled as the officer hauled him to his feet. Bulky and bistre-skinned, the new officer seemed oddly uncomfortable in his uniform.

To Chet's surprise, the officer began leading him away from the car. "What are you doing? Where are you taking me?"

"Hush. I'm getting you out of here, Chet," the guy murmured in his deep bass. He was carrying a large paper bag in his other hand, marked "evidence."

Chet stared as he was hustled forward. The policeman's uniform exactly like the others, only he wore his hat scrunched down to his ears. No sideburns, no hair peeking out from under the cap. Moreover, one of the cords was located right beside Chet, as was the Raptus.

"Journey?" Chet whispered with disbelief.

"Yeah. Come on, they'll be back any minute." Journey hustled him into the nearest building, an archaeology lecture hall with faculty offices in the basement. Chet knew the building inside and out.

"Can you get these cuffs off? I mean, can you shape your fingers real thin and break the chains in half or something?"

"I don't have extra-human strength," Journey growled in his deep voice. "I'd shatter bones doing that, and Pelin doesn't heal bones. I got this guy's keys, though, when I stripped him. Whoops!"

Journey swiveled around and walked the other way, but not before Chet saw the officer at the end of the hall. Fortunately, he was faced the wrong way. He'd been positioned like a man guarding something.

"Go left," Chet said in an undertone. "Now go right, straight down this hall. There's a stairwell we can take."

"Where are we headed?"

"Down to the steam tunnels. We can't get to the economy parking lot that way, but at least we can get out of this quad." The invisible bond to one of the others seemed to point downward. The other... Chet frowned, uncertain. He couldn't properly concentrate while hustling with his hands cuffed behind his back, but whoever it was wasn't in the archaeology quad anymore.

"Won't the police expect us to take those tunnels?" Journey said, glancing behind them. Chet could see the whites of his eyes.

"Don't know, but better than nothing." There had been two police cars and one security car, meaning... what? That there were four officers and two security guards out there? Or three, since Journey seemed to have taken one down, or whatever, for his clothes. They had to have called for backup, though, which would be arriving soon.

Chet and Journey turned the corner, and a policeman was standing right there. He was in the process of lighting a cigarette. "Hey, what are you doing, Myers? The kid's supposed to be locked up in the car!"

"I was told you wanted him," Journey said evenly.

Myers? Journey had apparently copied the appearance of the officer whose uniform he wore, which made sense. Chet had known Journey for only a short time, but it seemed to Chet that this current face and figure wasn't his *style*.

"Aw, Abyss with that. Take the kid back up," the officer growled. "We can't screw up this scene or admin will be all over us."

"Right." Journey swiveled and led Chet back the direction they'd come. "That was close," he whispered.

"Take a left up here. We can still get to the staircase via a roundabout corridor." Chet had often used that particular corridor while coming in and out of Professor Tibbet's office.

"Chet, *look*." There was a smear of blood on the floor near the corner, leading in the direction Chet was taking them.

He hestitated, then swallowed his fear. "Come on, we've got to keep going." They either went this way, or they didn't get to the steam tunnels.

They rounded the corner. Even though he was prepared for a gristly scene, Chet's mouth opened, and he felt blood drain from his face. Journey gasped, his hand reflexively touching his heart, an effeminate gesture belied by his current appearance. Chet couldn't believe it. He just couldn't.

Professor Tibbets sat against the wall. There was blood all over the floor, smeared and marked. By the mess, it looked like Tibbets had dragged himself into that position. His chest was bloody, marring his perpetual tweed suit.

He was dead.

# Chapter 11
# Getting Away from It All

"Oh, Pantheon," Journey said as they tiptoed around the body. "Oh, *Pantheon*." He sounded far too effeminate to be a policeman, now, though his voice was still low.

Numb and sick to his stomach, Chet took the lead. Journey trailed behind, not even pretending to be an arresting officer anymore. They trotted downstairs, and Chet led them through the double doors marked "Do Not Enter." The utilitarian corridor was silent and dimly lit by emergency lighting.

Chet stopped and leaned against a wall, unable to continue. His teacher, his mentor, was dead. Professor Tibbets had been a swell guy, completely affable. He'd never once expressed concern about Chet's non-affiliate status. Now he was gone. His body had looked so awkward, sprawled on the floor. Something inside of Chet wanted to protest the careless, almost accidental nature of the scene they'd just witnessed. Professor Tibbets had deserved to be more than a corpse, killed before his time.

Blood. There'd been so much blood.

Chet swallowed. "I think I'm going to be..." He barely had time to take a breath before throwing up. Coughing, his throat burning, Chet slowly straightened.

"You okay?"

"Not sure. I guess so."

"Turn around, Chet. Let me at those cuffs." After a few false tries, Journey found the correct key to free him.

Chet rubbed his hands and arms, chilled through. He could feel the invisible cord to the nearest person; whoever it was, they'd begun heading their way. They were on the same level, he was certain. Was the other person lost in the steam tunnels?

"Come on," Chet said, heading toward the sociology-anthropology lecture halls. By the loosening of the bonds, he was certain both Fenimore and Knife were in this general direction.

"Who would do that to poor Veyaon? He was a kind, generous man who wouldn't hurt a dium, not even if it was gnawing on his face."

His voice was a light alto, and Chet glanced back, startled. Journey was shapeshifting even as Chet watched. His skin color rippled back to flaxen, growing taller and skinnier in the process, though he stayed male. Now Journey looked much as he had last night. He stripped out of the button-down police shirt to reveal a white undershirt, but didn't discard the hat; the wig was nowhere to be seen. Myer's clothing was loose and baggy on him now, too short for his stature—Chet could see a sliver of Journey's midrift between his shirt and trousers. He carried the purse with the Raptus openly, the paper bag having been abandoned.

Chet licked his lips. Barring a random killing... almost *any* of them could have murdered Tibbets. "I know Fenimore has his blade, but does Knife carry any weapons?"

"Several. He even has a concealed gun. I know Knife doesn't have a problem hurting people while on Pelin's business, but we aren't on Pelin's business. Knife isn't a sociopath, you know."

"Um, you don't say." Chet shot her a sideways look from the corner of his eye. He'd never thought Knife *was* a sociopath.

Journey shrugged. "All I'm saying is, she doesn't enjoy murder. For that matter, I've killed men in my time."

"This lifetime, too?" They opened another set of double doors, paused, then entered the next set of steam tunnels. Somewhere in the distance he heard the rumble of pipes and a water heater turning on.

"Mmm. I survived the war, you know. You do things in war that it normally wouldn't occur to you to do," Journey said thoughtfully, his voice distant. "But I know it wasn't me. I don't think it was you."

"Good great Pantheon, Professor Tibbets was all that was standing between me and being expelled because of you guys. Plus, he was a fantastic person and a good teacher. Why on Uos would *I* kill him?"

"Motivation is a problem for all of us. What about if it wasn't one of us, though? What if it was Clementina?"

Chet chewed the idea over, wiping sweat from his brow. It was getting warmer now that the corridor led upward. They were probably near the boiler by the sociology faculty offices. "How do you figure?"

"What if she saw this as an opportunity to finger evil, perverted Flame for murder? The timeline works. She spots us, calls the police, murders poor Veyaon, then has enough time to meet the police in the quad."

A dark shadow stepped out from behind water and sewage pipes down the corridor. Chet jumped, heart in his throat.

"Did I hear right? Tibbets is dead?" Knife said quietly.

"Where have you been?" Chet said, glaring.

"Don't snap at me, boy. We got separated running from the police. This place is a maze. Finally thought to follow this bond thing to find you."

Chet let Journey do the explaining. The forth cord—Fenimore's—was definitely straight ahead and up a level. Apparently he was in the faculty parking lot nestled between buildings. Chet turned and led them through another set of double doors and up a stairwell. The problem was that Journey was right: they all had a problem with motivation. Journey could even be covering his own guilt. He and Tibbets had been old friends, or so it seemed. Maybe Journey had slept with Tibbets, too, when Tibbets had been younger. That would fit Journey's *modus operandi.* Yet Chet could have sworn Journey's reaction had been real.

But what did he really know about these Flame? He'd known them three days.

They emerged from the quiet building to the secluded faculty parking lot. After a few seconds, Fenimore emerged from behind a vehicle and loped over.

"Where have you been?" Fenimore was wild eyed and stranded looking. He seemed relieved to see them, his hair escaping the ponytail in puffy, frothy curls.

Journey explained again. Chet ignored them, watching Knife—he seemed to be casing the joint, or something like that. Chet had never seen someone do such a thing, but the phrase fit his behavior. Knife was looking over each vehicle the way a ceros thief looked over a herd. He paused beside a large luxury sedan.

Chet recognized it. "That's Professor Clementina's car. One of them, anyway."

Knife grinned and fished a leather wallet out of his pocket... only it wasn't a wallet, it held tiny metal tools instead of money. "Thought these female professors don't have the salary of their Literati counterparts."

"I believe she married into money," Chet said, watching with fascination as Knife picked the car door lock. "Her husband's family controls copper mines in the mountains."

"In that case, she can afford to lend us her ride." The door clicked quietly, and Knife opened it. "Come on, get in."

They piled inside except for Knife, who knelt under the steering column. He extracted another tool from the leather wallet and unscrewed a front panel, then ripped through the wires inside. He touched two wires together, and the car started.

Chet shut his gaping mouth. He really *had* fallen in with bad company. These were the people that mothers warned their children about. Well, not *his* mother, but mothers in general. Stealing cars, possibly murdering people and having sex like crazy... Chet couldn't help but grin at this last quality, despite his deep-set unease with sexuality, especially his own.

"Want to try for the rental car in the economy lot?" Knife asked. Chet nodded and gave directions.

Fenimore looked at them in disbelief. "Is it worth the risk?"

"Yes!" Journey and Chet said simultaneously. Chet didn't want to lose his books much in the way he didn't want to lose his right arm. Journey apparently felt the same about her things, too.

Except the economy parking lot was being used as overflow for the numerous police cars that had responded to the murder investigation. Policemen were walking between the lot and the archaeology quad. There was no way to enter without being seen. No way to retrieve their stuff. An officer glanced up at them even as he filled out paperwork on his dash.

"Shit," Chet said, wanting nothing more than to sink down in the seat.

Knife said, "Everyone, stay calm. Look bored."

Chet closed his eyes, waiting for lights and sirens to blaze up behind them. Nothing happened. Knife gently steered them down the hill, and they passed not one but three more police cars, sirens wailing.

"I can't believe we got aw—" Chet paused as they rounded the corner. Police were putting up barricades even now at the base of campus. A checkpoint crossing.

Knife glared at him. "You realize this is your fault, right?"

Chet swallowed and glanced at Journey in the backseat. He was the most conspicuous member of their party, with his police hat and bald head beneath. Journey knew it, too. He slipped to the floor of the car. Chet watched as he flattened out; it was a bit like watching pastry dough being rolled out. After a moment, Chet realized Knife was changing, too. The shape—and color—of his exposed skin was shifting, morphing. Chet stared, wondering what the results would be.

"Face forward, Chet," Journey hissed. "Act like nothing's wrong. Fenimore, take off your sweater and drape it over my head and arms, then put your feet on me like I'm the floor."

"Try to stay calm, everyone. This is going to get hairy," Knife said. Even his voice was changing—it sounded familiar, somehow. They were about a hundred feet from the officers.

This couldn't work. It would never work. Chet faced forward with wide eyes and a smile plastered on his face. What had Knife changed into? Who was he now? And how could the police possibly miss the lump—the flat lump, but still—of Journey on the floor behind them? Chet could *feel* cold sweat, something he'd never felt before, as Knife brought them to a complete stop.

"Morning, officers," Knife said in an entirely different tone of voice. Abyss, his voice was familiar.

"Step out of the car, please."

"Yes, sir."

Chet stared at Knife's back, jittering with unease. Knife seemed shorter in his new form. Chet glanced back and caught Fenimore's eye; Fenimore looked cool and collected. He either didn't understand the severity of the situation or—more likely—he'd experienced worse. Chet swallowed and tried to emulate Fenimore's nonchalant attitude.

"What seems to be the pro—hey!" Knife cried out. The officer had grabbed his hair—the wig—and swept it off his head.

"A Flame!" Both officers drew their guns and trained them on Knife, who'd raised his hands above his head.

"Yes, I'm Flame. But I'm also a student here." Knife had finally turned so Chet could see his profile. Chet gaped. He *knew* that face, knew it well. Knife continued, "My initiate name is Oak, but on campus I'm known as Steve."

"There are no Flame at Semaphore University." The officers seemed hesitant, the tips of their guns wavering.

Knife made eye contact with Chet. "That's my friend and former roommate in the front seat. His name is Chet Baikson. Could he step out of the car to verify my identity?"

The second officer moved around the stolen vehicle, his gun now aimed at Chet, and nodded once. "Keep your hands visible," he muttered as he opened the passenger door.

Chet rose from the seat, hands raised in the air. He was shaking. "Um, hello."

"Chet, *tell* them," Knife hissed.

"Okay, yeah. This is Oak, but I still call him Steve," Chet said valiantly, gazing at Knife. Knife short as Steve, but he was rounder: his belly protruded, and he had a bit of a double chin. Was it because he was usually taller than Oak? Maybe he had more mass. Chet continued, "Oak's a graduate student in the law degree program. We've known each other for three years, from before he initiated to Pelin last summer."

"What else?"

"Don't you guys know a student when you see one? Look, his last name is Irkshie and his student ID number is 772A-3-9G34," Chet went on, warming to his work. Of course he knew Steve's ID, as Steve had let him cheat off a test that first year. Chet was heartened that he still remembered it in the heat of the moment. *Knife isn't the only one who can pull this trick.* "You don't have to take my word for it. Why don't you call the law department on campus and *ask* them? Abyss, ask Professor Espies. Oak, aren't you're taking a test in Espie's maritime-trade class tomorrow?"

Knife nodded, hands still raised in the air. To Chet's surprise, he was crying and shivering, as if he really was scared out his mind. Despite the extra weight, he looked exactly like Oak when he was crying. "Y-yes. P-please don't hurt me. It's not a crime to be Flame! Not even outside W-Wetshul."

"All right, stay put while we check this out." Both guns had been put away, now.

One officer went back to the car to confer on his radio while the other walked around the car. "Hey, who's this?"

"Recent exchange student from Tache. He knows almost nothing of our language, and his name is Fenimore LaDaven," Knife supplied, as if eagerly.

Fenimore smiled and waved through the car window. In the Tache language, he said, "Very pleased to meet you, you son of a rabies-infested dium and a scrotum-dragging doedicu."

Chet glared at him, and even Knife shot him a sharp look, but the officer just shrugged. "Huh. Well, okay, then."

*That was close,* Chet thought. Fenimore had taken a chance, and not a small one. The officer might well have known the Tache language... or, more likely, he could have recognized some of the words Fenimore had used. It would have been easy for the guy to deduce he was being mocked. Doedicus and diums were universally thought of as common, stupid creatures across Uos, no matter the language.

They waited. They waited some more. Finally, the other officer came back. "What was your ID number, again?" he asked Knife.

"772A-3-9G34," Knife recited promptly. Of course.

The guy checked his pad. "Okay, I guess you're free to go."

An hour later, deep in the Monastery Mountains, Chet said, "So where are we going next? We can't go back to Wetshul." How strange it felt to be a wanted criminal. How strange to have his whole professional future swept out from under him. *Now* he could believe he'd be expelled. Abyss, he was probably going to prison.

Knife glanced over his shoulder at Journey, who was still rubbing the back of his neck. "We do the job. The plan hasn't changed. We visit the next council member on our list."

"At least Othnielia is relatively close. Only about eight hundred miles away," Journey said, coughing. He looked like he was in pain, and his voice cracked when he spoke. Apparently, he'd flattened out his lungs and throat with the rest of his body on the floor. "Pantheon, those wigs we just left behind cost me 2000 gilt. Not to mention my wardrobe. Knife, how much money do you have?"

"Some. The rental car and hotel took a chunk, though, and we may have to get a little inventive soon." By his tone, Knife didn't find the concept of stealing abhorrent.

Chet glanced around their stolen luxury car and sighed. He'd just covered for the crime. Aided and abetted, quite willingly. Even his family couldn't save him if he got caught with these people.

"*Inventive* would add more theft to the charges on the list," Journey muttered. Chet was comforted that he wasn't the only one evaluating their growing number of felonies.

Knife said, "They'll want our heads for this anyway. I mean, just think of the headlines. 'Flame Murder Beloved Professor After Stealing Ancient Relic.' A roll of cash will make little difference."

"Prison is not my favorite place," Journey said shakily. He was close to tears, Chet realized. "I don't like being locked up."

"I know, lovely one. I know." Knife glanced at Chet. "You and Fen will miss most of the blame. They might get you for being accomplices, that's all."

"My father's rich," Chet said reluctantly.

"There you go. You don't have a criminal record, right?"

Chet shook his head. Fenimore chuckled in the back, and Chet glanced over his shoulder.

"I never thought to leave behind my own deeds, but history has probably forgotten me," Fenimore said. "How untoward to have all my notoriety swept away in an instant."

Now there was a thought. If Chet really screwed this up, he could jump in the lucid mud river that Journey claimed ran beneath the city-state of Allistair. *And then what?* End up in some unknown future, all his friends and family dead? Chet wanted the past, not flying cars and spaceships. He wanted his *books.* Chet sighed and leaned against the window, watching life pass him by.

# Chapter 12
# Farmers

The stolen car broke down a few miles short of their goal, the engine smoking something terrible. It was early evening, insects chirping in the dimming light. Knife and Chet did the manly thing and popped the hood. They looked at the smoking engine, then at one another. Chet instinctively understood that Knife knew as little about engines as himself but had responded to the masculine urge to seem in charge of such matters. They vented a simultaneous sigh. There was a greenish yellow liquid dripping from a ruptured part inside. Who knew what kind of part? Certainly not Chet, to whom all engines were a closed book.

Knife cleared his throat. "Um. Maybe that's the radiator?"

"Could be."

The sun was setting. After escaping Semaphore yesterday, they'd driven thirty out of thirty-five hours on the road, taking short breaks and switching out drivers. Chet had bought snacks at a convenience store, but they'd avoided the few restaurants scattered in the mountains, let alone hotels. The results were hunger and seedy exhaustion. Knife had insisted everyone drive at the speed limit, which had been a pain. Nearly nine-hundred miles over the Monastery Mountains hadn't been a straight line, either.

Now they were surrounded by rolling hills and farm country. West Eicha was a decidedly civilized chunk of continent. On one side of the road, a herd of marauch watched them curiously from behind a picket fence. The graceful, seven-foot tall hoofed animals craned their long necks, probably hoping for carrots. One occasionally honked through its distinct droopy nose.

"Let's start walking," Journey said, touching her head nervously.

Journey was back in female form, apparently because she felt like it. Knife had given her back her jacket, and she'd fashioned a turban of sorts out of the white tee-shirt. It looked odd, but at least it covered her baldness. Nothing else could be done.

Knife sighed. "Walking is exactly right. We can't hitchhike like this—we're too memorable together."

Night settled as they hiked. Cars occasionally passed them. A few slowed down but Knife waved them on, smiling and bantering with forced cheer. They turned off the gravel byway for a dirt road. Chet hoped Knife and Journey knew where they were going, as there were no signs. Fenimore found a fallen branch and trimmed it with his hunting knife as they crossed through a wood lot, whittling a walking stick. Chet was chaffing and hungy, but at least it wasn't cold in summertime.

Chet gaped as they broke through the trees. The stars overhead were brighter than he'd ever seen in his life. Elderbeth hadn't yet risen on the horizon to drown out the night sky in green light. "We really are in the country, aren't we?" Chet said after a while.

"Yep," Knife said. "Our colleague, Othnielia, likes it that way."

"At least it isn't threatening rain," Journey murmured.

"That's true. We're being framed for murder with half the police force of Wetshul after us, we're bound to an ancient, blood-soaked magical relic, and separated from our luggage and transportation, but at least we won't burn to death tonight."

Chet scowled. "Hey, you didn't just see your professor's dead body bloody on the floor."

"Or wake up three-hundred years in the future," Fenimore added.

"Yes, I suppose there's that." Journey sounded like she wanted to cry, but was holding herself together. "Though now that I think about it, being pushed into lucid mud would be the most horrible of fates. I wouldn't want to wake up in the future not knowing what had happened between times. Centuries or even millennia, gone. Just like that. Or you might not ever wake up again, and you'd never *know* it."

"I went into lucid mud, once, and I woke up again," Knife said, sounding amused in the dark.

"*That* was under controlled circumstances, as I recall."

"Hey, my plan worked, didn't it?" Knife sounded hurt. "And the Watering Times could hardly be called 'controlled circumstances.'"

Chet frowned critically. "Wouldn't lucid mud burn you to dea—ah. Not water based, right." He was growing stupider by the minute to forget what he'd learned only last semester. "Knife, why did you go into lucid mud?"

Knife obliged. The story was followed by others; they took turns spinning tales, though Chet didn't have much life experience to draw on.

The stories stopped when they arrived at what turned out to be a farm. There were no exterior lights on the property, but by that time Elderbeth had risen. The gas giant dominated a quarter of the night sky. Without light pollution, Chet could see swirling details on the planet's surface, plus a scattering of silhouetted moons. More importantly, by Elderbeth's light Chet could see a large barn, exterior buildings and a cozy house surrounded by fields and rolling farmland. It looked like a calendar picture. He could smell wood-fire smoke and the odor of farm animals like the past come to life. No sounds of traffic. The front window was illuminated by an oil lantern, the others covered by gingham curtains; there was flickering light inside, as if from fire rather than electricity.

Journey knocked on the door. After a moment it was opened by an overweight, middle-aged, flaxen-skinned woman wearing what seemed to be a homemade dress and apron. Chet's heart froze: were they at the wrong place? Her graying hair seemed real.

The woman looked over her shoulder and called, "'Lia, they're here."

A gaunt man with a wrinkled, deeply tanned face appeared behind her. He had a distinct belly sticking out, though he wasn't fat. It was only by his wrinkled bald head that Chet would have ever guessed the guy was Flame. He didn't *look* Flame. Why would a shapeshifter want to appear so ugly? Yet he grinned toothily—he was missing an incisor—as Journey leapt into his arms.

"Othnielia!" she cried out. *Now* Journey was crying as she buried her face in his chest. "Oh, Pantheon, everything's turned to shit."

"There, now, lovely one. Come in and tell me all about it." The guy—Flame—held her tenderly. "Masie, get the fire built up? And let's heat some supper. I assume you haven't eaten yet."

"No, not yet," Knife said.

Knife was hanging back, Chet realized. He seemed vaguely uncomfortable. Chet noticed that Knife had changed back in his usual bistre-skinned, tall-and-skinny shape. The messy wig *looked* like a wig, out of context next to his skin tone.

"Well, come on in. Don't dangle on my doorstep and let mosquitoes inside."

Chet gulped and obeyed. The house didn't have any electric lights—instead oil lamps burned on the hewn dining room table and sitting room, which also had a fire in the grate. A younger woman attended to it as Masie moved around the kitchen, getting down plates and stirring a real cook-stove fire. Othnielia had his hands full with Journey. He crooned softly as she wept all over him. Chet wondered whether the Flame would help in the kitchen otherwise, if the division of labor was fairer in this house than with a real man and woman. *Or, um, women.*

Fenimore breathed in deeply beside him. "At last, a *real* place," he said. "I was starting to wonder if there was any normalcy left on Uos."

Chet found himself oddly in agreement with Fenimore. Despite its strangeness, this house seemed very real to him, too.

"Othnielia and his family are rare," Knife murmured. "At least they have glass windows rather than oiled cloth or rice paper, as if we still lived in the Cobalt Era."

The young woman who'd been building up the fire came over and shyly introduced herself as Saemion. Chet wondered how she fit into the picture. Was Othnielia involved with one woman or both? She couldn't be his daughter, after all. His curiosity fled as soon as the table was set and a pot of thick, bubbling stew placed on a trivet in the middle. It smelled alluringly of doedicu meat and vegetables. Pickled sides of all sorts were placed around it in little dishes. Fresh baked bread joined the rest, a rounded scoop of white butter placed beside the loaf. Chet's mouth watered unabashedly. When the older woman, Masie, finally invited them to sit and dig in, Chet nearly scrambled to his place at the table.

"I'll clean up afterwards, much as I'm able. You two go on to bed," Othnielia told Masie, hugging her tenderly. They finished with a loving kiss. Othnielia offered the same to Saemion, who accepted readily.

It didn't look like Othnielia had a platonic relationship with either of them. Were they... a threesome? Strange threesome, if true. Masie seemed to be in her late forties, Saemion maybe a few years older than Chet. Othnielia—who knew? Hadn't Oak said that Flame could live up to a hundred and forty years? Maybe he chose to appear as an old man because he was, in fact, old.

Othnielia listened to Journey and Knife explain as they ate. After they finished talking, he sighed. "Well, I can't do much about the mess you're in."

"You shouldn't have to," Journey said, her face darkening with emotion. "I have no wish to bring trouble upon you and yours."

"As it may be. Both of you are welcome to bathe in my hearth and bunk down in the front room. You boys can sleep in the barn," Othnielia said, regarding Chet and Fenimore with neutral eyes. "The hay loft is cozy enough in summertime."

Knife cleared his throat. "Othnielia, do you have a vehicle we can use?"

"No, sorry. I still stick to the old ways around here; the most I have with is a tractor, and that's forty years old. Picked it up after the war for almost nothing, old-fashioned as it is."

"It's so quiet," Journey murmured. "Ah! I know what's missing. 'Lia, where are the children?"

*Children?* Chet jerked in surprise then glanced around surreptitiously. Hadn't Journey said that Flame were sterile?

Othnielia took in Chet's obvious bewilderment."I generally have four or five orphans that I'm raising at any given time. That's what I do. I farm the land, breed animals and raise unwanted children. That's what I've done every lifetime I've ever lived when given a choice in the matter."

"Are they in bed?" Journey persisted.

"No, we have none at the moment. There's a lot of anti-Flame feeling just now, as you are aware—officials think we're perverts and abusers. It trickles down to the local level. You both know I don't go in for wigs or hiding my nature; I'd rather be burned to death, and of course I have been. When I take in orphans these days, a social worker from the providence shows up at my doorstep, soon as people notice. I've stopped trying."

Knife frowned at this. "You were the first among us to start that tradition. Why should you bow to such blatant ignorance? You could sue."

"Sue my neighbors and friends? Last time we had the social worker in for supper when she came by to cart another kid away. I figure, give them about twenty years or so. The pendulum'll swing our way again. Some horrible new disease will kill a lot of parents and taint a lot of kids, and they'll be stuffed into overfilled trains again, shipped out to rural regions. It happens. I'll go and sit in on town hall meetings and voice my opinion, as usual. They know me. Eventually they'll let me do it again." Othnielia chuckled. "Masie says we should take some of these new foster-parent classes to appease social services. I'll take the classes, but don't think they can teach me anything about raising orphans I don't already know."

Chet felt himself swaying as he finished the last of his stew and bread. Everything he'd thought he'd known about Flame was wrong. For mercurial shapeshifters, they sure were a mixed lot. Cunning as he was, Knife had kept the same face and figure for centuries, only changing when he needed to. Oak studied hard and tolerated administrative prejudice to finish her professional degree. Othnielia was the strangest of all: a craggy, ugly individual dedicated to only three things in life... or lives. Of all of them, Journey was the most stereotypically Flame, with her feminine tendencies and bi-sexed nature. Yet even Journey defied surface impressions. The way she'd fled into Othnielia's arms spoke of a long-term relationship. *Not a sexual relationship, either,* Chet thought. More like a child seeking comfort from a parent, which was bizarre, given that Journey was thousands of years old.

Othnielia retrieved an oil lamp and blankets, leading Chet and Fenimore out to the barn. Sleepy ceroses poked their heads out of stalls. Chet avoided them, wary of their horns, though they snuffled at him curiously. A pen near the back of the barn smelled distinctly of palaeoth, though nothing stirred in that direction.

Othnielia climbed up the loft ladder and Chet followed, Fenimore at his heels. "I'll be up before dawn to do the chores. It's best if you boys sleep in that corner rather than near the drop off, because I'll be forking down hay to ceroses in the morning."

"Okay," Chet murmured. He wanted to go to sleep as soon as possible but Othnielia seemed to be watching them with a measured, knowing gaze.

"I understand you've lost your luggage. If you boys have need, there's a grease bucket behind the barn. It shouldn't be rancid; just slaughtered a doedicu a few weeks ago."

"Um. Thank you?" Chet rubbed his arms and took the offered blankets gingerly.

Fenimore smiled far more sincerely and thanked Othnielia using flowery, old-fashioned wording. Were these his courtly manners? Othnielia grinned toothily and answered with the proper responses, though his accent in the Tache language was terrible—worse than Chet's.

Othnielia left, taking the light with him. Chet burrowed down into the hay and draped the blankets over himself and Fenimore, feeling vulnerable and decidedly strange. The hay smelled good, though it was scratchy. Fenimore spooned him, his body warm.

Just before Chet dropped to sleep he heard Fenimore murmur, "Grease, eh? Guess that one's Flame after all."

It rained the next morning, and Knife and Journey stayed in the house. Was it part of the plan to take things slow, or just necessity? Othnielia didn't seem inconvenienced, anyway; he wore bright yellow slickers and an enormous cone-shaped hat to do his chores. He'd covered every part of his body, including his face.

Later during breakfast, Journey confirmed Chet's assessment by saying, "We're not going anywhere right now. Think of it as a rest day." Knife grunted agreement, looking trapped and uncomfortable.

Chet could use a rest day but missed his books intensely. Saemion offered up her collection of lurid pulp romance novels for his perusal. There were several set in historic time periods—Chet studied their covers doubtfully before selecting one and retreating to the barn. He gave up around chapter three, grumpy at the historically inaccurate details.

Fenimore, who'd been sharpening his blade on a leather strop, glanced up. "Rain's stopped. Come on, let's explore this place."

The farm was beautiful, Chet had to admit. There were rolling pastures and bawling baby animals in pens. Masie came out with a bucket of scraps and fed the free-roaming palaeoth, who butted their blunt heads against her waist, nearly knocking her over.

"Get on with you," she said with mock anger, slapping their furry haunches.

Saemion was outside in another cone-shaped hat, weeding the enormous vegetable garden, domesticated peteinos sifting the soil and making mewing noises at her side. For a while, Chet weeded beside her, breathing in the scent of fertile, wet soil while Fenimore poked about.

After a time, Fenimore grew bored and cajoled Chet until he got to his feet. "Look, there's a lake over there."

"That's the doedicu range," Saemion said, pausing to wipe her brow. "Their tails are clipped, but stay away from the male enclosure on the far side of the lake."

Sure enough, Chet spotted his first doedicu as they wandered to the wooden fence. It was enormous, over six feet, its dome-shaped shell layered like ancient leather armor. More doedicus rushed the fence upon spotting them, shuffling quickly upon their short feet. Expecting treats, probably. Chet felt guilty about his empty hands and pockets. As Saemion had said, the doedicus' tails had each been cut short at five feet long and lacked their famous spikes. Chet hung back as Fenimore held out a fennel bulb pilfered from the garden. A doedicu stuck its head out of the shell and whiffled the vegetable curiously with its thick beak. It took the bulb delicately, then scampered away on its short feet, head retracted into its shell to avoid the other doedicus crowding in for a taste.

"They're really tame," Fenimore said, breaking out into a grin. "I bet they'll let us ride them. Come on, let's try it."

"But..." Chet swallowed as Fenimore vaulted the fence. Chet hunched. He was no athlete; he was a *scholar*, for Pantheon's sake.

Fenimore glanced over his shoulder. "Unbend, you milk-livered pumpion. It's time to grow a pair, eh?"

"If you think insulting me is going to make me do something stupid—"

"They're *tame,* cream puff! Don't make me come back there and get you."

"Right. Tame, right." Chet gulped and awkwardly climbed the rough, splintery fence.

The beasts sniffed him curiously. They were *huge*. Chet had once read that the coteries of Palister had required boys to ride an unclipped doedicu three miles before permitting him to be a man. In that culture, Chet would have been a boy *forever*. A baby doedicu, perhaps a season old, clung to its mother's side as she investigated Chet. Chet found himself breathing easier around the baby animal. It was so *cute*.

"Come on, let's ascend a big one together," Fenimore said. He grabbed Chet's hand and hauled him through the grazing herd.

Chet's shoes, already damp from the wet grass, were soaked through as they stomped through mud. Where did the lake start, anyway? Chet looked over and saw several doedicus—or at least, their half-submerged shells—in the water. Amphibious grazers, they were at home in the lake as on land.

Fenimore stopped and surveyed the herd. "There, that one, the castrated male. Seven feet tall if it's an inch."

Chet groaned. "Fenimore, I don't think this is a good—"

Fenimore grabbed his hand and hauled him to the doedicu. Then Fenimore let go and scrambled up its shell. The grazing doedicu ignored him. Chet bit his lip and followed—or tried, anyway. His feet kept slipping.

"You're not going fast enough!" Fenimore snarled. He grabbed the neck of Chet's sweater and hung on as Chet tried to find a foothold.

Perhaps it was his awkwardness that alerted the doedicu to their presence, for it stuck its head out, bellowed, and scampered on its tiny feet toward the lake. Terrified of falling to the distant ground below, Chet screamed up to Fenimore, "Don't let go, don't let go..."

Water splashed around them; the shell tipped as the doedicu dove. Fenimore didn't let go of Chet so much as he lost his hold on the doedicu. They both fell into the lake. Chet splashed down, accidentally gulping water. It was cold. Oh Pantheon, it was *cold!*

Soaked through, Chet gasped and swam toward shore until he found footing in the soft, muddy bottom. Where was Fenimore? Could he even swim? Something grabbed Chet's foot, hauling him sideways and underwater. Chet's scream was lost in the lake. A moment later, he fought his way back to the surface, Fenimore laughing beside him.

"The look on your face." Fenimore's beautiful eyelashes dripping water, cheeks dimpled with mirth.

"That's not funny!" Chet cried out, splashing at Fenimore. "I thought you'd drowned!"

"The venerable Countess LaDaven didn't raise her sons to be cowardly of the sea. I spent my childhood summers at the seashore in Torque."

"Bully for you," Chet grumbled, wading out of the lake.

Sardonic applause caught his attention, and he looked toward the fence: they had an audience. Saemion, Masie, *and* Othnielia had gathered there. Othnielia still wore his cone hat, yellow slicker and knee-high waders despite the fact that the rain had stopped.

"Good thing for you I clip tails and castrate my doedicus," he commented as Chet hauled himself over the fence, Fenimore following lightly. "If you two had tried that with one of the intact males, you would have ended up with broken bones."

Chet didn't reply, stomping back toward the barn. He was wet, muddy, freezing and didn't have a change of clothes. Not even a change of underwear. Undoubtedly, Othnielia could lend him something if he asked. *How humiliating.* Chet wasn't going to ask if it killed him. Fenimore cheerfully chattered with the others and followed them as far as the house. Chet stumbled into the barn. It was warmer here, anyway. He stripped off clothes and laid them over the wooden beams. They dripped on the distant floor below, his shoes helplessly wet. Chet huddled under a blanket, teeth chattering and attempted once again to read the historically-inaccurate romance novel. He set it aside after a minute, seething. How dare Fenimore make him a laughing stock!

As if in reply to his thought, Fenimore's head appeared in the ladder hole. He'd already changed into dry, borrowed clothing. "Here," Fenimore said, tossing up a bundle of clothes. "*These* are for you." He disappeared, grinning sardonically.

Chet unrolled the bundle, grateful despite himself, then froze. It was *women's* clothing. There was a purple skirt and a low-cut blouse, a white bra and sexy pink underwear. Chet couldn't breathe. Part of him was furious. What was this fresh humiliation Fenimore had dished up for him? Another part of him was... curiously aroused. The cloth was soft, the underwear and bra satiny. He'd never considered dressing in women's clothing, yet here was the perfect opportunity.

Fenimore poked back through the ladder hole, hauling up a covered wooden bucket. "Still not dressed? You'll catch your death."

"Why didn't you bring me regular clothes?"

"Is it not obvious? You scream so like a girl I thought you might as well dress like one as well."

Chet scowled at him. "You're so obnoxious, you, you..."

Fenimore touched him under the chin, and Chet abruptly lost his train of thought . "I had also thought how delightful it would be to pilfer you as a woman. Flame are not the only ones who can play such games."

Chet's muscles contracted at the thought, his penis hardening between one breath and the next. Fenimore noticed, grinning down Chet's naked body under the insufficient blanket.

"Get dressed," Fenimore ordered. "If you're good, I shall undertake to educate you most thoroughly, little girl."

# Chapter 13
# Loft and Cellar

Chet picked up the pink underwear, his chilled body suddenly warm with the thought of being fucked in women's clothing. He slowly drew them up. The underwear did not in any way cover his erect dick; in fact, his circumcised glans stuck out of the top.

Fenimore groaned at the sight. "Oh, you're a sweet package I'll enjoy tearing open. Go on, cover yourself. Be modest, girl."

The bra was difficult. Chet had to fasten it backwards just to see the weird clasps. He'd never actually taken one off a woman, he realized—Journey had done all the work when she'd fucked him. Now he wished he had more of an education in that area. But once the bra was on and the right way around, he realized just how sexy it was, even empty of breasts. Fenimore, apparently awaiting this moment, handed him two small, unripe persimmons. Chet tucked one inside each cup and grinned. Instant breasts, at least for show. He finished dressing, noticing how the blouse accentuated those little bumps even further, the skirt brushing against his legs alluringly.

Fenimore lay back in the straw, hands behind his head. "Go on, walk up and down the loft. I want to see you wiggle your hips at me, girl."

Chet walked, his face warm. He felt... sexy. He tried to wiggle his hips, and Fenimore snickered; Chet grinned back ruefully. "I just need some practice."

"Mmm. I agree, practice is needed. You were always more feminine than me, even if Foex prevented us from living as actual women."

"What?" Chet stared at him. What a weird non-sequitur.

"Try wiggling again." Fenimore reached out a hand, and Chet

sauntered toward him, trying for slower, circular movements this time.

"Better," Fenimore said judiciously. "That's a good girl."

"Could I have your cock, please?" Chet said with sudden courage, ducking his head shyly.

He blinked, suddenly alarmed at the question that had passed his lips. How had this happened? How had he morphed from a student of archeology to a, a homophile asking for something forbidden from a male, um, lover? Had traveling with Flame changed him so deeply that he didn't even think before doing something like this? Journey had put her finger right on it: he had always been aroused by both men and women.

His courage would fail him, yet he was wearing female clothing now, too. The clothes had certainly given him the audacity to ask for what he wanted.

"May I have your cock, please, *sir*," Fenimore corrected.

Chet put his hands on his hips, deliberately keeping his wrists loose. "May I have your cock, please, sir? I am ever so hungry for it."

Yes, the clothing was definitely making a difference. How odd. The Flame weren't present—and they certainly hadn't given him this strange power—but they'd shown him the way of it, hadn't they? Chet remembered Knife pretending with everything he had that he was an innocent university student, even crying and shaking as the police held guns on him. Changing his shape hadn't done that, not entirely. Knife and Journey had shown him that shifting was more than magic. It was *attitude*.

"I think you need to dance for me first. Show off your body, and give me something to look at." Fenimore grinned up at him. "You need to earn my regard, girl. Only then will you get what you hunger for."

It was so easy to lose himself in acting, to bury himself in the performance. As an undergraduate, Chet had once gone into a men's club on a dare. Now he tried to emulate the dance moves he'd witnessed there. He ran his hands up and down his body, lingering at his breasts. He turned around and stuck out his ass in Fenimore's direction. He knelt before Fenimore and jiggled his chest so that the bra and persimmons shook, too. He acted like a slut, enjoying every moment of it.

No matter how shocked he was in the back of his own head.

Fenimore, thoroughly engaged, unbuttoned thefly of his borrowed trousers and pulled out his erect cock. "Good girl," Fenimore breathed. "Now take me lightly—lightly!—in your mouth. Cover those delectable pearls with your lips and swallow my sex. Do not brush me with your teeth, or I shall tie your hands together and flog you thoroughly with the ceros whip I saw hanging downstairs. Perhaps I shall do that anyway after I've had you."

Chet gasped at the thought. He knelt before Fenimore, legs spread under the skirt. Chet's dick popped free of the underwear, and he self-consciously tucked himself back in. Fenimore's cock bobbed before his eyes as Fenimore stroked himself. Chet gently took it into his mouth. *Oh, my,* he thought, eyes wide. The taste wasn't exactly to his liking, but the act was intensely sexual in a way he'd never experienced. In his surprise, his teeth brushed Fenimore's penis...

Fenimore growled, grabbing Chet's hair. "That's one stroke, doxy. I said no teeth."

*No teeth, right.* Chet tried to cover his teeth with his lips, but it was a struggle, especially because he wanted to feel Fenimore's cock with his full mouth, enjoy and explore the soft texture to the utmost. Fenimore had other ideas. He controlled Chet with both hands, fucking his mouth. Every few strokes, Fenimore pushed himself deeper inside. Chet mewled and struggled for air. He would be released and the cycle would start again. Fenimore kept count for every time Chet accidentally uncovered his teeth, which was often.

Fenimore pulled out of Chet's mouth when they reached twenty one. "That's enough or you'll be a bleeding mess by my hand."

"...Sorry."

Fenimore placed a finger over his mouth. "Little girls are to be seen, not heard. Turn around and show me your arse. On your hands and knees, mind."

Chet obeyed, shaking. He wanted Fenimore's penis inside him. Chet suddenly remembered that they didn't have any condoms, but he didn't want to stop now. Truly, he didn't. He especially didn't want to go banging on Othnielia's door and ask for condoms, his cock sticking up like a spike beneath the skirt. Othnielia probably didn't even have any; she didn't need them, after all. Besides, what venereal disease could Fenimore have that was so bad? Modern medicine had undoubtedly far outstripped any 73rd century plague.

Fenimore rose and retrieved the bucket, uncovering it as he returned. Chet caught a whiff of doedicu lard. "You're going to be a filthy little girl when I'm done with you," Fenimore murmured.

Chet felt Fenimore lift his skirt as cool air wafted between his legs. Chet wiggled involuntarily, his dick popping out of the feminine underwear once again. Fenimore swatted him on the ass, and Chet squealed.

"Stay contained," Fenimore ordered, tucking him back in. Chet almost came in his hands, gasping. Fenimore's fingers lingered on his buttocks, still covered by the underwear, rubbing Chet up and down. "Tell me what you want."

"I want your cock inside me." The words burst out of him without checking in with the shocked part of his brain, the rational side. Chet felt exhilarated and powerful. He'd never before experienced this freedom, and he might not get another chance.

"You are a slattern," Fenimore chuckled. "A little whore. Do you really want me to do a kindness to you?"

*Do a kindness?* Maybe it was an anachronism for fuck. "Yes, sir."

"Ah, that's my good girl. You've finally acknowledged me as your lord and master, eh? Such a sweet anuro. I think I shall have you after all." Fenimore let go of his ass with his left hand, moving the underwear to one side with his right. A greasy finger found Chet's ass, and Chet moaned, bearing down. The finger slipped inside him. The grease was both absolutely disgusting and the most sexual sensation Chet had ever experienced. Not that he'd felt many, but still. Fenimore greased him thoroughly, like a railroad engine.

"Oh sir, fuck me hard. Please fuck me. *Do* me a kindness," Chet moaned. His cock slipped out once again, but Fenimore didn't put it back. Chet could feel the front of the skirt against his dick, the underwear hem tight around his scrotum.

"Am I to fill your burning shame, doxy?" Fenimore's tone was low, alluring. He grabbed Chet's underwear and pulled it down to his knees, trapping them together.

Ew. *Burning shame?* Probably another anachronism, this one not nearly as sweet, but Chet was still aching to play along. "I'd give *any-*

*thing* for you to fill me."

"Perhaps I shall accommodate your base, hysteric lust, then. Spread your legs further and show off your civet. Wider. Wider. Good, like that. Common slut."

Fenimore spat, and Chet felt the wad his hit back, through the blouse. He half turned, shocked to be treated with such contempt, but Fenimore mounted him and drove inside. Chet shrieked, his high-pitch tone sounding girly even in his own ears.

It was like being fucked by a machine. Fenimore took him hard, without reprieve, plunging deep inside. Chet groaned at the pain, feeling terribly feminine in the clothing. He really could feel himself become a whore for Fenimore: power of suggestion was nothing compared to being encompassed in the blouse, the fabric of the skirt, the bra clinging to his chest. And like a woman, Chet was disappointed when Fenimore came less than a minute after entering him.

"That wasn't much," he said, sprawled beneath Fenimore. "Thought you'd have more in you, *sir*, with all your talk."

Fenimore grabbed Chet's hair and pinned his head to the hay. "Just for that, girl, I'm going to stay inside you until I'm hard again."

Chet frowned. He was compressed and splayed in this position. Surely Fenimore didn't mean—? He did. Minutes passed as the man lay on top of him, wiggling just a little, apparently enjoying the position of ascendency. Chet had all the time in the world to regret his dive into the obscene. Despite everything, he was still aroused. Fenimore reached around and grabbed the persimmons still bound by the bra, squeezing them. Chet bore his touch, his own dick so hard it quivered. He wondered why he hadn't come, why he didn't come now. Perhaps the clothing was once again responsible for his restraint? If he'd been naked, he would have shot off just like that, but somehow he couldn't quite come as a woman.

"You're not very impressive anymore."

"If you bait me, you should know what you get," Fenimore breathed in his ear. He reached into the low cut blouse and removed a persimmon, then pinched Chet's nipple. Chet squeaked and writhed. Fenimore chuckled. "Finally got a reaction from you, doxy."

"Did you used to do this often?" Chet asked breathlessly. His ass felt wide open, at the mercy of the half-erect man bearing down on him.

"Often enough. I best loved taking apart young fops new to court. Old bessies would hover over the girls during their coming out; they'd be guarded and locked day and night. But no one cared to hover over young men. They were especially sweet if they thought themselves the highest lords of Uos, swaggering drunk from one tavern to another. I could take that type all day."

"What about women?"

"Of course women. Whores by the boatload, naturally, and sometimes I had an older widow with multiple assets and a wet, ready civet. That's how I started, you know. Older women with assets."

Chet frowned critically, trying to match up what he knew from his studies against Fenimore's claims. It was really too bad he hadn't taken Clementina's class about that period in Tache history. "Didn't you ever marry? I thought it was almost a requirement back then."

Fenimore sighed. "They tried to drown me with a wife once. She was young and attractive. I carefully ruined her with my attentions, then lent her out to friends and sundry until she found a man who fit her better than I ever could. She learned to play the game rather well, I'm proud to say. Such a good student. I was quite sorry when she died in childbirth last... um. Three hundred and half a year ago."

"That's despicable," Chet said, scowling. He wanted to climb out from under Fenimore, but he could barely move in this position.

"Oh, it's far better to be despicable than boring. My love life is—was—considered absolutely notorious at court," Fenimore said congenially. "That way my other activities are well covered."

"You snooped for your prince, didn't you?" Chet said, thinking back to what Knife had said. Knife had called Fenimore a "colleague," and Knife was almost certainly a spy.

"Snooped?" Fenimore seemed confused.

"Um. You were a spy? An intelligencer."

Fenimore shifted his weight—uneasily, Chet realized. "It seems my past is more uncovered than I'd thought."

"Well, Knife said you and she were colleagues. And I just assumed..."

"Ah, Knife." Fenimore breathed a sigh of obvious relief. "I see. Yes, of course she would insinuate that."

Chet wondered if the man would fuck him again, or if they would continue lingering here conjoined like mating insects. "I'm growing tired," he said, tightening his aching ass muscles to emphasize the point.

"Good thing I am not." Fenimore began moving atop him. He lifted himself off and pulled Chet closer at the same time, so they were still connected, then fucked him at a leisurely pace.

Chet felt wide open, wider than he'd ever been in his life. The underwear was somehow gone from his knees. He gasped when Fenimore reached around and grabbed his cock, stroking up with a light touch. Chet thrust backwards, aroused once again. Fenimore laughed and took him at a swifter pace. This time Chet wasn't overwhelmed—he found that he preferred the rougher fucking. It felt better, the thumping against his ass reverberating through him with fantastic pressure. He came without warning, spurting messily all over the skirt. Fenimore bore down on him, coming with shuddered gasps.

Chet struggled away from the man, determined to break free. He heard an audible *pop* as his anus was released, and Fenimore didn't hold him back.

"Oh, Pantheon," Chet groaned. "I don't think I'll ever be tight again."

"Yes, you will," Fenimore predicted. "You will be tight, and I'll rend you open once again. That, or I'll lend you to another man who'll do the work for me."

Chet frowned. "I'm not your wife." Blouse, skirt and bra to the contrary.

Fenimore grinned at him. Apparently spotting something in the hay, he lifted up a ruined twist of the pink underwear. It was torn asunder. "You're rough on clothing, little girl. What will Saemion say?"

"She would say it's time you two came down and ate midday," Othnielia said, sticking his head through the ladder hole. Chet almost buried himself in the hay head first, he was so embarrassed. "Here, Chet," he said, tossing in a bundle. "Now that you and Fenimore have had your fun, perhaps you'd prefer something more suitable to your preferences."

"Thank you," Chet called as Othnielia disappeared.

"Abyss, I'm hungry. Guess I'll have to whip you another time."

Chet shrugged, still distracted by Othnielia's appearance. *He, or, um, she didn't turn a hair – if she'd had any,* Chet thought. Fenimore was putting himself back together; he wiped himself down with the torn underwear and buried it deep in the hay. Chet snorted. Othnielia would probably find it mid-winter, frozen solid. Repayment for her kind hospitality, Chet was afraid.

He bundled the rest of the soiled women's clothing together and descended the ladder, Fenimore following. Chet found himself mulling over Fenimore's earlier words, disturbed at the images they invoked. There was no way Fenimore would be *lending* him to anyone. Chet had chosen to explore this bizarre and riveting sexual world once, but he could stop any time he chose. Right? He was a free man despite their little games.

Midday was a hearty meal, featuring a doedicu roast with gravy and mashed parsnips. Othnielia turned to Chet while they were eating. Chet braced himself for questions regarding his sexual adventures, wincing inside.

Instead, Othnielia said, "I understand you're studying for your Ph.D. in archaeology, Chet. Have you dedicated yourself as an affiliate to Philapo, yet?"

Chet swallowed a suddenly dry bite of home-baked bread. It went down like ashes in his mouth. "Uh. No, good Flame. I'm unaffiliated and intend to remain that way."

The usual startled looks around the table followed this statement. Chet was used to them by now.

Journey said, "I'd assumed you were waiting to become Literati for some reason."

"I don't see the need."

"Are your family atheists?" Othnielia asked. "We have a clan of atheists a few miles away, bunking down and waiting for the end of the world. While I admire their survivalist attitude, I find myself dubious as to their goals."

Knife chuckled under his breath. "I'm dubious as to atheists' grasp on reality."

Chet agreed readily with this assessment: atheists on Uos were a paranoid lot with reason. They were alone in their assertion that the Pantheon were not really gods at all, but evil space aliens with too much power, playing with humans like children with toys. Some sects believed that there were no higher beings, while others argued that there was a bigger god somewhere in the universe who had originally created everything, including the Pantheon. Chet could only be glad he hadn't fallen in among a group of such weirdoes and kooks.

He cleared his throat. "No, good Flame. My father is a dedicated Merchant, and my mother is the only non-hereditary Scientist among my aunts and uncles on that side. All six of my sisters have dedicated themselves as Acia Nuns. My two older brothers have followed in my father's footsteps as Merchants, carrying on our family business."

People were staring in earnest now, even Fenimore. "All *six* of your sisters dedicated themselves to Acia?" Othnielia said.

Chet nodded glumly. "My youngest sister dedicated herself last midwinter. You could say my family is highly affiliated."

"You must feel like the odd man out when you go home," Journey observed.

Chet shrugged, playing with the remaining food scraps on his plate. "Yeah."

"How do you intend to pursue a teaching career without dedicating yourself to Philapo?" Journey said. "The Literati University System isn't partial to the unaffiliated, though you are the population majority. They don't like *us* teaching, even in more congenial locales than Wetshul. Do you plan to teach at an independent city or city-state university?"

"I don't know," Chet said, downcast. "My father keeps threatening to stop paying tuition and drag me home by the collar, but... the past holds so much. I feel it on my shoulders, like a weight. If I didn't study history, I think I'd drown under that weight."

The Flame at the table exchanged looks. "The past is the past," Othnielia said, rising to gather empty plates. "Mostly it's like layers of rock, pressed stratum of events piled atop one another."

Someone knocked at the door, and Masie rose to answer it, greeting the neighbor on the step. She closed the door behind her to speak to her friend; Chet could hear them conferring in undertones outside.

Journey was frowning deeply, gazing at Chet as if she wished she could see through him. "Chet... before I, um, took the initiative the other day to rid you of your virginity, did you... were you..." She gulped and looked away. "What I'm trying to say is, when you held a lit match or lighter to your fingers, *could* you burn?"

"Er, yes?" Chet was not a little freaked out by this line of questioning. "Yes, fire burns me like it burns everyone else."

"Oh, thank *Pantheon*," Journey murmured, bowing over until her forehead rested on the wooden table. "I didn't screw up, then."

Othnielia and Knife chuckled. Chet frowned at this. "Does someone care to explain?"

"To initiate as Flame, you have to be a virgin," Knife said.

Chet grew hot—his face probably almost matched his hair. Journey thought he might have been a candidate to be Flame? But... he was just a guy. A normal, everyday guy. Despite having just, um, cross dressed to experience anal sex with a man. Anyway, he *couldn't* initiate to Pelin now. Chet cheered up at the thought, grateful that he was no longer a virgin. His aching ass, so recently plundered, felt like an insurance policy in his pocket.

Masie closed the front door, calling goodbye to her friend. She turned and murmured in Othnielia's ear.

Othnielia went instantly still. "Is she sure?" Masie nodded, her expression serious. Othnielia took a deep breath. "You four had best climb down into the cellar. Our local sheriff is going door to door, asking after you. Not by name, but by description. He's my friend, and I'm sure he won't look further than he has to, but best we don't stretch his dedication to the badge, eh?"

Masie had already rolled up the rag-tied carpet in the kitchen to reveal a cellar door. She pulled the trapdoor by a ring to reveal a black void. "Saemion, light a lamp. We can't send them down in the dark."

Chet couldn't believe it as he descended the ladder behind Journey. The events from three days ago rushed back to him, and he gulped residual nausea. By the steady, dim light of the oil lamp, he could see the cellar was more like a large pantry. It was filled with wax-sealed canning jars, rotund barrels, packing crates of wizened melons, sacks of root vegetables, and dusty bottles that undoubtedly held alcohol.

Othnielia stuck his face in the hole. "You okay?"

"We'll be fine," Journey assured him.

The trapdoor closed, locking them in. Chet sat on the dirt floor, repressing panic. He took deep breaths, listening to the footsteps and murmured words overhead. Noise resonated just fine through the floorboards, anyway.

Fenimore glanced around. "Where's the Raptus?" he whispered.

"In the living room. My purse," Journey replied, glancing at the ceiling.

"If we had it, we could try to gain control of the sheriff's mind and send him away," Fenimore said. "If he discovers us and attempts to use force, the shielding power might work even now."

Knife sighed. "I trust Othnielia to cover for us."

"She's the reason I survived the World War," Journey put in. "Most Flame died, you know. That's why three council members just initiated. The medical experiments carried out on Flame were the worst of part..."

Chet jerked at a knock on the front door, and Journey fell silent. Chet's whole body was tense, his shoulders shaking. He pressed his face into his knees and waited.

# Chapter 14
# On the Road to Fengfu

No one spoke in the cellar as someone walked across the wooden floorboards to answer the door. "Jindo, welcome! We just finished eating midday—would you care to set in?"

"No thank you, Masie. I just need to talk to Othnielia."

More footsteps. "Yes, Jindo? How can I help you today?"

Chet blinked, sorry that he couldn't see anything. This was like listening to a soap opera on the radio. The strange male voice murmured, and Chet only caught a phrase or two. "Murdered," was the most prominent word, and also "renegades," "stolen car."

Chet heard Othnielia sigh. "Got it. I'll keep an eye out."

Jindo's voice rose in volume. "Of course, of course. I'm canvassing the whole neighborhood for clues, starting with the west end and moving east in a leisurely fashion. Can't miss a thing that way. The law enforcement up the mountains seems quite keen; they don't understand our way of doing things."

"I understand completely, Jindo."

More murmurs, a laugh. Someone was smoking by the smell of it. Discerning the pattern of footsteps, Chet decided they'd moved into another room. More talk. Doors opened and shut. Silence. Chet was going out of his head, waiting. Journey had her eyes closed and was taking deep breaths. Fenimore had his hunting blade out, his expression grim. Knife... Knife looked like a man—or an individual, rather—finally in his element after a long, dull day. His eyes sparkled with interest, and his leg jiggled, like a benched athlete waiting for a coach to put him in the game.

Movement overhead, scrapping. The carpet being rolled up? Sure enough, the cellar door creaked open. "All clear. Come on out," Othnielia said.

"What's the word?" Knife said, climbing the ladder first.

Othnielia had a distracted, unhappy look of someone being pulled in two directions. "Sheriff Jindo is being mighty good to us. He carefully visited all our neighbors first, including Masie's best friend, who is the biggest gossip in these parts. I gather that he's playing a delicate game, and a jurisdiction game at that."

"He's covering for us?" Journey said as she put the lantern on the kitchen table.

"Covering for me. He doesn't know you from a herd of macrauch, but he knows you're here, of course. It's obviously why you abandoned that stolen car in the neighborhood."

Saemion, who was leaning in the doorway, said, "Jindo owes you for a couple of solved cases, 'Lia, going back some years. You *are* the local expert on god affiliates."

"So when do we leave?" Fenimore asked, his whole body radiating pent-up energy.

Othnielia eyed Knife and Journey. "Well, now. That's a question, isn't it?"

Journey looked reluctant. "We need to go to Plainsdaugheau to see Aureate but don't have enough funds on hand. I have reserves in a cache near my home. So does Knife, of course. My place is closer than Knife's, but it's a long ways north to Eich Che, especially when we're wanted by the police and all."

Chet nearly choked. "Plainsdaugheau? We're going to *Plainsdaugheau?*" Half a world away, the city-state was located in the middle of the ocean, perched at the edge of an unassailable land mass. It was so far away they might as well have been headed to Elderbeth in outer space.

Knife eyed him speculatively. "Chet, you're from the Door area. That's half as far as Eich Che, *and* in the right direction."

"Um. Yes?"

"You mentioned before that your family is rich."

Chet dropped his eyes. "My family would rather see me locked in an insane asylum than accept the company I'm keeping."

Both Knife and Fenimore grinned in response; identical grins, in fact. Fenimore slapped Chet on the back bracingly. "I think we can slip through that net, fair enough. Lead us forth."

"My parents actually live outside of Door in the suburban community of Fengfu..."

"Yes, yes. We'll figure it out," Knife said. He turned to Othnielia. "We're headed west. Door is only about six or seven hundred miles away. The Arch Trade Route is near here, isn't it?"

"People call it Highway 1 these days, and yes, it's about ten miles via back ways, over fields and through orchards. I wouldn't want to take you by the front road anyway, what with curious neighbors just having been spoken to by the sheriff. You hitchhiking?"

Knife and Journey met eyes, and neither seemed overjoyed by the prospect. "Yes," Journey said. "Looks like I'll be taking the hit on this one."

Chet frowned, not certain what she meant. Knife and Othnielia each touched her gently: Knife took her hand and Othnielia her shoulder, supporting her. "Maybe it won't come to that," Othnielia murmured.

"Maybe. Think you can get us there tonight?"

"Best not risk it. Ceroses do better in daylight, and I'd like to get home before dark. Don't think it'll rain tomorrow, and Sheriff Jindo made it clear he's giving me space. He even outlined where he's searching next."

"Of course, that would be the best way to entrap you. And us," Knife muttered.

Othnielia gave him a long, measured look. "Can you think of a better plan?" The tension between them was subtle but present. Chet looked from one to the other. They weren't exactly having a staring contest, but it was a near thing.

Knife gave up first, dropping his eyes. "No. We are as you see us: without luggage or backup."

"Well then, you'd best trust my friends and not fool around here, making a mess of things." Othnielia's tone was sharp.

Knife turned away. Journey looked like she was being ground between two stones. Chet felt the same, though he lacked her insight. He'd always thought of the past as fascinating and intricate, all the battlefields comfortably far away. But to three—no, four—of the people here, the past was alive, tainting the present. Othnielia had been right about layers of rock, he decided. Whatever layer of past lay between the Flame, it jutted into the present in a distinct, geological fashion.

As for Chet, he was the same guy as always. Just the same no matter how much he delved into dangerous sexuality or conversed with historic men and Flame. Uncomplicated and unaffiliated, unknowing of the past as he'd always been. He might study hard as he pleased, but he could never seem to catch up.

Even now he was the odd man out.

While *up before dawn* might be normal on the farm, it was not in Chet's usual vocabulary.

Othnielia woke them while doing chores. Half asleep, Chet stumbled through the motions of dressing and eating until he was faced with a task he'd never had before: mounting a ceros. Othnielia had assigned him an older gelding, placid yet featuring a full rack of horns, which he and Fenimore were to share pillion style. The beast was nine feet tall even without accounting for the horns. Fenimore didn't seem at all distracted or even interested by the mode of transport, helping to saddle and bridle without comment.

Chet hung back. His ass was still sore from yesterday, but that would be nothing compared to what it would be tonight when—what? When they were riding in someone else's vehicle? Asleep—or dead—by the side of the road? *Today couldn't possibly get more intimidating,* Chet thought irritably.

Journey and Knife seemed to be in a sober mood. They both sported knotted kerchiefs under wide-brimmed hats. Saemion—who was up to see them off—had clearly lent Journey clothing. The fashionable purse had been replaced by an army-surplus duffle, which held the Raptus plus spare clothing and food rations. Knife remained exactly the same, of course, though he'd ditched the college sweater. *What's the use of being a shapeshifter if you don't ever shift your shape?* Chet wondered. Now was a great time for the Flame to take on different figures and faces. He kept his thoughts private.

Fenimore did not. He turned to Othnielia and inquired, "Why do you change to female to travel? Seems to me it's best to travel as male."

Chet blinked. He, too, had wanted to ask Othnielia why she'd turned female, but hadn't quite dared. She appeared to be third of the age she'd been before—in her mid-forties, perhaps. Still flaxen, she had a certain spare, wry beauty to her face and figure. She was still missing a tooth. Apparently, it was a real loss, not just for show. She, too, wore a kerchief under a wide-brimmed hat.

Othnielia shrugged. "You never know when you'll have to navigate unfriendly terrain. Being female means people will deliberately miss when they're shooting at you. Not that I expect to be shot at in peacetime, but territoriality is a timeless trait. Chivalry and sexism not so much, but still."

Masie and Saemion watched, unconcerned, as they mounted up. Or at least as everyone mounted up save Chet. Saemion giggled behind her hand as Masie encouraged him to ascend the beast. "You've got to stretch your legs wide open, once you're on the mounting block," she said cheerfully.

"*You* know all about that, Chet." Fenimore grinned down at him, holding out a hand to haul him up.

Fortunately, this beast was more placid than the doedicu yesterday. Chet almost popped his thigh out of its socket before he finally succeeded. He gripped Fenimore grimly, expecting to fall any minute. To his relief, Othnielia chose a walking pace.

Despite Othnielia's time-tested fears, they traversed territory without issue, cutting across fields and shallow creeks. Chet's leg muscles ached, but he managed to enjoy himself. It almost seemed like his childhood dreams of camping; a clear sky and real ceros riding. Chet's family had taken their vacations by a rural lake. He knew how to launch, handle and dock just about every kind of small boat imaginable, but riding a ceros through this rural area seemed a more authentically historic activity. He wondered whether they would see a pride of wild othnielias out here. Probably not, but he could dream.

As the day warmed, Chet grew cheerful enough to start reciting poetry under his breath. Fenimore gave him an odd look but didn't interrupt. Encouraged, Chet began another classical poem, this one written by the Magician Zang commemorating the construction of the city-state of Door by the honey-eyed Magicians and Foex. Fenimore joined in. Their emphases were different, and some of the little words had been changed—flipped around in translation?—but they were remarkably aligned with one another. At the end, the Flame applauded.

"Not bad," Journey said. "I've always felt Zang was best recited by a choir rather than read on the page."

Chet, recalling her background in the theater arts, felt immensely cheered by this professional opinion.

Fenimore seemed to have his blood up. He glanced at Chet over his shoulder. "Bet I can beat you in recitations. We each recite a verse no less than twelve lines long, and the other must guess the author and century written. Nothing after my time, though. No cheating."

"You're on," Chet said fiercely. Here was a game which he might have a chance of beating Fenimore!

They began with the easy stuff. Chet laughed out loud when Fenimore tried to trick him with the original Maansterdam city-state anthem, nationalist garbage that was a far cry from true classics. Fenimore, in turn, snorted when Chet just about handed him a Tache poet from his own time period. The Flame joined in after a while, and the game became truly hard. In the end, Othnielia stumped everyone when she recited repeating stanzas that sounded like they were from *The Book of Twelve* but clearly weren't.

Chet closed his eyes to think, then gasped. "It's from *Lament to the Metacors!* It's attributed to the mother of gods, Aerora herself, at the end of the Crimson Era. Say, the 3800s? Foex's millennium."

Othnielia stared at him with respect, and Knife whistled low. "You're good," Othnielia admitted. "I didn't know there were any copies left in the world."

"Only one. It's kept under glass in an air-tight vault deep in the Eich Che Independent University library. I gather they acquired it from the God Plain, though I don't know how or why. I was there on an entirely different research project. Couldn't resist taking a look, though. One of the oldest written texts in existence, all that." Chet nibbled on his lip. "You knew those verses pretty well, Othnielia. Are you that old?"

She laughed. "Abyss, no. No one is, except the gods themselves and Aureate, I guess."

"Chet, that was masterfully done. I think you just won the game," Journey said with the air of an umpire.

No one gainsaid this; even Fenimore looked a little awed. Chet leaned back in the saddle, grinning with pride. He didn't get to show off his knowledge often, not even among graduate students. No one wanted to talk about authors, poets, historians and ancient scholars for *fun*. No one really cared what they'd written beyond the immediately accessible classics in mass-print paperback.

Feeling bubbly as carbonated water, Chet glanced around and realized they were passing a series of buildings surrounded by cherry orchards. It almost certainly an Acia Nun convent; a small one, anyway. His sisters all belonged to a convent more than six times that size in Fengfu. Chet noticed a billowing line of Nun's habits on a clothesline. They were bright green, as per usual, with black trim. No one seemed to be around. Maybe the Nuns were praying inside as they did several times a day.

Inspiration struck. He struggled to get his leg over the ceros's haunch, then slipped down—down, down!—to the ground. Chet gasped and fell over, blood rushing to his head, his legs aching. He ignored the others' questions as he stumbled to his feet. Then he was off, running toward the clothesline in an ungainly fashion. Chet snatched the nearest two habits and headdresses and raced back, grinning like a boy.

"*What* are you *doing?*" Othnielia hissed, scowling.

"Saving Journey and Knife some trouble. Quick, let's get going before they come outside." Chet glanced guiltily over his shoulder. Stealing from Nuns wasn't the sort of thing he usually did... Fenimore must be rubbing off on him.

Indeed, Fenimore seemed nonplussed but not at all shocked. Chet wondered whether he was capable of feeling shock. "That low-lying walnut tree should work as a mounting block."

Chet was soon back in the saddle, aching and splendidly happy about his discovery. "Don't you see? If you Flame are disguised as Nuns, no one will question or bother you. And with headdresses you don't *need* wigs."

Journey and Knife exchanged uncertain looks, and Knife shrugged. "Emulating another god affiliate is no worse than the theft or murder charges, I suppose. The taboo would even serve to make our disguises more believable."

Othnielia still looked dour. "My family will need to make quiet donations to the convent. A gift of pies and one of my quilts, I should think. Bottles of Saemion's mead and dark ale, too. Look, I'm pretty non-political for a god affiliate, but we don't steal from Tutelary Party allies. The goddess Acia is on *our* side."

She didn't grumble for long, though, and no one made Chet give the habits back. *Needs dictate,* he thought smugly. Chet held onto the black-and-green bundles until they stopped for lunch. The peaceful glen apparently represented the last of the trees before the land flattened out into prairie. Journey shook out both habits: one was short and the other... shorter. And wide. Very wide.

Journey tossed this one to Knife with evident glee. "I don't have the body mass to fill that one, even at the required height. You do. Congratulations, you get to be short and fat for once."

Knife blanched as he assessed the habit. "Abyss," he muttered. He shot Chet a dirty look. "You should have made a more careful selection, Chet."

Chet frowned at him. "I don't understand. I thought you could change your shape to just about anything."

"Not so," Journey said. "Our bodies aren't nearly as flexible as you might think. We can't pour ourselves through the eye of a needle or even a chain-link fence. Muscles and tendons can be manipulated but still need space, and bones are rigid no matter what. Anatomical structures exist for a reason, and breaking those rules is painful. Back when I flattened myself out in the car, I was in pain the whole time. As far as these outfits go, we only have one body mass. Shape tall and you're thin, shape short and you're fat. It all has to go somewhere. I weigh a little under ten stone, but Knife is thirteen stone six. Ergo he gets the smaller, fatter habit. He'll need all that weight to shape outwards, you see."

"I hate being fat," Knife grumbled. "I hate big breasts. They *sweat.* And *jiggle.* I don't like the way men stare at them, either. You can't even sleep on them; it's like sleeping on enormous, sweaty tumors. I like long legs, the better to run fast and escape."

"Too bad." Journey grinned at him, stripping down to her underclothes without a trace of self consciousness. Chet realized everyone here had seen her naked before. "You don't mind the distraction of big breasts when you're tracking a mark."

"That's taking care of Pelin's dirty laundry, which is my passion. I'm willing to make sacrifices like that in the short term, but I draw the line at having voluntary sex as a woman with big breasts. Or as a woman at all, really." Knife shuddered. "The jiggling and pawing is enough to make me throw up. Then when you throw in the issue of vaginal penetration... gah. I'll do it, just never ask me to like it."

Othnielia and Journey giggled uproariously. There was no other word for it: they clutched at one another's arms and gasped for breath. Knife, looking prim, went behind the bushes to change into the habit.

Chet watched as Journey shaped herself downward, simultaneously growing portly, aged and soft in the process. With Othnielia's help—as she didn't have a mirror—Journey shaped a slightly asymmetrical face with vague, watery eyes. She looked like a Nun who'd never heard of the concept of makeup. The headdress went on, and voila: one elderly Nun. As before, Chet couldn't see anything of Journey in that face, except maybe deep in the eyes. He realized that he'd grown used to her preferred visage, both in male and female forms. It seemed that Flame created a cozy home space within their own bodies, remaining the same far more than they became different.

Knife, when she—she!—came out from behind the tree, was even more of a contrast. Chet snorted, his hand over his mouth to keep from laughing out loud. Fenimore grinned, not bothering to hide it. Knife was indeed short and quite fat now, squat and maybe even bowlegged. Flaxen-skinned, she had shaped the ugliest face Chet had ever seen. A completely asymmetrical, lumpy visage with jowls, large bags under her eyes and a permanent scowl. Her stitched boots seemed incongruous under the ankle-length habit; Chet hoped no one would notice them.

Knife waddled over to her ceros and sighed. "Someone want to give me a hand up?" she said in a warbling alto.

As promised, the last leg was mostly flat and hot under the clear, poppy-colored sky. Highway 1 appeared after a time, a ribbon etched upon the rolls of prairie. Not long after that, Othnielia pulled up her ceros. "You can find your way now. I don't want to get close to the road, as we're too visible and easily remembered like this."

Chet slid awkwardly to the ground. His whole body ached, even the little muscles he'd never knew existed. "Thank you for everything," he said. The others made their goodbyes, including the typical kiss from both Flame and a long hug from Journey. Then Othnielia galloped away with her string of ceroses behind her.

They reached the road an hour later. Knife had worked out a reputable cover story as to why elderly Nuns and young men were hitchhiking together: Chet and Fenimore were supposedly volunteers who'd been driving them to the Fengfu Convent on Acia's business. They'd broken down up the road, and the elderly Nuns had insisted upon continuing forward. It didn't seem likely to Chet, but he couldn't think of a better story, so he kept his mouth shut.

"Four is an awkward number to grab a ride," Journey sighed after a while.

Chet nodded agreement, turning once again to stick out three fingers in the usual sign. He knew this highway well. He'd driven it enough times, although he'd never picked up a hitchhiker himself. Chet wondered whether his own reticence was coming back to haunt him. At last, a big-rig truck slowed to a stop, and they hustled—or waddled with dignity—up the road to meet it. The rig had a closed cargo hold. Were they were all going to climb into the back with the cargo?

The driver was a middle-aged man, oily and unkempt. He looked exactly like the kind of man mothers warned their teenage children about—Chet got chills just looking at him. "Need a ride, sisters?" he said.

"Why, thank you, young man," Knife warbled, wiping her face with a handkerchief. Knife explained their problem as the driver opened up the back of his cargo hold. It was filled with industrial barrels, the hold half full.

Was he a smuggler? Chet scrunched his shoulders as little hairs on the back of his neck stirred.

"Everything is tied down, no problem," he said. "You sisters can bunk back here. One of you two young guys come up front." He gave Chet and Fenimore an appraising glance, his eyes lingering on Chet.

Chet gulped. He instinctively knew that he didn't want to be the one up front. Fenimore patted him on the shoulder and whispered in his ear, "You be a good girl for our carriage driver now."

Fenimore, slimy dium, turned away and made a show of helping the awkward, elderly Nuns into the cargo hold, then followed them inside. He was clearly uninterested in sitting up front... with reason. Journey shot Chet a worried look. Chet tried to smile back at her. He recalled her words back at the farm that she would be the one "taking the hit." Chet suddenly realized what she'd meant: hitchhiking was free with some drivers, but not with others. Bartering sexual favors was the coin of choice it seemed. Swaddled by her habit, Journey was no longer the target here. Chet was.

Apparently, it was time to take another one for the team.

# Chapter 15
# The Trouble With Hitchhiking

The cab smelled of stale beer and body odor. There was a rumpled bed in the back of the tiny compartment covered by dirty clothes. The man beside Chet kept giving him sideways glances.

"What do they call you, son?" he asked after a time.

"Chet. And you?"

"You can call me Rhiys." The man seemed to be evaluating him.

Chet looked down, his mouth dry. How personal would this get? As if in answer, Rhiys reached out and put a hand on Chet's leg. His touch was warm and had some pressure behind it. He rubbed Chet's leg up and down.

"You ever hitchhike before?"

Chet shook his head truthfully. Rhiys lingered at his upper thigh, and Chet couldn't help himself—he squirmed. "I don't like that," he said experimentally. "Please stop."

Rhiys put his hand back on the steering wheel, but his expression didn't change. "You been volunteering with Nuns all your life, boy?"

"All my sisters are Nuns," Chet said, sticking with the truth.

"You want to get those ladies where they're going, you're going to need to follow some rules, here. For one thing, this cab is my home. You're to be polite and respectful to me. You're to call me sir. Do you understand?"

Chet didn't like where this was going. "Yes, sir."

"I want you to undo my fly, boy, and pull out my dick."

*That was quick. No foreplay or anything, right down to business.* Chet nibbled his lip, uncertain. What would Journey do in this situation? She'd defended herself readily against Fenimore, yet she'd implied yesterday that she be the one handling this exact circumstance while hitchhiking. Not willingly, but from necessity. Would Journey open this guy's fly and take out his dick? Chet was afraid the answer was *yes*. Journey would probably make sure to set some boundaries, though. Both Knife and Fenimore had neatly—and cruelly, in Fenimore's case—avoided this situation entirely. If Fenimore were up here, he'd probably unsheathe his hunting blade and threaten the man to keep driving. Knife would have employed a subtler tactic with equal results. Lacking a weapon or tactical knowledge, Chet decided to try setting boundaries as a partial solution.

"Look, I'll suck your dick for you. But I won't take it in the ass."

Rhiys glanced at him with surprise. "Thought you were a blushing virgin. Ah, well. Suck me off, and I won't hurt you too badly."

*What does* that *mean?* Chet felt his breath stop in his throat. Was the guy a killer? They'd sure chosen the wrong truck to climb into, that was certain.

His fingers shaking, he unzipped the man's fly. Rhiys lifted his pelvis helpfully as Chet pulled his penis out. It was midsized and starting to grow hard, the glans head unusually square and large, like a hammer. It didn't smell very good. Chet gulped and lay down on his belly, then took it in his mouth. It tasted exactly the way it smelled. Chet made sure to cover his teeth with his lips, the way Fenimore had taught him. Rhiys rumbled in appreciation, stroking Chet's head one-handed, the other hand still steering the truck forward.

"Not bad, boy," he murmured as Chet suckled and pumped him with his lips. Rhiys was completely erect now. "Aw, Abyss with it," Rhiys growled after a while.

Chet felt the truck start to slow down, and he looked up, confused. They were pulling over to the shoulder. "What are you doing?" His lips felt oily and unclean.

"Next stop is too far away, and I want your dick *now*." Rhiys parked the truck and reached for Chet.

Chet backed away. "Hey! I said—"

"Yeah, yeah, no fucking. I heard you. But I still want to play with your cock." Rhiys grabbed at his fly; Chet struggled reflexively for a minute, but Rhiys was stronger. His penis was limp as Rhiys pulled it out.

"Look, I—*oh,*" Chet gasped. Rhiys had him in both hands now, pumping with one hand, the other rubbing the tip of his penis. It felt overwhelming to be touched by a man he feared, yet he was still turned on. Chet writhed, his empty hands opening and closing as Rhiys manipulated him.

Rhiys put a hand on his shoulder, pushing him down. "Lie face up on the seat."

"Y-yes, sir."

Chet did as he was told. He'd delved into the darkness of sexuality with Fenimore. Now he was diving deeper... deeper... could he ever surface from this depth?

*Yes.*

*I* will *survive,* he decided. It was a comforting thought with no basis in reality. He was surrounded by people who frightened him, events that had turned his world inside out. Professor Clementina's threats. Fenimore's insistent ways. Even Knife had scared him when he'd stepped out of line. The things Chet loved most were gone, starting with his degree, his ex-girlfriend, and Tibbets. And yet he would survive this. *I vow it.*

Rhiys climbed atop him, his crotch in Chet's face. His penis dangled on Chet's lips. "Suck me off while I play with you."

Chet lifted his head and took his dick once more. Rhiys's oily taste and smell filled his nostrils. He felt nauseous and involuntarily aroused, his cock again trapped and pumped. Rhiys fucked his face indelicately, smashing himself into Chet's nose and cheeks. There was an implicit assumption in Rhiys's actions that Chet was a puppet to play with, an object without emotions or opinions of his own. Chet gasped for air, fighting against the, the *illusion* that his mouth was nothing but a hole for the man to fuck. An illusion, yes. Had to be.

"Swallow me, boy. Swallow what I give you," Rhiys said in a breathless tone as he came, spurting semen into Chet's mouth.

Chet swallowed, gagging and sick to his stomach as he tried not to bite down. *Pantheon, that was cruel.* Would it end now? Rhiys didn't climb off—instead, he leaned over and took Chet in his own mouth. He didn't bother lapping his teeth, and Chet cried out, squirming, as the man half-bit, half sucked him. Aroused and laid open, Chet came with Rhiys's scrotum mashed against his cheek. *Well, that was unpleas-*

*ant*. Strange that the same physical reaction could be so different depending on who had caused it.

Rhiys let him up. "I'm tempted to fuck you anyway, boy. You're too a fine dumpling to eat only half."

"I'll suck you again whenever you want, *sir*. But leave my ass alone," Chet said, trying to keep his voice steady.

The ride continued. Rhiys fingered him occasionally. The guy was just gross. Chet wished he were back on the ceros, reciting poetry with the others. He wished he were anywhere but here, yet this wasn't too bad. Despite his greasiness, Rhiys didn't alarm him anymore. Rhiys respected Chet's imposed boundary, a fact which Chet found comforting.

"There's a principality ahead where I fill up and get some food," Rhiys commented after a long silence. "Want something to eat? Do you think your friend and the sisters will want something, too?"

"Sure, I'll have something. The others have food in the duffle bag." Chet didn't want the Flame exposed when they didn't need to be. Besides, why should they get hot food when he was the one doing all the work? *Fenimore can eat dry rations and sit on it,* Chet decided grumpily.

"Whoops," Rhiys muttered, clearly alarmed as they rounded a hill.

Chet blinked. Twelve police cars, their lights on, blocked the highway ahead. A long string of cars crept forward, the queue controlled by the officers who were checking each one.

Rhiys grunted, his expression hard. "Wonder why they have a roadblock *here* of all places. No alternate routes on this stretch."

*You just answered your own question,* Chet thought, frowning at the police cars. Yesterday Sheriff Jindo had said police forces had been scrambling to find them. Now there was a roadblock on Highway 1, the only viable road that ran east to west across the Eicha continent.

Chet squinted, trying to see what was happening. Each officer had a canteen in hand. They leaned into the windows of cars with the canteens, doing—what? Checking for Flame by sprinkling water on people? It seemed a likely and fool-proof way to seek out disguised shapeshifters. There would be no mistaking the Flame as anything but what they were... nor was there a convenient doppelganger at hand, like Oak.

A line of closed-cargo trucks had been waved off the road, the cargo doors open as they were searched. *Shit, shit, shit,* Chet thought wildly. He had no way to warn the others. He could only wait, but the wait wasn't long; an officer waved them off road as they crept forward in the line of cars.

Rhiys growled to Chet, "You say nothing, understand? I can't believe my bad luck..."

Chet nodded. *The guy's a smuggler after all,* he thought dryly. At least Rhiys had an internal motivation not to stir up trouble in this police blockade. Chet frowned, distracted. The cord he'd forgotten about—the cord linking his navel to the Raptus—shifted a little. Then it jumped. Chet glanced over his shoulder at the closed cargo hold. Was someone back there messing with the Raptus?

A policeman waved at Rhiys and Chet to get out of the truck, which they did. Rhiys presented his license and travel permits upon request. The officer eyed them alertly. "And who are you?" he asked Chet.

Rhiys said, "This is my son, Chet. He's on summer break from school and wanted to make a run with his old man. Eh, Chet?"

"Yeah." Chet shrugged, trying to look bored and slouch like a secondary-school student. For once, he was glad he looked younger than he really was.

"What cargo are you carrying?"

Rhiys cleared his throat. "Empty barrels. I make stops all along Highway 1 to ice makers and other folks like that."

"Please hold out your hands," the officer said, a canteen in hand. They followed instructions and enduring a sprinkling of water on their hands.

"Say, what's this about anyway?" Rhiys said, shaking off his hand. "You doing a hygiene test of some sort?"

"Tracking possible fugitives. I'll need you to—to open the... ba..." The guy blinked, as if uncertain. Then he looked *very* uncertain. The feeling in Chet's belly, the link to the Raptus grew stronger. The officer shook his head. "Excuse me. I need you to open the back of your truck."

"Sure thing, sir." Rhiys strode around the side, Chet and the officer following.

The cord extending from Chet's belly was almost vibrating now. Chet held his breath as Rhiys opened the cargo hold.

The officer glanced inside, his eyes vague and unfocused. Even Chet could see that someone was hiding behind the roped-down barrels: there was a tiny swatch of color in the back of the hold. Fenimore, by the look of it, but the officer didn't seem to see him.

"Yep, looks good. You can be on your way."

Rhiys didn't speed while driving away. He also didn't stop in the small principality they passed, or the next one, either. Thoroughly spooked, Chet decided. After a while Rhiys seemed to calm down.

"What a doedicu," he said after a time. "I can't believe how dumb he was."

"Guess you have good luck after all."

Rhiys frowned at him. "They were looking for someone. They were looking with *water*."

Chet had nothing useful to say, so he kept his mouth shut. Rhiys's appraisal had become narrow-eyed. "Those Nuns in the back... they're not really Nuns, are they, boy?"

Chet swallowed, his throat dry. "Of course they're Nuns, sir."

"Yeah, right. The way I see it, I covered for your little group back there. You owe me." Rhiys pulled off the road to the shelter of a lonely grove of trees. "I need to take a piss."

"Okay," Chet said. *Just a piss. Right.*

Rhiys looked at him closely, and Chet stopped feeling relieved. "You're a good swallower."

"... Sir?"

"Take out my dick and swallow my piss."

Chet blanched. "Oh, gross." Well, this trip was certainly opening up new horizons to him, wasn't it? Like the sewer.

Rhiys grinned, his teeth mossy. "Tell you what. You owe me, boy, but you've been such a willing lad that I'll give you a choice. You either drink my piss, or I fuck you in the ass. No rubber, no nothing. Your choice."

Chet found himself crumple inside, his heart pounding in his ears. Despite himself, the guy had won. He *couldn't* drink piss, which meant... which meant he was going to be raped after all.

"You can't fuck me without lubrication," he said after a minute, thinking about Fenimore's earlier complaint to Knife.

Rhiys grinned wider. "Good choice, boy." He riffled around the cab and found a bottle of hand lotion, which he dropped in Chet's lap. "Make yourself nice and ready for me on the bunk."

Chet didn't move as Rhiys climbed down and slammed the door behind him. Feeling more like an object than ever, he slowly climbed back onto the filthy, stinking bed. He took off his pants and shoes, though he left his socks on, and rubbed his anus with lotion. Fortunately it wasn't the perfumed stuff. Chet couldn't believe this. He couldn't believe he was about to be fucked by a dangerous, oily smuggler on Highway 1. How many times had he driven this road between his family's home and the university? He would never drive this way again without remembering...

No. He was just going to have anal sex with the guy. He'd done this before with Fenimore and Journey; there was nothing new about the act. Really. Rhiys hadn't threatened him, exactly, except with vague guesses about the Flame. Chet still wondered whether Rhiys was a killer, but he didn't know and had no way to find out. Except the hard way, he imagined. *I'll take it in the ass, but I'm no smaller for this experience,* Chet thought stubbornly, his lower lip sticking out. *I'm not weak.*

And if it came to killing... well, Chet would keep his eyes open. He'd be ready to do whatever was needed. Before this week, he'd never imagined himself murdering another human being, not even in his own defense. Yet hadn't Journey said it herself? "You do things in war that it normally wouldn't occur to you to do." This was a kind of war, too, and if Journey could kill a man, so could Chet.

The cab door opened and Rhiys stuck his head inside. "Good, you're ready to go," he murmured, undoing his belt buckle and letting down his pants.

Though he'd resolved to keep quiet, Chet groaned involuntarily as the man clambered on top, his weight and smell pressing down on him. Chet closed his eyes tight. It didn't help as much as he'd hoped. Rhiys grunted as he pushed himself inside Chet's ass. The head of his cock was hard to take—it was too blunt. Chet wished Rhiys could shape down the way Journey could, or at least take his time. Rhiys fucked him without hesitation or compassion. Chet gritted his teeth and bore the unclean touch. He wasn't hard at all, he realized. Being fucked by Rhiys wasn't arousing; it was to be endured.

At least Rhiys came quickly. "Sweet Chet," he whispered in his ear, licking it.

Chet grimaced and tried to turn away. *Survival sure isn't pretty,* he thought, straining under the weight. Rhiys grabbed his hair and hauled his head back, then proceeded to lick his ear out thoroughly, nibbling on the lobe. Chet closed his eyes again, enduring both the man's tongue and dick still lodged inside him.

After a time Rhiys rose, dressed and started up the truck again. Still no threats or attempts on Chet's life. *Good enough,* he thought muzzily. He dozed on the bed as the sun set. After a while, he felt the truck slow and make several turns. The engine cut. Chet sat up, blinking sleepily. Rhiys had stopped at a gas station and diner, dusk deepening into night.

"Come on, let's have dinner. Since you're whoring your sweet ass to me, I'm buying." Rhiys grinned at him.

Chet didn't know how he'd be able to eat, but once the food arrived, he found he had an appetite. The meal almost felt normal, sane, as if the world hadn't turned upside down. Yet when they were returning to the truck, Rhiys grabbed Chet's belt in a proprietary manner, as if he owned him.

"There are kids here! Families," Chet hissed, his face going red. The parking lot wasn't *that* dark. Though there was no one directly in their path, he could hear their conversations and smell their cigarettes.

"You want to protect those people in the hold? Then your ass is mine."

"Yes, we've already established that." Chet bit his tongue against a more sardonic response. "I just don't want to be reported for indecency."

The argument seemed to hold water until they climbed into the cab, when Rhiys grabbed him with a move akin to wrestling, his touch savage. "Take off your pants. I'm going to fuck you right here where everyone can see."

Did he have a choice? Chet decided yes, he did, but almost every path he could conceivably take would lead to the police, exactly what he didn't want. Nevertheless, Chet's eyes narrowed. "You can fuck me in your bed."

"Shy, are you?"

"Yeah, I am."

Chet moved toward the back of the cab, and to his surprise, Rhiys let him. Rhiys climbed in behind, and Chet let him take off his pants. *Abyss, he gave in to my demands, so give the man what he wants.* It was almost sexy to spread himself over Rhiys's lap; he even helped insert himself. Chet relaxed. Being fucked like this was gentle compared to other positions. He glanced at the forward windshield and smiled. They weren't under a street light, and it would be too dark to see inside the cab. He felt protected and safe from the public eye.

Despite the danger, he was in control. Very nearly in control, anyway.

Rhiys pumped Chet's dick in his fist and fingered his nipples through his shirt. Chet was undisputedly aroused. He moaned, enjoying the feeling. Before being fucked by an oily smuggler had been a bad thing, but now it was almost tolerable. The guy accelerated the tempo of this fist pumping, and Chet abruptly forgot the litany in his head. He threw his head back and made little needy sounds. The dick inside him, the hands upon him, everything made him light up like Elderbeth in a clear sky. Chet came, spurting in Rhiys's hand. Rhiys pushed him down into the bed—Chet felt like he had no bones left in his body to fight. Not that he wanted to fight. Chet fell to his stomach with a little grunt, and Rhiys fucked him harder in the new position.

"Yeah, boy. Take it like a slut, boy. You're my whore tonight, you and your hot cock belong to me..."

The words washed over Chet. Fenimore wanted to own him, this guy wanted to own him, the police wanted to cuff him down and drag him away. Everyone wanted a piece. He grinned at his own private joke.

Rhiys grunted and came, spurting deep into Chet's ass.

"Hey, don't fall asleep," Rhiys said after a while. "Come to the front and keep me company. Oh, and your pants stay off. I want your bare ass on this seat for the rest of the night."

*What?* How long could he keep this up? Chet shouldn't be surprised at this point. "If my pants are off, how will you concentrate on driving?"

"Pantheon, you got a mouth on you. If you'd stick with me, kid, I'll pummel those smart-alecky ways right out of you, but not tonight. I got to make my schedule."

They reached Fengfu an hour after dawn. Chet was filthy, tired, his muscles sore, his ass exposed and wet, his lips oily as abyss. Survival no longer had the shine it had held earlier in the night; Chet held on doggedly nevertheless. Rhiys pulled off at the correct exit and had Chet suck his dick one more time. Chet honestly didn't care if the man killed him. He swallowed semen with dull exhaustion, no longer remotely aroused by the act.

Rhiys zipped up his fly."Good boy. Let's let your friends out of the back, and you can be on your way, eh?"

*Really? My fears were for nothing?* Chet found his pants and shoes, dressing himself in jerky movements. He let himself out of the cab and joined Fenimore, Knife and Journey by the side of the road. They were rumpled and smelly from uninterrupted hours in the cargo hold, but otherwise unruffled. Rhiys drove away without saying goodbye. On the whole, Chet preferred it that way.

"So, girl, did you have a good time?" Fenimore asked Chet sunnily.

Chet didn't even think about it. He curled up his hand, pivoted and punched Fenimore on the face. Fenimore dropped to his knees, obviously surprised. Chet yelped, shaking out his hand.

"Great good Pantheon, that hurt," Chet hissed. He glared at Knife with unvoiced accusation.

Knife grunted. "Next time, curl your hand so your thumb is outside your fist, like *this*."

Chet watched the movement of her hand. "Yeah. Next time."

Fenimore picked himself off the ground and began whistling a cheerful ditty. "Everyone ready? Let's head back to civilization!"

# Chapter 16
# Family Values

Chet had expected his parents to be home on a weekend morning. What he had not counted on were his two older brothers with their families. That meant two sisters-in-law and the eleven assorted children between them. Pantheon help them, one of his sisters-in-law was pregnant again. Chet could only be grateful that none of his actual sisters were home. With the Flame still in Nun costume, he didn't want anyone taking a real close look at them.

"Chet!" his mother cried out. "What are you doing here? We thought you were doing that silly dig thing out in Wetshul, burrowing in the earth like some common construction worker."

"Waste of time," his father put in, stuffing his mouth with sausage and whitefish. "I could put you to better work here as mid-level management. You'd have fifteen employees under you tomorrow morning."

His brothers echoed this sentiment, adding brotherly comments about his lack of intelligence and motivation. The in-laws ignored the name calling and focused on the children, who were running wild. Chet kept his still-oily mouth shut and glanced at Knife, Journey and Fenimore. Journey's eyes were wide and fascinated, vague no more. It was hard to tell what Knife was thinking behind the ugly visage, but Chet rather thought she was taken aback by the noise and bustle of the family weekend breakfast. Fenimore was truly taken aback. He looked appalled by both the children and uproar.

It felt bizarre to be home. Chet's mother had put her finger right on it: he hadn't expected to show up for a long time with the dig of the century going on. He felt out of time as a man who'd fallen into lucid mud.

The sensation was especially intense with Fenimore and the Flame trailing him. His parent's house somehow made recent events more real, not just a dream he'd wake up from any minute. Despite the pain and uncertainty of the last few days, he felt proud of himself. He'd endured with newly acquired friends and skill sets, yet he couldn't help but feel this rise in self esteem was a soap bubble about to burst. Chet always felt smaller and insignificant at home, outshone by every other family member. Abyss, even his sisters—the Nuns—were blazing extroverts. Not like him. He'd been the odd guy out from the cradle on up.

Even so, he felt reasonably optimistic. Maybe now that he was traveling in bad company—dastardly Flame and a libertine courtier—he would have the spine to stand up to his family. *Maybe.*

Chet cleared his throat."Uh, I brought some friends home."

"We can see that, Chetling," his mother said. She hugged him and frowned, trying to straighten his hair. "I swear, you seem to be covered in grease. There's something matting your hair, too."

*Semen,* Chet thought sourly. He ducked away from his mother's reflexive grooming. "Do you mind if I go upstairs and take a shower? My friends wouldn't mind having some breakfast, if that's okay."

"There's plenty, help yourselves," his father said congenially.

One of Chet's brothers, Brae, made eye contact and smirked, then let loose a belch, purposefully winding Chet up. Abyss, Chet hated how crass his brothers were. No one else seemed to mind, though; his wife just sighed and the younger family members giggled. More competitive burping followed. Chet ignored them. He wasn't anyone's favorite uncle, and—though it kind of hurt—he didn't want to be. Sometimes he felt like Brae was training the next generation to make fun of him, too.

Chet stayed long enough to make sure the Flame received loaded plates and were seated at the table. The Baikson family had servants but preferred to only be served formally at supper. Or rather, his father preferred to eat breakfast, "With everything hanging out," as he liked to put it.

Fenimore followed Chet upstairs, presumably to flee the Baikson circus. "Your family is insane. The house is stately enough, but they act like peasants," he commented in undertone.

"They're my folks, okay?" Chet said, put out.

"Well... I suppose they're more like minor hangers-on of the court, the type who'd ferry a commission to a brothel owner or pilfer through a rival's jewels. For a fee, of course. I used to employ the type all the time."

Chet supposed Fenimore was attempting to be diplomatic. Too bad he was so lousy at it. "There's nothing *minor* about my family."

"My words sting, do they? The truth can be hard to swallow, I know. Like swallowing my sweet jam."

Chet wrinkled his nose, catching the reference to semen without difficulty. He was getting better at this. As for his family... Chet paused at the top of the grand staircase and looked down at the noble foyer with its twenty-five foot high ceiling and massive crystal chandelier. Seeing it not only for everything it was, but everything it symbolized.

He lowered his voice and said, "Not at all. I think you misunderstand the suffering my family has inflicted. My father and brothers cheat and steal for a living, not just from a few people but from millions. No one is safe, not even their own employees. They've learned to be subtle about it, that's all. Why do you think my sisters chose to be Nuns? It wasn't for the eye-catching habits."

Fenimore blinked. "Ah. Puffed-up hangers on, then."

Chet rolled his eyes. He was still pissed at Fenimore, and didn't intend to do anything but shower and get rid of the icky, awful clothing that clung to him like rags. Being arrested, dunked in a doedicu lake, rubbed against a ceros for five hours, and fucked by an oily smuggler hadn't done his clothing any good.

Once inside Chet's room, Fenimore glanced around with curiosity. "That's quite a collection," he said, gazing at the books in the floor-to-ceiling shelves that lined the walls.

Chet unbent a little. "Thank you." As a teenager, he'd fought with his father to have those bookshelves installed.

Chet grabbed a change of clothes and started into his private bathroom, then paused, eyeing Fenimore. Fenimore seemed to be innocently studying the titles in the bookshelf. If Chet took his eyes off of Fenimore, would he get in trouble? Or get Chet in trouble, which was far likelier. Fenimore seemed to have a knack for it. Chet sighed and closed the bathroom door behind of him; he was not Fenimore's keeper and, Pantheon curse it, he wanted his *shower*.

Feeling almost human again, Chet emerged to find Fenimore in the exact same position as when Chet had left, unlikely as it seemed. "Want to shower? I'll lend you clothing,"

"Certainly!" Fenimore grabbed the proffered fresh clothes and disappeared into the steaming bathroom.

Feeling obscurely that it would be bad manners to leave his guest, Chet lay down on his bed and gazed at his ceiling. It seemed so strange to be in his childhood home after everything that had happened in less than a week. In that short time he'd bonded with an ancient magical relic, been deflowered by men and Flame, watched his ex-girlfriend disappear into thin air, witnessed the dead body of his professor, and... everything else. Too much, too fast. Chet turned over and pressed his face into the pillow. It smelled nice, like lavender. One of the servants must have changed the sheets in his absence.

Chet felt dirty and corrupted after last night, yet he also felt strangely free. He'd survived, just as he'd intended. Horrible things had happened to him—he'd been taken without his consent—but he'd lived through the experience. Like... like the Flame themselves. Even when they didn't survive, they ended up living again, remembering all the same. They dealt with the hurts and moved on. Chet had survived one night, but Journey had survived over two-thousand years. Clearly not all of that had been pleasant.

It was like tasting a slice of eternity. Chet wasn't sure he liked the flavor.

What would Rory think of him now? He was warm and tingly at the thought. He missed her. Chet felt like all his ties to life had been cut: Professor Tibbets, his archeology program, Steve, the university and Rory. Her common sense and self efficacy would come in really handy about now. Too bad she wasn't here.

What had she said about the Raptus? That it was more important than her degree, her own life. Chet frowned—he could barely feel the cords anymore. How far could he travel away from the Raptus before he'd have to return? It was unnerving that even the Flame didn't understand the nature of this binding. Why had the Raptus waited until he'd grabbed it to tie them together? He'd never heard of four being a traditional magical number; not that there were any Magicians left to tell him, but still. Six and twelve were numbers laden with far more ancient power, thanks to the gods, each of whom had an extra finger on each hand.

Why, why, why? Chet glanced at the books—and by proxy, the authors—surrounding the walls of his room. So many secrets between those pages, hidden between the lines. He didn't have a key to unlock them. Yet for whatever reason, the Raptus wanted him. Unaffiliated or not, it wanted him. Personally.

Someone jumped onto the bed beside him and Chet yelped. Fenimore grinned at him. "Startled you, did I?" he purred.

Chet sighed, eyes narrow. "I'm *so* not fucking you right now. You realize what an asshole you were back on the road, right?"

Fenimore raised an eyebrow. "I believe we've established that I'm here to—what's the charming word you use? Ah, yes—I'm here to fuck, not to *be* fucked."

"Knife had you first thing, back in Wetshul."

Fenimore actually blushed and looked away. Chet was impressed by the show of emotions and wondered whether it was real. "Knife is... special. She knows what a predator I am. She *likes* predators, the way I like innocent young men."

Chet raised himself on his elbow. "At this point, I'm not innocent by any stretch of the imagination. Why are *you* still around?"

Fenimore clasped his chest. "Ah, you've sliced me to the quick! Such a sharp sword you wield this morning, Chet."

Chet paused, taken aback. "I don't believe you've ever called me by name."

Fenimore nuzzled Chet's chest, almost as if he were an inofe—an enormous cat that had once roamed rural Uos. "What, must I call you by demeaning pet names all the time?"

"You tell me." Chet frowned at Fenimore. This behavior was very unlike him. "You want something from me, don't you? Not sex. You'd just take that, if that's what you wanted. No, you must want something else."

Fenimore blinked up at him with his long eyelashes and didn't answer. *Those eyelashes ought to be illegal,* Chet thought. But all Fenimore said was, "I think we should go have breakfast before it is either set aside or disappears entirely."

*No, he definitely doesn't want sex,* Chet thought as they descended the staircase. Whatever Fenimore was after was lost in the general uproar and chaos of Chet's family. Chet was alarmed to see Journey missing from the table—her plate thoroughly emptied of breakfast—until he heard her voice from the rumpus room. He ducked down the hall and around the corner. Sure enough, Journey was surrounded by his nephews and nieces. Even as an elderly Nun, she drew attention: singing and acting out the lines to something silly and rhyming. The children were spellbound and clearly delighted. Bemused, Chet returned to the dining room to find that Knife, meanwhile, had struck up a conversation with his father. They were talking about stocks and bonds on the Genis Exchange in Allistair, a subject his father knew a lot about.

Knife seemed incongruous as a bowlegged Nun while saying things like, "Simeon Brothers has really gone downhill since the war. I don't think their stock has ever topped out since the faulty arms scandal of '587..."

Chet snorted. All was well, apparently. He even managed to eat something before his mother descended upon him once again.

"Chet, the police just called. Something about stealing a valuable artifact and some sort of other investigation. Also, a woman from the university called last night about your whereabouts. A Professor Clemena? Claminata? No, that's not right."

The police? *Clementina?* Chet froze instinctively. "Did you tell them I'm here?"

She managed to glare while straightening his collar. "What do you take me for? Of course I wouldn't tell the authorities you're here. When the family is in trouble with the law, we back each other up. But I don't know why you'd steal anything—we give you everything you could possibly desire, and more."

His father, alert to the conversation, turned to Mother and said, "You know, I wish he would steal something. Far as I can tell, Chet's life is all about scurrying around like a filthy dium, scrambling in the dirt for ancient trash and reading his old books. No one should live like that. In fact, I think prison would do him good. When I was Chet's age, I'd already done six months for tax evasion and bank fraud. There's nothing like prison to make a man of you, to focus your ambitions and help you make connections in the business and political world."

Chet looked at the table, feeling tears rising to his eyes. Apparently, he couldn't count on his father to bail him out. His father wanted him in prison for his own reasons. Chet's life might be dour and colorless compared to the flashy, let-it-all-hang-out attitude his family strove for, but it was his life. No one else's.

"I don't want Chet going to prison," his mother said in a wavering voice. "He's my baby. Men do horrible things to boys like Chet in prison."

Chet nearly rolled his eyes. *Too late, mother.*

Brae seemed to perk up at the subject matter. "What, Chet's going to prison? About time you stopped being such a goodie-goodie, you little prick." He leaned over and cuffed Chet on the head. Hard. Chet breathed through his nose and tried not to react, as usual. Brae continued, "Last season, I had to testify in front of the magistrate for the usual litany of tax loopholes. It would do you good to be accountable to that kind of inquiry, doedicu. You can finally stop being such a sensitive fruitcake."

Chet covertly swiped tears and glanced at Knife, who was staring at Chet's family with disbelief. Knife cleared her throat and said, as if she couldn't help herself, "You clearly care about Chet's future prospects."

His father slammed the table with his open hand, making everyone jump. "What I care about is if he finally chooses a god to affiliate himself with! Genis *told* me he'd have you, boy, no questions asked. At least choose Philapo, already! It's expected for a professor, which is what you seem bound and determined to become. Our family pride is at stake."

This inspired a whole chorus of agreement and the endless questions. Chet hunkered down and weathered the storm, as usual. He didn't want to be an affiliate for Genis—the god who specialized in commerce—any more than the rest of them. Less, all things considered. Fenimore, gulping breakfast rabidly, nudged Chet with his foot, as if to remind him why they were here.

Chet took a deep breath. "Actually, Father, I was wondering if I could possibly float a loan."

His father glared. A long pause went by, then he said, "You can have all the money you want... once you become a god affiliate. I don't care if you jump in a fireplace and become a stinking pervert of a Flame, so long as you make up your abysmal mind. Though I'd obviously prefer if you took up with Genis."

Chet felt something inside of him snap. "No. You can't have that," he muttered toward the floor.

"What?"

He looked up into his father's face and yelled, "I said, *you can't have that*. I'd rather peddle my ass on the streets of Door before becoming a god affiliate. My life and my, my *soul* are my own! I will not declare myself in a god's camp until I'm ready. And I never will be."

Chet was almost too angry to watch for reactions around the table, though his heart twinged when his mother put her hands over her mouth and turned away. His father, on the other hand, seemed unmoved. "So be it. I'm putting my foot down and pulling your tuition for fall term. You can go join the ranks of unaffiliated and work for a living, far as I care, though I'd prefer if you didn't throw it all away. I've paid too much for your private schools to squander an investment like that."

"Fine," Chet growled. He could almost feel the last tie from his old life give an audible *ping* as it was cut from him. "I can find work in a library or as a research assistant. Pull my way through and earn the degree on my own."

"Not at Semaphore, you won't. You'd never make tuition."

"Then I'll go to an independent city-state university! I'll make my own way in life. You can't make my choices for me, do you hear?"

What was he doing? He'd never intended to yell, not at his family. They may be messed up, but he loved them and disliked them so much. Why did they make everything more difficult? Yet he felt a glimmer of satisfaction because he'd stood up for himself at last. Chet's face was hot and his whole body tingled with rage.

At that moment, the backdoor opened and all six of Chet's sisters piled inside, one after the other. They wore their Nun's habits though only two wore headdresses; the others had their hair down. All were chattering away. The tension broke in the room as the noise increased six fold. Chet's anger began fading abruptly, giving way to fear. Sisters hugged and carried on with the family already present, drawing a crowd from sisters-in-law and various children trickling in from other parts of the house.

*That does it,* Chet thought. It was clear they weren't getting any money from his father—thanks to his outburst—and the game had changed with his sisters home. Though he liked some of his sisters more than other members of his family, he and the others couldn't stay. Chet glanced at Knife nervously, and Knife returned a wide-eyed look. Definitely time to go.

Chet nudged his head to the left, indicating the escape route, then murmured in Fenimore's ear, "Come on."

Getting up from the table, Chet spotted Brae's car keys on a side table. He quietly pocketed them, feeling a twinge of satisfaction course through him. Was being a criminal getting easier, or was it just because it was Brae? Knife was already ahead of him, retrieving Journey from the rumpus room.

They'd almost made it to the garage when Chet's second-youngest sister, Silvie, popped out of a side corridor, cutting them off. "Hi, Chet. I didn't know you were coming home. My, this is different company for you, isn't it. Who are these strange Nuns?"

Chet gulped. His favorite sibling wasn't a dummy. "Um, Silvie, could you let mother and father know I've gone?"

Silvie squinted at the two Flame, frowning. "This doesn't seem right, Chet. Excuse me, but what convent do you two come from?"

Journey smiled, watery and vague to the extreme. "It's a tiny one west of the Monastery Mountains, a little south of Highway 1. I doubt you've heard of it..."

"Oh, the Arch Convent? The thing is I've visited that convent a number of times. I've never seen either of you there. Could you describe your mother superior, please?"

Knife sighed and stepped back from the group while Journey extrapolated wildly. "I hate to do this," Knife murmured, drawing up her habit.

Chet's eyes widened as Knife withdrew a tiny, snub-nosed pistol out of her boot. Is *that* where Knife had been keeping her gun all this time? No wonder she rarely took those boots off. Did she have a blade in her other boot? Tibbets had been stabbed, after all.

"You're *not* going to shoot my sister," Chet said, almost hyperventilating. Thankfully, Silvie hadn't noticed the pistol yet, still arguing in a loud voice with Journey.

"Your family is big enough to be a mob, and to judge by your father, a dangerous mob for us to be caught by. Best nip this in the bud now. We'll have to bring her with us. We don't have much choice."

Fenimore touched the duffle bag on Journey's back. "No need," he murmured, somewhat smugly. Chet stared at him—what was he going to do?

Silvie was yelling, "It's a felony to imitate a god affiliate! My sisters and I are going to tie you up and call the pol—"

She stopped abruptly. Silvie had the same bewildered look on her face as the officer back at the roadblock. As before, Chet felt an odd vibration in the region of his navel. He touched his belly, uncertain, and gazed at Fenimore with awe. Though Chet had been around the Raptus as long as Fenimore, he hadn't even tried to make it work. It was a hesitation Fenimore didn't share, apparently. Knife, he noticed, didn't seem surprised that Fenimore had a degree of control over the Raptus. She was expressionless though she watched him closely, the gun held loosely at her side.

Fenimore smiled. "You are going to eat breakfast with the others and forget all about us."

"Yes, I'm going to eat breakfast with the others and forget all..." Silvie wandered off mid-sentence.

Chet gazed after his sister, worried. Would this brush with the Raptus hurt her? Would she even remember? He didn't know the answers. Pantheon, did anyone? He wished he could go after her and make sure she was okay, except he was already committed to their escape—not to mention the rest. At least Knife holstered her gun.

Chet led them to the garage where several assorted vehicles awaited. Knife already had a familiar, abstract look on her face, appraising. Chet touched her shoulder and shook his head.

"I already got it." He tossed his brother's keys in the air and caught them.

"Hah. You learn quick."

It felt weird to steal Brae's car, but Chet could still feel the spot on his head where Brae had cuffed him. Chet had stood for up himself—

sort of—but some things were more personal than that. His anger, repressed when his sisters had walked in, bloomed within him like a spring bulb. It just wasn't fair. Father gave everything to Brae because Brae had followed him into business and had done everything Father had ever asked of him. Chet did not. And Chet got nothing for his troubles... well, almost nothing. He supposed a high-priced education wasn't small change, but still. He sure wasn't going to have an education now, was he?

Everyone followed Chet to Brae's family station wagon, complete with crumbs and sticky seats. Chet backed it out of the garage without further incident. "Where are we going?"

"Door International Airport. Should be about an hour and thirty minutes away, right?" Knife said.

"But I didn't get the money! I suppose we could sell Brae's car." Chet frowned at the thought. A brotherly prank was one thing, but selling Brae's car was something else. Bad crowd or not, he didn't really want to cross that line, much as his family pained him.

"Fen?" Knife murmured, glancing at the backseat.

Fenimore extracted a wad of cash, a checkbook, his father's watch, some jewelry and several papers from his shirt pockets."I found a copy of his signature, sure enough, Knife."

Chet opened his mouth and left it open. Fenimore must have gone through his father's study while Chet had been in the shower. "But how did you know to look for a checkbook, Fenimore?" Had they even *had* checkbooks in the 73rd century? Chet didn't think so.

"Knife told me what to look for."

"We had long hours in the truck cargo hold to plan," Knife said smugly. "Get us to the airport, Chet. We're going to Plainsdaugheau."

It was only later—as they were crossing the tarmac to board the airplane—that Chet remembered Fenimore's odd behavior in his bedroom. Fenimore had never told him what he wanted. Chet stared at Fenimore's back and frowned.

## Chapter 17
# Flaming Dance

Chet approached yet another bald-headed Flame on the muddy street. "Excuse me, good Flame, do you know someone named Aureate?"

The Flame paused and eyed him curiously. Chet noticed that though she wore bright, colorful clothing, she had also taken the precaution of wearing knee-high rubber boots to protect herself from the pervasive mud.

"I know *of* her. Why, what do you want to know?"

"My friends and I are wondering where she's performing tonight with the Intako Dance Company. We'd like to see them in action," Chet said. Over the past hour he'd repeated the same question many times. Lacking a phone number and address, they had to find Aureate the hard way.

Fortunately, Plainsdaugheau was an easy city-state to search for a Flame. Chet had seen more Flame in the last hour than in his entire life. At first, he'd found it rather alarming to see Flame openly walking down the street, ducking out of doorways, kissing, talking and riding bicycles like normal people. The Silk District was brimming with them. Despite this—or perhaps because of it—finding one Flame among many had turned out to be its own challenge.

Indeed, the Flame he was questioning shook her head with a shrug. "Sorry," she said, moving on. Chet sighed, watching her go.

Fenimore whistled at him from the street corner, and Chet slopped over in his muddy shoes. "Come on, Journey found our answer. The Intako Dance Company is apparently performing aboard a luxury passenger ship tonight. They're launching off Syn Port's Pier 24 at sunset."

"Flame at open sea? That doesn't seem right," Chet said. Fenimore shrugged and Chet could only agree. If this Aureate didn't care about such things, who was he to judge?

Chet glanced around him as they moved off down the street, admiring the city-state. Now that he was here, Plainsdaugheau was breathtaking in an eclectic, handmade way. Houses stacked up like shipping containers, trimmed with decorative gingerbreading and stained-glass windows. People walked about in similar, gaudy styles. Chet had yet to see a man wearing a suit—instead, they wore bright colored pants or gradient sarongs. Everything seemed home dyed or otherwise modified. And the women! Toplessness seemed normal among women of all ages, even among mothers with half-grown children traipsing behind them.

They met Journey and Knife on the next street corner. "Now that we know where we're headed, let's go shopping before we find somewhere to eat," Journey said with enthusiasm. "We can't possibly attend a party in these awful clothes." She'd changed back into Saemion's clothes and Knife had his outfit from Wetshul, but they both looked rather wilted. Not to mention the smell.

"If it's a private party, will we be allowed on board?" Chet said.

Knife shrugged. "Aureate'll get us in."

Chet thought the Flame would shop for themselves but found himself roped in, too. Journey held up clothing and regarded Chet narrowly. "I think we'll go with warm colors for you. Oranges and reds with black for contrast. How do you feel about prints, Chet?"

"Uh, what?" Chet slouched, feeling trapped and panicked by the many choices available in the boutique.

"Just let Journey dress you. It's easier," Knife advised him cheerfully. Knife was naked to the waist with black dress pants and his ever-present boots on. He was back in his favorite bistre-skinned, tall-and-skinny male form. By his relaxed stance, Knife must feel relieved about this.

Journey hit Knife playfully on the shoulder, and they engaged in a brief tussle. Then Journey deliberately turned her back on Knife and pressed a pile of folded clothes into Chet's hand. "Go try these on, Chet, and see what you think." As he left for the dressing room, Chet heard her turn to Fenimore and say, "Now for you, how about white and black..."

An hour later, Chet had to admit that Journey knew what she was doing. He'd never been dressed by someone head to toe. He felt *stylish*. When two young women—with perky, exposed breasts bouncing above their crocheted skirts—stopped to giggle and stare at him behind their hands, his back automatically straightened.

"Miss, miss," he said, nodding his head in their direction. More giggling before they moved off.

"You should have asked them to step around the corner into the alleyway," Fenimore said from where he leaned against a wall. "I'll bet they would have let you under those skirts."

Chet blushed. "You'd do that kind of thing. Not me."

"Why not? You should take initiative, Chet, and stop being such a pansy."

Chet brushed imaginary dust off his new jacket. "I will when I'm ready. Don't push me."

Syn Port's Pier 24 was crowded as the sun sank in the poppy-orange sky, spectacular with reflective blues and greens of sunset. It was pretty, but Chet felt his heart sink at the crowd wandering around the wooden pier, though they quickly spotted the luxury passenger ship in question. Chet eyed it curiously. Older members his family had been passengers on such ships and had hosted many a dull slideshow based on their travels. This one seemed compact. It was more like a private yacht than a luxury liner. It was only four decks and two-hundred feet long. At least it was still at port, though the gangplank not out yet. Closed for now.

After employing the same tactic of spreading out and questioning the crowd, someone pointed them to a hand-painted van at the end of the pier. The van was rocking. Maybe the troop was practicing dance moves in there.

*Yeah, right,* Chet thought, feeling a new kind of cynicism. *Different kind of dance.*

Knife knocked. A middle-aged man, his thinning hair dyed in orange and green streaks, slid open the door. He was naked to the waist and wearing a long grass skirt, two smaller grass skirts tied around both knees—obviously a costume.

"Yes, good Flame? May I help you?"

"Is Aureate around?"

"Knife!" a voice squealed from inside the van. "'Scuse me, people, I gotta say hello!"

Chet's first impression of Aureate was a moving streak in a grass skirt. She was wearing a similar costume as the man and others in the van, some of whom were still entangled together in a half-dressed state. She was bald, of course. Her tits were enormous and bouncy, Chet noticed instantly. Unfortunately, they were covered by another part of the costume: a halter top with woven rhamph fur-feathers.

Aureate ran between Knife and Journey, kissing and hugged them with enthusiasm, chattering away the whole time in some other language that Chet didn't understand. It was different from the tongue Knife and Journey had spoken before, full of clicks and glottal stops. Knife grinned at her fondly, and Journey replied in a rapid patter of the same tongue.

Aureate turned to Chet and Fenimore and asked a question in the unknown language, gesturing at them. Chet felt his heart stop. All of him just—stopped. Aureate had honey-colored eyes. Yellow eyes like a Magician. *But... there are no more Magicians,* he thought. What had Othnielia said about Aureate being the oldest living thing on Uos that wasn't a god? Fenimore, he realized, was standing very still at his side.

Journey held out her hand to Chet and switched languages without missing a beat. "This is Chet Baikson, who's a student at Semaphore. I met him on the lucid mud dig site. And this is Fenimore LaDaven, who was *in* the dig site."

"Got it," Aureate said with a grin.

They switched back to the unknown language, Journey waving her arms in illustration. At one point, she shot Chet a sly look and made big-breast motions with her hands. Aureate smirked and gave him a fleeting, assessing kind of look.

Chet blushed furiously. He could only hope Journey was relaying his enjoyment of her breasts and not his cross-dressing, which she hadn't been witness to, anyway. Were they deliberately being rude? Chet stepped away from the group and kicked a bottle cap in the gutter.

Why hadn't anyone *told* him there was a Flame with yellow eyes? He would have wanted to know! It seemed a terribly important fact. Apart from Othnielia, who else had been talking about Aureate? Oh yes, Journey had wanted to consult with her about the Raptus and why it was acting so strangely. Aureate was an expert—why? Who was she *really?* No one these days had those classic honey eyes, no one. Something stirred in the back of Chet's head; some poem or passage wriggled in his mind, half forgotten...

"Oh, Journey, we have an opening in the troop tonight! Venitte broke an ankle," Aureate cried out. Chet found her language switch almost dizzying this time. "Can you fill in?"

"Yes!" Journey clapped her hands together, her whole face radiating delight.

The other members of the Intako Dance Company—now outside the van, watching the Flame with much the same expressions as Chet and Fenimore—seemed less enthusiastic at the prospect of dancing with a stranger without an audition or even a rehearsal. "So you're Journey, eh? How much do you know about the *goncang?* How about the *tersenyum dan menipu?"* said the man with the orange-green hair, arms crossed.

Journey immediately dropped the duffle bag, loosened her fancy new clothing and demonstrated. Even knowing nothing about dance, Chet was impressed. Her body—her whole self—was involved in the movements. She reached out a hand to the man and swung him into action. That's when the dance became truly intense, both athletic and blatantly sexual. Passersby began gathering around, curious and alive to the possibility of a free show. They actually applauded when Journey and the man finished, arms outstretched dramatically. Even members of the Intako Dance Company applauded. Aureate shamelessly grabbed Knife's hat—he yelped—and passed it around the audience for change. Meanwhile, Journey conferred with the dancers, speaking the same technical language. Though Chet understood their words, he didn't really *understand* what they were saying.

Aureate flipped a coin into the air and put in, "We all do a solo to start the second act. You can skip that part if you like."

"You kidding? I don't have anything prepared, but I can do flick-flacks!"

Journey kicked off her shoes and demonstrated. She could even touch her feet to the top of her head. Chet didn't know how she could pretend like gravity didn't exist, but it clearly worked. Again, a crowd gathered, and again, Aureate passed around Knife's hat. By this point the dancers were grinning. Journey was clearly good—or at least good enough—in their eyes, too.

Chet, Fenimore and Knife retreated to the main lounge while Journey went to prep with the rest. The passenger-ship lounge was almost full: about a hundred well-dressed people of every race, size and shape were nattering away, drinking and snacking.

Getting into the spirit of things, Chet volunteered to fetch the first round of drinks. On the way back to the table, all three drinks balanced in his hands, he noticed Fenimore was chatting up a young man sitting at the table behind them. Seeking fresh blood, was he? Chet was so distracted that he didn't watch where he was going. He tripped over their duffle bag and fell directly onto Knife.

"Abyss!" Knife cried out as the drinks splashed. His whole front was wet. He jumped out of the seat, staring in horror at his soaked shirt, and by proxy, his chest beneath. The crowd around them grew silent and whispered to one another, watching.

"Knife, I'm sorry, I'm sorry!" Chet cried, upset. He tried to wipe Knife off, but Knife swore and batted his hand away.

"You'll only make it worse," he said, almost hyperventilating. "I have to get out of this shirt."

It was the only clean shirt Knife had, Chet realized."Let's go out to the deck and I'll switch shirts with you."

Without a word, Knife stumbled toward the door. Chet followed, wringing his hands. He glanced back; Fenimore had resumed his conversation—or his softening up—of the young man. Chet frowned, wishing Fenimore would *care* more. *Might as well wish the sun rose at night,* Chet thought with a snort. Fenimore didn't care about anyone, save himself.

There was only one other person on deck. She was smoking a short distance away, a long, fluttery silk scarf around her neck. Knife stripped off the wet shirt and rubbed himself dry with the expensive dinner jacket Journey had insisted upon purchasing. His chest was blistered, Chet was alarmed to see. If Knife weren't bistre colored, his skin would probably be very red. Chet felt worse by the second. Knife fished a lighter out of his pocket, began running the open flame against his chest, and sank to the deck with a sigh. Chet followed him down, hands outstretched helplessly.

Bereft of direction, Chet glanced around and abruptly realized they were at sea. The ship had set sail already, the sea calm under a clear, windless sky. Other boats, large and small, were sailing on the nearly still waters. Chet understood with a start that the Flame were surrounded—completely and totally surrounded—by a deadly substance. It was as if they had set sail in the center of a bubbling volcano. One little slip over the deck rail and they would—what?

Knife glanced at Chet. "Don't look so scared, boy. I'm fine. Or I will be."

"I really am sorry, Knife. I didn't mean to do that,"

"I know, Chet." Knife put a consoling hand on his shoulder.

Chet relaxed. Despite the incidentback at the Wetshul hotel, Chet discovered how much he cared about Knife's opinion of him. The Flame had a crispness about him—a brevity of words and actions—that Chet admired. He felt better knowing that not only was Knife okay, but his opinion of Chet was apparently unchanged by the event.

The smoker finished her cigarette and was heading back into the lounge. Knife glanced up as she passed. "Excuse me, could I bum one of those?" He looked startled as the woman handed him a smoke, but murmured, "Thanks," all the same. Knife lit the cigarette and leaned back against the deck, still running the lighter over his chest.

Chet eyed him. "Knife, could I ask you a question?" Knife waved a *feel free* gesture. "What do you do for a living? I don't mean the work you do for Pelin. How do you make money?"

Knife grinned around the cigarette, his teeth and the whites of his eyes almost glowing against his dark skin. "I trade stocks and bonds. When I'm low on petty cash, I trade stocks and bonds for other people. Besides paying my way, it puts me front-and-center of Genis' business in Allistair. Which comes in very handy in doing my other job—as you say, Pelin's work."

"You, um, track *marks* on Genis' Exchange?"

"Some of them. Merchants have this bad habit of assuming Flame are still commodities that can be bought and sold. We're too vulnerable to that sort of thing, always have been. It's not just Merchants, either. There's bad behavior all around when it comes to Flame. We're too easily controlled, you see, physically and otherwise. We have this tendency to be emotionally sensitive and, as they say these days, co-dependent, which leads to all manner of abuse."

Chet tucked his chin. "I can see the physical part of the problem." Even *he* could kill the Flame at any time, he realized with a sinking heart.

"Yeah, but the physical is only the tip." He took another drag and added, almost as an aside, "My problem is, I'm Flame, too. I get so emotionally involved with my prey that I tend to lose sight of the original purpose in tracking them down. I like my prey a little too much for my own good. Been blindsided and murdered that way more times than I can count. I keep promising to myself it won't happen again, then it does."

"What's it like... to die?"

"Much as you'd imagine." Knife gave him a sharp look and stubbed out the butt. "It hurts, then I go back to Pelin. Don't really remember the between times. We're flesh like everyone else, and it's the flesh that dictates what's important and what's not. I'll have your shirt, now, thank you for offering, Chet."

After the clothing switch, they reentered the lounge. The lights had been dimmed and someone was introducing the dance troop. Chet and Knife slunk back to their seats as the music started.

Chet forgot that he was wearing a wet shirt that was a little tight for him. He forgot to breathe, even. The Intako Dance Company was *spectacular*. From the first moment, the men and women—and Flame, he reminded himself—stole the entire room. Chet gulped, his mouth dry. After a time he thought to look for Journey. Though he spotted Aureate right away—she hadn't changed from before—he couldn't see Journey. They were all wearing fancy headdresses, effectively masking the Flame from view, though he doubted that was the headdress's original purpose. Chet finally leaned over and asked Knife during a slower dance. Knife grinned and pointed out one of the men. He was so similar to the others Chet hadn't even considered him. *Oh.*

A musical interlude followed the first performance. Then the solos began. Aureate's solo was a comedy act centered around her big tits, set to accompanying music played by the live musicians. It was hilarious to watch, especially with her ability to control how large or small they were. She mimicked accidentally deflating a tit, then looked up at the audience, eyes round with exaggerated horror and shock. Chet couldn't help but be drawn into the grotesque, exaggerated story she told without words; he found himself leaning forward in his seat, giggling like a child. Chet was very sorry when her solo wrapped up. Journey's solo was far less impressive, but Chet knew that Journey had made it up at the last minute. It was pretty good for all that.

After a dazzling finale, when the lights came up, Chet enthusiastically joined the standing ovation. He hadn't realized... he hadn't realized that Flame could be like *that,* too. They kept surprising him. He wondered whether he'd ever surprised Journey, then felt the smile slide right off his face. *Probably not.* There was nothing special about him. He was—and would always be—just another guy.

Chet drank alone at the table, still filled to the brim by the performance. Knife was chatting away with some guys at the bar, apparently a gentlemanly discussion about livestock prices and ceros betting. Fenimore had left with his target a few minutes ago, trailing the young man out as if he were an animal—indeed, a predator—tracking blood scent. Chet hadn't felt as bad about that as he thought he would.

Someone sat down next to him, and Chet jerked awake. It was Aureate, in the same form as before. She was dressed in tight fitting street clothes draped by a loosely-woven crocheted sweater, artfully ripped in all the right places. Aureate's bald head was bare, and she still had stage makeup clinging to her face.

"Here, give me that," she said, grabbing his drink and slugging it down.

Chet sat back in his seat, curious and slightly alarmed. Aureate seemed larger than life, especially after that performance. Was she always this way? He remembered when she'd snatching Knife's hat earlier to beg change from the crowd and decided that yes, she probably was. Aureate turned her mesmerizing gaze upon him, and all thoughts fled from his head. Her honey eyes glittered in the dark; a trick of the light, he decided after a breathless second. *Not magic. There is no Magician-style magic left in the world.*

"So tell me, Chet Baikson, do you like Flame?"

"I didn't think I did, until I met Journey," he answered truthfully, not sure what she was getting at.

"You seem like a real charmer. Tell me about yourself."

Chet's face grew hot. He'd never seen himself as charming—Fenimore matched that description far more than he did. Studious, serious, bookish... he'd answer to any of those adjectives. Why was Aureate trying to flatter him? She seemed to be playing a game with him, but what? He couldn't play along until he knew the rules. Yet something inside of him—a facet beyond his rational self—sat up and took notice. Whatever it was, it had a ready-made answer for Aureate. Chet surrendered to instinct and smiled.

"What's to tell? Apart from the past few days, my life has been rather dull." Moved by the same instinct, he leaned forward and touched her arm; she was very warm indeed. "I'm far more interested about you. Tell me about yourself."

She giggled. "What, you want the whole *Book of Twelve* or just the footnotes?"

"Flame, I can read just as fast as you can."

It was like diving into the depths of the ocean while feeling an astonishing confidence that he could swim. Had he really learned this much in a week? He was *very* close to her now. She smelled fantastic. Ichor probably went into overtime when sweat was involved. Her lips were close, too.

Chet leaned in and kissed her.

Aureate kissed back, her tongue enthusiastic and highly active. He found himself being pushed back in the chair, her hand raking his hair. When they parted, Chet realized he was panting.

Her eyes were glazed with longing. "That was *exactly* the right thing to do. Come on. I have a key to a more private space."

# Chapter 18
# Yellow Eyes Speaking

They stumbled out of the lounge together, holding hands like teenagers. Except Chet had never actually held a girl's hand as a teenager, or anyone's hand, for that matter. Rory had come much later.

People were everywhere. They'd spilled out onto the decks and were drinking, smoking and chattering away. No one could leave the ship until it docked. Chet vaguely wondered whether the patrons were planning on staying up all night. He'd heard someone say there was gambling on the deck above with a piano act starting in an hour. Maybe the ship would calm down after a while, but Chet doubted it.

A couple of people in grass skirt costumes burst out of a door. They were—*what* were they doing? Aureate grinned and called out to them, but she was ignored. Chet's eye finally decoded their tight cluster as wild kissing. Three women were kissing one of the men, his headdress still on. No, that wasn't a man, it was Journey! Journey was the one being kissed—almost attacked, really—by the dance-troop women.

They banged against the deck railing, and Journey gasped, crying out, "Wait, stop. Don't want to fall over the rail! Not in the wa—mph. Mph! Here, let's move to the other..." He yelped as they pulled him back toward the ship.

One of the women reached under the grass skirt and grabbed hold of—well. Chet was fairly certain she'd caught his penis with both hands, but he couldn't see in the dark. They slammed back through the door they'd just come out of, the woman with the handful of cock leading the way. Journey followed—by necessity—with a breathless grin, not protesting.

Aureate was laughing and shaking her head. "You get those girls going and they *go*. Journey should have figured that out before starting. They'll take Journey apart, piece by piece."

Chet drew Aureate close. "Glad I'm with you, then!"

She grinned up at him, her teeth showing. It was less a grin and very nearly a territorial snarl. "Oh, I could take you apart, too. I'm just not in that kind of mood tonight."

*Message received.* He followed her down to the lowest deck; this area was much quieter. More private. She unlocked a door and snapped on the lights. It was a tiny room—a closet really—decorated as someone's office space. An enormous, empty desk was built into the wall with a chair and not much else. It had a nice view featuring the sparking lights of Plainsdaugheau out curved windows, several of which were cracked open.

Aureate sighed. "Sorry there's no bed. The troop is bunking down together in a communal room. I have a key is because the owner is a personal friend."

"That's okay. At least it's private." Chet realized that he hadn't experienced privacy with a woman—or a female-shaped person, rather—since these events had begun. They could do anything they wanted without an audience.

Aureate pulled off her crocheted sweater, then removed the skin-tight shirt underneath. She wore no bra. Aureate leaned back against the desk as Chet stared at her naked breasts with rapt attention. She grinned and crooked her finger at him. "Come on, then. Journey says you're a tits man. Try me out. Taste me."

He approached and sank into the desk chair, scooting it closer so his head was exactly at the level of her chest. Giving in to his aching desire, he buried his face in her breasts. Both his hands engaged, he took a nipple in his mouth, then the other. *Oh, Pantheon, that's good.* He couldn't get enough. Chet rubbed her tits up, down and sideways, endlessly fascinated by how they moved and bounced. After a time, Aureate pushed him away. He reluctantly let go.

"I want you to fuck me in the ass."

Chet paused, taken back. "I don't want to hurt you." He'd been fucked in the ass so many times since this had begun—by Fenimore, Journey and that dickhead smuggler in the truck—but had yet to inflict such treatment on another.

She smiled, her expression rather smug. "You can't."

*Oh, yeah. Shapeshifter. Right.* Chet smiled uncertainly. He turned off the lights, self conscious at the lack of curtains. "Um. I'm not sure how to begin."

In answer, she pulled down her skin-tight pants and let them fall to the floor, then kicked off her heels. She was naked, now. Chet caught his breath. She was *serious*. Aureate turned her back and stuck out her behind, leaning against the desk.

This was going too fast. Chet touched her back and ran his hand down to her posterior. She had the *best* ass. Well, of course she did: whether she was twenty or a hundred and twenty, she could shape exactly what she wanted. It was heart shaped and firm, yet round and soft in the right places.

Chet realized he was in control. Aureate had her back turned, waiting for him to take the upper hand. He could do anything. As long as she let him, he could try something... new. Freedom rippled through him, and he grinned. Moved by instinct, he drew back and spanked her, his open hand slapping her firm, bouncy buttocks with an audible crack.

Aureate cried out in shock. Chet shrank away, a hand at his mouth. "I'm sorry! I didn't mean to... uh..."

Aureate hadn't moved. She was grinning, he realized, as she looked over her shoulder. "Why, Chet Baikson, I didn't realize you had it in you. Do that again."

He exhaled, his hand falling to his side. She'd liked it. *He* certainly liked it, now that he knew it was allowed. He liked being in control: it was such a new feeling to be in control of a sexual situation. Of any situation, really. Chet started rubbing her ass in earnest. He swung back and spanked her again. She cried out, but this time she undulated her hips and pelvis, obviously enjoying herself. He spanked her a few more times, then realized he wanted a different position.

"Climb on the desk," he said. As she did so, he shed clothing rapidly until he was down to his boxers and tee-shirt. Chet arranged himself so that he was beside Aureate. "Drape yourself across my lap. Face down."

She obeyed. She obeyed him! It was possibly the sexiest thing anyone had ever done with him. His cock was achingly erect, but he wouldn't let it out yet. The pressure of her body draped across his lap was wonderful, yet he wanted to enjoy her, not focus on his own pleasure.

*Her* pleasure was what he really wanted.

Chet began spanking her, softly at first, building up to a faster crescendo. Aureate moaned and gave little sexy screams that sent chills up Chet's spine. He wanted more. He did want to fuck her in the ass. Journey had told him days ago in the prostitute's van that Flame basically lubricated their own rectums. That seemed... kind of gross. Yet what did he have to lose by investigating the claim? Women did the same thing in the front end, after all.

Chet rubbed Aureate's ass and pulled her cheeks apart. She squeaked, hands splayed on the desk, attentive to his every movement. Her attention was sexy as her body. He fingered the outside of her little pucker of an anus. Then, taking a courageous breath, Chet stuck a finger inside. It was wet in there. He withdrew and rubbed his finger and thumb together; the wetness was thick, viscous. A lot like the way Journey's cunt had felt, actually, not that he'd touched her there with more than his dick. That seemed like a bad call, now. Chet smelled his finger, still suspicious. It did smell of ass but also strongly of ichor. *Well, then.*

"Get up. I'm going to sit in the desk chair and you're going to be on top of me, with my cock in your ass."

"Yes," she agreed instantly, drawing herself up.

He climbed down and settled in the desk chair. It was solid and didn't have armrests, fortunately. Chet pulled out his erect penis and held out his other hand to Aureate. With luxuriant, leisurely movements, her tits bouncing ever so subtly, she climbed off the desk and turned her back to him. Aureate sank slowly onto his lap. He found her rectum with difficulty, but once he fingered it open, he didn't let go. Chet tucked himself inside of her, breathing harder as he did.

"You are to do all the moving, here. I'm not going to move at all."

"Oh, yes." Her face turned so that he saw her profile. On cue, she barely moved atop him, undulating just a little.

Chet reached around and rubbed her breasts, his hand open on her nipples. He slapped a tit and she cried out, sinking fully on his penis.

"Do that again," she said, her breath coming faster.

He grinned and took her at her word. After a time, curious, Chet felt down her body until he reached her hairless pubic area. It was very, very wet. He fingered her, and her breath caught. He brushed against the raised mound near the front, and she let out a little scream.

"You like that, huh?" he whispered in her ear. She whimpered in response.

Chet loved this. He felt entirely in his element for the first time in his whole life, the odd man out no more. He brushed against the tiny, erect mount again, and she leaned back into him, making wimpering noises.

"Please, please," she said in an unending litany.

He began rubbing her there. Endless circular movements, that seemed to be the trick. He realized his other hand was still hovering over her breasts. Reminded of their presence, he slapped her tit again. She moaned, head thrown back. Aureate's reactions drove him on—every sound, every breath she took—let him know what to do next.

Her body was a roadmap in the dark.

Chet had almost completely forgotten his cock... but she hadn't. Aureate pulled herself up, until just the glans head was inside of her, then settled down upon him again, so he was enveloped.

He rubbed Aureate harder, and she thrashed in his arms. Tit slap, rub, slap, pinch, lots of rub. Playing Aureate was far more interesting than woodwinds or the brass section. Chet's hand—buried in her hairless sex—was so wet he might as well have been under water. He was enveloped by her, surrounded by her power, yet he was also in charge of the situation. Aureate was thrashing with such intensity, Chet feared he might accidentally come. The next time she arched up, he pulled out on purpose. Then he plunged both hands into her sex, still rubbing, his other fingers buried in her cunt and ass.

With almost clinical curiosity, Chet squeezed his fingers together. Aureate went insane. Her body became an electrical arc. She screamed in his ear.

The screaming stopped. Everything stopped. She sank into his arms, her body limp. "Thank you," Aureate said, sounding surprised in the dark.

He wasn't sure what to make of it. "Are you okay?"

"Better than. Do you know how long it's been since a man *did* that to me? Not this lifetime, for certain." Her words were slurred, and she cuddled against him, her knees drawn up. "You know, I usually like women. I don't normally pick up guys, if I'm the one doing the choosing. Guess I knew something was different about you. You did well."

Chet settled back in the chair and breathed out. He wasn't exactly limp, but he wasn't erect, either. He felt absolutely no desire to fuck her again or come. It was as if her orgasm had somehow illuminated him. Made him larger. Probably the effect of little sleep and lingering alcohol, but still.

They dressed out of necessity in the cool room and settled on the desk. It was hard and lacked covers, but Chet dozed, warmed by the soft, perfect Flame curled in his arms. He'd never felt this way about another human being. Not even Rory, though he felt a twinge of guilt at the thought. A piano tinkled upstairs. People were laughing and talking, their voices blurry noise that merged together.

The windows were still cracked open, and cool air moved over Chet's bare feet, keeping him from sleep. An occasional wisp of cigarette smoke drifted into the room. Chet should really get up and shut the windows, but that might disturb Aureate.

She was breathing evenly, her body curled against him with implicit trust. Her crocheted sweater had an interesting texture under his hands. He stared upwards, the lights of Plainsdaugheau making strange patterns on the fabricated ceiling. Chet closed his eyes and lolled against her bald head, loving how soft she felt against his body. A breath of poetry sped around his head like a cynodict on a race track. Who'd written it? The Magician Zang? No, that wasn't it. The Magician Tene, that's right. Something about eyes. Traitorous honey eyes, not of magic but sex...

Chet's eyes sprang open. His whole body came awake, though he didn't move. Tension rippled through him, his muscles contracting involuntarily. "I know you."

"Mmm?"

"I know you. You're the traitor! The affiliate turncoat."

Aureate sprang up as if she were being attacked, her hands reaching for weapons that weren't there, her eyes wide in the shadows. "*What?* What did you call me?"

Chet could recall the whole verse now that he was awake. He gazed at her, dark legend come to life. "The Magician Tene wrote about you. I'm sure it's you! You must be the Magician who turned away from the fold..."

"Stop." Aureate looked like she wanted to leap out the window, glass and all. "You can't—you don't—who *are* you? Answer me! Answer me *now!*"

Chet blinked. She was shaking. Hard. He realized what he'd said, what he'd done. "Aureate, I'm sorry, I didn't mean to scare you. I read it in a book years ago. Since I met you, I kept thinking something about you was familiar. I just figured out what it was."

A pause, then Aureate began breathing again, though her shaking grew worse. Chet hadn't realized she'd been holding her breath. She murmured, as if to herself, "That's right, Journey said you're an archaeologist with a really good memory for classics."

"Is it... is it true? *Were* you a Magician?" Now he was the one holding his breath.

She stared at him in the dark, then quietly crept back into his arms. He accepted her—she was crying. "Yes," she said, sniffing.

He held the forgotten past in his hands, yet she still breathed. It was strange and wondrous and scary as Abyss. "Tell me about it. I—I think I need to know."

*Why* did he need to know? Such a frightening question to ask himself. He'd been obsessed with the past far too long with an intensity that had—for all intents and purposes—kept his own life in check. Now that he was in a position to learn the answers he craved, he wasn't sure what question those answers pertained to. It was like staring down the fabled Abyss: Chet felt excitement and fear in equal parts with a sprinkling of horror, though regarding what he could not say. If Aureate asked, how could he assure her he was serious? He had nothing. Chet held his breath, awaiting her reply.

Aureate was silent. Then she whispered, "For a long time, it was easy. I liked it. Blood magic was... very powerful. But there was this little problem, you see. I don't think anyone ever wrote about the problem. It's not the sort of thing most Magicians worried about."

"What was it?"

"Death," Aureate said with a shaky laugh. She sniffed again.

Chet found a handkerchief in his jacket pocket, silently thanked Journey for its existence and offered it to her. Aureate sat up to wipe her face and nose. He said, "What do you mean, death? You face death as Flame, too. What's the difference?"

"As a student of the classics, you must understand that Magicians, like Flame, were reincarnating affiliates. Yet all Magicians were men. Did it never occur to you to ask why?"

"Um." Chet blinked. "No. I—I guess... there aren't too many women represented in the classics anyway."

"Foex was a sexist asshole who didn't like women except to fuck them. Oh, and he also liked pregnant women because they popped out babies to carry on the line of whatever race he was sculpting. He tinkered with the flaxen race for millennia; his hands are all over the roots of your racial memory, did you know? Foex had no other use for women. But the thing is, if you pick up a reincarnating soul over and over again, half the time they'll be born as a girl."

"He couldn't control that?"

"No. Don't know why not. One of the larger rules I guess the gods cannot break or sully. Pelin doesn't care—never has, never will—but Foex did."

"You said... the problem was death."

"When his Magicians were reincarnated as girls, he killed them. Us." Aureate took a deep breath. "Me."

"Oh."

"Usually, he'd bring the baby girl to a practicing Magician to use in blood magic. That's how Foex liked it. He utilized every resource and didn't waste energy. He had an appalling amount of energy; that's why I liked him as an affiliate. But... sometimes the girl wasn't a baby. Sometimes she was older. Sometimes she *remembered*."

"You remembered."

"Oh, yes. I didn't really think about it until I was born female six times in a row. Foex was mindful about finding us early, but I escaped once during that streak of lives. I grew up and found a really good man. I miss him sometimes or at least the memory of him, which isn't the same thing. I was pregnant—near term, in fact—when Foex found me."

"He killed you."

"Of course he did. He killed me the next time and the time after that. By that point, I was going out of my mind. Then I was born a boy. Foex was much happier. He let me grow up and instructed me personally in changes in magical workings that had taken place while I was out of circulation. I smiled and took his instruction until his back was turned, and then..."

"And then?"

"I grabbed the first ship to Palister and rode like abyss until I reached the first Flame node I could find. The nodes are an old thing we used to have back in the Cobalt Era, before our current system with the Flame Council. I *begged* them to hear me out. The Flame, I mean. Pelin was curious and came down to talk with me in person. I was absolutely raving mad, but she listened. And here I am." Aureate took a deep breath. "Well, here I am a few thousand years later. My eyes were permanently dyed yellow by Foex, no helping that. They're with me every lifetime, thus my initiate name. Pelin gave me the name knowing full well what I just told you. I don't remember the last time I've told this story to an outsider. I hardly ever talk about it."

Chet could barely think or breathe with this living legend in his arms, sharing real secrets from the past. Nevertheless, he frowned. "They must not have liked that. The Magicians, I mean."

She chuckled ruefully. "You've been reading Tene, have you? He was such a doedicu. He hated everything I stood for, waging his own private smear campaign against me, to use the modern phrase. I haven't heard the accusation 'traitor' in ages."

"Oh." Chet blinked. He hadn't considered the authors of his books as biased, somehow. As political. *I should have,* he thought with a snort. No god affiliate on Uos had the luxury of being apolitical.

"Chet, you said you needed to know all this. Why?"

"Because... because I'm bound to this weird Magician's tool, and I don't know why. I don't know why it chose me. Did Journey tell you what happened?" Chet was distracted by an odd noise outside. Was that a motorboat? It seemed incongruent that someone would be messing around with a motorboat in the middle of the night. Well, they were at sea. The motor cut, and Chet ceased worrying about it.

"Briefly. Tell me more."

Chet explained how the Raptus had reacted when he'd touched

it during the tug-of-war. "I can't get the feeling out of my head that it *wants* me for something. It didn't bind us until I touched it. But I'm just a guy!"

Aureate grunted. "I have guesses, but you have to understand I was never at that kind of skill level. Even Zang and Tene were really pushing the envelope to create it. They must have sacrificed a lot of girls to do so."

"Oh. Yes, I can see that. Blood magic always sounds so romantic in the abstract, but it must have been horrible and messy on the practical end." Chet chewed it over. "I was always taught Foex's brand of magic stopped working when he died, but the Raptus is still operational."

"I don't believe in perpetual motion, so my best guess is that they must have linked it to its victims in an endless loop. The more blood it spills, the more powerful it becomes. There are problems with that theory, the most obvious being that the Raptus has been mired in lucid mud for three-hundred years, yet it hasn't run down. Don't know how they did *that*. I would have been curious about it—once."

"Aureate, I hate to ask, but is it possible for you to find out? Journey said back in Wetshul that you were the best consultant on why the Raptus is acting this way."

She looked away, fiddling with her crocheted sweater. "Yeah, Journey asked me before we went on stage."

"What did you say?"

"I told her no. I really don't want to meddle with the Raptus. I expect she and Knife will ask me again, try to talk me around. But my answer is final."

Chet jerked back, then glared. She didn't want to *meddle* with it? He and the others were linked by an invisible umbilical cord by a mind-control device—like being strapped to a ticking time bomb—and she didn't want to even try? *Screw that,* he thought. "Why not?"

Aureate looked him in the eye. "Because I don't want to kill someone to find out."

"You're kidding."

"No."

"You can still... *does* blood magic still work?"

For a long moment, he wasn't sure whether she'd answer. Her

shoulders slumped, her athletic, dancer's body curled away from him. Then Aureate nodded once, her eye downcast. "I don't practice it. Much. Hardly at all. Only in dire emergencies, and most the time not even then."

The answer seemed to cost her much. It occurred to him that Aureate's reaction—her whole being—was consumed by shame. Based on everything she'd said, he could understand why. "I see."

"Obviously the Raptus isn't a toy just anyone should be using, or using at all. I'm glad Knife and Journey are set on destroying it. Good riddance."

Chet sighed. "Did Journey have you unlock it with your words and blood, backstage earlier?"

"Yep." Aureate stretched, then climbed down from the desk. "I gotta take a piss, Chet."

"Is there a bathroom around here?"

She snickered. "There's the ocean. Flame can aim and fire just like a guy, you know. When I come back, maybe we can play some more. Me on top, this time."

He grinned at her. Though she hadn't specified a gender, he rather thought she'd be fantastic as a man. His cock stirring at the thought. "Sounds good."

Chet hummed under his breath as she strode out, leaving the door open behind her. The summer breeze was a little too cool. He rolled onto his belly. If Journey could do all sorts of tricks with a penis, maybe Aureate could, too. Maybe they'd...

A scream, a splash. Chet scrambled to his feet, eyes wide. There was more screaming outside. Real screams.

# Chapter 19
# Chaos

Chet raced outside and slammed against the waist-high railing, staring down at the water. Elderbeth had risen in the sky hours ago, green and luminous, three of her moons visible. In her light he could see... Chet gulped.

Something human shaped was thrashing in the water. Chet caught a glimpse of a bald head and face, nearly unrecognizable. Almost a horror mask, covered in lumpy boils. Chet couldn't believe it. Was that—was that *Aureate?* She was struggling, screaming in the night; even her eyelids had erupted in boils.

*I see,* Chet thought breathlessly as her instantaneous transformation from sexy Flame to horror show sank in. He couldn't imagine how much pain she must be experiencing; even a few drops of water had made Journey and Knife whimper.

Chet looked up and down the deck. He was alone, he'd have to save her himself. He checked his first impulse, which was to dive in, grab her and pull her back to the ship. The best possible way to drown. Aureate was panicked, out of her mind. Chet raced along the deck, looking for floatation devise or even a decorative donut-shaped life preserver. This was a ship, there had to be *something*.

He gaped. A motorboat was tied up just around the corner. Chet recalled the noise he'd heard earlier... maybe someone had lowered a lifeboat into the water? If so, it was to his good fortune. The boat was tied to one of the emergency ladder rungs along the ship's hull. Chet swung over the railing and scampered down, grateful beyond measure that he was at home in all manner of boats. His family's vacations by the lake had done that much good, anyway.

Aureate was still screaming. Why didn't anyone come? Chet needed *help*, for Pantheon's sake."Knife! Journey! *Help!*" he screamed at the top of his lungs as he untied the rope.

The motor was a brand he was familiar with. Chet primed the warm engine and ripped the starting cord. The motorboat roared to life—not a sputterer or a reluctant starter, then. *Good.* Next came safety. Chet's eyes roved around the little boat, seeking lifejackets. Nothing. Not a single one. Chet swore, cursing whoever had outfitted this lifeboat. What did they think people needed most during an emergency at sea anyway? Canapés, mixed drinks and a parasol?

After he'd successfully fished Aureate out of the water and saved her life, he was going to have a little word with the ship's crew about that. But the first important step in the customer-complaint process was *not dying*. Right.

Chet swung the boat about and renewed his yells for help. Aureate's screams seemed to be tiring. Or was she... Chet gulped. How long could a Flame survive in water?

The thrashing lessened as he aimed toward her. He hove to right by her side, let the throttle go, and reached down to grab her crocheted sweater, glad she'd dressed after they'd had sex. She didn't grab hold of him, didn't acknowledge his grip. In a burst of desperate strength, Chet pulled her into the motorboat without the usual flailing about. Aureate—he assumed it was Aureate more by her clothing than her face—was twitching violently, her screams quieter once she was aboard.

Her face was a nightmare. He couldn't see distinct features anymore: no eyes, nose, lips or ears. Half of the massive boils were in the process of bursting, ugly puss running everywhere. Her exposed skin was bubbling off, pustulating and sinking, an active process taking place before his eyes. A chemical reaction. Chet had expected smoke or steam, but no. There was only a sound, a low hissing to accompany her fading screams. Chet wondered what he should do. This wasn't a heart attack or a stroke! What did you do for a water-soaked Flame? Get her clothes off? Dry her? It would do for a start. Where was a fire when you needed one?

"Chet!" It was Knife, fully dressed and a little seedy looking, his collar open. He raced across the decks and ladder-like staircases to reach them.

"Thank *Pantheon!* Come on, she needs your help," Chet cried out. Knife would know what to do! He'd help Aureate.

A flash lit the sky and there was an explosive thud not far in the distance. What? Chet anxiously looking up: the sky was starry and clear. It hadn't been thunder. But the ship was rocking just a little, as if in response.

Knife grabbed hold of the railing. People from the other side of the ship began screaming, and a clearer voice than the rest yelled something about a fire. *Was there an explosion onboard?* Chet wondered. Then he looked at the motorboat itself. *Oh. This isn't a lifeboat, is it?* Someone had boarded them. The same someone who'd pushed Aureate into the water? Chet assumed she'd been pushed. Aureate hadn't been drunk and no sane Flame would have jumped.

Chet steered the motorboat toward the nearest emergency rung ladder. "You'll have to climb down," he called up to Knife, tying the boat up to the ladder with a sailor's hitch knot. He deliberately cut the engine. Pantheon knew how much gas the motor had left, and they'd need it to get Aureate to a hospital on the mainland.

Knife climbed down slowly, reluctantly. Chet wanted to scream at him to hurry, but held his tongue. There seemed to be a lot of commotion on the upper decks of the ship; he could smell fire and something like gunpowder. In contrast, Aureate had ceased making noise and moving. Well, except for a minute hissing noise as her skin continued bubbling off. Knife gripped the side of the motorboat stiffly and gazed at Aureate. His expressions radiated the same horror Chet felt, only intensified. Knife didn't move.

"Do something! Quick, do you have the lighter?"

Knife jumped at the sound of his voice. Then he closed his eyes, his expression grim and resolved. He said in a low voice, "Chet, I need you to grab hold of Aureate and raise her up. Her head needs to be clear of the hull of both the ship and this boat. Can you do that?"

Of *course* he could do that. Grateful for direction—at last!—Chet grabbed Aureate... and cried out. Her skin reacted to his touch: it was sinking, popping and receding at the same time. A sensation he'd never felt before and instantly hoped to never feel again.

Her face was worse than ever. In Elderbeth's light he could see...

Chet closed his eyes. He thought he'd seen a flash of skull, through a pustulating bubble. *It can't be true, can it?* The Flame he'd just had amazing sex with, the Flame who'd been a Magician, who remembered thousands of years of history... she couldn't really be dying, could she?

*No.* Fire would fix her. Knife would make it all better.

After all, Aureate still breathed. She was alive. She moved in his arms, independent of the bizarre chemical reaction. Against all reason, she opened her eyes. Close enough to see every detail, Chet noticed one of her eyeballs was clouded and ruined, probably because the eyelid had melted off. In hideous contrast, the other eye was intact, bizarrely unharmed in the mess of her face.

The single eye focused on Knife. "Knife..." she whispered, her voice raspy but clear. "*Please.*"

Knife rolled up his pant leg, reached into his boot and pulled out the tiny pistol. Chet stared, aghast. He didn't understand what Knife intended until he aimed carefully, using both hands.

Chet screamed, "Wait—" as the shot reverberated. The gunshot had been shockingly loud in his ears.

Aureate's body still hissed. Chet let it fall to the bottom of the boat, his hands twitching. He looked at Knife. Knife sat on the wooden slat, holding his gun in both hands, staring at nothing. Not even the body.

Chet found his voice. "Why? Why, Knife? She would have... you could... she was asking you for help!"

"It was too late," Knife whispered. "Fatal exposure." He looked at the gun in his hand as if he'd forgotten it was there, then holstered it carefully.

"But she was still conscious."

"Yes. She might have remained conscious to the very end." To Chet's shock, Knife began crying. He gulped tears, his shoulders drawn inward, his body rocking back and forth.

Chet wiped his wet hands on his pants and joined Knife on the central wooden slat. He put an arm around Knife's shoulders, though it felt awkward to do so. The Flame smelled of cigarette smoke and gin.

Knife laid his head on Chet's shoulder. "Abyss. I thought we'd have time to catch up in the morning, after she'd had her way with you. I thought... oh, Pantheon. I just shot my best friend."

Chet regarded the corpse at the bottom of the boat with reverence. "She was a spectacular person," he said, feeling tears rise in his own eyes.

"She will be again. That's the beauty of it." Knife sniffed, rubbing his nose on his sleeve.

"Knife! Aureate! Chet? Where are you guys?" It was Journey's voice.

Chet and Knife looked up simultaneously. Knife called out, "Journey, down here."

"Oh, thank Pantheon. There's the strangest stuff happening, and the *weirdest* people on the upper decks. I couldn't find you. Are we leaving? Is that why you have the boat? Where's Aureate?" Journey glanced over the railing; she was back in female form, worse for wear. She wore only an undershirt and panties, her feet and bald head bare.

Chet blinked. Were those burns on her clothing? On what little clothing she had, that was.

She tossed the duffle bag onto the motorboat and carefully climbed down the emergency-rung ladder. Chet wanted to warn Journey, to say something, but found that he couldn't speak. Knife stirred beside Chet but also remained silent. Journey turned from the rung ladder to step into the boat and caught sight of the corpse. She screamed, her face radiating shock and terror.

"Journey, stop," Knife said.

Journey put a hand over her mouth, eyes immense in the dark. "S-s-sorry. Wh—wh..."

"I'm not... I don't... Chet, what happened?" Knife turned to Chet as if realizing he didn't know the answers.

Chet shut his eyes to make reality go away. It didn't help: his hands still felt the sensation of melting flesh. "Aureate went outside to take a piss off the deck. I stayed in the room. We'd been talking after we—I heard a splash. She was, was screaming. This boat was right around the corner, and I think maybe someone's on board who wasn't before. An enemy of some sort? Though why—and how—I think someone pushed her in. Maybe someone was listening at the window, I don't know. I don't think it would have been hard to sneak up on her if they were quiet. She was so relaxed."

"Abyss," Journey muttered. "Yeah, there're these violent people on board. About five or six of them, dressed in black with masks on. Not affiliates of any sort, I don't believe. They seem to want the Raptus. Or me personally, it's hard to tell."

"Why—" Knife's question was cut off as a figure appeared on the deck above them, holding a gun pointed in their direction.

"Don't move!"

Chet's eyes widened. Though a colorful theatrical mask covered her face, he knew that deep, two-packs-a-day voice. "Professor Clementina?"

She jerked in place and her arm swung up—as if automatically—to point the gun at the deck roof above her. "Chet Baikson, you little dium. Why aren't you back in Eicha where you belong?"

"Abyss," Knife muttered under his breath. "This is what comes of traveling at a slow, plodding pace."

Out of the corner of his eye, Chet saw a shadow of movement from the walkway's rounded corner, creeping closer to Clementina. From what little he could see, it looked like Fenimore's shape and size. *Distract her so he can get closer,* he thought wildly. What bait would she respond to? Based on what she'd said back on campus, she'd paid hundreds of thousands of gilt for the dig site, all for the Raptus. Did Clementina want to rule the world?

"What's the story, Professor? You couldn't get the Raptus by throwing money at it, so now you've resorted to murder?"

She jerked back as if shocked. "We've no intention of killing anyone unless we're forced."

Journey snorted, glaring. "Shouldn't have come armed then, should you?"

"You've *already* murdered," Chet put in. "We have a dead body on our hands."

She shook her head as if to discard their words. "Toss up the Raptus and I won't hurt you."

Whoever was creeping up on her was about six yards away, almost near enough to pounce. The mask must be cutting off any peripheral vision Clementina might possess, and the conversation was doing the rest. Chet *must* keep her occupied. He rose to his feet, arms out for balance. The Flame clutched each other, and Chet self consciously tried not to rock the little motorboat.

"Professor Clementina, you'd better shoot me because I would die before seeing you rule the world!" He pointed at her—more of a stabbing gesture, actually—and raised his voice to a full roar. "You are *not* a fit guardian for the Raptus!"

Chet couldn't see her expression with the mask on, but her body language radiated sarcastic exasperation. "We're not *trying* to—"

She screamed as she was tackled. Chet watched breathlessly from the odd angle, craning his head up. There was a flash of Fenimore's hunting knife. Clementina seemed to be below him. Was she struggling with both hands to keep from being stabbed? Muffled yelps emerged from the deck.

Thundering footsteps rang out. More masked people dressed in black ran toward the struggling pair. On instinct, Chet scrambled to the stern of the motorboat and grabbed at the rope securing them to the ship. Journey yelped at the motorboat's rocking movement, and dove into Knife's arms. Knife was—rationally enough—sitting in the exact center of the boat, far away from water as possible.

A gunshot went off above their heads, and Fenimore bellowed.

There was no time. Even as Chet unhitched the line and pushed them away from the larger vessel, someone dove into the water only a few feet away. One of the black-clad attackers? Both Flame screamed, clutching each other as the boat rocked violently. Chet yelped as a wet hand slopped over the side.

"Knife, your gun," Journey cried out. Knife clawed at his pant leg.

"Don't shoot, don't shoot!" said a familiar voice. Fenimore's head popped up, thoroughly soaked. "Get us out of here now! *Row,* I tell you!"

Chet glanced up just as a black-clad individual dove off the railing in pursuit. Another was climbing down the emergency rungs. Chet turned to the motor, his fingers fumbling through the ignition process. Someone on deck was yelling about the Raptus. The motor turned over and Chet hit the throttle.

Fenimore yelped, his head disappearing as the boat leapt forward.

Only his white-knuckled hands remained wrapped around the edge. A small wave of water splashed inside the boat with the momentum. Both Flame screamed at the top of their lungs, curling themselves into a splayed huddle on the bench. Shamefaced, Chet eased off, gaining control of the momentum. Gunshots rang out behind them, rekindling his panic. Chet ducked instinctively but kept a hand on the throttle. They needed to get out of range, out of range *now*. Not caring which direction they went, so long as they didn't go in circles, Chet kept at it, his head down.

After a minute of silence, he looked around, careful to keep his profile low. The ship was a good distance away—maybe a quarter mile? Chet exhaled. Both Flame were huddled together on the middle seat, sobbing. Chet hoped their reaction wasn't due to burns. Fenimore's hands still clung to the hull near the front of the motorboat.

Chet cut the motor, carefully climbed past the Flame and navigated around Aureate's body to reach the bow. "Fenimore? Are you alive?"

"I think so," came the hollow response. "I... oh, Pantheon. Chet, they shot me."

"Where?"

"Below my left knee. Get me out of the water. Please, get me out."

Chet hauled Fenimore into the boat, every muscle in his body protesting. Water slopped as Fenimore clambered aboard. Chet couldn't tell whether his leg was bleeding between the dim light and wet trousers. Fenimore was dripping wet. The Flame jerked away but didn't move off the wooden slat, their eyes wide. Chet breathed deep and gazed at Fenimore, who was lying in the bottom of the boat. Was he really bleeding out?

They were almost completely alone on the water, Chet noticed, glancing around to assess their position. The Plainsdaugheau coastline was perhaps two or three miles away. It must have been after midnight based on Elderbeth's position in the sky. Few other boats were out sailing, none nearby.

Fenimore coughed and rolled over... only inches away from Aureate's body. His eyes widened as he gazed straight into her ruined, melted face. Fenimore shrieked at the top of his lungs. Chet tried to grab Fenimore as he attempted to scramble away from the body. They almost went over the side. Chet had to hold Fenimore back by his jacket as the boat rocked violently. Chet splayed his arms out, praying they wouldn't flip over.

Fenimore switched directions. The Flame screamed in earnest as he scrambled toward them, panicked by his sopping clothing and erratic movements. The Flame, in turn, stumbled toward the stern. Journey cried out, clutching her bare feet. The bottom of the boat held a considerable amount of water, Chet realized. His bare feet and pant legs were wet, too.

Fenimore kept advancing on the Flame, looking back with horror. Cornered, Knife untangled his gun from the boot and wet pant leg, turning it on Fenimore. "Stop!" he yelled, voice raspy with pain.

"Fenimore, *calm down!*" Chet cried. "Knife, put that thing away. Fenimore isn't getting near you. Are you, Fenimore? Fenimore!"

Fenimore still seemed wrapped in blind panic, his eyes rolling white as he gazed at the gruesome remains. Any second he might jump toward the stern again, gun or no gun. Chet couldn't let him. Chet snagged Fenimore's sopping jacket, hauled him around and slapped his face. Fenimore hissed outrage. He unsheathed his hunting knife with a quick flick of his wrist. Chet held onto Fenimore grimly as cold steel was pressed against his throat.

Everyone froze. The boat rocked under them, water splashing against the sides. Chet looked Fenimore in the eye. "You're not going to kill me. You need me. I'm the only one who can get us out of this mess."

The knife was slowly lowered. Fenimore wheezed and looked over Chet's shoulder at the body. "What... what on Uos *is* that?"

"Our friend. She's dead. She cannot possibly hurt you," Knife growled from the stern. He holstered the gun and held Journey in his arms, his expression twisted with fear, anger, pain and outrage.

"Oh." Fenimore breathed out, seeming to crumple into himself.

Chet had to take charge. No one else could. The Flame were useless at sea; the extreme danger was evidenced by the corpse at their feet. Fenimore didn't know modern motors, and he was injured, although how badly Chet couldn't tell. Besides, Chet didn't trust him. Especially not after what he'd just done.

Chet sighed. Even simple maneuvering around the boat required a strategic upper hand. He wanted the Flame back on the central wooden slats where they'd be at the least risk of injury, but asking Fenimore to sit beside Aureate's body was right out. He didn't want an argument. He also didn't want to move the body again, mostly because he didn't want to touch it. A useless wish. Chet suddenly understood he was the only one who'd be able—and willing—to get rid of the body... if that indeed was what needed to happen.

*Abyss. Take it one step at a time.* If he tried to do it all at once, he'd sink and take everyone down with him. Chet needed to put one foot in front of the other. He could get them out of this. He could. They just needed to calm down, to see each other as human again. Chet glanced at the duffle bag at his feet. It held the Raptus, but he didn't think that would help just now. What would?

"Journey, do you have any food in this bag?"

"Uh." Journey seemed to switch gears with difficulty. "I think so. A paper bag of nuts and dried fruit."

Chet riffled through the duffle. The outside was wet, but it was lined with rubber, sparing the contents. He felt soft clothes, the hard, thorny Raptus, and... there. The small sack seemed promising. He pulled it out and poured a handful of fruit and nuts into his hand. Then he passed the bag to the Flame. "Have some."

"Chet, we need to get out of here."

"Eat," he growled.

They hung their heads and obediently took a handful each. Chet could see precisely what Knife had meant about Flame being too easily controlled. They both seemed cornered, their personalities flattened in the face of the immense danger surrounding them. If Chet were the kind of guy into abusing Flame, it would be absurdly simple to gain the upper hand with psychological and physical manipulation. Knife grimly handed the sack back to Chet, and he offered it to Fenimore.

Fenimore stared at it blankly. He was clutching his leg, his face deeply etched in the dark. "Um..."

"Eat."

Fenimore, too, obeyed. Good. Now they were getting somewhere. Minute crunching sounds filled the boat. Chet glanced up at the clear sky and could only be grateful that there was no wind. If there had been the sea would have been rougher, and the motorboat would have probably tipped over in the chaos, instigating more deaths. Chet issued up a quiet prayer to the Pantheon, grateful beyond measure for smooth sailing.

After a minute, Chet sighed. "Fenimore, you are to strip out of your wet clothes. Everything goes." On impulse, he said, "Throw the wet clothes over the body."

*Yes,* he thought, *that's right.* Best get Aureate's ruined face out of sight where it wouldn't be so alarming. As Fenimore obeyed, Chet reached into the bag and pulled out what proved to be Fenimore's dirty trousers, the same pair he'd had on in the lucid mud. The puffy shirt followed. Fenimore hissed as he drew the wet pants off, and Chet took a closer look at his leg. The wound didn't seem large: the emerging blood was more trickle than gush.

"I think the bullet grazed the side of your calf. You're not bleeding too badly, anyway. Knife, what do you think?"

Knife reluctantly craned his neck, then crept forward for a better look. "I agree that it's a graze. I don't see entrance or exit wounds. You're lucky; we can bandage you with something for now, but you'll need stitches later. Here, um..." He felt through his pockets and extracted a fluttery silk scarf.

Chet blinked. It was feminine and kind of familiar. Had Knife been sleeping with someone when Chet's cries interrupted him? And hadn't Knife said he didn't like women? No, he'd said he didn't like *being* a woman, which wasn't the same thing at all. Anyway, one scarf did not mean a sexual tryst. Maybe he'd won it while gambling with other passengers.

Reminded, Chet glanced back toward the ship. Whatever fire there had been seemed contained now, or at least, he didn't see evidence of it. "Knife, you bandage Fenimore. Journey, in a moment I'd like to switch places with you. I'm going to get us out of here."

"*Finally!*" someone—or several someones—muttered.

Chet grinned as he stood up. "While I'm getting us out of here, I think we'd all like to hear what happened to each other tonight. Who wants to begin?"

# Chapter 20
# Coming Clean

Pregnant silence followed. "I'll speak first," Journey volunteered after a few seconds, her voice shaking. "But Chet, could you lift me up and put me on the other seat? I'm, um..."

Chet blinked down at her. By Elderbeth's light, she seemed very uncomfortable and, looking closer, he swiftly realized why. Her bare feet and legs were blistered, and some of the angry spots were bursting. Blood trickled even as he watched.

Chet jerked back, alarmed. "Are you—will you..."

"I'll be fine," she said, clearly containing her pain.

Chet could see by the little lines around her eyes what it cost Journey to remain calm. He immediately felt ashamed of his actions, making them eat before triaging her wounds. "I'm sorry."

"No, it's okay. I know why you did it," she murmured, touching his lips. "You had to get control of F—of the situation."

Chet sighed, silently agreeing with her slip of the tongue. Very, very carefully, Chet took Journey in his arms and transferred her to the middle wooden slat. She was wet in other places, he noticed, her skin covered in blisters where she'd been hit by spray and splashes. She was dressed in just undershirt and panties, after all.

"Knife, do you have that lighter?" Chet asked tightly.

" One moment, let me finish this." Knife was wrapping up Fenimore's leg tightly with the scarf, knotting it with care, though he seemed to be using only a few fingers to do so.

Blistered hands, perhaps? Knife's feet were touching the bottom of the boat, encompassed by his boots, Chet noticed. The boots he never took off. Apparently, they'd been water-proofed to the point where Knife didn't worry about puddles. His pants legs were going to eventually soak all that water up and hurt his legs, though Chet snorted was sure Knife would know what to do in that contingency.

Chet wished he had a light other than fire to check inside the motorboat's gas tank. He just had to assume they had enough gas to make it shore. He began angling toward the Plainsdaugheau skyline. Fenimore slouched on the edge of the middle rung while Knife tended to Journey. Knife held her hand while working the lighter between her toes, his expression radiating gentleness. In turn, she murmured over the blisters on his hands, worried at the pain he was feeling. Chet sighed, envious of their tender grooming. At least they weren't freaking out anymore.

"Journey? You said you'd go first," Chet said.

"I did. It's like this. I was really, really occupied for a while, okay? And afterwards I was pretty sweaty. I wanted a bath, but there's nothing like a real fire on a modern vessel like that. So I thought, why not try the galley? They sometimes have these little cans of jellied chemicals that are used under chafing dishes, perfect for hours of contained flame. I wondered whether they might lend one to me. Or if no one was cooking and they had a gas stove, that would work fine, too.

"No one was cooking, which didn't surprise me at that hour. I spoke to the last employee wiping down; the kitchen had closed an hour before. Only the bar was open all night. They had a gas stove, and she was fine with me bathing there, being used to Flame and all. After she left, I stripped down and climbed onto the stove. You can get almost clean if you lie down and roll over the burners, you know, depending on how greasy it is. I wish I'd put my clothes in the bag, instead of folding them on a counter. And my *new shoes*. Oh, well."

"Were you interrupted by those guys in black?" Chet said.

She nodded. "I heard noises, at first. They were trying to be quiet and weren't very good at it. They had these radio transceivers; old ordinance from the war, I think. They kept crackling, which is what alerted me at first. I didn't want to be caught in the nude, so I started dressing, but I wasn't fast enough. One of them barged into the kitchen and cried, 'Flame!' He drew an army-surplus pistol on me and ordered me to sit on the floor, then called his buddies on his bulky transceiver radio."

Chet frowned, wondering how Journey had known where the pistol had come from. She'd talked about surviving the war but had never shared *how* she'd survived, he realized. Now was not the time to ask. Chet made a little noise to encourage her to continue, not that it made a difference. Journey was in full story-telling mode.

"They grabbed the duffle first thing and began searching it, which is when they found the Raptus. They seemed very pleased and called over the radio that they'd found it. They stopped paying so much attention to me; I saw my chance and rushed them. Whoever they were, I didn't want them to get the Raptus." Her mouth compressed into a thin line.

Chet glanced down at the rucksack on the seat, thinking about what it contained. The Raptus was the reason they were all here. He'd almost forgotten *why* Journey and Knife were putting their lives on the line, risking death and prison sentences.

"It was a mess. I was dressed as you see me now, and it's been too long since I've been in combat. I kept wishing I had Knife or, or Aureate with me. The guys managed to get me down and were tying me up—silly doedicus to tie up a *Flame*—when Fenimore burst in." She looked over Knife's shoulder, smiling at Fenimore. Fenimore blinked and smiled back, seeming almost as surprised as Chet at her positive regard. Usually, she looked at Fenimore with cool, critical eyes, probably because of their—misunderstanding—in the Wetshul hotel.

"Fenimore was *fantastic,*" she continued. "He kicked them up, down and sideways. He grabbed the Raptus and tossed it to me. I stuck it in the duffle bag and was about to go out the backdoor when another one of those guys rushed in, blocking me. By that point, Fenimore had forced the others to retreat out the front. I could still hear them out there, fighting.

"It was just me and the new guy. He had a big bag slung over his shoulder, bristling with weaponry. Maybe he was their ordinance logistics man, I don't know. The guy had at least three stones on me, so I danced out of the way and jumped on a table to keep the Raptus—and myself—out of his grasp. He flung the bag down on the nearest surface and came after me... the nearest surface being right beside the lit gas stove." Journey paused, her face breaking into a grin. "He was clearly not the brightest doedicu there ever was."

Chet blinked, remembering the explosion he'd heard. Journey's burnt, hole-stricken clothes seemed evident of an explosion as well; even the wet duffle was speckled with little black burns. "He had something explosive in his bag?"

She nodded. "First we ran around a while. I don't know why he didn't just draw a gun and threaten to shoot me. He had enough firearms in that bag, I should think. He seemed to really be enjoying himself, chasing after me in my underwear. He was getting off on it—at one point he told me exactly what he wanted to do to me once I was pinned. Asshole. During our scuffling around, I kicked his bag onto the gas stove proper. It caught fire, and about a minute later—boom."

"You weren't hurt in the explosion?"

"I saw it coming in advance—not by much, but enough—and ducked out the backdoor into the hall. The big guy had just made it to the doorway when the galley exploded. He was a great shield for me, though of course it wasn't so good for him. The shockwave was the worst part, but the fireball that followed was more helpful than not. From my perspective, you understand."

Journey, of course, would not have been affected by the fireball, and had probably felt perfectly at home inside of it. Chet nodded succinctly.

Knife frowned, though. "You were lucky not to get hit by shrapnel. And you might have a concussion from the shockwave."

"Yes, thank you. I have the headache of a lifetime, anyway. *He* was knocked out, or dead, what have you. The galley and hallway were on fire. I fled and went looking for you guys. Fenimore and the other attackers weren't anywhere in sight or earshot by then."

Journey fell silent, her expression grim. Remembering what she'd found next, Chet assumed. He took a breath, wishing they didn't still have the body on board. He wondered what to do with it. *No, one thing at a time.* The shoreline was growing closer by the minute.

"Knife, want to go next?"

"Sure," he shrugged, "but mine's real brief. I was in the lounge: drinking, gambling and considering a mark. She's a Tarro affiliate known to me who evaded the law about a decade ago. Ran a string of brothels and ruined what Flame she could draw in. It would have been a perfect time to make the first move; she was relaxed and only had two lackeys on board. She was considering her own mark, a professional gambler whom I gather owes her money. I decided not to pursue her, though. I figured she'd complicate things, and we don't need complications. I'll circle back to get her later, now that I know where she's located."

"I see. Thank you." Chet could make out the Plainsdaugheau shoreline, now. He headed toward one of the many docks. Chet glanced at Fenimore. "Fen?"

"Yeah." Fenimore glanced up, his eyes glazed and tired. "I, too, was busy for quite a while. That didn't end well and I left. I thought to locate one of you, anyone who was still up, but got turned around. I heard strange noises and looked through this cunning glass window in a door. I saw those men holding Journey down. As she said, I rushed them." Fenimore shrugged. "Some night in the future, when we're deep in our drinks and carousing wenches, I'll share each move in detail. For now... they were neither daring nor competent fighters. The explosion and fire with the chaos of the other passengers kept me from coming sooner. I apologize for my lateness. But at least I was able to catch that Metacor-like strumpet of a professor before she got the Raptus or injured one of you."

"I see." Chet angled around docked boats and ships, looking for an opening at which they could dock. He, too, privately thought Clementina resembled one of the ancient, legendary monsters, first children of the mother of gods, Aerora. "We need to figure out what we're going to do with, with Aureate's body. Should we... I mean, should we go to the police? She was a Plainsdaugheau citizen. I assume that means something around here."

Knife and Journey looked upset and depressed at the thought of getting rid of the body. Journey said, "I've been in Plainsdaugheau enough times to trust the local police force with our affairs. There are Flame here who are *on* the force, eccentric body as it is. That said, I would rather not have to explain ourselves. Her death was mysterious enough to elect questions, and they'd want to detain us for further details. We need to keep moving and keep control over the Raptus. We should get transportation to Ventris next, to talk to Doyen, then on to Knife's home in Allistair to complete our journey. We can't stop now."

Knife grunted. "They might speak to the police in Wetshul by telephone. They can do that quite easily now. I'd rather not have to lie, starting with our names. It would only make us look guilty of murdering Aureate if they uncovered contrary evidence. The best way is to avoid the issue entirely."

Chet spotted an opening on the dock and headed in. "How do we get rid of the body, then?"

"Open sea," Knife said immediately. "Should have dropped the body in earlier except we didn't have weights. It'll float, you see."

"Won't the body disintegrate?"

"No. Bones, muscles, organs and tendons don't melt. We need to find something to weigh it down. Rocks are good. They can be tied in to that loose sweater she was wearing."

Chet docked the boat and helped the Flame onto the wooden dock. He scouted around, barefoot on the splintery wooden, Knife at his side. They found a substantial length of discarded string—nylon pilot cord by the feel of it—and, at Knife's urging, Chet trespassed onto several boats until he found a modern sea anchor. Chet also grabbed a lifejacket. His years on the lake had taught him prudence, and he felt itchy without one. Making his way back to the motorboat, Chet realized how exhausted he was; he ached all over from exertion and emotional turmoil. In contrast, his genitals felt oddly satisfied and relaxed. So inappropriate, considering what had just happened.

"How far should I go out? About half a mile, say?" Chet asked.

"I guess."

Knife sounded strange. His shoulders were drooped and shaking. He sank on the dock next to Journey, and she curled into his arms. They were both crying, Chet realized. Now that they were no longer at sea, they were free to let their feelings out. Fenimore sat to one side, holding his hurt leg. He looked uncomfortable at the display of emotions. The silk scarf wasn't soaked with blood, nor did he seem in excessive pain.

Chet bowed his head as he faced the Flame. "Do you want to say goodbye to... to her?"

"That's not Aureate anymore. We'll see her again," Knife said, his voice cracking. Despite his tears, his expression radiated assurance, his spine straightening at this statement. "Pelin willing, we'll see our friend again."

Chet climbed back into the motorboat, feeling empty inside. Knife knew his goddess personally. His faith in her abilities was rock solid, beyond reproach. Chet almost wished he had a god on *his* side. Not that gods were particularly comfortable people to talk to, he imagined. To judge from their footnotes, Magicians had considered Foex a prickly character, his temper vivid and always bursting to the surface. No one could have equaled him as a teacher, though. *What a random thought.* Chet sighed and cast off.

He glanced back at the distant dock, determined to remember it. If there was anything he'd learned during lakeside vacations, it was terribly difficult to distinguish one dock from another from a distance. Especially in the dark. The image he saw was vivid: the two Flame were rocking and crying in each other's arms with Fenimore sitting off to one side. The scene somehow struck him as odd. As wrong.

Chet faced forward, frowning. He just needed to focus on one thing at a time. It was the only way to get through this.

It was quiet in the boat. Chet's only company was the corpse, hidden by Fenimore's wet discarded clothing. He wondered whether Aureate's ghost lingered near her body... yet Knife had said that Pelin took up souls. Chet felt nothing of Aureate's presence. Not that he'd expected to.

*This is insane.* Of course, when had dumping a dead body in the ocean ever been a sane activity? They had been on the move for about ten days—a whole week—yet they'd left two bodies in their wake. The first two dead bodies in Chet's life had occurred since they'd found the Raptus.

The deaths were too personal to be random events.

Were the Flame responsible? Chet compressed his lips. Flame probably *could* go insane, given the pressures, prejudice and pain they faced on a daily basis, but Chet could have sworn that both Journey and Knife were on the level. He trusted Journey almost implicitly at this point. Certainly she was a thespian with a masterful ability to act and control her facial muscles, but her reaction to both Tibbet's body and Aureate's ruined remains had seemed genuine beyond any skill as an actor.

As for Knife, he—no, she—was too slippery for such trust. It was probably due to her nature; she seemed most comfortable in the shadows, a lone hunter tracking nocturnal prey. She'd certainly cornered him back in Wetshul, buttoning his mouth with an efficient hint of force. Knife's alibi both times had been vague. If Chet asked other gamblers on the passenger ship, would they have confirmed Knife's presence in the lounge?

Wait. She'd had a silk scarf in her pocket. Chet *had* seen that scarf before: it had belonged to the female smoker they'd seen before the performance. The Tarro affiliate? Knife's story was too consistent for the peripheral evidence to be coincidental.

Fenimore seemed the most likely candidate for murder. He grew uncomfortable and relieved at the oddest moments. Chet was willing to bet Fenimore was a sociopath, functioning without emotion or moral values. Hadn't Knife said something of that nature back at the dig site? What words had she used? "He is a libertine who will lie, cheat and steal to meet his ends." Given Fenimore's words and actions since then, Chet could readily believe each accusation.

Then again, perhaps Chet was judging the mores of Fenimore's vanished culture rather than his personality. Had a bad first impression prejudiced Chet's opinion? And a bad second impression, and a bad third impression...

Fenimore was a tougher nut to crack than the Flame, but what on Uos might have motivated him to murder Professor Tibbets? They hadn't even formally met. As for Aureate, the timing fit. Fenimore could have listened at the window, pushed Aureate to her death, then found the galley where Journey was being attacked.

No! He could have *followed* the black-clad group up through the ship, tracking them silently. Then he could have watched through the galley door *while* Journey was attacked. That was much more believable than happening on the galley randomly.

*But... but* why *would Fenimore murder Aureate?* That made no sense, either. Fenimore didn't hate Flame. Not like a certain professor from Semaphore University.

Professor Clementina had been present both times. She'd had the means, opportunity and even a certain amount of motivation. Who was she really? Chet had always assumed she was exactly what she'd seemed: a bulky woman frustrated by an artificially dead-ended career, married to wealth. Yet she was surrounded by strange, unaffiliated thugs who wanted the Raptus.

She'd seemed shocked when he'd insinuated she wanted to rule the world. What did she intend with the Raptus? No one made tea and dumplings with the thing, after all.

This was ridiculous. He didn't have enough information. Fenimore had complained back in Wetshul that scholars asked too many questions. Chet's lips turned up at the memory. Of *course* he needed to ask questions; he had even more questions waiting in his queue as soon as these had cleared out.

Like... what was he doing with his life? That one was too hard. He'd dived into the deep end of the pool of both history and sexuality, yet he had no direction. Worse yet, he was barred from returning to his old life. Even if he didn't land in prison, his father had trashed his educational prospects. There was no turning back, but he had no answers. Rory was already lost to him. He'd given her up—less than twenty days ago?—of his own accord. Such a stupid thing for him to do. He wanted Rory at his side even now—her presence would be soothing, helpful. Chet had flubbed their relationship without help from anyone, let alone Fenimore, Professor Clementina and the Flame.

To ask what he was doing with his life was almost as bad as asking why the Raptus had chosen him. And it *had* chosen him. Him specifically. The more he thought about it, the more personal the binding seemed.

Chet glanced back at the shore; he seemed far away enough now. He cut the motor and uncovered Aureate's body. It seemed smaller, and the hissing sound had ceased... because the body had no skin left. Chet gulped, nausea rising in his throat. It occurred to him that he'd made love to this body less than two hours ago. He turned, swallowing hard, but there was nothing in his belly to throw up. He had to do this. He had to touch... it.

What would Aureate have thought? In the short time he'd known her, she'd been funny, graceful and intelligent. Aureate might have sighed and rolled her eyes skyward toward the God Plain at being dead again, he thought. Perhaps she'd say something like, "I only *just* initiated!" Chet grinned. Yeah, that's what she'd say. Knife was right—this body wasn't Aureate at all.

Chet tied the anchor into the crocheted sweater with the pilot cord. Gathering his courage, he lifted the body and tipped it into the sea. It sank slowly, feet first. Chet watched until he couldn't see it anymore in the dark water.

He had to say something. It was traditional, wasn't it? Chet licked his lips and murmured, "May Pelin keep you. Thank you for everything, Aureate."

He turned the boat around and touched the throttle. It sputtered. Chet swore as the motor abruptly died. He tried it again. Nothing. Again. Nothing.

*Shit.*

# Chapter 21
# Struggle of Wills

There was no help for it. He could either wait here until daylight when a boat or ship might just happen to come by and rescue him, or he could swim. Considering he'd sunk a body on this very spot, he was disinclined to wait for a random rescue. At least he'd thought to grab a life jacket, and he was already barefoot; he wouldn't have to tie a pair of shoes around his neck. Even knowing what he had to do, Chet sat in the boat a long time. He was tired, hungry and distraught. He didn't want to do this.

*Come on. It's not going to get any easier.* Chet took a deep breath, stood, aimed for what he hoped was the direction of the dock and jumped in. Unsurprisingly, it was just as chilly as before, but at least Plainsdaugheau was close enough to the equator so that it wasn't *cold* cold. Chet swam. He'd always considered himself a strong swimmer, but had never taken on the open sea or such a distance. His mind was caught in an endless loop, recalling the last moments of Aureate's life... no, this would never do. Chet focused on poetry.

A verse by the Magician Zang popped into his head, unbidden.

"Will, I hail thee
Lend me the strength
To see this twisted bough into a house
To crack stone into a pathway
Yea, lend me the strength
To throw open gates to the lost city of El
Rendering god barrier to splinters of light
So Metacor bones and all Mother Earth's works

may see the light of day
And be mystery no more."

Though pure doggerel, the verse seemed to help more than any other. Chet repeated it over and over again as he swam. The sea was endless and seemed to go on forever—surely an illusion. He could see the Plainsdaugheau skyline growing infinitesimally closer. Sort of. Chet closed his eyes and kept swimming.

After a time, he frowned. He could hear a motor in the distance, growing louder by the minute. Chet paused and gazing around him. A large, dark boat was zooming across the water at full speed, headed directly for him.

"Abyss!" Chet said out loud, accidentally swallowing salt water.

Why, why, *why* with all this open sea was someone bearing down on him? Undoubtedly it was random—no way they could see him. Smugglers or drug dealers, maybe. They seemed to be pursued by a blocky craft. Chet couldn't see much from his perspective, but he thought it was a law enforcement vessel.

They were almost on top of him. If they hit him, he'd be dead.

A new verse rose unbidden in his mind:

"Will, I hail thee
Lend me the strength
To deflect these boats from my path
And gain ascendency once more."

Chet repeated the new verse as the boats bore down on him. They were coming closer, closer. He bit his lip, tasting blood. Chet wanted to close his eyes but couldn't. At the last minute—only feet away—the boat in front swerved. He gasped as a deluge of wake hit his face; Chet went down momentarily, his lifejacket bouncing him back to the surface. The second boat was already swerving in pursuit as he reoriented himself.

The motors grew faint as they swung off into the distance. *Huh. That was lucky.* Chet bobbed a minute, regaining his strength. Then he started back toward Plainsdaugheau one stroke at a time.

Booking a flight to the city-state of Saene turned out to be impossible. There was a general labor strike at Saene International Airport, and flights to nearby airports were booked solid. The best they could do was fly across the ocean and land on the western edge of Tache, then take a transcontinental train over land.

Chet slept on the flight, losing all sense of time. He felt itchy and uncomfortable in his skin and kept sneezing. Chet didn't make any decisions, not even when to eat. He felt drained of initiative, grateful that both Journey and Knife were competent travelers. They took a taxi to the train station and bought tickets, including a private train compartment and bunks in the sleeper car with a plan to sleep in shifts.

Journey frowned at Chet as they boarded the train. "You look terrible, sweetie."

"I don't feel so good."

"Why don't you rest on one of the bunks. We'll save you some dinner from the dining car, okay?"

"Okay."

The white noise of the train lulled him to sleep immediately. When he woke, the sun was up. It seemed to be closer to noon than morning. They were traveling through a civilized rural area, everything neat and tidy, land portioned in precise orchards, fields and houses. In contrast, Chet felt seedy and awful. He stumbled to the bathroom, then found their private compartment. Fenimore was the only one there, reading.

He glanced up when Chet entered. "You look like a strong breeze would knock you down."

"I feel it." The promised dinner—and breakfast—sat in take-out boxes on the seat. Chet opened a box and frowned at the food; it didn't look at all appealing. He closed it, swallowing nausea.

In contrast, Fenimore seemed smug and contented. He was reading the newspaper like a modern gentleman, his locks tied in a plait down his back, a fresh drink with ice cubes in hand. They were on his home continent, and he appeared far more at ease here. Yet for all Chet knew, he might have committed atrocious crimes. How did you ask someone whether they were a murderer?

Chet sighed. "So we only have one more Flame to go, eh?"

"Three," Fenimore corrected mildly from behind the newspaper.

"Three?"

"This Doyen Quor person, then Knife and Journey. They have not yet said their verses or shed blood on the Raptus."

"I didn't realize you were tracking these procedures so closely."

Fenimore shrugged, frowning. "I don't know why Journey is waiting. She *said* she remembers her verse."

"Okay, so three to go. Then Knife will destroy the Raptus. Do you think she'll need our help? I wonder if Pelin will come down from the God Plain in person." Except Rory had made it clear that Pelin couldn't destroy the Raptus, and Knife had been bluffing, but toward what end? What really awaited them at the end of this slow, plodding race?

"Mmm."

Chet nibbled on his lip. "You *are* going to assist in destroying it, right, Fenimore?"

"Why should I do otherwise?"

Evading the issue, Chet noticed. Feeling reckless, he decided to push. "Well, you could try to take it by force."

Fenimore closed the paper with a crackle, folding it. With the bulk of the newspaper out of the way, Chet realized Fenimore had the Raptus on the seat beside him. The Raptus... *and* the bottle of lubricant from the Wetshul prostitute. Chet's heart fell.

Fenimore watched him steadily. "What makes you say that?"

"Uh. You didn't want to destroy it in the first place. You seemed to like using it on my sister, and you enjoy doing things—forcefully." Chet shouldn't have brought this up. He should have kept silent. Fenimore's calmness was like a flashing red light seen too late. Chet looked out the train window, burning hot although he felt chilled; he hadn't felt warm since climbing out of the ocean.

Fenimore steepled his hands. "Chet, are you accusing me of something?"

"No."

"Because it sounds like you are. Very serious accusations, too. I have no wish to rule the *entire* world."

"What do you want, then?"

A slow smile spread over Fenimore's face. He leaned back and said, "I'd like you to unbutton your shirt. Now."

Chet frowned fiercely at him. "I don't feel well, Fenimore! I'm not going to have sex with you."

Fenimore touched the Raptus at his side. "Take off your shirt. One button at a time."

The cord at his navel vibrated—hard. A fog settled over Chet's head. In fact, it felt almost like a cartoon icon of a personal, dark cloud hovering above him. Chet's fingers unbuttoned his shirt without his consent. Fenimore watched, his eyes predatory slits. *This can't be happening,* Chet thought mussily. Where were the Flame?

How had Fenimore gotten such total control over the Raptus?

As Chet pulled his shirt off, he remembered that moment on the dock when he'd left to take care of the body. Knife and Journey had been curled up together, weeping and unstrung, while Fenimore had been sitting off to one side with the duffle bag. Two emotionally distraught Flame left alone beside a predator.

Now Chet was alone with him, too.

"Very nice. Remove the rest of your clothing."

Chet obeyed helplessly. He glanced at the windows; the shades were up so anyone outside could see them. The country homes and communities they passed looked so peaceful... Chet shut his eyes.

"Fenimore, may I close the shades?"

"It does not please you to be seen naked by everyone?" Fenimore's voice was a low purr. "Perhaps you should learn to enjoy it. Perhaps I will make you rub your naked body against the window."

"Please don't."

Fenimore licked his lips like an inofe eating a meal. "You know, I believe you owe me from a few days ago when you used your teeth in exactly the wrong manner. It's time for me to collect on my debt. Turn around, hands on the seat in front of you. Stick out your arse so I can have access to it. Oh, and when I tell you to do something, you are required to answer. Call me 'sir'."

"Yes, sir." Chet turned and took up the position, his genitals dangling, exposed and vulnerable.

Fenimore was quiet behind him. Chet wanted to turn and look, but he was frightened of what he might see. Fenimore had proposed to flog him with a ceros whip back on Othnielia's farm. He didn't have a whip here. Would he use his hands to spank as Chet had done with Aureate?

Chet yelped, startled. An entirely different, painful sensation touched his buttocks. It was ice. Fenimore had fished an ice cube out of his drink and was running it up Chet's ass cheeks. Chet looked over his shoulder. Fenimore was grinning. He ran the ice over Chet's ass crack, then popped it inside his anus. Chet mewled, writhing at the sensations. Fenimore fished out another ice cube and grabbed Chet's genitals, rubbing it all over his penis and balls. Chet squeaked, unable to stop squirming. Again, the ice cube was inserted inside him.

"Tell me you like that," Fenimore said.

"I... like that, sir."

"Very good. I notice you have a belt, Chet. Journey kitted us out beautifully, did she not? Untangle the belt and pass it to me."

"Yes, sir." Chet did, his ass tightening convulsively. He could feel the ice melting inside of him, rendering his anus numb.

"Twenty-one strikes, was it not?"

"Sir."

Fenimore stood and moved to one side of him, undoubtedly to gain leverage. He stroked Chet's ass lightly with the folded belt. "You are not to make noise while I mete out your punishment. It's about time you started being a man instead of a milk sop. Oh, and you're not to close your eyes, either. If someone sees you through the window, I don't want you to miss the opportunity to view yourself being exposed."

"Yes, sir," Chet whispered. He could feel his throat shutting down. He *couldn't* make noise with that kind of command laid upon him. His eyes felt dry already, forced open.

The first strike was a shock, and a second followed swiftly. Each strike made Chet jump and flail. The silence was the worst part, he decided. If only he could yelp, swear and scream, he'd feel better, letting loose some of the energy being invested in him. He bit his useless tongue as he took another stroke, and another, and another. Fenimore moved to his other the left side and began again, focusing on his left buttock. After a time, he stopped. Was it over?

Fenimore said, "Turn around, boy. Let me see your sausage and potatoes."

Chet did so, trembling. Fenimore took Chet's dick, stroking before he hit it with the belt. It was painful and grotesque beyond measure. Chet wanted to protest—this had to be more than twenty one strikes! Fenimore wasn't playing fair. Of course, Fenimore wasn't *playing* at all. He'd ceased playing when he started using the Raptus.

At last, Fenimore tired of his game and sat back down in his seat, taking a sip of his drink. "Very good. Circle on the spot and let me see my work."

Chet obeyed, burning with fever and humiliation. How far would Fenimore go? He couldn't have Chet parade up and down the train corridors for everyone to see. Surely Fen didn't have *that* much control over the Raptus—did he? Where on Uos were the Flame? Why weren't they barging through the door to catch Fenimore in the act? Unless... unless *they* were already under Fenimore's control.

*No!* Chet thought with a frown. Fenimore had complained about Journey holding back her verse. Journey wouldn't *be* holding back if Fen were in charge. She was still out of his reach, and Knife probably was, too, but Chet wasn't. Chet was squarely in his hands.

As to echo his thoughts, Fenimore glanced at his watch, the one he'd lifted from Chet's father's study back in Fengfu. "I believe we have time for a little more... enjoyment. Down on your hands and knees, Chet."

He obeyed, expecting Fenimore to take him. Fenimore didn't move from the plushy bench, instead instructing Chet to angle himself so his ass faced the door and his face was almost touching the wall. Fenimore ran his hand along Chet's naked back; Chet shivered, shrinking away.

"Ah, ah. No." Fenimore reached over to slap him on the ass in the exact spot where he'd been whipped. Chet whimpered. "You are to remain perfectly still, Chet. Keep your back flat and available to me. You are nothing but an object. Do you understand?"

"Yes, sir."

Chet remained still—though his butt muscles clenched and his dick quivered—as Fenimore spread the newspaper on his back. It *tickled*. Then he gasped as Fenimore set the drink glass upon his back.

It was freezing cold and wet with condensation. Chet wanted to do something, but the fog clamped down upon his mind. He could do nothing but remain perfectly still. Fenimore had exactly what he wanted: Chet was an object, a table.

To his shame, he realized his cock was quivering hard. It was so hard he ached.

Freezing cold wetness tricked upon his back, and Chet mewled deep in his throat."Whoops," Fenimore murmured. Chet could hear his grin—Fen had poured a dribble of water onto his back on purpose, hadn't he? *Asshole.*

Being an object was slow, yet elusively sexual. He was intensely available this way. Alas, his body wasn't nearly as happy as his cock; Chet blushed, embarrassed when his belly gurgled and he let out gas, his feverish system protesting the unnatural pose. Fenimore didn't seem to care. Chet wished he could scratch his nose. He was hot and sweating, yet he couldn't *do* anything. Lacking a viable alternative, Chet relaxed into the role.

What would Rory do if she saw him now? Chet was supremely glad she wasn't along on this little journey. If Fenimore could control her... he shuddered as his mind generated a plethora of sexual images. His breathing grew ragged as he imagined her in the same position: being forced to strip, made to act like a table. What if Fenimore had ordered Chet to fuck her? Chet squirmed at the fantasy.

"Mmm. I think you're enjoying yourself a little too much. I'd best join in, or you'll be frolicking and squirting without me."

Something was jammed into Chet's ass. The pressure was fantastic, and he gasped, unable to swear aloud. It had to be Fenimore's fingers—at least two of them. Maybe three. They were wet, and Chet remembered the bottle of lube from Wetshul had been on the seat beside the Raptus.

"Like that, boy?"

"Y-yes, sir." It hurt, but that was beside the point. Chet was an object. The fog insisted as much.

"I'm so glad we've come to an understanding."

Fenimore set aside his newspaper and the glass disappeared from Chet's back. He moved behind Chet, and Chet braced, waiting. He didn't wait long. Fenimore grabbed his thighs, rammed his dick inside. He fucked Chet with the indifferent, unemotional fervor of a hammer pounding nails. A subject fucking an object. Chet took it, his eyes watering, guts protesting, whole body aching. But he took it. Fenimore slowed down and sped up again, not once but several times. The sound of their silent fucking filled the cabin. Chet's dick was full to bursting.

"You're nothing. Say it, boy."

"I'm nothing, sir."

"You're a hole for me to fuck. Say it."

"I'm a hole for you to fuck. Sir."

Pantheon, Chet was hard. He'd never been so hard; not even while cross dressing, not even with Aureate riding him like a ceros. He wanted to come yet hated how much he yearned for it. His cock seemed to love the attention Fenimore was paying him. Fenimore knew it, too.

"Sit up, boy. Let me look at your knob."

Chet pushed upright, hands loose at his side while his body shuddered with Fenimore's every thrust. His dick was sticking upright at a forty-five degree angle, dripping with pre-come. Fenimore gazed at it from over his shoulder, and Chet could almost feel his smirk. He ceased thrusting, pushing all the way into Chet's ass. They were conjoined like animals on the floor of the train.

"Here," Fenimore murmured, pulling something off his wrist.

It was the watch Fen had stolen from Chet's father. Fenimore flung it around Chet's penis as if he were playing the carnival game involving throwing a ring around a milk bottle. Chet gasped. It had been warmed by Fenimore's body heat, but it was also heavy and metallic. Fenimore rubbed the watch up and down Chet's dick, and Chet squirmed, horribly aroused by his father's possession.

"Now you're abusing time with your carnal urges," Fenimore said in his ear. "To use your singular word, *fuck* time, boy. Fuck it."

Abyss, how had Fenimore figured this out? How had he *known* that Chet had always had a love affair with time itself, with the past? He was too good a listener. Chet couldn't help it. Aroused beyond reason, he let loose a wordless yowl as he came, squirting like a fire hose, pumping his juices at the cabin wall. It took a surprisingly long time to empty out as Fenimore milked him for everything he had.

Then Fenimore sped his own pace and came deep in Chet's ass.

"Look what you've done, boy. At least I am circumspect as to where I deposit my seed, whereas you have sown it far and wide." Fenimore slapped his belly in mild reprove. "Is that something an object would do?"

"N-no sir."

"Clean it up. With your tongue."

Chet knelt over and lapped up his semen. With it came grime, sand and dust. Tears slid down his cheeks as he followed orders without recourse, the fog thick within his head. Forcing him.

Chet was permitted to visit the bathroom and clean up before returning to the passenger cabin. In fact, he was compelled to return to the passenger cabin. There was no choice in the matter.

The Flame were back from wherever they'd been; the dining car by the conversation they were having. They were clearly in a cheerful mood, relaxed, their footwear off. Journey was reading a book she'd picked up at the train station while simultaneously shaping her fingers and toes. It seemed like some kind of exercise: she shaped long, short, long, short. Knife was painting his toenails – his toenails! – dark green. It was the color of mourning in Tache, Chet recalled. A tribute to Aureate? Fenimore was still reading the paper, clearly for show.

He beckoned to Chet and whispered in his ear, "You are to be silent about what has happened, my flaxen catamite." Chet nodded glumly and sat beside Journey.

"Secrets with Fenimore?" she asked lightly. "Chet, you're still not looking well."

"You're telling me."

Fenimore caught his eye and smiled, then went back to his paper.

# Chapter 22
# Dreamtime

By the next morning, when they arrived in Saene, Chet was delirious. He only knew they'd left the train because he had to walk. Journey was guiding him... or possibly half carrying him, he didn't know which. He thought it was Journey but couldn't quite make out faces. Everything was blurry and words flew over his head like anuros. Thoughts flickered through him, never-ending and incomplete. Chet found himself squashed with the others in a taxi, uncertain how they'd gotten there. Was Fenimore still controlling him? Chet couldn't tell.

Someone placed a hand on his forehead.

"Think we'll have to leave him in Saene? What about the Raptus?"

"The connections are pretty loose by now. We may be able to go halfway around the world and not inadvertently pull him behind."

In his fuzzy suffering, Chet sunk into a more reasonable reality. Escape seemed vital, and he did not struggle against it. Better than existing in this world. Flickering hallucinations around him resolved into a more stable form.

Chet—only he wasn't Chet anymore, he had another name—smelled smoke and mushroom porridge. He opened his eyes. He was surrounded by a hand-hewn wooden building with opaque windows. They were opaque because they'd been covered with rice paper. He wasn't sure how he knew that. Chet touched the rice paper; it was thin and delicate, dry under his hand.

Someone was speaking to him. "...in charge of the ritual killing."

"What?" Chet turned and looked at the person.

It was an elderly man with an elaborate combed and plated beard. He was flaxen and had honey-colored eyes. He seemed oddly familiar. Chet realized that he knew him... but the man was speaking, looking rather peeved. "I *said,* we must finish the ninth prong tonight, so you're in charge of the ritual killing. Another girl."

Caught in the mechanics of the dream, Chet felt no horror at the idea of a ritual killing. He only felt weary. There was something tiresome about the situation as if he'd done this too often and the man was asking for more of the same. More blood. Always blood and viscera. Drugged drinks lessened the screaming and carrying on, but the blood was vital to their operation.

He slid into the conversation as if on oiled wheels. "How old?" There seemed to be an internal logic behind his words, contextual and aligned with the reality around him.

"Three and a half. Not one of Foex's, I'm afraid. This one was bought from poor charcoal burners."

Chet felt himself sighing. "I'll be glad when this is over and we can go back to peteinos and palaeoth. I'm tired of slaughtering children."

"Yes, well, magic propels us forward, not back." The phrase seemed a pithy truth, repeated a thousand times without communicating anything.

Chet made a face. He knew perfectly well the man was his superior, that the work they did would make the world a—different place. Not a better place. But progress, progress. Always progress. The Metacors smashed and destroyed; they were enormous and far too intelligent. Aerora sheltered the monsters she'd borne from her womb, while Foex—her second born, always striving to be first—challenged their right to exist. Terrifying creatures. Somehow Chet knew he'd seen Metacors, that he'd been killed several times by them, mauled by their tusks and flung about like a sack of rice flour.

Endless war raged on between the Metacors and gods while humans—affiliate and unaffiliated alike—were trapped in the middle. There was only one best way to fight: create magical weapons like the one they were currently laboring upon.

The war was a distant reality in this time and place, though. Chet watched from the back of his head, bemused, as he went about his day. He spoke to a servant, checked ongoing magical workings, and stirred something foul and herbal in a pot over a fire. Chet felt awed at the sight of wild othnielia at the gate, though his dream doppelganger apparently saw them daily. He always fed the othnielia—upright reptiles, standing only a few feet higher than men with intelligent eyes, their babies clinging to their backs—this time of year during their migration across the continent.

Everything was vivid under his hands, his eyes. Chet sank deeper into the reality, comforted. He was deeply in love with this. It felt so *right.*

Then... he laid a little girl on a stone slab.

She was asleep. Drugged. The girl was tiny and—despite her famine-rounded belly—wonderfully perfect. She was at that phase in life when she looked more like a fairy-tale creature than a human being. He checked her eyes beneath her eyelids, mostly out of curiosity than any real need—yes, they were dark eyes. Not the honey yellow of a reincarnating Magician's soul. He'd killed colleagues before, of course, trapped in minute female bodies; best to release them into their next life as Foex decreed. Chet sighed, knowing he needed to do this. It was necessary. He was a responsible and respected individual who did what needed to be done. Chet recited the correct incantation. He took up the ritual knife, tightened his grip, and—

*No!* Chet cried out as the person—not himself, *not himself*—cut her throat, a swift mercy stroke. More ritual cuts. The body bled into purposeful grooves on the table, dripping into a pan at the end of the table.

Chet lost his grip on the dream reality, panicked and screaming inside.

There was something cool and wet on his forehead. A washcloth? But... but there were no washcloths in Crimson-Era Eicha. As if by naming the reality he'd experienced, the remainder dissolved around him. Chet felt as if he was rushing back into his body.

Yet he'd been in his body all along.

His confusion palpable, Chet opened his eyes. He was lying in a stranger's bed in a thoroughly modern space. There was a high roof with exposed pipes and blocky walls of concrete. The bed itself was large and airy with a white comforter; it was set on a platform, raised above a living space below. Everything around him was pewter grey or white, with geometric, burgandy-and-green prints thrown in for good measure. A loft apartment? It was in an urban area to judge by the traffic noises and honking outside the frosted, sheet-glass windows.

Chet licked his lips. They were crusty... so were his eyes for that matter. Something wet fell off his head. It *was* a washcloth. So that hadn't been his imagination. He was naked below the comforter except for a pair of underwear, not his own.

"Oh, you're awake."

Chet looked over his shoulder, his neck aching as if he'd slept on it wrong. A Flame was descending stairs from a higher platform. Her skin tone was light bisque and she wore blue scrubs. Her manner was brusque and professional as she took his hand, her fingers touching his wrist. She paused, looking at the clock on the wall. Chet relaxed after a minute. She wasn't seducing him—not that he wouldn't mind being seduced by her, at least in her current face and figure—she was checking his pulse.

"Who are you?" he said, his voice raspy.

"My name is Doyen Quor. As you are not a god affiliate, you may call me by my given name, Quor, and not my title," she said, reaching over to grab something from the bedside table—a blood pressure cuff and stethoscope. Quor fastened the cuff around his upper arm and began pumping, handling the stethoscope with practiced professionalism.

"Are you a doctor?"

"Used to be. It's too hard to get a license these days, and I have no money at the moment. Therefore I'm a registered nurse. Just got off graveyard at the hospital."

Chet glanced around the loft apartment; they seemed to be alone. "Where are the others?"

"Gone. You've been delirious almost two days. They left early this morning when I got home from work to catch a train to Allistair. They seemed to feel their errand was more important than seeing you well." Quor frowned. "If you ask me, they're acting a little strange. I've rarely known Journey to be so uncaring. It made me wonder if you've done something to offend her, and, of course, now I'm stuck with you."

"Abyss," Chet whispered. Fenimore had to be in control. He

grabbed Quor's arm as she removed the blood-pressure cuff, upset beyond measure. "Why didn't you say anything? Why did you let them go?"

Quor blinked. "Journey and Knife? They know what they're doing. Why should I stop them?"

"...Never mind." He wanted to tell her about the Raptus but *couldn't*. Fenimore's order of silence was apparently still in effect. Such a powerful tool.

He blinked tears. Fenimore had told him to grow up, to be a man. He'd faced similar criticism all his life. Now his friends were gone, and he was alone in a foreign city-state under the care of this cold stranger. He still felt sick and weak, his body wrung out. Undone, Chet rolled over and sniffed into the pillow. To his relief, Doyen Quor set a box of new-style paper tissues on the bed and left him be. Chet snuffled into tissues, gulping sobs until they were nearly inaudible whimpers.

Journey and Knife had *left* him. They'd left with Fenimore. Did they know they were the only people standing between Fenimore and full control over the Raptus, and therefore control over the people of Uos? It was too late for him to say something: Chet was sundered, rejected, left behind. He had no value. What could he do? Go home? Follow them? How could he do anything when the Raptus still controlled him?

Quor puttered around the apartment, in earshot if not sight. He felt unwelcome, an annoyance for her. *I should go.*

Though it made his head spin, Chet was attempting to climb out of the bed just as Quor popped up the stairs, a big tray in hand. "What are you doing?"

"You didn't ask for me to stay here. I should go find a hotel or something..." *And, er, my clothes.* Did he even have money? Had Journey and Knife left him *anything?* They were sort of being funded by Chet's father, after all.

"You stay put. You had a fever of a hundred and five at one point. You're lucky your brain isn't fried. I was all set to take you to the emergency room at my hospital when you started cooling off."

"Oh, wow. That explains the dream. It seemed so real."

"Mmm." Quor set down the tray. It held dry toast and a big glass of lychee juice—an invalid's breakfast. "Here, you need to rehydrate."

Chet sipped, eyes half closed as he tried to recall more of the dream. "It was like... I was in Eicha during the Crimson Era. There were all these little historically accurate details." He could even remember a few that he hadn't noticed during the dream proper: the woven rush mats on the floor, for example, sprinkled with herbs for cleanliness and good humors. The curved blade the other guy had worn, slung across his chest like Fenimore wore his hunting blade. The man had had honey eyes and had spoken to him like he was—

"I was a Magician!"

"What?" Quor cried out, startled.

Chet smiled apologetically. "Sorry, didn't mean to yell. I mean I was a Magician in my dream. This other Magician was talking to me. I, um, I killed a little girl. Pantheon, she was little: only three and a half years old. That's what made me wake up. I couldn't... I mean, I've never hurt anyone in my life, yet it was so clear. The person I was in my dream—he didn't do it out of malice. He didn't even *like* doing it, but he felt like he had to, as if it were just another chore to get out of the way."

"Abyss." Quor's eyes narrowed, and she regarded him curiously. "I understand you're wrapped up in this business with the Raptus. Knife and Journey are both confused as to why you and the other guy, LaDaven, became bound to the Raptus."

"I wish I knew," Chet sighed. Aureate hadn't been able to answer the mystery for him. Now he'd never know why he'd been chosen.

She raised an eyebrow. "Chet, has it ever occurred to you that you really were a Magician?"

## Chapter 23
# Professional Opinion

"What?" Chet cried, staring at Doyen Quor in shock. She sounded so certain; it was less a question and more a statement of fact.

Quor sat and folded her hand. "You need to keep drinking."

Chet glared at her. "I'm not doing *anything* until you explain what you just said."

"Very well. Tell me, where do human souls come from before we're born? Where do we go after we die?"

He couldn't fathom why she was bringing up these sorts of irrelevant doctrine questions now. "Is this a trick? We come from the black ether between the stars. We return there when we die." The rote answer rose readily to his dry lips. He was thirsty at that. He self-consciously gulped lychee juice, and Quor nodded approval.

"That's an answer any Literati might have given me. I'm grateful you've not pledged to Philapo yet—" She held up a restraining hand as he opened his mouth. "Yes, yes, I know, you're not at all interested in becoming Literati, Journey told me. In any case, I'm grateful you're not because they'd argue about this *forever* with me."

"Argue about what?"

"If human souls come to and from the ether, how do you explain gods like Foex and Pelin engendering reincarnation?"

"Obviously, they catch you before you go and push you back to Uos again." Chet licked his lips. He wanted more juice but didn't want to end the conversation.

Though he hadn't asked, Quor picked up the glass and walked downstairs. Her voice called back, "Has it ever occurred to you to question how they do that? I mean, it seems a huge expenditure of energy, even for a god. There are about twelve hundred Flame who reincarnate on a regular or semi-regular basis, yet Pelin still needs to take care of other business in her life. How can she be on the lookout for dying Flame all the time?"

"You couldn't possibly think I know the answer to that."

Quor reappeared with both a glass of juice and the bottle in hand."You're such a good scholar. I like the way you don't assume you know the answer when you don't."

He ducked his head shyly. "Thank you."

"Look, I've been around a while. You start to notice patterns. There are plenty—plenty!—of people walking Uos who've been here before. People who are not Flame and never have been. Some were Flame once or twice but chose not to initiate again. We call them loopers. Privately, of course, as it's not ethical to tell people this sort of personal information. Journey and Knife would never share with you what I just said. They told me they have no doubt whatsoever that you're a persistent and voracious looper."

"They said *what?*" Chet recoiled, wishing he could pull the covers over his head. "No, wait, back up. How can there be such a thing as randomly reincarnating people?"

"Yes, exactly. How *can* there be unless the gods have nothing, absolutely nothing, to do with it? Listen, you've studied the works of Magicians in detail, yes? You know something of Foex's style. He never consciously wasted energy. He was like a card player who used every single card in his hand and wasted no moves, counting and tracking every card in the deck. What if instead of expending gregarious amounts of time and effort grabbing people before they returned to the ether, he simply utilized a natural phenomenon? Twisted it around to meet his needs. What if, instead of instigating reincarnation, he simply made his human affiliates aware of their past-life memories?"

Chet frowned thoughtfully. "So he didn't have to keep teaching the same people the same information."

"You got it." Quor smiled approvingly at him. "Pelin does the same thing, mostly because she feels we have a right to know and enjoys deepening relationships over time. We remember our past lives upon initiation."

Chet lay back in bed. "So I'm a looper?"

Quor sighed. "Don't take my word for it."

"But—but you said..."

"What possible good could come of knowing about your past? You're in this body now. This life."

"I think I have a right to know." He glared. Hadn't she just said her goddess believed in freedom of this sort of information? "Why do *you* get to have automatic access to this knowledge, yet *I* can't? Don't trot out that old garbage about how you're a god affiliate and I'm not. That's an answer I've never accepted as anything but begging the question, worse than when a parent says, 'Because I told you so.'"

Quor quirked a smile. "Bear with me, Chet. *Why* do you need to know?"

"Because... because the past is impacting my current life. My current body." She'd been leading him on.

Quor spread her hands. "Obviously, I can't tell you who you were. Only you can answer that question. Eat your toast. I should go out and do some errands, then I'll need to sleep. *You* are to stay in bed. Bathroom's through that door. If you feel cold, there's clothing in the closet on the upper level, and I have male clothing almost your size. I like a longer inseam and narrower waist, personally, but the fit will be close enough for practical purposes."

"Thank you," he muttered, annoyed. Why had she led him on if she hadn't intended to answer his questions? It was almost as frustrating as if she hadn't said anything, letting him stew forever in his ignorance.

"I'll be back in a bit."

He lay flat in bed as she left the apartment. Was it true? Had he been a reincarnating Magician before Foex died? That would explain an awful lot in his life. His psychological block from wanting to become a god affiliate, for one thing. Next to Foex all the other gods did seem pale and measly. Aureate had been drawn into Foex's service out of passion, at first, anyway. Had Chet felt the same?

He remembered that moment when he'd accused Aureate of being an affiliate turncoat. "Who *are* you?" she'd asked, her voice strained. She'd gazed at him as if she'd wanted to drill him open and see what was inside. He'd run on instinct when flirting with Aureate, and everything had been so easy with her. Maybe they'd known each other in the past. In the dream, Chet had remembered killing girls who'd been his colleagues born in female form. Like Aureate had been.

*If that's true, I was, um, sacrificed in female form, too.* Chet blinked, his world tilting in a way that had nothing to do with the apartment around him.

This was crazy.

His brain churned on regardless. Being a looper would explain his obsession with the past. Chet blinked. He could see his bookcases in his mind's eye, the titles laid out before him. More than half of his collection had been penned by Magicians. He'd never noticed the sheer numbers before, the oddly high percentage.

Then there was the Raptus.

"It should not have called upon any but god affiliates," Journey had said in the prostitute's van."I cannot believe that the makers of this object would wish to endow it upon random, unaffiliated people."

Chet was unaffiliated now, but if he were a looping soul, then the past had its fingerprints all over him. Perhaps... he was reaching now, but perhaps the Raptus had recognized him as a Magician, one of its correct guardians. Maybe the Raptus even *knew* him. Personally. The idea was delightful and frightening beyond belief. Did Chet know the Raptus?

Chet closed his eyes. He obsessively recalled every detail of his dream. The smells, the sounds. The other man had talked about shaping a ninth prong. The Raptus had twelve spikes—like the twelve fingers of a god—only it was shaped like a doedicu's tail. The spikes on a doedicu's tail, he recalled suddenly, were often translated as *prongs* in the ancient tongue of Door. Maybe he and the other man had been in the process of creating the Raptus? It seemed too big a stretch, yet Chet had been traveling with the Raptus for a week. Had his subconscious mind had chosen that memory on purpose?

Who had that other man been anyway? The other Magician, rather. Chet thought he'd seemed familiar...

He sat up in bed, stunned.

The other man seemed familiar because he *was* familiar. It was Fenimore LaDaven. Only not Fenimore: he'd had a different face and body, a different name. Like Chet. It was obvious... yet not so.

Chet settled down again, frowning. There was a definitive lack of solid evidence, for one thing. How could he prove it? Reincarnation had no physical proof to draw on. Yet beneath Fenimore's mannerisms was the same energy. He was the same *person* as the Magician in Chet's drea—no, his memory.

Fenimore had been a Magician, too. That explained Fenimore's role in the binding, at least. The Raptus may have recognized him, too.

If it were true, did Fenimore *know?* Chet nibbled his lip, thinking about Fenimore's words, his silences. He had the same silences as Knife only laid out in a different pattern. Fenimore had tried to grab the Raptus back at the dig site. He'd acted as if he'd owned it. Hadn't Fenimore said something about Foex in the barn? About how Foex prevented *them* from being women? It made sense, given Aureate's story.

*For the sake of argument, I'd say he knows.*

If that was true, it followed that Fenimore had long-term plans for the Raptus. A magical relic that could control humanity... Chet could see Fenimore enjoying that kind of power.

How long had those plans been laid? It was a good bet that back in 7305, Fenimore had been seeking the Raptus for himself, not his prince. Chet considered Knife's version of the story. It still felt wrong, but it was the only information he had, far more complete than Fen's account in the ambulance. Fenimore and Knife had split up in Eich Che, taking different paths. Chet decided that it wasn't a coincidence that Fenimore had found the Raptus and Knife hadn't.

Pantheon, Fen wanted the Raptus so badly. The physical evidence said that Fenimore had dove into lucid mud—into the unknown future—holding it in his hands. He'd held on so hard that the graduate students had had to tie a rope to his legs to pull him from the dust.

*Fenimore has the Raptus even now, this very moment. He also has Journey and Knife,* Chet thought wildly.

Wait. Something wasn't quite adding up. It was like looking down at a half-finished jigsaw puzzle to try and see the picture without the missing pieces. *Did* Fenimore have Journey and Knife? "I don't know why Journey is waiting," Fenimore had said on the train. She was holding back both her blood and verse—for a reason? Chet knew Journey and Knife were currently unaware of Fenimore's heightened control of the Raptus. Abyss, he'd been there. But had they always been ignorant of his actions and intentions?

No.

Oh, Pantheon, it all added up. Knife had been keeping an eye on Fenimore since day one. Chet remembered Journey whispering in Clementina's house about how "he" was Knife's meat. It was so simple. Journey had called Knife in not just because of the Raptus—she clearly hadn't known the Shadow Dancers were keeping an eye on things until she reached the site—but because of Fenimore. Knife had been called in to handle a very old problem indeed: the double-faced courtier who had craved the Raptus beyond rational thought and reason.

But things hadn't gone according to plan, had they? After becoming bound by the cords, Knife had switched up her game. She'd made noises about destroying the Raptus, sure, but she'd also offered the incentive of unlocking it. Luring Fen along.

To what? Who was trapping whom?

Did Knife and Journey know Fen was a reincarnating Magician, too? Um. Chet found himself going cross eyed at the possibility. The Flame had treated Fenimore with a careful respect as they'd watched him, nothing more. It was likely Knife considered Fenimore a greedy, entitled, immoral loose cannon, exactly the way she'd described him earlier. The Flame were not Syche affiliates, and they could not read minds. The only reason Chet suspected Fenimore was because of his dream.

In the end, it didn't matter what Journey and Knife's intentions had been. Fenimore had sat on that dock with two weeping Flame and had somehow gotten the upper hand on them using the Raptus. Maybe. The last two verses, the last drops of blood, were the only things locking the Raptus. They were headed for Allistair at this minute to retrieve Knife's verse.

*Shit, shit, shit.* He had to get there. He had to get there *now.*

Chet threw his feet over the edge of the bed tried to stand up, immediately collapsing. He was weak, his body wrung out. It wasn't just his body—Chet's head swam. *One step at a time,* he thought, breathing deep. Just like the motorboat. Clothing was upstairs. He stood again, bracing himself against the wall and walked slowly on shaky feet to the staircase. It was such a modern apartment that the stairs appeared to float in the air, connected underneath somehow. There was no railing. Chet eyed the stairs, nauseated and nervous. What if he lost his balance?

He turned around and sat on a riser, then lifted himself to the next stair backwards. Scooting up the steps like a child.

A child... he remembered the face of the young girl he'd slaughtered like an animal. He'd told Fenimore that he was tired of killing children. Chet swallowed nausea. Magicians had practiced blood magic for millennia; it was what they were notorious for.

*I murdered children,* he thought. Lots and lots of children. Little girls, mostly.

Chet crawled back down the stairs as fast as he could. He could see a bedpan on the floor beside the bed. His whole world had narrowed to that single goal. Reaching it, he vomited his guts out. Then he sank, head resting on the floorboards, moaning.

*If only Rory could see me now,* he thought. He'd been a god affiliate after all. A murderous, horrific god affiliate. What would she say if she knew? Rory would probably never accept him with good reason.

There was so much blood on his hands... no, wait. *Was* there blood on his hands? Chet had never hurt anyone in his life. He was completely innocent, just a graduate student with a rich family. *That's right.* Except he didn't believe it. The Raptus had called him out, hadn't it? The Flame, while discrete with their circular reasoning, had done the same. How could anyone live with this kind of legacy? Chet had wallowed in history, but history, it seemed, was full of nasty surprises.

*I will be paying for this for the rest of my life,* Chet thought grimly. What could possibly balance his terrible deeds? Growing up, he'd been surrounded by family members who either enjoyed breaking the law for the purpose of making money, or who'd despised this mindset and turned to a higher calling. His sisters had become Nuns for more than just legal and financial independence from their father's dealings. Chet, too, had always identified with a higher calling, as his finely honed conscience wouldn't have had it any other way.

So he wasn't a normal guy, the same guy he'd always been. Chet was worse. A murderer of children, and another Magician was about to unlock a powerful magical tool to help him do—what? Kill more people, Chet was afraid.

He was too sick and weak—with both remorse and illness—to do much about it.

# Chapter 24
# Taking the Upper Hand

It took over an hour, but Chet got dressed, visited the bathroom and descended the stairs to the ground level. How was he going to get to the train station? He had no money on him. How was he to buy a ticket?

The front door opened and Quor strode through. She was wearing a knit cap in proxy of a wig. She still wore her scrubs and cradled paper grocery bags, a newspaper tucked under her arm. "Abyss, what are you doing?"

"Journey and Knife are in terrible danger. I've got to..."

"You're going back to bed," she said firmly, putting the bags down on a counter. "Come on, I'll help you upstairs."

"You don't understand." To his horror, he started weeping *again*. Fenimore was right, he was a pansy. Chet swiped his eyes angrily, sniffing.

Instead of forcing him up the stairs, she pulled out a chair and gestured him into it. "Tell me what you think is going on while I put away groceries, okay? I want the whole story. Front to back."

Chet was incredibly grateful for the chair. The story had started at the lucid mud dig site when Professor Tibbets had introduced him to Journey. So much had happened since then. Trying not to feel daunted by his own experiences, Chet cleared his throat and began. Doyen Quor was an appreciative audience. She scowled at the discovery of Tibbet's body and smiled wryly at his dunking in the doedicu lake. He had a feeling she already had most of the facts; it was his opinions and understanding she was looking for. Though he attempted to conceal the sex stuff, he had a feeling Quor saw right past him.

"You know," she said, "you really ought to go get tested."

"Tested?"

"For VDs. I wouldn't be surprised if you've caught something. For the sake of any potential partner you might have—apart from Flame—go see a doctor pronto. Okay, Chet?"

"Yeah. Fine." His face was hot enough to melt tar, and she looked away as if preserving his privacy. It helped him continue with his tale, anyway.

He got to the part where Aureate had left to take a piss... and halted. He literally could not continue. It wasn't a Raptus thing—the fog seemed to be fading for some reason—but he couldn't speak.

Quor put a gentle hand on his shoulder. "Knife told me you tried to rescue her."

"Yes." He closed his eyes. "I can still feel... oh, Pantheon."

"Aureate and I have rarely gotten along, but I'm sorry that she's dead. Such a waste of a good body. She was pushed, wasn't she?"

"I think... I think I know who did it, too. Maybe."

Quor lifted an eyebrow. "Pray continue."

He found to his relief that he could explain what had happened on the train. Fenimore's words and actions were just as gut wrenching after the fact. The mind-control fog seemed irrelevant now. Why was the Raptus's power over him reduced and diluted? Chet didn't know, but he guessed it had something to do with distance. He could still feel the Raptus—and the others through the cords—though the connection was quite stretchy. He certainly wasn't in physical pain. Through the connection, he could tell the Raptus was several hundred miles away, and the distance was growing greater with each passing minute.

No one in the old days had been able to travel seventy miles an hour as people did on modern trains. Chet and the others had started this trip wondering what effect modern technology would have on the Raptus. It seemed this was one of them.

Chet finished his story, saying, "So you see, Journey and Knife are all that remains between Fenimore and the unlocked Raptus. This is just a theory, but I believe Fenimore was a Magician, too." He explained his dream in more detail.

"I... suppose that might be possible. LaDaven seemed a little jittery while he was here. Didn't say much."

Fenimore had hardly been speaking at all, Chet realized with a start. For a guy with such high energy, he'd been surprisingly quiet. Patient. "I know I need another day in bed, but I don't want more people to die for the Raptus. Especially not my friends."

"Mmm, but Knife knows all this, too. This is Knife's forte."

"Yeah, I figured out that Knife was called in to look after Fenimore. Though I wonder why Knife didn't just kill him outright." Chet shot her a covert look.

Quor blinked. "You look awfully innocent, Chet, but you aren't, are you?"

"I used to be. Last week, say."

"Huh. Knife likes to get the lay of the land before acting, and the Raptus caught you all long before she was done with her assessment. None of us know how to deal with that. Hopefully the Shadow Dancers will come through."

Come through with what? And what would he do if they didn't? Chet chewed on his inner cheek. "If Knife can't destroy the Raptus, why have we been unlocking it, anyway? I wasn't there for that part."

"Apart from keeping LaDaven occupied—which is Knife's game, no one else's—we're trying to make it easier to destroy the Raptus. For a goddess, Aiena is kind of ornery, you know? She won't do anything unless the abysmal thing is gift wrapped."

"But didn't Aiena have you lock it in the first place?"

"She did, but that doesn't mean she can unlock it on her own. You have to understand, Foex and his Magicians left tens of *thousands* of items when they died. Aiena was overwhelmed. It took her a decade to even triage the mess and two centuries for a decent sorting. The process is still going on, really. Aiena has been forced to work for decades to get rid of things that Foex could have destroyed in seconds not because she's less powerful but because she didn't make them herself. Different energy and methods, you see. We—the Flame Council—took on the Raptus as a favor. We didn't want to hold it ourselves, though, as reincarnation doesn't allow one to hold onto material items. Also, we were very clear that if it did anything wacky, to use modern parlance, it would go right back on Aiena's plate."

"That's what it's doing now."

"You got it. We're not in the business of getting Aiena's attention, though. It might be a fatal error for us to try. Like I said, she's prickly."

"So remind me again why Journey and Knife aren't in deep trouble?" Chet was vividly reminded of the old fable of the farmer, the peteino feed, the peteinos and the inofe. Trying to keep everyone from eating one another was a problem.

She snorted. "Didn't say they weren't. But Aiena was very careful in setting the ritual when we locked the Raptus. Fenimore LaDaven cannot possibly control Knife and Journey in direct ways, though he might be influencing them in little ways if he's found a loophole, and I don't doubt there is one. Aiena tried hard to close all the loopholes, but the nature of Foex's magic was based on very specific wordings. Anyway, it's my belief that Knife and Journey are going to Allistair of their own free will."

"So... he's got to trick them before he can actually do anything." Could Fenimore trick Journey? Maybe. She didn't like him and was unlikely to turn her back. Could he trick Knife? Probably not.

Quor smiled at him. "Come on, back to bed with you."

"I do need to get to Allistair soon, though," he mumbled sleepily as she helped him up the stairs. The cords were tightening in a slow, subtle way, pulling him west. "I wish... I wish I had something to counteract the Raptus's influence. I'll just have to sneak up on Fenimore and hope he isn't paying attention."

Chet woke in the late afternoon and stretched. Then he froze—someone was in bed with him. He glanced over and saw the back of Quor's bisque-colored head. She was curled away from him, lightly snoring. *Oh, of course.* She'd said she worked graveyard shift, so this was her sleeping time. Chet did feel better, he had to admit. Getting to the bathroom was easier than before, anyway. He slid back under the covers, grateful to be warm and clean.

Pantheon, he had the biggest erection imaginable. He felt embarrassed, though no one was around to see it.

He regarded Quor curiously. She was less intimidating asleep. It was funny... even Oak, perched in her single dorm room, had a poster on the wall depicting the past. There was nothing of the sort in this loft apartment: everything was scrubbed and aggressively modern as if Quor preferred to forget rather than remember. She seemed very alone. Though she'd complained about having no money, this urban apartment had to have cost something substantial. Chet wondered why she required so much space for just one person. Wasn't she lonely?

He crept closer to Quor. She was wearing a loose cotton shirt. His breath came quicker as he wondered what she else was wearing—or not. Would it be creepy to check? Chet's dick grew harder at the thought. He felt like fucking, and Quor was Flame. There was no way she could catch any disease he might have. She didn't seem to be in a relationship at the moment, and she lived alone; in fact, she was in bed with him, available. He nuzzled the back of her neck. She snorted, still asleep.

Chet began thrusting against her just a little bit, and reached down to feel... *oh.* She wore a lacy thong and nothing else down there. His fingers accidentally—almost accidentally—brushed against a tit, and his breath caught. Would she mind? Abyss, she was Flame. They all had a maniac sex drive. Well, all of them except Oak, but Oak was just weird.

Quor woke with a snort. She looked over her shoulder, eyes drooping with sleep. "Chet?"

*Stop being such a pansy,* Fenimore had told him. Everyone thought he was too shy, too reticent. Chet firmly took hold of Quor's shoulders and rolled her onto her back. She blinked at him, suddenly expressionless. He kissed her on the lips, working his way down. He couldn't wait. He mounted her, fingered the lacy thong aside and entered her swiftly. Her breath caught. Chet fucked her hard, gasping as he bore down on her. She was tight and wet as any Flame. In fact, she felt *phenomenal.*

Quor's expression did not change. She looked at him steadily. Then she looked away. A tear slid from her eye down to her ear, the wet track tinged purple with ichor.

Chet paused, confused. He realized... he'd never asked her consent. Was this rape? He wasn't raping her, was he? Chet remembered—with an intensity that encompassed his whole being—lying under Rhiys while being penetrated. But this was different! Maybe he could just finish... but she was crying. He was causing her pain. He'd never wanted to cause anyone pain. He wasn't a bad person despite his past lives. Was he? Chet felt a wave of nausea, his hands and knees aching at the memory of being Fenimore's table. Of being an object waiting to be fucked, unable to change his fate. Of having no choice.

He had a choice now. Withdrawing from her wet, tight sex was one of the toughest things he'd ever done. He found the strength to do so.

Chet turned away, hands covering his face. The depths of his shame scored him, sharp as a blade. Nothing he could say would make this any better. Nothing. Pantheon, he'd murdered girl after girl when he'd been a Magician, and now he was a rapist.

*I should just go home and dedicate my life to Genis, like my father wants, and be my brothers' butt boy until the day I die,* he thought. It would be a punishing and miserable existence exactly the way he deserved. Self flagellation at its finest. Abyss, maybe he should just acquire a gun and end his life swiftly, get it over with. Out of nowhere, he felt a wet sweater gripped in his hands, the sensation of Aureate's bubbling skin. There had been an utter finality to it when Knife had fired his gun, killing her. The flashback made him sway in place.

"You stopped," Quor said as she sat up. "You stopped before you came."

Chet looked over his shoulder, hardly seeing her through his misery. "Does it even matter? I thought once... I didn't *ask*."

"It matters to me. I'm male, too. I know how hard it is to stop in the middle."

There was something about her tone that wasn't quite—present. The words were casual. *Almost too casual,* he thought, frowning. Chet dared take a second look, peeking at her like a dium about to have its elongated nose chopped off. Quor looked... *odd* was too simple a word. She was rocking in place in a subtle way that barely registered as movement. Her expression was a fusion of clinical analysis and raw, gapping vulnerability.

"For whatever it's worth—probably nothing—I'm sorry," he

whispered, eyes closed tight.

Quor made a small noise low in her throat. He glanced over in surprise and couldn't look away. She was *shaping*. It wasn't anything like Chet had seen before. She—the pronoun didn't quite fit—was changing her race, gender, facial features, body type, *everything*, by the second. Chet felt like he was going crazy, and all he was doing was watching. What did it feel like on the inside? He suddenly understood Quor was instinctively trying to shed her skin—to distance herself from her own physical sensations and emotions—but couldn't. All she could do was *this*.

"Quor, stop."

"You... don't get... to tell me what to do!" she hissed. Pantheon, her voice had gone from bass to soprano in a single breath. Didn't it hurt?

He didn't know how to react, except to walk out of the apartment with his metaphorical tail between his legs. Then what? Take a vow to a god he disliked? Buy a gun? Who knew? Chet began sliding to the edge of the bed and was stopped by a hand clasping his wrist. Tight. Chet looked at Quor. She'd gone back to her bisque-skinned beauty, yet there was something sharp and pinched about her face, or maybe it was just her expression.

"Oh, no, you don't get off that easy."

What did she want with him? Revenge? Chet hung his head. "Go on. I deserve whatever you do to me."

She snorted. "You're a self absorbed twit."

He could hear the amusement in her voice, though he honestly didn't know what was so funny. What could he possibly say to tell her how bad he felt? Words clotted in his mouth."I don't disagree. It's just whatever you do *can't* be worse than what I'm feeling now, even if you did horrible, unspeakable things to me." Like a Flame villain in a melodrama? Her rapid shapeshifting had looked unhinged, scary.

Was she going crazy? And would she take him down with her?

Quor paused. To Chet's surprise and discomfort, she put her arms around him and drew him downward, so they lay together on the bed. Her other hand traveled down his body until it was just above his cock. He jerked away, wanting to fight, wanting to protest—this was getting creepy—but he was breathless with anticipation. A beautiful

Flame held her hand right above his penis. Chet grew hard as if his dick wanted to meet her halfway.

In a sudden movement, she grabbed his scrotum with the accuracy and speed of a rhamph—a large, flying mammal that hung around the seashore—picking a snail out of its shell. Was she going to castrate him with her bare hands, the way Journey had threatened Fenimore? Quor gripped the base of his ball sack firmly, but her touch was light and lacked a crushing, squeezing quality. Yet.

"What are you doing?" His voice squeaked up at the end.

"Is it not obvious?" Quor's voice dropped—though it was still feminine—to a low purr. "My bed, my apartment. My rules."

Chet's heart pounded in his ears. He'd invited her to do whatever she wanted to him, but he wasn't so sure that had been a good idea in retrospect. Yet the part of him that still shuddered in horror and despair at his own actions was mollified. "I guess that's better than my plan."

"Which was what, exactly?"

"Um." Now that she'd invited him to say it out loud, Chet realized how stupid it sounded. "To go shoot myself in the head. Or dedicate myself to Genis and live out a miserable existence just like my father wants. Either way."

Quor chuckled low in her throat and patted him on the chest with her other hand. "Yep. I called it all right. You're a self-absorbed doedicu."

"Hey!" Chet glared at her. "If I'm an idiot, how about you? You could have slept—elsewhere. Or turned male, or something."

She gazed at him so long he looked away, uncomfortable. "Chet, are *you* blaming *me* for your lack of judgment?"

"I'm just saying the lack of judgment wasn't mine alone. I mean, you should know I'm dangerous."

"Is that how you see yourself? Point of fact, I did think about the couch, and I considered turning male. But the first is very hard and modern, plus it smells like ass when you put your nose right on it. The couch came with this apartment. As for the second... by all accounts, it wouldn't have made a difference to you. Would it."

"I—no."

"There you go. Chet, have you thought this through? You were raped several times in rapid succession this week. You're attempting to compensate, re-learning your boundaries, probably trying to sort out the negative messages from the positive ones. Trust me, I know the feeling. On top of everything, you've suddenly discovered your past. Not just any past, either, but blood-soaked lifetimes serving a drunken, abusive asshole of a god."

Chet stared at her. "You make it sound like... Quor, did you know him? Foex, I mean?"

"I did." Her mouth was tight. "There was one lifetime when he really got to me. I had a thriving herbal import-export business based in Door, which was the center of the Magician's world back then. My business was a little too successful. I came to the attention of Foex, and he proceeded to break me down over the next twenty years. Speaking of rape. He was psychologically abusive in so many ways. I went from a secure business owner who rode with her own caravans to a degraded shut in. All that, and he just wanted two things."

"What?"

"Big tits and a tight box." Her free hand, lying on his chest, had curled into a fist.

"Pantheon. I'm sorry."

"Oh, not your fault." Quor smiled at him, and it was a genuine smile. "Have you figured out your name yet? Your old name? You have all the pieces in your hand, you know."

Why was she being so congenial toward him? She was treating him like, um, like a friend, or at least a benign acquaintance who'd lost his way. "Does it make a difference when I did those horrible things?"

She snorted. "Listen, the power-hungry sociopaths are always with us. Doesn't mean you've ever been one of them. Think."

With her hand cradling his scrotum? Not likely. Yet his mind was racing forward, trying to put the puzzle pieces together. He and Fenimore had been killing girls—he shuddered at the memory of blood running down table grooves—and making prongs, possibly for the Raptus. The Raptus... of *course* he knew the two Magicians who'd made it. Even if he hadn't heard about the Raptus until this week, he'd long been obsessed with the Magicians Tene and Zang. He knew their writings by heart, and...

*Oh.* He looked at Quor, utterly dumbfounded.

She smirked back. "You got it."

But which one was he? Zang or Tene? Chet wanted more than anything to have been Zang for his wisdom and delicate prose, not Tene in all his fear mongering. Yet he didn't want wishful thinking to lead him astray. It occurred to Chet that—if this were true—he'd lost much: his honey-colored eyes to start, and many other attributes as well. Like fame and power? *Pantheon.*

Quor let go of his balls. Chet sighed with relief and was about to say something about getting up when Quor took hold of his cock. All thoughts left his head. She stroked him slowly, making each movement count.

"What are you doing?"

"I told you, my bed, my rules. You took me without my consent. Turnabout being fair play, notice how I'm not asking for yours."

"Are you sure?" He gasped under her practiced touch. Her other hand was playing with his nipples, making him writhe. He was so, so hard. "After what I did?"

"You don't get to decide for me. This is not about you, either as a reward or punishment. It's about me. I'm in control, you are my meat, and you will take whatever I choose to do to you."

"Y-yes, good Flame." It felt strange to be put back on the bottom, but didn't he deserve it?

Quor looked like she was pondering the situation. Chet watched her for clues, both terrified and elated as to which way she'd jump. He no longer feared for her sanity. She'd survived Foex and undoubtedly many others, so she'd certainly live past his aborted, botched rape. He waited upon her whim.

Her first move was to shapeshift to male. Quor remained bisque skinned and many of his facial features remained the same, only thickening his chin a bit. A feminine kind of masculinity. Despite this, there was nothing womanly about Quor as he positioned himself at the base of the bed and parted Chet's legs, lifting them above his head to study his ass. Chet's anus tightened reflexively at the thought of being penetrated again, and Quor grinned in reaction.

Quor grabbed a bottle of lotion from nearby bedside table and applied it with verve. Chet loved the idea of taking another cock, but he couldn't help feeling disappointed. Abyss, Quor had been so hot under him as female, though he cringed from the thought. Quor positioned Chet's feet on his shoulders and was about to enter him, then paused.

"What?"

"Nothing."

"I mean it. What?"

"It's just... you were so hot before. As a girl."

Quor's lips quirked up. "Ah, I think I know what you want."

He pushed out his chest and—Chet gasped. Tits! Beautifully rounded breasts, big enough for him to hold securely. Was Quor still a guy? Yes, his erect penis hovered over Chet's thighs. Chet couldn't believe it, yet it made sense, all things considered. Quor smirked and slapped his belly, making him yelp.

"Put your feet on my shoulders. Now."

Chet scrambled to obey. Quor penetrated him with a grunt; he didn't mess around with a small cock like Journey had. Chet whined under his breath, grimacing at the pain. Quor settled himself above Chet with a satisfied expression and began pumping him. The movement made his tits jiggle and shake. Chet's eyes nearly popped out of his head. *So* hot to be fucked, his ass fuller than full with those amazing tits bouncing over him. Loving every moment, Chet took hold of those breasts, caressing and kneading them. Exactly what he'd always wanted, even if he'd never admitted it to himself.

Pleasure washed over him in waves, and he came, basting their stomachs with his juices. Quor didn't even pause. Chet lay back, his hands full of tits and his ass full of cock, and just took it.

So perfect.

He came twice more before Quor shot deep inside his ass. To his shock, Quor didn't withdraw. Instead, he rocked gently inside Chet's ass, subtly pumping. Making himself hard again? Chet groaned, but he had no choice. Quor was in control. After a time—a shorter span than Chet had thought possible—Quor began humping him again with vigor.

"Oh, please," Chet moaned, his ass protesting.

Quor didn't hesitate: he slapped Chet lightly across the face. "Who's in charge?"

"You are, good Flame."

"Don't you forget it." Nevertheless, he slowed down. Long, toe-curling strokes that made Chet feel like his hair was writhing like a sea creature.

Would it ever end? Did Chet want it to end? All his nerves were singing, fully awake and alive. He'd never felt more feminine, not even doing drag under Fenimore's exuberant care. Chet came again. His scrotum felt flaccid, emptied of semen.

Chet let go of his thoughts, his very being, and let himself be fucked. It was like being a table again but better. Quor didn't ask anything of him, and Chet didn't have to give anything. It was pure fucking, nothing more.

When Quor finally released him, Chet glanced at the clock, then looked again. "Pantheon."

Quor was already burrowing into the bedclothes, and covered them both with alacrity. "You're lucky it's a weekday for me. If it had been a weekend... well. Your ass would never be the same."

Chet rolled onto his side, amazed he could close his aching legs. "Thank you," he whispered as Quor spooned him.

"You're welcome. Now shut up and let me sleep; the alarm's going to go off in an hour."

"Yes, good Flame."

Quor was shaking him. She was back in female form and wearing scrubs again. "Come on, Chet. Get dressed, and I'll feed you something. Then I'm putting you on a plane to Allistair before going to work."

"Wha—? I thought there was a strike."

"It ended a few hours ago. Hopefully we can squeeze you in, and maybe you'll even get to Allistair an hour or two before the others arrive."

"Oh." Chet blinked, remembering why it was so important to get to Allistair. "Yes. That would be good."

"Chet... considering what's at stake, do you think I should come with you?"

It would make sense. Quor would be resistant to the Raptus's influence, thanks to Aiena's attempt to close all loopholes. Chet was not. She might solve all his problems for him, and that was an issue, wasn't it? "Don't take this the wrong way, but I kind of feel like I have to do this myself. Like it's my own nut to crack."

"This is your manhood rite, eh? Like we used to do in the coteries. You need to ride your doedicu three miles and dismount successfully without getting walloped by the tail."

"Yes!" he cried, staring at her. She understood. Her turn of phrase clicked in his head; it could be a curious exercise, speaking to Flame. "Did *you* ever do it? Ride a doedicu three miles to become a man?"

"Oh, yes. Didn't stay a man long, but so it goes. Come on, food first and the rest follows."

"Right." Chet frowned. He was forgiven one transgression. Perhaps he could make this work after all.

# Chapter 25
# Allies

Chet wandered through the airport, a knapsack on his back, literally kicking his heels while waiting for his delayed, overbooked flight. It was four hours overdue. *So much for getting to Allistair before the train arrives,* he thought dourly. He still felt wrung out from the fever. While his ass ached deeply, it was a satisfying kind of ache. Fortunately, Quor had given him snacks and some cash. He also had Knife's home address in his pocket along with a map of Allistair. He was prepared as he could be for whatever came next.

Chet wondered what Journey, Knife and Fenimore were doing at this moment. Sleeping, if they were smart. Was Fenimore toying with the Raptus even now, working on his goal to gain ascendency over the Flame?

If Fenimore hurt Journey, Chet would—what? What would he do?

He was too tired to keep pondering such things. There was a fancy, sunken conversation pit with chairs and tables for passengers to use; it currently held several families and business people. Chet wondered whether he could nap with his head resting on one of those tables. He paused, staring at a young, bistre-skinned woman who was sitting with her back turned to him. She looked familiar.

*Oh!* It was Rory.

Chet swallowed. He didn't know how he felt about seeing her again. He'd missed her terribly. Chet was not unaffected by their break up as he'd originally thought. On the other hand... Rory had shown her true colors by becoming invisible and rushing right through him. Then she'd met with Knife under a street lamp in the most cliché god-affiliate scene he'd ever witnessed. She hadn't even stopped to say anything to him, let alone apologize. Rory's Cluster was supposed to follow their group, to keep an eye on them as they unlocked it, but so many bad things had happened without their intervention. Was that why she was here? She was late if that was the case.

There wasn't anything around that looked like a pulsating black hole, but she wasn't alone. Rory's companion... Chet's mouth opened and shut in rapid sequence. Her companion was Professor Clementina. No longer wearing black, the frumpy professor was dressed as any Tache citizen in a red skirt with a rustic pattern and a fur-lined muff. Clementina and Rory were chatting as if they were travel partners awaiting their flight. Exactly the way he was.

They hadn't spotted him yet. Chet considered his position. Were they booked on the same flight? A distinct possibility, especially since the recent strike had narrowed everyone's choices. Chet decided he preferred to make the first move rather than be discovered. What would Knife do in this situation? Knife would approach them in a casual, quiet manner to see how they reacted, playing by ear. Knife would trade information for information, a game of checks and balances. *Right.*

Chet headed for the conversation pit at a moderate pace. He grabbed a spare chair—there weren't many—and approached their table. Rory's face when she finally caught a glimpse of him radiated shock and... was that fear? Clementina kept talking, her words trailing off as she realized her companion's attention was elsewhere. Then she, too, grew silent, her eyes wary.

Chet positioned the chair backwards and sat, legs spread wide and hands clasped across the back. "So, how've you been, Professor? Rory?"

Rory licked her lips. "Chet. You're here." She touched a bracelet around her wrist. It was a pretty piece, bronze with a turquoise stone. Chet gauged it five or six hundred years old.

Having secured the first word, he intended to continue on the offensive. Chet smiled. "Rory, glad to see you're visible again. Professor, good to see you, too. Murdered any more Flame, lately?"

"I do not know what you're talking about." Clementina's fallow skin was pale and she looked rather clammy. She, too, touched a bracelet at her wrist, identical to the one Rory wore—an oddly vulnerable gesture. Were the bracelets significant somehow?

"So, what are you two doing here?"

They glanced at one another. Rory seemed to be holding her breath. Clementina looked a little stuffed, but her eyebrows were starting to descend into their typical, pissed-off position. Why were they so frightened?

Chet decided to push. "Oh, wait. I know exactly why you're here. You've got tickets to Allistair, just like me. A little late off the mark, aren't you, Rory? You must have lost us somewhere along the line, I'm thinking."

Another significant silence, neither denial nor confirmation of his supposition. Rory seemed to pull herself together. "Perhaps we should go somewhere more private to speak."

Chet had expected Clementina to treat him like the enemy, but Rory was a different story. Hadn't she and Knife decided they were all on the same side? He frowned at her. "No, I don't think so. Rory, where's your Cluster?"

Rory's expression hardened. She appeared to be waiting for him to do something. Clementina kept looking at his knapsack as if waiting for it to explode. Why were they treating him this way? What would Knife make of their behavior and their silences? There was certainly a lot of silence here. If he didn't speak, no one did. Rory wasn't a passive individual, yet she was waiting for him to—what?

Chet understood. *They think I have the Raptus! They're waiting for me to issue orders.* No wonder they were frightened.

"Pardon me, ladies. I think we have a problem, and I'd prefer to speak more openly. With that in mind, I'll take the first step toward trust."

He slowly took off his knapsack, aware that they were inching back in their chairs, their eyes hard. Rory had her hand wrapped around the bracelet on her wrist. Was it something that could help protect against the Raptus's influence? *Hmm.* As carefully as he knew how, Chet unzipped and emptied the knapsack onto the table. Three pairs of men's underwear. One paperback novel (historically accurate, Quor had assured him.) One doedicu-and-processed-cheese sandwich with sliced radishes, just the way Chet liked it, wrapped in wax paper and sealed by masking tape. One map of the city-state of Allistair, and a bag of nuts and dried fruit.

The women seemed to relax as each item appeared. Chet shook out the empty knapsack. "There. I'm not here to assault your minds and remove your free will. I'm here to talk."

"So it seems," Clementina murmured.

Chet decided to start with her. He repacked the knapsack and folded his hands together, feeling like a character in a spy novel. "Who are you really, Professor? Who are your people? Why have you been trailing us, and what do you want with the Raptus?"

"You would not understand."

"Try me." Chet spread his hands. "What do you have to lose? Notice I'm not strangling *you* for the information."

She glared at him. "I have a great deal to lose!"

Rory put a restraining hand on her arm. "Professor, please. I think Chet has a right to know."

*How long has Rory known – what?* Was Clementina another Steve, a secret Rory had kept from him? Clementina sighed, a long and theatrical venting of wind. "This is confidential information. Not for the ears of the university administration, Chet Baikson!"

"Mmm." He wasn't making any promises, not with this enemy turned enigma. Then something clicked in his mind. It was exactly like a riddle: who on Uos moved in groups like affiliates yet reviled all gods? "You're an atheist, aren't you, Professor Clementina?"

Clementina gaped. He'd never seen her at a loss for words; she looked rather like a fish. She snapped her mouth shut. "Yes, my husband's family and I are atheists."

"Your family is using its money to fight the Pantheon?" It seemed a safe bet: Clementina's wealth, gained through her husband, was common knowledge at Semaphore University.

She regarded him with a frown. "Of course. Unaffiliated people are the vast majority upon Uos – over eighty percent of the population is not committed to a god – yet we are treated as second-class citizens. Evil affiliates must make room for us! We *must* be heard."

While he agreed with her statistics and general thrust, he wasn't sure about the other parts. Evil affiliates? Chet glanced at Rory and raised an eyebrow. *Nice ally you have here,* he wanted to say. She seemed to get the point anyway; she rubbed her face and looked tired, her shoulders slumped.

Chet turned back to Clementina. "You work with god affiliates all day, both among your colleagues and students. Why did you choose to teach at a Literati University when you hold these political views? You can't get tenure at Semaphore anyway."

"There are more important things in life than tenure." Her mouth snapped shut as if she hadn't intended to say anything regarding her true purpose.

Chet, however, could make an educated guess. "You're a spy for your people. Your family wants to know what's going on in the world of Literati."

Rory shot him an expression of pleased surprise. "Hanging around Flame has made you smarter, Chet."

He didn't like her condescending tone. "Oh, by the way, Rory, I ran into our mutual friend Steve the other day. *She* told me how loving and caring you've been to *her* lately. I'm impressed at your thoughtfulness. There's nothing like a well-kept secret between friends, is there?"

Rory folded her arms, looking disgruntled. "Oak told me not to say anything. You wouldn't have taken the news well."

"Thank you for your vote of confidence." He glanced back at Clementina. "So, back on the subject of espionage, how did you know the Raptus was going to be found at the Lucid Mud Dig Site?"

"Of *course* I knew. I know everything there is to know about the Tache royal family."

Chet grunted. "That's right, you're a fan of Emperor Konstantine."

This time her glare was especially withering. "I am *the* world expert on Konstantine. I've read every scroll, every little reference I could find, even traversing underground tombs in Allistair to discover evidence long buried. Konstantine wrote in secret about sending two courtiers to fetch the Raptus, and one disappeared in Wetshul. I followed up, utilized my own resources to figure out where the courtier had lost it."

Chet caught his breath. "Did he have special orders for Fenimore LaDaven, the courtier who disappeared in Wetshul?"

"How did you know that name?"

"You know Fenimore, Professor. You fought him on the passenger ship in Plainsdaugheau. He nearly stabbed you with a three-hundred year old hunting blade."

Her eyes went wide. "Oh. My. Well, that answers my main questions. I hadn't realized the Lucid-Mud Man was Fenimore LaDaven. No one told me," she growled, glaring accusingly at Rory.

"You didn't ask. I don't routinely give away information."

Chet couldn't help but smile dourly. Now that he'd been around Knife a while, Rory's way of doing things made much more sense. He had so many questions for her, but Chet turned back to Clementina.

"*Did* Konstantine write of why he'd sent Fenimore in the first place?"

She blinked, apparently taken back. "Not that I found. He wrote that one of the courtiers, whom he called Uncle Flame—I've never been sure if he referred to a real Flame or a perverted relative *like* a Flame—was suited to find the Raptus due to cunning and knowledge. He mentioned in passing that the other courtier, LaDaven, had made a study of the Raptus. Which I was uncertain how to interpret, since Fenimore LaDaven was a well known satirist and libertine who'd been sent to a famous gaol several times due to a variety of transgressions."

"Ah." Chet sighed, ignoring the crying baby at the next table. Konstantine hadn't known then. It was a point lost to history. "Do continue, Professor."

"After purchasing the site, I hosted you little diums in my house to keep it well contained. My family is certain that we do not want the Raptus in the hands of god affiliates. Even Professor Tibbets would not have made a good guardian. He was too old and would have had a hard time defending it."

"What would your people have done with the Raptus if you had it?"

"Our plan had been to bury it under the mountains in a place only we know about. We would have kept it buried. A sacred trust for our grandchildren's grandchildren. We do not otherwise have god gifts to otherwise contain such an object." She glanced at Rory, who smiled benignly, then back to Chet. "Do you even know what it does, Baikson? Do you know what you've been harboring?"

"At this point, I know with my entire body and soul, which was not a fun ex—" Chet paused as the overhead sputtered to life, announcing that his flight was going to be board in ten minutes. *At last!* he thought irritably. Rory and Clementina, also alert, started gathering their carry-on bags. They were on the same flight after all.

Chet repressed a grin."I suggest we resume this conversation at the boarding gate."

As they were walking, Rory looked him over; she seemed to be gauging him. Chet wondered whether she noticed how tired he still was, post fever. "Chet, I am actually glad to see you."

"Are you?" Though she was a breath of home in this strange city-state, he felt decidedly grumpy about the way she'd frightened him back in Wetshul. She'd had no right to turn invisible and run through his body like that. That was just *rude.*

"Do you think I wish ill upon you?"

"Honestly, I don't know what to think." Chet studied her right back. She wore neutral taupes and white in the manner of an Eich Che independent citizen, which she was. The style looked good on her. "Where *is* your Cluster, anyway? I thought they were supposed to tail us."

"They're elsewhere," she said evasively. He shot her a dirty look which she readily ignored. They reached the gate before she spoke, this time to Clementina. "I believe we all want to sit together, Professor. Do you mind negotiating with the airline staff?"

"Not at all,"

Chet refused to be distracted as Clementina trod off. "Your Cluster lost us, didn't they. When?"

"During the uproar at Semaphore. When... when Professor Tibbets..."

"I know." He offered his hand, and she gripped it tightly. They stood a moment in silence.

"Chet, I really am impressed with you. I thought you were a..." Rory paused, shamefaced.

"What, that I was an unaffiliated idiot with my head stuck up my ass? It's true. Rory, I was stupid as Abyss and twice as blind. Now I'm playing catch-up and the stakes are astronomically high. I've lost Tibbets, I lost Aureate, now I might lose... well."

"Who's Aureate?"

He ignored the question; she'd learn soon enough. "When we were at the dig site, you knew about the Raptus, didn't you? You were stationed there by your Cluster to watch over it, right?"

"Of course Rory knew. She took my class on Konstantine, smart girl that she is," Professor Clementina said, straightening her cuffs as she came to a halt beside them. "I cover the Raptus in the third week."

Chet's mouth dropped open. "You're *kidding*."

Rory grinned at him. "Don't look so surprised. My people knew about the Raptus well in advance of the good professor's course. We figured even if Clementina's people got hold of it first, we could track them into the mountains." The women traded ironic looks.

"Huh. So the dig really *was* an arms race."

"Oh, yes."

Airline officials threw open the outside doors, and a cool breeze traveled through the terminal as the line moved forward. Chet could see the plane as they stepped onto the tarmac.

"Chet?" Rory said as they reached the rollaway staircase.

"Yeah?" He held his breath, hoping she'd say how much she missed him. How much she wanted him.

"Back in the terminal, you'd said you knew what the Raptus did with your whole body and soul. When did you learn this information, and who used it on you?"

He exhaled, feeling crumpled. Rory was right, though, it was his turn. In lowered tones, he explained what had happened after Semaphore while they boarded the plane and settled into their seats. Chet found that he *couldn't* describe Aureate's death with Clementina sitting in the aisle seat with only Rory sitting between them.

Clementina seemed to twig to his reluctance. "Of course we decided to raid your little ship. You were traveling with Flame, Chet Baikson. Wholly unfit to be guardians of such a stupendous magical item."

Chet felt as if his body had turned to ice—he was numb all over—and his hands curled into fists. "There was no need to assault us like that."

Her eyes were cold. "I'll have you know one of your friends killed my nephew in the galley. He didn't survive the explosion."

"*You* people struck first." Chet glared at Clementina. Though he was fairly certain of the answer, he had to eliminate his final variable. "Aureate was just pissing over the balcony. She was no threat to you."

"Who?" Clementina squinted as if squeezing her memory. "I do seem to recall some kind of accusation when we were yelling at one another over the railing, but I honestly don't know what it was."

Rory waved her hands as if trying to clear the air between them. "Chet, instead of being so cryptic and passive aggressive, it might help to simply say what you are accusing Clementina and her people of doing."

"Fine advice from a spy." Chet realized his arms were crossed over his chest. "The fact is, Professor, you had the opportunity, method and motivation to murder Aureate. My... my friend. She was pushed into the water just as you were boarding. I tried to save her, but..." He looked away.

"I did no such thing. Nor, to my knowledge, did any of my people." Clementina shrugged, unconcerned. It was clear the death of a Flame was of no interest to her. She certainly seemed to lack the passion of cold-blooded killing.

"Do you also deny murdering Professor Tibbets?"

This time Clementina looked deeply affronted. "You think I killed Veyaon? I did no such thing! You must believe me. Veyaon was harmless—even for a Literati—and he was one of my favorite colleagues. Chet Baikson, you are a horrible person to believe I could ever harm him!"

Her reaction seemed genuine. "Sorry, Professor."

She harrumphed and settled back into her seat, still scowling.

Rory looked back and forth between them, apparently amused. "Now that we have that all straightened around, I believe we can focus on the most important subject: defending ourselves against the Raptus and taking it back. My Cluster is ready to call Aiena as soon as we have it secured. We have this time to plan, and I *suggest* we use it well. As we're about to face off against a mind-altering magical relic designed to rule the world, we need all the brainpower we can get."

Chet shot her a pointed smile and gestured at her bracelet.

"Sounds good. I can't wait to learn about your secret defense against the Raptus."

Rory gave him an unsettled look, and he couldn't help but feel vindicated. She may be a spy who'd been pursuing a magical relic and tracking atheists the whole time they'd been dating, but he was up to speed now. He was asking the right questions, which might very well lead to the correct responses. Hopefully.

# Chapter 26
# Into the Breach

Chet's mouth was dry as he hammered the knocker on Knife's front door. The house was in a shady, well-established neighborhood of the city-state of Allistair, surrounded by ornate residences at least a few centuries old. Knife's house, too, appeared to be well aged: tall and thin like its owner, it had a dingy presence that might be easily overlooked.

There was no answer. Chet glanced over his shoulder at Rory and Clementina. "Maybe they stopped for breakfast at the train station, then went shopping." Nevertheless, he double checked the address on the slip of paper Doyen Quor had given him.

Rory raised her eyebrows. "Feel for the magical cords that bind you together."

What an elegant idea. Why hadn't Chet thought of that? He closed his eyes and concentrated: sure enough, he could feel the bonds. "They—they're close. All three of them. But it's weird, like two of them are muffled, somehow." It was the same feeling, Chet realized, as when Knife and Fenimore had been in the steam tunnels at Semaphore. "The other one is kind of faint. I think that person is upstairs in the house."

"Let's try the backdoor," Clementina said, already heading in that direction.

Chet followed the women. It was a strange sort of commando team they'd formed out of necessity. Rory was convinced she was in charge, and Chet was content to let her believe it. Her Cluster was apparently on the way, though when she had contacted them—and how they would find her—remained a mystery. Then there was Clementina. She'd had them stop the cab from the airport at a small house;

she'd knocked on the door and been admitted, appearing a while later with a long, bulky bag. Clementina had shaken her head when they'd asked what it contained. Back when they'd been making plans on the airplane, she'd volunteered to distract Fenimore while Rory snuck up from behind. Chet could only assume the contents of the bag were part of her strategy.

As for Chet, he was no longer an ordinary guy, but he wasn't exactly special. *He* couldn't turn himself invisible and pass through solid matter. Nor did he have a mysterious bag. What he had was untapped but latent memories—buried under many lifetimes—of how magic really worked, and the determination to overcome Fenimore. For whatever it was worth.

At least he now matched the others: he wore the same type of bracelet, too. It looked like a feminine accessory, but according to Rory, the bracelets had been created by Shadow Dancers specifically to withstand the mind-altering influence of the Raptus. Chet felt far more secure with the band upon his wrist.

"Look," Clementina hissed as they made their way through the garden gate. The backdoor was hanging open.

"I should reconnoiter," Rory said, mouth set at a determined angle. Chet could see her outline thinning even as he watched.

"Wait, I don't think the person upstairs is Fenimore," he said swiftly before she turned invisible altogether. "In fact... the other two seem to be headed away from us in that direction." He pointed away from the house. "But the one in the house isn't moving at all. The bond feels... fluttery."

"Like the person is injured?"

"I don't know." Chet stared up at the house, wishing he could see through walls. "We go together or not at all."

Someone had made a mess in the back hallway. There was an overturned chair, crooked paintings and a smashed glass vase with silk flowers scattered on the floor. There were also puddles of water underfoot. *That can't have come from the vase,* Chet thought.

After a quick survey of the first floor—which seemed untouched, apart from the chaos on the stairs—they made their way to the second landing. The women followed Chet's lead, while Chet followed the tugging of the magical bond. The house was quiet despite the wreckage. Anuros were peeping outside the windows and someone was raking leaves next door. A faucet was on in the second-story bathroom, gushing water. Chet shut it off, frowning. There was water on the floor here, too. *Why does a Flame need a water tap in the first place?* he wondered absently. A propane torch had been installed in a homemade fix above the toilet; perhaps the sink was just for visitors.

Rory poked into the two rooms on the opposite side of the hall, and shook her head. Clementina looked uncomfortable but alert, jumping at the slightest sounds. Her hand rested inside her bag—there had to be a weapon, or weapons, inside. Heart racing, Chet led the way upstairs to the third floor. A noise stopped him on the landing. It sounded like... heavy breathing? It came from an open doorway off the hall. Chet looked inside.

He froze.

The room was furnished as a study: an enormous wooden desk, filing cabinets and an open safe in the corner. A familiar figure sat in a chair, clutching at his stomach. Knife's hands and button-down shirt were covered with blood. Gore also soaked his trousers and the upholstery of the chair he sat in. The priceless antique carpet, too.

He opened his eyes and focused on Chet. "Abyss, but I wish... you'd gotten here sooner," he rasped. His breathing sounded bubbly as if there was blood in his lungs.

Chet rushed to his side. Why hadn't he asked Doyen Quor to come? She would have known what to do! "Knife, do you have a first-aid kit in the house? Should we call an ambulance? Or, um, light a fire or something?"

Knife simply sat. Chet noticed he had a modern rotary phone on his desk, and none of the cords had been cut. "Fen found a way... around Aiena's safety measures," Knife said, each word labored. "He's better than I anticipated. He must have... gained ascendency while we were mourning Aureate. I was ordered to sit here... until time ran out."

How *cruel*. Fenimore could have slit his throat, but he hadn't. Instead, he'd cut Knife's belly open and—by the sound of it—nicked a lung in the process. Chet looked around and saw Knife's gun on the floor across the room, as if someone had kicked it there. He wondered whether Knife had gotten a shot off first, or if Journey...

"Journey," Chet said urgently. "What about Journey?"

"He has Journey. Journey fought. Still fighting, I assume. Hope. Fenimore was subtle until... last minute. Don't think he has... a full hold on her. She hasn't said her piece yet," Knife's eyes flickered behind Chet, and his lip twitched upward. "Meeting old friends, I see. Shadow Dancers... are finally coming, eh? Good."

"Knife, we need to get you to a hospital," Rory said from behind Chet.

"Too late." Knife coughed up blood. It ran down his chin, soaking his shirt. "*Abyss.*"

Chet sat back on his heels. "You will live again," he said, his voice distant in his own ears as if he were reciting an ancient poem he didn't quite understand.

The statement seemed out-of-place, inappropriate given the context. Yet Knife grinned, blood staining his teeth. "That's exactly right. Chet... go underground. Underground!"

That made sense, given what he'd been feeling from the magical bond. "How do we get there, Knife? Where's the entrance?"

Knife's gaze focused inward. His hand on Chet's arm slumped and went limp. Chet waited for the next bubbling breath, but it didn't come. Knife grew still, a subtle but palpable process. An odd noise emerged from him. Chet wondered whether it was some sort of Flame thing—the holy hand of Pelin?—then realized what it had to be. A death rattle.

Chet stood. "Shit," he said in a detached, oddly calm voice. His shirt was bloody where Knife had grabbed him.

Rory stepped forward and closed Knife's eyes, her attitude respectful, even reverent. "Now we know why the other bonds were muffled. Underground indeed. Must be sewage tunnels under the city-state."

"Let's go," Clementina said from the doorway.

Viewed in the context of Knife's words, the mess on the stairwell was actually comforting. Journey had fought Fenimore. The fog hadn't taken her completely, so Fenimore had used water to distract and secure her. But why not just stay in the bathroom where he could torture her to his heart's content? Even if Fenimore had felt Chet coming through the magical bond, he wouldn't have been afraid of Chet.

He'd already dominated Chet into a fugue state.

Which meant that Fenimore was acting on a plan of some sort. And that, Chet decided, was a far less comforting thought.

The women were already fanning out across the back garden. It was a surprisingly large plot for a city-state: at least three acres, Chet estimated. The garden was overgrown, almost a wilderness of vines and shrubs at points, though someone had been keeping the grass trimmed and the grounds clear of fallen branches.

"Which way?" Rory asked.

Chet pointed, then realized he was pointing in the general direction of a shed. It was in the most sheltered, overgrown region of the garden. Inside the shed were the usual shelves with garden tools, but there was also an open trapdoor. A spiral staircase led down into darkness. There were several flashlights lined up on the shed shelves alongside other tools, batteries sitting beside them in neat rows. Knife had clearly used this underground... sewage pipe? Cave? The Abyss itself?

Rory handed flashlights to Chet and Clementina but didn't take one for herself. "Chet, how far away are they?"

"Maybe three hundred yards."

"Are they still moving?"

"No... well, I'm not sure. One of the bonds feels weak." What was Fenimore doing to Journey?

"It's time I got out of sight," Rory said.

Chet watched as Rory grew invisible, but Clementina did not. She knelt and pulled items out of her bag, two pistols with belt sheaths, and a hefty rifle which she assembled and strapped to her chest. Next came a string of—those weren't grenades, were they?

"Professor, I trust you're not going to set off explosives in a closed space. Please?"

"They're flash bangs. In terms of being an explosive, they're about as strong as cherry bombs, mostly designed to distract and disarm. Shouldn't trigger a cave in or anything."

"You do realize we're just going after one guy." Chet felt nervous at the sight of so many firearms.

"One man, yes, but also a powerful relic with shielding properties. Have you not researched the very treasure we are up against,

Baikson? The Raptus isn't just a mind-control device. When it is either fully or nearly unlocked, it's designed to defend itself—and its owner—from physical assault."

*Oh, yeah.* Hadn't Journey said something about shielding powers back in the prostitute's van in Wetshul? "I hope you won't shoot me by accident."

"LaDaven caught me unprepared before," she said grimly. "He will not do so again. I believe it's my turn to... what's the newfangled phrase? Kick his behind?"

"His ass," a disembodied voice said just beside Chet. He jumped before he realized it was Rory.

"This is so strange." He tried to touch the air in front of him. He didn't feel anything. Not even a crackle of energy like he'd felt back in Wetshul.

He heard a chuckle. "You're cute when you're spooked," she said in his ear. "I'll go first and you trail behind me, okay?"

Chet waited the obligatory moment before starting down the stairs. Luckily, he wasn't claustrophobic. Clementina followed behind, bristling with weaponry. The staircase spiraled downward for a long time. Chet shone his flashlight around; there were natural rock formations on all sides. The place didn't look like it had been drilled by human hands.

"I wonder how LaDaven knew this was here?" said Rory's disembodied voice.

"Maybe Knife managed to hold onto this property a long time. Over several lifetimes, say?" All the furnishings and pictures in the house had been old, Chet realized. The only evidence of progress in the last eighty years had been plumbing, the telephone and electricity. Plus there was the surprising amount of land that came with the house. Journey would know for certain.

The stairs ended in a tunnel. It was lined with locked wooden drawers, built directly into the walls. It looked as if Knife were in the process of installing electricity: there were industrial rods and cords piled to one side of the tunnel. A folding table held a brand-new circuit box and a series of wrenches, tri-squares and nut drivers. A long-term project, Chet suspected.

An arched door gaped open at the end of the hall. By all signs, the old-fashioned door had been recently kicked in. The floor began winding downwards, broadening and curving. There were square nooks carved into the walls. Tombs. Chet caught his breath. Skeletal remains lay within the nooks, whole and carefully laid out, their hands folded neatly over their chests. Knife hadn't touched them, it seemed.

Chet paused beside one, curious despite their hurry—the archeologist part of him couldn't help it. The consistency of the arrangements was troubling, especially since there was a decided lack of identity markers. Despite this, the bones had been laid out in careful, ritualistic manner. There were no visible artifacts left for the dead soul; no metal items, ceramics or stone markers that might yield clues as to the person's station in life. Had the bones belonged to peasants? They didn't show signs of having been malnourished in life, nor were there the usual markers of poverty. No pitting, no missing or ground-down teeth. All the skeletons were faintly purple in color, but that was probably just a trick of the light.

"I wonder... I wonder if these are Knife's bodies," Rory's voice whispered in his ear. "Not people she's killed, but her own bodies. From past lives."

Chet jerked back from a skeleton he'd been studying. "No!" he said, barely remembering to keep his voice down. "Knife couldn't—she wouldn't. Would she?" It seemed obscene. *Would* she have kept her own bodies, preserved under her property? *Ew.* He started down the tunnel again, his eyes directly forward.

He blinked. There was a light ahead: it seemed to be an indistinct, ambient light, not a flashlight or even electrical. He crept closer, turning off his flashlight, Clementina following suit beside him. Chet heard noise, a bubbling, churning sound. The light grew brighter, and the wall of the tunnel opened abruptly on one side. They stopped, clinging instinctively to the edge, poking their heads out just a little to see what lay beyond. There was an enormous body of... not water. *Lucid mud,* Chet realized, gaping. The ambient light seemed to emerge from the lucid mud itself.

What had Journey said, back at the dig site? "There's still an active system beneath Allistair, you know. Quite the churning river of lucid mud."

A lone figure stood beside the river of mud, reeling in a length of rope. It was Fenimore. The Raptus wasn't visible, though he did have the duffle bag slung over his shoulder. Was he fishing in the lucid mud? Something was being pulled in at the other end of the rope. A hand... an arm. It was Journey! Chet gasped, then touched his mouth, hoping Fenimore hadn't heard him. She—her tits were vivid through her muddy shirt—was breathing heavily, eyes closed as Fen reeled her in.

Fenimore knelt beside her. "You ready to sing your little song, Journey?"

"Never." Though her voice was low, Chet could hear her clearly through the churning of the river.

"Then back you go. Crawl into the mud; you have my permission to hold onto the rope again. *This* time. Though I might just grow weary of holding it myself."

"Then... you'll never unlock... the Raptus."

"Mmm. You're growing weak, Journey. I think next time you surface, I'll dance a jig with your diddly pout. You should still have enough energy to shape your ass to suit me, but not enough to be tiresome. I grow weary of being rejected by you."

"Abyss... to that."

She was crying, Chet saw, as she crawled backwards into the roiling mud. Journey was under the thrall of the Raptus, or very nearly under its thrall. How long was Fenimore planning to keep this up? Hours? Days? Journey couldn't hold out forever, especially if Fenimore raped and abused her. Chet watched as she vanished beneath the surface. Hadn't Journey said sleeping in lucid mud would be a horrible fate? Fenimore clearly remembered, too. He must have taken note of her words, patiently mapping out her fate even as they walked to Othnielia's farm.

*Asshole,* Chet thought fiercely.

"Professor, you go first and distract him just like we planned," Rory's voice whispered. "Chet, you're in charge of rescuing Journey."

"Right."

They hadn't known in advance what kind of situation they might face, but Chet had been clear that if Fenimore took Flame hostages, he should be the one to save them. Rory was focused entirely on the Raptus, and Clementina just didn't care. Chet wasn't a fighter, and he had no knowledge of weaponry, but he could help Journey.

"I'll get him from behind, Professor after you stop shooting," Rory continued. "The bullets won't matter while I'm invisible, but I don't want to get shot once I'm corporeal again."

"Certainly." Clementina unslung her rifle. "I'm going in."

Chet wanted to call her back. He wasn't ready! He didn't feel up to facing Fenimore, even with Journey in danger. Chet realized it was because Fen had been dominating him all week. His strength of will was stupendous, exponentially more powerful than anything Chet could summon. The protective bracelet around his wrist seemed thin, flimsy, barely anything at all, but Clementina was already striding out to into the cavern.

She didn't waste words. Clementina simply began shooting with the rifle. Chet crammed his fingers into his ringing ears, shocked at her lack of honor and chivalry. Except she was right: a pure frontal assault was more practical than warning her foe in advance. Fenimore wasn't a moving target, though. He stood, looking smug, as Clementina fired shot after shot. Chet could even see the streaks of light as bullets rebounded off the... yes, that had to be the infamous shield.

Fenimore faked a yawn, patting his mouth. "You seem familiar, madam. Have we met? Ah, yes. The frumpy strumpet from the ship."

Chet watched the rope from the tunnel, holding fast as bullets flew. The end of the rope disappeared in the middle of the muddy torrent. How could Journey breathe in there? *Lucid mud,* he thought grimly, *is a preservative.* Journey didn't need to breathe. She would hold onto the rope because she'd been ordered to by the Raptus's master. Fenimore had *definitely* planned this.

"You can't keep it up forever," Clementina growled through gritted teeth, loosening three more rounds in quick succession. "The Raptus was created thousands of years before bullets."

Fen touched the duffle bag at his side. "Abandon this arsenal and walk into the lucid mud, madam."

"I don't think so, LaDaven." Clementina threw down her rifle and unslung her pistols.

The rope wasn't fairing well under this new barrage—it unraveled as bullets grazed it. The fibers parted and Fenimore was left holding a short, slack rope as the other end slithered along the bank, headed downstream.

Swearing, Chet broke from the safety of the tunnel and ran for the trailing end of the rope. His pace turned into an all-out sprint as the rope slid into the mud. He dove and caught it, spattering mud down his front in the process. Chet began reeling in the rope hand over hand. It was hard. The current was something fierce.

The gunshots had ceased, at least. Behind him, he heard the unmistakable sounds of a struggle, and he looked over his shoulder to see Fenimore fighting with a half-visible Rory. She had him in a headlock, her legs wrapped around his torso. Why hadn't she grabbed the bag as planned? Fenimore must have prevented it while Chet was pursuing the rope. Fen was cursing—maybe from the electric-like shocks in her half visible state—and had his knife out. He was trying to stab Rory without injuring himself.

Clementina advanced grimly while sheathing her handguns. She attempted to grab at his knife-wielding hand. The women were calling directions to one another, trying to work in concert.

It was almost over, Chet reassured himself as he pulled the straining rope.

Moments later there was a wild yell. He glanced back in time to see Fenimore bowing in a fight move, effectively flipping Rory into Clementina like bowling pins. He grabbed at Clementina's bracelet and *twisted*. She cried out in pain as it parted from her wrist.

Fen threw the bracelet away; it clanged as it hit a rock wall. "Fling yourself into the lucid mud, woman, fast as you can. Now, where did your Shadow Dancer friend go?"

Rory had grown invisible again, effectively disentangling herself from the scene. With nothing to impede her, Clementina turned and raced toward the lucid mud. She splashed through the shallows, then belly flopped into the churning river. Not even bubbles marked her passing. Clementina was gone.

Chet swallowed. Clementina was the first to go, but was she the last?

# Chapter 27
# Loopholes

Chet needed to get Journey out *now* so he could help Rory. Since Fenimore had figured out the bracelets, it was only a matter of time before Rory would go the same way Clementina had. At least his efforts were panning out: he could see Journey's hand as it surfaced, still clinging to the rope. He pulled harder, bracing himself.

"Chet," Fenimore called. "What are you doing? Saving Journey? What a *romantic* gesture, cream puff."

"Shut up, Fen."

"By all means, oblige me and keep my meat fresh while I figure out where your little friend has—"

Fenimore yelped as Rory engaged him again. Rory was up against Fen on her own. She needed his help! Journey was close enough that Chet thought he could—yes. He grabbed hold of her be-slimed clothing and pulled her in. She coughed and wheezed, her eyes closed. Frantic, Chet abandoned her and raced up the tunnel to where Fenimore and Rory were grappling.

Rory could *fight*. Chet could see she was far better than himself—no surprise considering he was a scholar above all—but she was also better than Fenimore. He had his knife, while all she had were her hands and feet, yet she used them well. Plus she kept turning translucent when he got close enough with the blade.

Chet hovered at the edge of their battle, uncertain how to be of assistance. His toe hit something—one of Clementina's flash bangs. He bent to pick it up... there was a blow to his face, then another on back of his neck. Chet collapsed, gasping. Fear flooded his body as he was lifted by the hair. Fenimore's blade was cold at his throat. Something was dripping from his nose—blood? He didn't know what Rory was doing, but she certainly wasn't attacking. Fen had traded one hostage for another.

Would Fen keep him as a hostage, though? The answer was immediate; Fenimore reached over and plucked the bracelet from his wrist. "There. Chet, walk into the lucid mud and let it take you."

"Don't do it, Chet!" It was Rory's voice. She'd turned invisible again.

Mind-clouding fog descended, a very familiar feeling. Chet regained his feet and began making for the mud river. He could move slower than Clementina—Fenimore hadn't specified a speed—though he echoed her course with the same results to come. Abyss, his face hurt, his nose bleeding freely. Would the pain still be with him when he woke from lucid mud?

Behind him, he could hear Fenimore yelling to Journey, ordering her to return at once. Somewhere in the back of his mind Chet had hoped that Journey had made her way out. Given Fen's exasperation, she may have been running the other way, farther down the cave. It might have worked if Fenimore hadn't had the Raptus.

The Raptus. The very thing that was about to deposit him in lucid mud. His feet had almost reached the bank. Chet was about to be preserved for decades... centuries... millennia... a curiosity for future generations. Canned archeologist.

There was something was in his hand. The flash bang, he realized, gazing down at it. A corner of his mouth turned up. Fenimore had only told him to walk into the mud, but he hadn't issued any other orders. Such as, "Don't fight me," perhaps? The trick with magic, Chet remembered, was *loopholes*.

Chet turned to face Fenimore, his feet still walking backwards into the mud, now up to his ankles. Fenimore was holding onto the duffle bag with both hands, gazing about with an alert expression, a livid mark on his cheek. Rory had marked him up, and still might, Chet realized. She was loose in the cave, awaiting her chance. Journey was slowly striding through the cavern, too, headed toward Fenimore, her expression grim. He wished there was some way to warn her in advance. *Ah, well.*

"Hey, Rory," Chet called out. "Now."

He pulled the pin and tossed the flash bang to Fenimore's right. Fen followed the movement, his expression quizzical. "Hah. Chet, you doedicu, you miss—"

An unbearable sound filled the cavern, accompanied by the brightest flash Chet had ever seen. He threw up his arms to protect himself, then lowered them, blinking to clear his vision. He couldn't hear anything except ringing in his ears. When Chet's eyes were working again, he saw both Rory and Journey were fighting Fenimore. A desperate, knock-down struggle.

Even as Chet watched, he realized the mud was well above his knees, almost to his hips. It was churning, the undertow fantastic. The fog still upon him, and Chet knew he would surrender to it. He had to let the river take him.

A triumphant cry resonated through the cavern, breaking through the ringing in Chet's ears. Rory held the bag in her hands, leaping away from the fray. Fenimore socked Journey—her head snapped back as she collapsed—and threw his knife, stabbing Rory in the back.

She gasped, her face ashen. Chet cried out her name, his hands flung out, helpless as she fell...

He lost his feet. The lucid-mud river swept him away.

The sensation of lucid mud was astonishing. Chet was pulled under. He had a single lungful of air. He'd let the lucid mud take him, as ordered, but he didn't have to breathe out yet. Loopholes, loopholes.

Unbidden, a verse filled his brain:

"Will, I hail thee<br>
Lend me the strength<br>
To see this twisted bough into a house..."

It was the same stanza that had saved him in the ocean after dumping Aureate's body. Chet scrunched his face at the memory. Who had written the line? It hardly mattered. There was no fighting the urge to sleep. His last breath had been a futile gesture. The mud had him securely in its swirling grasp; he didn't even know which was way up.

"Yea, lend me the strength
To throw open gates to the lost city of El
Rendering god barrier to splinters of light..."

The Magician Zang had written it. *No,* he thought wildly, grasping the truth as if it were a slippery fish in his hands. I *wrote it.* He was the right Magician after all. With his last ounce of strength, he mumbled into the mud,

"Will, I hail thee
Lend me the strength
To rise through the lucid mud
And breathe fresh air once more."

Chet's feet kicked of their own volition. He had nothing left in his lungs. He blindly trusted the imperfect, fragile sense of gravity within his head, heading *up.* Breaking through the surface of the churning river, Chet gasped air.

The others were nowhere in sight. Chet must have been moving down the lucid-mud river with the current. The shoreline was relatively close, and it looked like the same cave. The mud wasn't nearly as turbulent here; he could swim if it let him. If it didn't hold him back. The mud was all around him, sucking him down with surprisingly strength.

"Will, I hail thee
Lend me the strength
To swim to shore
And cease the bloodshed
Of the Raptus upon Mother Earth."

He swam. As he did so, he considered the situation. Chet found solid, if muddy, ground and sloshed out of the river. He took measure of himself: he was slathered in mud, just like Journey. Blood still dripped down his face. Despite this, he felt remarkably in control. Aureate had complained that she didn't want to kill someone to figure out what made the Raptus tick, but Chet—the Magician Zang—didn't need to kill anyone. He already knew everything he needed to know to defeat Fenimore. This little bit of blood would be enough for what he had in mind. Chet smiled and began walking back upriver.

Chet could hear them long before he could see them. Grunting, repetitive sounds that made his groin tighten even before his brain realized what was going on. Chet peeked around the corner, heart contracting.

Rory was crumpled off to one side. He couldn't tell whether she was breathing, but he could see blood on her fawn-colored jacket. The knife was gone, though, probably back in Fen's sheath. Fenimore had his back turned to Chet, pants around his ankles. He was lying directly atop a muddy figure that had to be Journey. Her legs were parted and Fen was... Chet licked his muddy lips, tasting dirt and iron-heavy minerals. His cock was visible as he pumped, and Chet could see every detail at this angle. Journey was making little noises as Fenimore slapped her tits with his free hand. He reached up and slapped her face, then his hand slipped around her neck. Journey grew abruptly silent.

"That's right, doxy, I can strangle you while my dick takes you for all you're worth."

Chet couldn't see his face from his vantage point, but he could hear Fen's grin. It was the tone of a predator thoroughly enjoying his prey. Chet closed his eyes, nauseous. Fenimore was certainly a man of his word. Chet *knew* Fenimore was the Magician Tene, and the knowledge didn't make anything better. Just different.

All his life, Chet had thought that if he could only know *why* he felt this way, things would be wonderful. Now he knew, yet he was still covered with mud and blood, two friends dead and another being raped only yards away. There were no miraculous turnabouts here. Not without direct intervention anyway.

Well, if direct intervention was what was needed, Chet would make it happen.

Chet strode forward, angling his approach so Fenimore couldn't see him. Fen was again wearing the duffle bag slung on his back, and both of his hands were occupied with Journey. Journey seemed to see Chet, though; just a quick glance before she looked away. Tear marks trailed down her muddy face to her ears, but at least her expression was alert.

It was the easiest thing in the world. Chet unzipped the bag, reached in and drew out the Raptus. He gaped, blinking. The Raptus was glowing green, its doedicu-like spikes shiny like stained glass, the light gently pulsing. Almost completely unlocked.

Chet drew back even as Fenimore muttered, "Hey!" One of his hands patted the bag while he attempted to look over his shoulder.

Journey's legs, which had been flung open in helpless supplication, wrapped around Fen's torso, her feet locking together to secure him. She grabbed his wrists. "Oh, Fen, don't go. Stay here with me."

Chet grinned and set down the Raptus a short distance away, then leaned over Fenimore. "I could fuck you in the ass, you know," he whispered. Though he couldn't bring himself to hump Fenimore and drive home his point, he did nibble on Fen's ear and squeeze a nipple through his shirt.

Distraction, misdirection. Fenimore twisted to look him in the face even as Chet slipped the curved blade out of Fen's sheath and retreated, taking the knife with him. It joined the Raptus on the ground. Chet had no need of the blade, just as he didn't require the Raptus. He never had.

"Chet!" Fenimore said. "But—but I ordered—oh, Pantheon. I could have sworn you didn't know..."

"I can't hold him long, Chet," Journey called out, her voice ragged.

"Don't let go, yet. Can you get him on his back?"

Journey grunted as she rolled, taking Fenimore down while simultaneously straddling him. She pinned his arms at his sides with her knees, apparently squeezing hard. "Whatever you're going to do, do it quick," she said. Fenimore was struggling, helplessly encompassed.

Chet settled at Fenimore's head so he was looking at Fen upside down. There was just enough congealing blood left from his nose to make this work, but it didn't take much, really. Just a dab or two.

Fenimore flinched as Chet wrote ancient letters upon his forehead in blood. "What are you doing?" he whispered, eyes wide. Fenimore looked like a child now. He'd always been so deceptive that way.

"Fenimore LaDaven, I lay a geas upon you, binding you by every name you have ever known. You are restricted from touching or using the Raptus from this time forward. To you, the Raptus is a locked door without key or keyhole. Any usage will mean the instant death of this body or any future body reincarnation might bring you. In laying this geas upon you, I bind myself to your soul again, as, indeed, we already seem to be bound." Chet cleared his throat and admonished himself to focus. "In addition to the Raptus, you are henceforth restricted from holding or using weapons of any sort for the duration of this lifetime. This includes any object that you might use with the intent of inflicting physical harm upon another living being. Again, the usage or even the touch of a weapon will mean your instant death. This geas is binding from now until the end of Uos." Chet cleared his throat and sang the correct hymn in the ancient Eicha language used by Magicians. He was off key and his voice wavered, but it was still binding. At least he remembered the words. His memory had always been good for things like that.

"Wow, Chet," Journey murmured, staring.

"You can let him up." Chet sighed and sat back. Now that Fenimore was no longer a threat, Chet turned to Rory—except she wasn't there. The body was gone.

*What?* Was Rory still alive? Had she turned invisible, choosing to die in non-corporeal form?

Fenimore threw Journey off, and she shuddered as she rose. Chet helped her as best he could, a supportive hand under her arm. She stumbled away a few feet and vomited onto the cave floor.

Still bent over, she mumbled, "Chet, find my pants. He tore my underwear in half, but my pants should be fine."

As Chet searched for mud-slathered fabric on the cave floor, Fenimore regarded him closely. "You think you're clever, don't you?" Chet expected him to look enraged, but Fenimore had his pleasant face on, again.

"I am myself," Chet said shortly, locating Journey's pants.

"You swam out of the lucid mud, yet my orders were to let it take you."

He was trolling for information, meaning—what? Chet didn't trust this apparent mood swing. But Journey, skinning into her pants, gave Chet a puzzled look. "How *did* you do it, Chet?"

"I..." How could he explain?

"Wait, I know. You found a loophole in my command, Zang." Fenimore smiled sunnily.

"How did you know?"

"I've known since we were bound by the Raptus. Why else would it choose a little nothing like you?"

Chet frowned at him. "That makes very little sense. None at all, actually."

Fenimore remained silent. Journey turned to Chet, her expression obstinate as Abyss. "Chet, you know something. You need to tell me what's going on. Please. Knife and Aureate have been murdered along with your professor. And your other friend, that young Shadow Dan—" she turned, apparently to look at Rory, and froze.

"By all the grace and goodness of the Pantheon, where did she go?" Fenimore's pleasant face had slipped into a more anxious expression. His tone sounded oddly frantic.

"What does it matter to you?" Chet scowled at him.

"Shadow Dancers can't become invisible if they're badly injured. At least, not on their own," Journey explained in a low voice. "I don't know why not."

Fenimore was distracted, walking over the spot where Rory's body had been. Heartened by his apparent discord, Chet told Journey about his feverish dreams and his conversation with Doyen Quor, though he skipped the part about the girls. It was his private shame, to be shared later or not at all.

She frowned. "Fenimore called you by a name—Zang. He was one of the more famous Magicians, wasn't he? He wrote a ton of stuff, anyway."

Chet felt his face grow warm. "I *am* Zang. I just didn't know for certain until I was going under in the lucid mud."

"Zang wasn't famous," Fen said over his shoulder. "He was a timid little nothing."

"What's it to you, Fenimore?" Journey said.

"I'm *not* Fenimore LaDaven. I am—"

"The Magician Tene," said Chet and Fenimore at the same time. Chet continued, "No wonder you killed Aureate. You hated her. You always did. But what I don't get is why you killed Professor Tibbets."

Fen shrugged, nonchalant. "It was an accident. I was going around the corner with my knife held outwards from my chest like this," he demonstrated with his bare fist held to his chest, staring at the blade on the ground. "The old man ran into *me*."

Chet met Journey's eye. He didn't know what she was thinking, but to his mind the evidence matched what Fenimore was saying. The murder scene *had* looked reckless and accidental.

Journey turned back to Fen. "But that doesn't explain how you knew Chet was the Magician Zang in his past lives."

"What's the information worth to you?" Fen wandered about the cavern as if aimlessly.

Journey glared at him. "You've murdered my friends, and raped and tortured me. I'm not *negotiating*, especially if you want some kind of clemency from the law."

"Then you can stick your head under a water pump, Flame."

Chet blinked, taken by a new thought. "You knew me back in the ambulance. You said something like, 'Pantheon, it's *you* again.' That's when you started talking to me like a person, not a disposable servant. So it *wasn't* when we were bound by the Raptus."

"So smart, Chet? You can guess forever and still not know the answer," Fenimore said in a sing-song tone. He was standing right beside the Raptus and knife. "Except you don't have forever, do you?"

"Oh, please." Chet rolled his eyes. "That's an empty threat if I've ever heard one. You're not going to touch those things. The geas was no bluff."

Fenimore smiled and picked up the Raptus. He tossed it in the air once and caught it. "A little dicey, sure, but... loopholes, my friend. Loopholes."

Journey's mouth dropped open. "What? How did you—I heard Chet. I *heard* him. He bound you by your name."

"Ah, see, if you're the *inventor* of a powerful relic like the Raptus, you build in layers of personal exemptions. Especially if, say, other Magicians come to you and insist upon locking your creation, lead by none other than Zang himself." Fenimore's smile twisted, growing bitter. "I've been fighting to regain the Raptus too many years, especially against *you*."

Chet drooped. All his hopes were shattered just like that. But he couldn't help protesting, "I helped create the Raptus, too. I shed the blood to make it a reality. All those girls murdered by my hand. And for what? To help you rule the world? Some reward."

Journey gazed at him, her eyes round with horror.

Fen laughed. "Scut work. You were always good at such things, Zang. Now, to business. Journey, you are to pick up my knife and stab Chet in the belly. Stab him ever so slowly, as please you. The geas shouldn't hurt me, as *you* will do the dirty work. I'm going to have you play with him a long time before I allow you to kill him. We're going to measure out his entrails length by length, you and I. Maybe I'll insert various parts of his body into your twat. Then, when you're so sick you'll want to die, we'll see if you'll sing for me. If you don't, I'm sure I can imagine worse things for you to do with his corpse. We can play games for *weeks*."

"Oh, Pantheon. Chet! Chet, do something," Journey cried out as she walked toward the knife.

Chet began backing up, but Fenimore nailed him with a look. "I order you, Magician Zang, by all the names you've ever known, to stand fast. Don't move. Just *stay*."

Chet stood, distraught as Journey picked up the curved blade and approached him one step at a time. He tried to think of a loophole—any loophole. "Um. Will, I hail thee, lend me the strength to..."

"You may not speak a word in your own defense."

"Chet, I can't stop." Journey was nearly within arm's reach, the knife held in her trembling hand.

Chet opened his mouth but couldn't speak. He couldn't move. He couldn't do anything. He had failed and would die for his failure.

# Chapter 28
# Lost Souls

Journey reached him, and Chet held his breath. Journey wasn't fully under the influence of the Raptus. Would she really slide the blade into his abdomen? He'd been threatened repeatedly by this same weapon since Fenimore had woken in the ambulance. Was he to die—gradually—on its edge?

Journey was visibly sweating through the drying mud. She slowly drew back, her eyes closed; Chet could see her shaking from the tension in her body, her clenched teeth. He closed his own eyes, waiting to be impaled.

Noises erupted all around them. Journey yelped, and Chet opened his eyes. They were surrounded by people in long grey robes, hoods covering their faces. One stood so close to Chet they were almost touching, chest to chest. Then he realized the strange person—the Shadow Dancer—was between him and Journey, effectively blocking Fenimore's order.

The person drew back the hood. It was Rory. She smiled at Chet and kissed his cheek.

He touched his face in awe, then he reached over and caressed her, making sure she was real. "B-but you were stabbed in the back. I *saw* it."

She grinned without answer and drew away. Journey had been disarmed by the Shadow Dancers on either side of her. She was slumped over, apparently with abject relief. Fenimore was fenced in by Shadow Dancers. He was yelling—trying to give orders—but no one was listening. Chet would bet everyone had bracelets on under those voluptuous robes. Fenimore was moved swiftly... then he stopped and screamed, disappearing from view.

What had happened? Chet traded looks with Journey and stepped closer, even as the Shadow Dancers around Fenimore drew back. He was lying on the ground, eyes open, staring into nothing. Dead. There was no blood or sign of injury. Some kind of dagger lay in his curled hand, the Raptus in the crook of his other arm.

"He tried to fight and the geas got him. *Finally,*" a Shadow Dancer said, letting down her hood. She looked awfully familiar... Chet blinked as he realized he knew exactly who she was. Rory's mom.

"Zamie, why didn't you appear sooner?" Journey said—or whined, rather. Her tone was one of deep complaint.

Zamie raised an eyebrow. "Hello, Zamie, nice to see you, Zamie," she prompted sarcastically.

"Mom, stop it. They've had a long day," Rory put in.

"But Rory, what are you doing up and about?" Chet asked, feeling like he'd missed a beat. "Even if you're alive, you should be headed for the emergency room!"

Everyone around them snorted. Chet wasn't sure how fifty hooded and robed people could convey sarcasm with body language, but they did.

Journey glared at them, frowning. "Give the guy a break. Look, it isn't *that* well known that you're able to heal in your own space," she said defensively. She turned to him and murmured, "Clusters are walled-off portions of the God Plain. The spaces have healing properties, like fire does for Flame."

"Oh." Chet realized he was hungry, tired and emotionally overdrawn. It was high time to go upstairs and get cleaned up... except there was still a major threat at hand: the Raptus itself. He wasn't the only one gazing at it, either.

"Right," Zamie said. "Well, time to make some decisions. Knife begged us to hold off doing anything about the Raptus until she'd figured out how your cord things work. We know now that nothing seems to happen to the others when one of you is killed. And apparently you can travel far away from the Raptus without injury. I think it's best that we take it into our Cluster to avoid further power grabs."

"Sounds good to me," Journey said wearily.

"Journey, go ahead and complete the unlocking process, then it'll go into our storage area. We can only hope Aiena responds to our request sometime in the next decade. She tends to not answer our call when she doesn't want to."

*What?* Chet stared at Zamie, then at Rory. "You mean the Raptus isn't going to be destroyed any time soon?"

Rory spread her hands. "We don't command the goddess. In fact, it's the exact inverse."

"But what if someone else grabs the Raptus while you're waiting! Like whatever happened before, when the Tache royal cousins got it. Your Cluster didn't do so great back then, did it?"

Again, he wasn't sure how a bunch of hooded people could thoroughly communicate wincing and glaring, but they did. Rory shrugged as if to say, "What do you want from us?" Both her expression and Zamie's expression were sardonic, bitter. Neither of them liked the idea of holding onto the Raptus so long, he could tell. But what choice did they have?

Journey took hold of the Raptus. "Abyss, it feels *awful.*"

"Is it really that bad?" Rory looked anxious. So did her mother, actually. Chet blinked; it hadn't felt painful to *him.*

"I'm afraid so. Fenimore already made me bleed," Journey said, frowning at the memory. Then she looked around at her audience, and sighed. "This is going to sound terrible."

Chet frowned. "Just spit it out. What's so bad about a children's poem? I mean, you act and dance in front of audiences all the time."

"Yeah. Okay, here goes nothing:

"A rake went cavorting with a Flame
Until she said 'You are too tame
I'll make you scream
You'll provide me with cream'
Now the rake has gone quite lame."

People snickered as the Raptus flashed bright green in Journey's hands. She hastily dropped it, hissing with—fear? Pain? It lay on the cave floor, inert as ever.

Chet frowned at Journey. "What kind of a children's poem was *that?*"

"An easily remembered one."

"But—but—a *children's* poem, Journey!"

"Hey, that ditty was popular among street urchins and school boys for centuries. I should know. I've *been* a street urchin and school boy, respectively."

Zamie reached for the Raptus—then yelped, drawing back and shaking her hands. "It *bit* me."

One Shadow Dancer after another attempted to pick up or even touch the Raptus with similar results. Tools were brought out from the pulsing black hole of the Cluster, which had apparently been hiding in the tunnel. Tongs, leather gloves, even a rubber-insulated box. It was like an engineering exercise with a live power line: ten people groused and yelped as they attempted the task of containing it.

When they finally managed to get the Raptus into the box, Chet felt as if his guts had been ripped from his belly. He squeaked, his hands automatically gripping his navel. Journey made a similar gesture. They looked at one another with much the same expression. The bonds that bound them to the Raptus had tightened exponentially. It *hurt.*

"I don't think the Raptus wants to go into the Cluster, somehow," Journey said.

"What's the alternative?" Rory shrugged. But she—and every visible Shadow Dancer in the cave—groaned when the box was popped into the Cluster itself.

"Oh, Pantheon," Zamie hissed. "That's *horrible.*"

Others were swearing, even collapsing to the ground. Chet wasn't surprised when the box was shoved out of the Cluster so hard it bounced a few times before coming to a stop. Luckily not in lucid mud—someone in the Cluster must have been thinking, even through the... pain?

"We can't have *that* in our Cluster. It felt like a collective kidney stone," Zamie said shakily.

"So what do we do? Toss it in the lucid-mud river and let someone else deal with it, years down the road?" a Shadow Dancer asked.

"No!" several others protested.

People threw back their hoods to argue with one another, gesturing and raising their voices. Chet was fascinated to find that Rory's family was amazingly diverse, racial wise. Did people marry into a Shadow Dancer Cluster? How many members existed in their little pocket of the God Plain? What was it really like inside the Cluster? Chet smiled at Rory and took her hand, squeezing it.

Rory responded by resting her head on his shoulder. She felt *fantastic* there, but Rory clearly wasn't happy. "Here we fought and shed blood for the thing, and it's *still* causing trouble. We're stuck with the Raptus for years to come, one way or another."

"Not necessarily," Journey said, her mouth set at a decisive angle.

Zamie was close enough to have heard her. "What do you mean?"

Journey pointed at Chet. "We are not using all of our available resources. We have a real, live, reincarnating Magician who is still with us despite the death of Foex."

Chet blinked, singled out. Journey had pitched her voice to carry—her thespian abilities had certainly survived the abuse she'd experienced. People in the cave quieted down, listening attentively.

"We *had* another real, live, reincarnating Magician here just a few minutes ago, and look at the destruction he was about to unleash on Uos," Zamie shot back, glaring at Fenimore's sprawled body.

"Chet isn't like that." To Chet's shock, it was Rory who'd spoken up. She faced down her mother, her spine straight as a board. "Chet doesn't want power, and he never has. Fenimore regarded him as a long-time enemy. If Chet *was* the Magician Zang in his past lives, then he has always been a thoughtful, philosophical soul with a keen mind for history. He has—or used to have—an intricate understanding of blood magic if his writings and epic poetry are any indication. That kind of knowledge isn't something any of us here possess."

Chet stared at Rory, taken aback. He felt absurdly pleased and embarrassed at her regard, yet he'd just found his old name. Now it was being bandied about the room with dozens of strangers looking on. *Could* he destroy the Raptus? Chet remembered the odd feeling when he'd taken it away from Fen. The Raptus had felt... alive. How many children had died in the making of it? How many people had been tortured, raped and slaughtered under its aegis? Abyss, he'd almost become a member of that endless list minutes ago. He honestly didn't know whether he could do anything about it.

Zamie looked skeptical. "What guarantee do we have that he

won't just grab the Raptus and use it to his full advantage?"

Rory rolled her eyes. "Mooom," she groaned, sounding half her age. "The family far outnumbers Chet, and everyone out here has a bracelet on. How on Uos could he run, let alone use the abysmal thing?"

"I'm sure he'd figure out something," Zamie muttered, but around her people were whispering amongst themselves, eyeing Chet thoughtfully. Zamie raised her voice to be heard. "Magicians were clever, murderous bastards who killed children for their rituals. They were never trustworthy."

Journey snorted. "You know, horrible things have been whispered about Flame, too. We're said to kidnap children and molest them. And, of course, there is a drop of truth to the old stories: young people have always run away with us to be initiated in fire, while older adolescents sometimes fall in love with us. You Shadow Dancers don't have the best reputations on Uos, either."

Chet cleared his throat and everyone in the cave went abruptly silent. "It *is* true. When I was a Magician, I did kill children. When I found out what my past held, I could barely believe it. I feel sick and guilty as Abyss—probably always will. We did horrible things back in those days."

"You aren't helping," Journey whispered out of the corner of her mouth.

A Shadow Dancer stepped forward. "Look, these claims are pretty incredible. You don't *look* special."

"I'm not," Chet agreed readily. He wasn't sure where he was going with this, but he needed to rise to the occasion, if only to be the person his friends believed he was and to validate their trust in him. "I was an archeology graduate student at Semaphore University before the Raptus turned my life on its head last week. I was deeply in love with the past, with history and antiquities of old. But you know something? No matter how beautiful the past might have been with its mysteries and secrets, the present is far more important." He reached out and took Rory's hand, emboldened. "This is what the Raptus takes away from us. It doesn't just remove our free will, no, not at all. Its power is divisive. It's easy to split a family, to split friend from friend, when people are hypnotized to hurt one another."

"Do you want to destroy the Raptus, Chet?" Rory said, pitching her voice to carry. A public question.

"Yes. To have it used upon you is a terrible experience. No one—not now, nor future generations—should suffer because of our pride and false notions of progress. I don't know if I *can* destroy it, but I vow to try. If it swallows me whole, if I try to use it to hurt anyone... you can kill me." He looked Zamie in the eye.

Her eyebrows rose, her expression a tad less skeptical. Maybe she'd noticed Rory hadn't let go of his hand. "That's unbelievably brave of you."

"Ma'am, I've had two friends and a mentor recently murdered—and an ally flung into lucid mud—because of this thing. The fate of the world is at stake if we fail. Our lives, our futures, our children... all endangered by the Raptus."

"But no pressure or anything," Journey murmured, grinning.

Zamie nodded, arms crossed over her chest. "All right, you have one shot. Guys, bring the box over here."

Rory drew close to Chet and kissed him on the cheek. "Good luck," she whispered. She let go of his hand and stepped back.

Chet gazed down at the unlocked Raptus. It was glowing a deeper green but seemed otherwise unchanged. He closed his eyes and took a deep breath, then lifted it out of the box and into his lap. He still didn't feel any pain—indeed, the thing seemed to be at home in his lap. The Raptus, as if sensing his readiness, pulsed at him through the bond. The bond. It had grabbed him first thing, it had wanted *him*. Why?

The answer was instantaneous, though shy. *Mama,* someone whispered.

"What?" Chet jerked back, staring at the glowing magical relic in his lap.

"No one said anything," Rory murmured. She was kneeling a short distance away, watching him closely.

"Just—something unexpected. Give me a moment," Chet said, closing his eyes again. Maybe he could *think* at the Raptus to communicate with it.

*Who is Mama?*

The answer was clear, though there were no words. The voice—voices?—inside the Raptus were certain that *he* was Mama.

"But I'm a guy," he mumbled aloud.

It didn't seem to matter to the voices. The other parent was mean, harsh. The other parent, Dada, wanted to dominate and hurt, and he used them to do it. There was a distinct feeling of being trapped, forced. Violated.

*Dada... is Fenimore? The Magician Tene?* Chet thought.

There was an affirmation, though a little quizzical this time. The voices didn't know names—they felt energy.

"That's how you knew me. That's why you wanted me, bound me to the others. You wanted me to protect you... to follow you."

*Yes. Mama, we're tired. Please, we're so tired.*

*Who are you?* he asked.

Pictures formed in his head. The faces of little girls, and Chet knew those faces. He especially recognized the one from his dream. These were the girls he'd killed—by his own hand—for their blood, the energy to fuel creation of the Raptus. *Oh, Pantheon.*

"You've been trapped inside this whole time?"

The affirmation was more than instantaneous, it was *loud*. The girls were screaming at him, crying and upset. They were fully awake for the first time in centuries, and they were hurting. Chet wanted to cover his ears but couldn't. The noise was inside his brain.

What did they want? Well, what did every small child want? They wanted *Mama*. Chet was the only person around whom they liked and trusted, despite everything. Fenimore had been the disciplinarian, demanding obedience from the Raptus as he would from any tool. Chet knew without question that the Magician Tene had never spoken to or interacted with these lost souls. Instead, he'd worked his will on the Raptus.

It was Foex's way, wasn't it? Foex had been a high-energy, economizing, misogynistic ex-general in a war that he'd eventually won. Foex, who'd drank himself to death when even being a god had lost its shine. Chet, as the Magician Zang, had been loyal to Foex. He'd been loyal to the end, though he'd experienced the same conditions Aureate had described; he, too, had been killed when he'd been born a girl.

Just like these children had been, their souls trapped for thousands of years. Cornered and forced to hurt people on a daily basis.

"Shhhh," he murmured to the children—his children. His girls. "I'm here. Mama's here."

"Chet? Are you still... yourself?" Rory was gazing at him with a worried look. The Shadow Dancers around her were bristling with weaponry, all of it focused on him. They, too, looked worried.

"It's okay, Rory." Chet found that he was crying. "It'll be okay. Please, just let me work."

He could feel their little bodies clinging to him. Gathering in his lap. Some were sucking their thumbs. Chet sang them the first song that came to mind, an old lullaby. The Flame had guessed right, even in their ignorance. They'd chosen children's poems and nursery rhymes to lock the Raptus, sending these girls to sleep in the best manner possible. At least *some* of the centuries had been bearable.

*You've a right to be tired, babies. People have been so cruel to you. I was, too, though I didn't mean to be. I'm very sorry for putting you in here. Now I'm going to set you free.*

*How?* they asked sleepily.

Good question. Chet cradled the Raptus in his hands. He took hold of a spike and exerted pressure. The girl who had been slaughtered to create that spike sat up in his lap, her eyes round. He didn't want to cause her more pain, but how to free her from this... this matrix? How had he and Tene created it in the first place?

An answer emerged from deep inside of him beyond conscious thought. Chet's fingers began undoing the intricate, web-like magic that held the spike together. It was like a body memory, the way his feet recalled a dance long after his head had forgotten; some part of him knew exactly what to do. *It's easy if you know which string to pull,* a voice said from within him. *Unmaking is always easier than making. Can't reverse the chaos of the universe, you know.*

The girl grew translucent as he worked. Then—as the spike disintegrated in his hands—she gave a little sigh and was gone. Chet sat on the cavern floor and worked, freeing each girl from the Raptus. He wept freely, snot running down his chin and dripping to his muddy, ruined clothing. The final girl, not by accident, was the charcoal burner's daughter from Chet's dream.

*Oh, beautiful,* he murmured into her hair. *Maybe you'll come back to Uos – to Mother Earth – in a new form, with a new mommy and daddy. I hope they'll be good to you.*

She smiled up at him, her expression trusting and open. *Thank you, Mama.*

He freed her as he had the others, the spike crumbling in his hands as she vanished.

The Raptus was less impressive now. Chet held it up and let go. It hovered in place. He breathed on the Raptus and it crumpled, growing smaller and smaller until it was a tiny, spiraling hunk of metal. Chet clapped his hands once, and it vanished. Winking out of existence.

Shadow Dancers applauded. People slapped him on the shoulders, cheering. Someone helped him to his feet. They were chattering all around him. But Chet couldn't celebrate. He closed his eyes, tears still streaming down his cheeks.

Someone touched him gently around his waist, pulling him into a hug. He caught his breath, hoping it was Rory, but when he opened his eyes, Journey smiled at him. "Hi, sweetie. You just saved the world. What would you like to do next?"

Chet laughed at the unexpected question. He wiped his tears, which had turned the dry mud wet again—sort of. Non-water based indeed. "I'd like a *shower*."

# Chapter 29
# Three's a Crowd

Chet emerged from the second-floor bathroom of Knife's house, wrapped in a towel. The Shadow Dancers had left a few minutes ago. Before leaving, they'd gone upstairs to the third floor with Journey, and they'd spent a long time up there. Chet assumed the Shadow Dancers taken care of Knife's body—maybe they'd taken the body into their Cluster for later disposal.

Chet didn't want to go to the third floor himself, not yet. He'd do it after he'd slept. He'd sit in Knife's study and drink, maybe even shed a private tear or two. Chet had been able to say goodbye when Knife had been alive, but it had been an aborted goodbye. There hadn't been time for every little matter. It still peeved Chet that Knife hadn't trusted him enough to take him into her confidence back in Wetshul, instead of slamming him against the wall and making threats, but Knife hadn't had a reason to trust him back then. Chet knew he'd miss Knife no matter what. Would Rory be there with him, or would he be drinking alone? A good question.

He found Rory lolling on the bed in a guest bedroom, wearing a plush bathrobe, her hair still glistening from her own shower. She was lying on her belly, looking into the roaring fire in the fireplace. Chet glanced that way, too—a figure was curled upon the lengthy andiron.

"How does Journey breathe in there?" Chet said.

"I don't know, but she occasionally reaches out for another split log and places it in a strategic location near her body. I'm not hungry yet, are you?"

"I'm not sure," Chet admitted. He was all tumbled up inside.

Shaky. It had been the strangest week and a half of his life, and it wasn't over yet.

"Chet... could you tell me what happened when you destroyed the Raptus?" she said, eyeing him with a worried expression. "When you were talking to it, it didn't sound like you were fighting. It sounded *strange*."

Chet settled beside her on the bed. He'd fought at Rory's side, but they hadn't really reconnected, not in an emotional way. Though nothing was resolved, he felt *fizzy*, as if being in close proximity to her was a drug. Chet didn't want to screw this up.

"It's difficult."

Would she judge him his actions from when he was Zang? Why not? Chet did. He'd been Zang for umpteen lifetimes, and Chet Baikson for only one—a short one at that. Was he, Chet, a real person, or was he a mask for the long-gone Zang? *I'm real,* he thought, bristling at the thought. Young but no longer untested, he'd overcome the challenges in his path. Zang was more like a dead ancestor than a ghost living inside him, he decided. A famous, pushy kind of ancestor, sure, but dead all the same.

Now if only the rest of his past would settle down and quit bugging him.

"Tell me." Rory reached up and brushed a stray hair off his forehead.

His heart beat harder at her touch; he realized he was hers to command. Chet bowed his head and explained. At one point he choked up, and Rory squeezed his hand. It gave him strength to continue.

"Wow," she said when he'd finished. "That's not how I thought it was at all."

"Me, either. But I'm glad they're free. I'll always feel guilty about it, but at least they're not in pain anymore."

"It wasn't you who killed them, Chet. You're your own person with your own experiences and ambitions."

"Yeah. Except everything's a little too close to home, too many coincidences. I figured out how I knew Fenimore last time around." He shook his head. "No wonder Knife's explanation of how Fen ended up in lucid mud always seemed off to me, why Fenimore's version was so different."

"What do you mean?" Rory blinked at him, her expression bemused.

"I remembered just now in the shower. It's like I'm a colander and information from past lives keeps trickling down through me. I think—no. I *know* I was the servant who accompanied Fenimore to Wetshul back in 7305. The one who betrayed him."

"Huh. Clearly, I'll have to get the full story some other time. Did you figure out you were Zang then, too?"

"No, I was an agent working for Prince Konstantine. His court really *was* hip-deep in spies. I remember pursuing Fenimore in that carriage we uncovered in the dust—I think I must have stolen it—before cornering him against the lucid mud pit. He went in and I didn't. I'm the one who lied about it, years later, to Knife." Chet vented an ironic chuckle. "Think about the course of events from Fen's perspective. One minute he's fighting me in the monsoon rain and darkness, then he loses and dives into lucid mud bearing his prize. Next thing he knows, Fenimore wakes up in the ambulance next to *me*—with a new face and body—three centuries later."

Rory shook her head, lips pursed. "Crazy."

"Yeah. I almost slipped in the shower because of it. I wonder if this sort of thing will keep happening."

"Who knows? Look, all god affiliates deal with weird shit. The trick is to not let that stuff get in the way of living your life."

"She's right, you know." Journey said, rising from the fireplace with a long, feline stretch.

Journey had changed to male, and he was absolutely *gorgeous*. Lithe with ropy musculature, a substantial penis and a sensitive, enduring face. Chet's breath caught and his dick hardened at the sight. He put his hands in his lap to cover his erection, hunkering down. The towel wrapped around his waist felt way too small all of a sudden.

Rory, on the other hand, sat up and whistled. "Nice. You look hot enough to start a forest fire."

"Thank you, Rory. I try." Journey settled next to her on the bed, smiling. He didn't seem shy about either his proximity or beauty. Well, he wouldn't, would he?

Chet's teeth clenched, his body tensing up. He was attracted to both of them, yet he felt intensely jealous of Journey. Ridiculous but true. What had Oak said about Journey? That he wasn't exactly discriminating. This was moving too fast... he'd never imagined Journey might seduce *Rory* for Pantheon's sake. It was funny because Rory had been on his mind all along, yet this contingency hadn't occurred to him.

Rory, however, turned toward Journey like a flower following the sun. "You seem to be feeling better."

"I will eventually." He looked away, gazing into the fire. "We were both in trouble for a while there, weren't we? You bleeding out, and me... under him."

"I remember. No wonder you've turned male. Do you think... I mean, will you ever be female again?"

"Oh, of course. Just not right now." They made eye contact, and it lasted a while. A long while.

Chet squirmed. Rory's back was turned, and Journey wasn't paying the slightest attention to him. Chet felt the childish desire to point out that *he'd* been in trouble, too. He also wanted to puff out his chest and claim that he was the one who'd saved them, except it wasn't true. Rory was a fantastic fighter, and Journey had been impressive considering the tortures Fenimore had heaped upon his head. But as the eye contact continued—the moment was lasting *forever*—Chet felt isolated and left out.

Rory leaned over and kissed Journey on the lips.

Chet wanted to growl like an animal. Rory hadn't kissed *him* on the lips yet, not even when they'd been going out. They'd been too shy and reticent, only holding hands and cuddling. Now she was kissing a *Flame*, and the Flame was kissing back. Journey stroked the back of her head, his hands meandering up and down her body. It looked fantastically sensual. Chet's penis threatened to pop out of the towel entirely, which now resembled a pup tent. His face was blistering hot.

Rory reached down and stroked Journey's exposed cock, caressing up to the tip. "Oh, wow. That's really soft, but it's got this hard, springy core to it. Is it soft for all guys, or just Flame?"

Journey drew back from her. For a moment, Chet thought he was backing off entirely, and an intense spike of relief surged through him. Then he realized it was an invitation. Journey lay down, arms crooked behind his head. "I have what every guy has. Please, feel free to explore."

"What if I hurt you?"

"I'll let you know if something's uncomfortable."

"Um. Okay, then!" Rory grinned and started touching up and down Journey's body. She seemed most fascinated by his cock and balls, playing with them intently.

It was too much. Chet shouldn't feel this way. He liked Journey and had enjoyed his company this week. Journey had been his first and he'd always remember that, but by the Pantheon, Rory was different! He felt so possessive of her. Protective and jealous, too.

Who did Journey think he was, anyway? Anger rose in Chet, hot as the fire crackling in the grate. He felt dirty and sundered. He'd appeased Fenimore in the prostitute's van, and no one had ever thanked him for doing so. He'd surrendered himself to the truck driver, saving Journey from having to submit to him. No one had acknowledged that sacrifice except Fenimore, who'd been an asshole about it, as usual. Now Journey was seducing his... well, his ex-girlfriend.

Rory would be the first person to point out that Chet had broken up with her, not the other way around. They were no longer going out. He had no right to feel this way.

"It's so *big*," Rory said, her tone detached—an almost clinical observation—yet she was clearly delighted. Like an archeologist with a splendid find in hand.

"It doesn't need to be, but I like it this way. Makes me feel all manly." Journey snickered, his manner ironic and effeminate. His body—his whole self—seemed relaxed and comfortable.

Rory laughed outright. "Here's to manliness."

Journey looked up at Chet with a smile as if about to say something irreverent. He paused, frowning, though his eyes were still glazed with pleasure. "Chet, sweetie, you look like you're eating a spoonful of bugs."

Chet sighed. This was ridiculous. What was he, twelve? His victimhood felt a little extreme, even to himself. Hadn't Journey just noticed him? Prompted him to talk about it? He wished Rory had said something, but he couldn't have everything.

Chet cleared his throat. "I guess I'm not sure what—"

"Oh, Pantheon!" Journey gasped and arched his back, making little mewling sounds. "Rory, don't stop!"

"What, *this?*" She grinned from ear to ear.

Chet leaned over to look: one of her hands was firmly holding Journey's dick and ball sack while her other hand was circling the tip. Any second now it would occur to her that she could use her mouth on him, too. Chet felt tears rise to his eyes, then blinked them away angrily. They didn't want him, didn't need him. He was undoubtedly contaminated anyway; Fenimore or the truck driver had, in all probability, given him a VD. Just what he'd always wanted.

Rory shot Chet a grin over her shoulder. "Looks like I'm pretty good for a beginner," she chirped.

"He's a *guy,*" Chet... yelled. His tone was so loud they stared at him with mutually shocked expressions. Chet lowered his voice self-consciously. "It doesn't take any skill to do that."

"I beg to differ," Journey said from his reclined position, frowning.

"What's eating you, Chet? You don't need to bite me, you know."

"Nothing." He crossed his arms and looked away.

Journey said, "You want to come here, cuddle and tell us all about it, or do you want to go away and sulk? Because I'd prefer if you didn't make a scene just now. We've all been through too much today for passive-aggressive nonsense like that."

"It's stupid."

Journey sat up and Rory, in turn, backed away. He threw his legs over the edge of the bed, still naked and looking good enough to eat. He gazed from Chet to Rory and back again. A corner of his mouth turned up. "Ah. I get it. I think I'd better let you talk this over yourselves. Want me to step out?"

"No!" Rory cried out, arms crossed. "I was having fun, and I don't *want* to have to talk things over."

Journey raised his eyebrows. "I believe Chet has something he wants to say to you and is having a hard time spitting it out. I'm in the way here."

"You stay put. What is it, Chet?"

Chet's face was hotter than ever. He felt like he was on stage in front of an audience. How could he reveal his tentative, heart-felt emotions like this? But denying how he felt would just make matters worse. "Um, Rory? I really like you. I, uh, was hoping we could start dating again."

She stared at him, and he wilted. She rolled her eyes. "Abyss, Chet. You have the worst timing *ever*."

Chet opened his mouth and shut it. He just sat there like a doedicu. A small sound caught his attention; Journey was covering his mouth, his eyes crescents. Chet realized he was trying hard—very hard—not to laugh out loud.

"What am I, the best show in town?"

Journey took several visible deep breaths before he was able to say, "No, sweetie, I'm sorry. It's not funny to you, I know. We've all just had a day from the Abyss. But may I make a suggestion?"

"What?"

"Let's fuck one another silly, order take out and sleep before making any kind of big decision."

Chet snorted, but he couldn't help smiling. "Just like a Flame. You're such a hedonist."

"Pantheon, yes. I'm the biggest slut you've ever seen. I enjoy myself mightily, so why be ashamed of it?" Journey shrugged, grinning unrepentantly. He turned to Rory and said, "I suggest you squash him flat in the morning instead of now."

She straightened indignantly. "I never said I was going to turn him down!"

Chet, who'd froze at Journey's words, straightened and threw back his shoulders back at her tone. She wasn't going to turn him down!

"Oh." Journey looked amused and a trifle smug at this exclamation.

Chet realized he'd worded it that way on purpose. Reverse psychology? Journey was on his side without doubt. Chet relaxed. As he did, he realized how astounding Journey was in this form. He gazed up and down Journey's muscled body, eyes lingering on his dick. What would Rory think if Chet did what he really wanted to do: grab hold of Journey and fuck him hard?

It was an invigorating notion. Fenimore had been brutal while raping Journey. Chet knew it, but the sounds and sight of it had detoured his brain and leapt directly to his cock. He was hard at the thought.

Journey seemed to sense his mood. He met Chet's gaze. Then he stood, turned his back and leaned against the bed, hands on the mattress, his ass decidedly pro-offered.

Chet stood and ran a hand up and down Journey's back. His back was fucking *hot,* lithe and muscled, everything Chet had ever dreamed. Well, when he'd admitted to himself that he dreamed of men. Definitely better than Fenimore.

"Are you sure?" he whispered in Journey's ear.

Journey wriggled in place, his shapely ass sticking out farther, his penis so erect it touched his flat belly. "Oh, yes."

"Uh, guys? What's going on, here?" Rory was staring at them, her expression everything Chet didn't want to see—alarmed, concerned, almost revolted. The woman he liked was witnessing his desires, and she was unhappy with what she saw.

*Not good,* Chet thought, crestfallen.

# Chapter 30
# Lusting for the Present

Chet swallowed, though he didn't draw away from Journey. He almost couldn't. Chet felt like a magnet attracted to the correct side of another magnet. Journey was spread and ready for him, and Chet's dick was so hard, the need frantic within him.

"Uh, Rory. I hope you don't mind..." There was no end to that sentence; it trailed off into the ether between the stars, horribly incomplete.

"Mind what?" Rory looked about ready to freak out.

Chet's shoulders slumped. Rory deserved more, yet Chet wasn't sure he could adequately explain. He'd been fucking men and Flame all week, yet his inner orientation remained murky, opaque to inner reflection.

Journey glanced over his shoulder at Chet. "Guess we need to keep talking and *processing* our *feelings*," he grumbled, spitting out the words like a curse. He sat on the bed again, scratching his chest with a disgruntled expression. "Abyss, I'm never going to get fucked, am I?"

"Is that all you care about?" Chet had been looking forward to fucking Journey, too.

"It was on my list this evening, yes. Guess I'd better get us started." Journey rubbed his face. He turned so he was facing both of them and addressed Rory directly. "Rory, how long did you and Chet go out before he broke up with you?"

"About a year."

"You're from Eich Che, too, right?"

"Yes?"

"Flame aren't at all rare at home like they are in Wetshul. There's

Flame everywhere, just like in Plainsdaugheau," he said, glancing at Chet.

She shrugged. "Of course. Where are you going with this?"

Journey was gazing at her with the air of a doctor looking to make a correct diagnosis. "Bear with me. Because you're from Eich Che, you *must* know that same-sex pairings are more often than not the norm, especially—though not exclusively—with Flame. Which tells me you understand what we want, at least on a cognitive level. I'm guessing you're not so much shocked by what's going on as that Chet here wants me as male."

Her expression reminded Chet of his own reaction to Oak's revealed identity. As if she'd been lied to and didn't like it. "That's it exactly."

Chet gulped. Could he explain this? He had to try. "I kind of knew I liked both men and women before Journey—and Fenimore—showed up, but I didn't want to admit it to myself. Let alone anyone else, especially you. Someone I liked. I mean, what if you thought it was creepy?" What if she *still* thought it was creepy? Chet almost wished he didn't like men, but he did. Whether she turned him down in the morning or not, he'd still be himself. Her acceptance or rejection wouldn't make a difference, and she should know that. It was only fair.

"Uh. Well, I guess that's... understandable." Rory looked like someone eating fish stew when the bones hadn't been properly taken out.

"It's been an eye-opening week, and *I* don't even know how to feel about it. It's unfair to expect you to accept me when I'm having trouble with this myself."

Journey took his hand. "I'm sorry, sweetie. Didn't mean to open a can of worms for you."

"It's not your fault." Chet straightened indignantly, gazing at him fiercely. He squeezed Journey's hand. "Don't ever apologize for being yourself."

His mouth quirked up, then down. He looked away, his expression abstract. Sad.

Rory looked from Chet to Journey and back again. "Are you two in love?" she whispered.

Chet blinked at her, then back to Journey, almost aghast. Journey was gazing at him with a similar expression. It should have made him feel bad, but it was actually comforting. "No," they said at the same time, dropping hands. Then they smiled at one another. *Consensus achieved!* Chet thought, a grin slowly spreading over his face.

"Well." Rory took a deep breath and let it out in a puff. "*That's* okay, then. Go ahead, Chet. This isn't something we're going to be worked out tonight. But... you know, I guess we'll figure something out, some kind of compromise. *If* I decide to take you back—and that's a big if."

Journey barked a laugh. "There's the old Eich Che spirit."

"You'd better believe it." She grinned at him and yawned. "Come on, let's do something. I'll fall asleep if we keep sitting still."

Chet's heart lightened until he was almost floating with happiness."Could you, um, do me a favor, Rory? Grab Journey's dick and enjoy him in the front while I take him from the rear?"

"Oh. Okay," she said, eyes wide.

"You have it all worked out, I see." Journey's tone was ironic, but he smirked as he scrambled upright. He resumed his position at the edge of the bed.

Chet's cock was so hard it quivered, like a cynodict following an exciting scent. He grabbed Journey and rubbed up and down his ass crack. He glanced around to find that Rory had her hands full. Journey groaned, his breath catching at her touch. At *their* touch.

Chet fingered his ass. Abyss, Journey was wet; the smell of ichor filled the room. There was no need to wait. Chet pushed his cock inside with an audible sucking noise. Journey let loose a small mewl, shuddering. Chet thrust all the way in, loving how tight he was, then drew all the way out, his dick coming loose. All the way in, all the way out of Journey's muscular ass. Journey squirmed, occupied at both ends.

"That's right, slut," Chet murmured. He didn't want to sound like Fenimore, but Journey was too hot to just fuck in silence. "You want it, don't you? Tell me how much you want it."

"Oh, Pantheon, I want it. Fuck me, Chet."

"I didn't hear you. What was that again?"

"Fuck me! I need to be fucked! *Hard.*"

"Really? You want it hard?" Chet pushed himself inside to the hilt and held still. "Hmm?"

"Oh, please. Please." Journey was gasping like a fish. He cried out and Chet peeked over his shoulder, frowning. Had Journey come? No, Rory was licking his dick. Trying something new, was she? Just like an ice-cream cone, only saltier.

Chet upped the pace, fucking Journey with precise blows. He loved this. Journey took it, took everything he had. Doyen Quor and Fenimore—not to mention Journey himself—had taught him how to time a good fucking. Chet varied his speed: he slowed down before upping his pace, then slowed down again. He didn't want to come, he wanted to fuck. Journey's ass muscles clenched hard as he came, squirting ichor-tinged semen across the bedspread. Rory jerked back as if uncertain how to deal with the event. Chet grinned and began fucking him again.

"Wow, Chet. You've got him good," Rory murmured, wide eyed. She repositioned herself at the edge of the bed, watching the show from a different angle. "Now *that's* hot."

Chet smirked at her, feeling like the luckiest man in the world. He loved that she wasn't horrified, witnessing the act. Her hand had disappeared into her bathrobe—between her legs—and she rocked in place.

Chet turned back to Journey, who was sprawled under him, taking it. Chet pummeled him harder with his hips, and Journey gasped. Then Chet snarled and fucked him so hard they fell to the bed together, legs waving unsupported in the air. Chet was on the verge of coming... he was coming... he held very still until the moment passed. He was still hard, his semen as yet unspilled.

"Oh," Journey moaned. "Oh, Chet. Oh, oh *Chet*."

If he wanted to keep fucking, he'd need better traction. "Journey, you and I are going to crawl to the center of the bed, so I can continue enjoying you. Go slowly and don't let me slip out of you."

Moving like conjoined insects, they reached a spot where their legs were firmly secure on the mattress. Chet settled over Journey like an inofe eating its prey. He felt a hand on his back and glanced over his shoulder. Rory, of course. Her eyes were sparkling with ambition, the same drive that had taken Fenimore down. She climbed on top of him and lay on his back, spooning him. Journey groaned, pressed under two bodies.

Chet paused. "You okay down there?"

"Keep going!"

He did. It felt wonderful to be sandwiched, to have Journey flattened under him and Rory writhing on top.

"I kind of wish I had a dick," she said into his ear, giggling. "Then we'd be a complete circuit."

"You'll lose all your hair if you went to fire." He grinned at her over his shoulder.

"I don't want a dick *that* much, thank you kindly."

Journey's hands were balling up the bedding. He yelled—orgasming again, Chet decided. After the spasm ended, Journey went limp. "Pantheon. Chet, are you ever going to come up there?"

"Do you want me to come, Journey?" he purred in his ear. "I thought you were disappointed when I came too soon, last time."

"There's some kind of turnabout-is-fair-play action going on here, isn't there?"

"Be careful what you ask for," Chet said in a sing-song tone. "I like being inside you, Journey. You're so warm, wet and tight. You feel *way* too good for me to back off."

"That's what I get for being hospitable."

"If you really feel that way, I guess I can speed up." Chet did, electing more groans from beneath him.

"You two are cute." Rory had responded to the change of pace by rolling down Chet's body until she was humping his upper thighs. She slapped Chet's ass, and he groaned, back arching.

"Do that again, Rory!" Journey cried out.

She spanked him harder this time. The pain felt like the deepest pleasure he'd ever felt. Chet screamed, arcing like an electrical current as he came.

He slumped, and Journey crawled out from under him. They were dripping with sweat, Chet realized. Journey left faint purple marks on the bedspread wherever his body had touched the fabric.

Chet rolled onto his back and let loose a satisfied sigh. "That was good."

"Thank you, sweetie." Journey kissed him on the brow. "You

gave me precisely what I needed."

"My pleasure."

Rory looked a little disappointed. "That was *it?*"

Chet groaned, sore and exhausted, but Journey grinned and crooked his finger. "Come here, Rory."

She crawled over, her bathrobe gaping open. Chet enjoyed the view from his reclined position. Despite everything, her expression was troubled. "Um, no offense, but I don't think I want to lose my virginity tonight."

"I wasn't planning on going there, not with matters so unsettled between you and Chet."

"What, then?" She pouted, looking like a schoolgirl hoping for a treat.

Journey slid his hand under her bathrobe, and she gasped at the touch. Chet watched, holding his breath, as Journey's hand disappeared into her nether regions. She lay down on her back, her legs open for his perusal. Journey maneuvered himself between them until his face was at the same level as her cunt. Grinning, he sank between her legs. Rory yelped, thrashing.

Chet wasn't sure how to feel, but Rory decided for him.

"Chet, get over here!" she gasped.

He cuddled closer, uncertain what she wanted from him. She grabbed hold of him and held on tight—tight!—making little needy sounds as she writhed.

Journey paused to look at him. "Chet, suckle her tits," he ordered, then disappeared once again.

It was what he'd always dreamed of doing. Chet opened her bathrobe all the way and regarded her breasts, jiggling before him. Rory gazed up at his face as if nervous.

"Am I... am I okay?"

"You're *perfect,*" he said, sinking upon her.

He took one tit in his mouth, rolling it around with his tongue while gently pinching the other. Her breasts were firm and moved under him in the most alluring fashion. Rory was screaming, her head flung back. Her body snapped like a rubber band. Had she come? Journey didn't stop, so neither did Chet. She snapped again, then again, still screaming.

Finally, she pulled away from Chet and pushed Journey out from between her legs. "Enough," she gasped.

"How many was that, Chet? I didn't count." Journey looked smug.

"I didn't, either," he said, thinking about what her reactions had meant. "She jerked in place maybe three or four times. Rory, how many times did you come?"

"I don't... I've never felt anything like that. I didn't know it was *possible*."

"You mean you've never orgasmed?" Journey crawled up the bed to lie beside her, curling into her body.

They looked so comfortable. For a moment, Chet felt another spark of jealousy, except he was comfortable, too, nestled up against Rory. Chet snuggled closer, and she put her arms around both their shoulders.

"Is that what it's called?" she said. "It felt astronomical."

"Huh. I'd have gone easier on you if I'd known you were pre-orgasmic. Sorry about that."

She shook her head. "No problem. No problem at *all*."

Chet gazed at both of them, secure and replete. He frowned, freed for the moment to think about what would happen next. Well, Journey would probably go back to his own life in Eich Che. Rory would undoubtedly return to Semaphore to complete her degree, now that the Raptus was destroyed. What about himself? Though he'd been struggling with the question all week, the answer was suddenly simple.

Chet cleared his throat. "Tomorrow morning I'm going to call my father and apologize. Then I'll tell him I'm pledging myself to Philapo as a Literati. Philapo doesn't have the same intensity of Foex, but you know, I think I'd do well under him."

"Fantastic." Journey reached over and squeezed his hand. "Knife and I noticed your, ah, Literati-like qualities in our travels. I'm glad you've made peace with yourself."

"Yeah. I'd love to return to Semaphore and complete my degree if I can work it out with my dad. I mean, unless I'm going to prison for the high jinks and murders."

Rory shook her head. "We recorded everything said in that cave. Fenimore's confession will stand in a court of law if necessary. The

Cluster is going to Plainsdaugheau to speak to the police there, then to Semaphore to discuss both Tibbets and Clementina with officials and the university administration. My mom has already contacted Professor Espies to work out a deal for both of our returns. Espies was her thesis chair when *she* earned her Ph.D. at Semaphore, so she has some pull with him."

"Oh." Chet blinked. "I—that's wonderful."

Journey added, "Don't forget to remind me to pay you back, Chet. I can draw upon Knife's funds to replace what we stole from your father."

Chet nodded, miserable at the thought of Knife.

As if feeling the change in mood, Journey sat up. "I'm hungry. Let's call for take-out!"

After they'd ordered in food from a nearby restaurant and ate it with hearty appetites, Journey sighed and folded his napkin. Rory was washing dishes in the kitchen; though no one had asked her to do so, she seemed to feel obliged to lend a respectful hand in Knife's house.

Chet studied Journey, not sure what to make of his expression. "Are you okay?"

"I was just thinking I'd best take care of the body before I go to bed. Can't do it in the morning because of the neighbors, and it'll start getting manky if I wait too long."

Chet stiffened. He'd assumed the Shadow Dancers had taken Knife's body from the third floor. "You mean... you mean while we were showering and talking and eating and, and fucking, Knife's been up there the whole time, *dead?*"

"Yes. Knife is very clear about her wishes in this matter."

Chet blanched, recalling the tombs. "You're not going to—I mean, all those skeletons underground. They aren't all..."

Journey shot him a dour look. "This is a private matter and none of your concern, Chet Baikson."

He folded his arms and scowled. "Knife was my friend, too."

"I... yes, you're right. You have to understand, Allistair is the oldest city-state on Uos. They have *traditions* here. One of those traditions is what people do to Flame corpses once we're dead. They do... the most disgusting things with our bodies. Prolonged and personal actions are taken in a traditional sequence. Very personal."

"Oh."

"Knife has lived in this city-state since her first life when she was born to the Tache royal family right here in Allistair. She has connections and carefully renews them life after life. They call her 'Uncle Flame.' How do you think she's able to maintain a long-term residence in this city-state? This place is worse than Wetshul for us."

"I didn't think. I didn't know."

Journey shrugged, his expression uncomfortable. "Death takes so many things, including dignity. Her royal connections can't—or won't—help her after she dies, yet Knife likes to be control over certain matters. The tomb might seem grotesque, but it's a lot better than the alternative. I wouldn't even trust a modern-day morgue to deal with us respectably in Allistair. They might sell the body, or lend it out. You never know when someone's going to get all *traditional*. By the time Knife initiates again, the body will be decomposed." He sighed and glanced upwards as if recalling the layout on the third floor. "Pantheon knows how I'll get her down the stairs, let alone the circular staircase in the cave. I'm so tired."

Chet laid a hand on his arm. "You have a right to be tired."

"Yeah, but this still needs doing. I guess I'll wrap her in the carpet. It has to be thrown out anyway."

Chet scowled reflexively and drew back. "You can't throw away that carpet! It's a priceless antique!"

"Chet!" Journey said sharply. "It's just old. Get over it."

Journey was right, of course. Chet looked up, visualizing how Knife had bled out in the study. "Leave her until tomorrow morning. The carpet will conceal everything from the neighbors, anyway. Would you like help taking her down to the tomb? It's kind of awkward getting rid of bodies, you know."

Journey stared at him, then chuckled. He leaned forward and ruffled his fingers through Chet's hair. "Thank you, sweetie. Somehow, that's very fitting. When Knife initiates next time—if you're around and interested in seeing her again—I'll try to make sure she knows what you did."

Chet ducked his head shyly. "You're welcome."

If you enjoyed this story, you can sign up for a free membership at ForbiddenFiction and discuss it with other readers and the author at *The Artifact of Foex* story page at http://forbiddenfiction.com/story/JLW-1.000183.

We do our best to proof all our work, but if you spot a text error we missed, please let us know via our website Contact Form at http://forbiddenfiction.com/contact.

# Glossary and pronunciation guide

### The Forty

Due to how Uos came to be, there were originally only forty land-based animal species. As a few have gone extinct, there are now thirty-eight land-based species. Despite this, the term "the Forty," which includes human beings, has remained the same.

**Anuro** *(an-NER-ōh)*: Small birdlike reptiles with tiny, sharp teeth and stout beaks. Highly colorful, they roam in enormous flocks and fill the ecological niche of songbirds on Earth.

**Ceros** *(SER-ōs)*: Cloven-hoofed, elk-like mammals with an impressive rack of antlers. They function much like horses do on Earth.

**Cynodict** *(sin-ŌH-dict)*: Hairless canines with whip-like tails, often kept as pets.

**Dium** *(DEE-um)*: A fast moving, high jumping, reptilian-like mammal. About eight-inches long, they have elongated noses and a penchant for garbage.

**Doedicu** *(dōe-DE-kū)*: Enormous humpback, armored amphibians. They have beaks, a shell like a turtle, and a cluster of razor-sharpened spikes at the ends of their tails. Doedicu meat is universally considered tender and tasty.

**Indricoth** *(in-dri-COTH)*: The largest mammals ever to roam Uos, these herbivores have been extinct since the World War. Indricoth toys are staples of childhood across all Uos cultures.

**Inofe** *(in-ŌH-fee)*: Giant, predatory felines with saber teeth. Humans have historically been a favorite food of the inofe.

**Marauch** *(MA-rach)*: A horse-sized, deer-like herbivore with an elongated, droopy nose. Humans have long bred macrauch for their meat and leather.

**Othnielia** *(oth-nee-LEE-ah)*: Herbivorous reptiles about seven feet tall, standing on two legs with short forearms and a long tail. Othnielia are the fastest creature on Uos, reaching over eighty miles an hour in short bursts.

**Palaeoth** *(pal-EE-oth)*: Palaeoth are multi-toed hoofed mammals, about two and a half feet tall and three feet long. They occupy the same niche as donkeys or goats on Earth. Because of their sexual displays when in heat, palaeoth have often been linked to brothels, prostitutes and Flame.

**Peteino** *(pet-EE-nō)*: Reptiles with long tails and leathery wings, peteinos occupy the same general niche on Uos as chickens on Earth.

**Rhamph** *(ramf)*: Winged mammals with cartilage "beaks" and extensive wingspans, there are more varieties of rhamph on Uos than any other land-based creature. The smallest can fit in a human hand, while the largest variety has a wingspan of over eight feet.

**Geography**

This section has three parts, including countries/continents, cities and city-states, and Pantheon-related geographical features.

**The countries/continents**:

**East Eicha** *(ĀY-cha):* Filled with vast, deadly swamps with extreme temperatures and vicious wildlife, East Eicha is a poor land. Fortunately, it also features the Monastery Mountains, which are havens in comparison.

**Idryss, or The Forbidden Lands** *(IH-dris)*: Ringed by a continuous mountain range, the Idryss continent is enclosed by a god-barrier specifically designed to keep gods out. Reincarnating affiliates—Flame and Magicians—have long confirmed there is an intense, thriving civilization in Idryss despite the fact that no one goes in and no one comes out.

**Jantrael Straight** *(jan-TRAL)*: A pincer-grip of two peninsulas with a six-mile stretch of ocean between them. There is no way around the Jantrael Straight if one wants to get from one side of Uos to the other via the sea.

**Palister** *(pal-IH-ster)*: To the north, the city-state of Maansterdam has long been an economic draw to Palister. However, the rest of the continent is much poorer and far more rural.

**Tache** *(tash-ĀY)*: A wealthy country with a bustling economy and an epic history. A traditional monarchy, the emperors and empresses of Tache have often been a driving force instigating international conquest and colonization.

**Ventris** *(VEN-tris)*: A traditional matriarchal nation, Ventris has a long history of feudal "households" with a strict caste system. Ventris and Tache are almost always at war.

**West Eicha** *(ĀY-cha)*: Much of West Eicha is a peaceful, agrarian society typically composed in small, rural villages. West Eicha is thought to be the continent where the Forty were originally released.

**Cities and city-states:**

**Allistair** *(al-is-STAIR)*: Located in the center of Tache, Allistair is among the oldest and richest of the city-states.

**Door**: Located in the center of West Eicha, Door struggles to remain relevant in modern times since the death of Foex and his Magicians. The interior of the city-state suffers from urban blight while the suburbs—a wide-spread sprawl—thrive.

**Eich Che** *(ĀY-chāy):* Located on a peninsula at the edge of the Ventris continent, Eich Che is a city-state independent of the gods. The premiere monetary and cultural center of Uos, it surpasses even Allistair's riches.

**El, the lost city of**: At one time, El was a thriving city deep in the Eilthera Mountains of West Eicha. Currently surrounded by an impenetrable god barrier, El is lost not because no one knows where it is, but because no one can get inside.

**Maansterdam** *(MAN-ster-dam):* Located in Northern Palister, the city-state is named for the Maan River, its main source of trade and travel.

**Plainsdaugheau** *(PLAINS-daw-ow):* Located on the southern tip of Idryss, Plainsdaugheau is the only livable space on the continent outside the god barrier. Founded as a free, independent city-state, Plainsdaugheau has a constitution—the only one on Uos—and is a radical democracy.

**Saene** *(SĪGH-en-āy):* Saene has a lengthy history with many rises and falls of power, wartime renewal and cultural institutions. It is the seat of the Ventris monarchy.

**Shul** *(shool):* Located only fifty-seven miles from Allistair, Shul is an industrial city with a long history of espionage activity.

**Torque** *(tork):* A seaside city on the southeastern edge of Tache, Torque has a long reputation as a resort.

**Wetshul** *(WET-shool):* Once a camp for the First Conversion Army, Wetshul was carved out of the rainy, humid, muddy, miserably cold swamp of East Eicha.

**Pantheon-related geographical features:**

**God barriers**: Aerora, mother of gods, cordoned off sections of the planet from her god children and every other living thing, including humans. There are two major god barriers upon Uos: the lost city of El, and nearly the entire continent of Idryss.

**God Plain**: The God Plain is a dimensional fold close to but not physically present upon Uos, where—as the name suggests—most gods spend their time.

**Abyss**: Unlike the God Plain, the Abyss is an actual geographical feature on Uos. Located in the lost city of El, no human or god has had access to the Abyss in thousands of years.

**The races of Uos**

**Bisque**: The lightest skin tone on Uos, a pinkish beige comparable to white people on Earth. Light-haired individuals often have streaks of sea green in their hair, thus the nickname "greenies."

**Bistre**: Extremely dark-brown skin with an underlying purple tone, most often found around the Jantrael Straight. Thanks to the economic stronghold of Eich che, this race is considered to be the second most powerful people on Uos.

**Fallow**: A light-brown skin tone, usually with curly hair. As fallow people emerged from Tache as a colonial power, they are considered the most powerful race on Uos.

**Flaxen**: Much like Asian people of Earth in skin tone, they have universal red hair. Flaxen people have similar features and tend toward highly eroticized primary and secondary sex characteristics.

**Gamboge**: Orange skin tone with black hair and hatchet-shaped noses, originally found on Palister.

**God affiliates:**

**Flame**: Affiliates of Pelin, Flame are among the most designed, highest maintenance people on Uos in terms of physiological divergence from the norm. They are human-form shapeshifters who can heal most injuries by bathing in fire. Flame reincarnate and remember past-life memories during initiation in fire.

**Literati**: Belonging to the god Philapo, Literati are among the least designed affiliates. Literati are more like a religious order than anything else: always male, they almost always take up the profession of teachers, philosophers, professors, researchers or administrators.

**Magicians**: Extinct thanks to the death of their god, Foex, Magicians once ruled large chunks of Uos. Magicians reincarnated like Flame.

**Merchants**: More a vocation than god affiliates, most Merchants conduct business independent of their god. However, Genis has a tendency to be extremely obsessive and becomes personally involved if a Merchant is in a field of his current obsession. They have no outward marks or body modifications.

**Nuns**: A new affiliation—less than a century and a half old—Nuns are a sisterhood of women organized into local orders that are more like artist's colonies than anything else. Nuns take vows as a "time out" from relationships, family, monetary obligations and work in order to grow as individuals.

**Shadow Dancers**: Affiliates of Aiena, Shadow Dancers often reside in a Cluster: a living space invisible to the naked eye in a sectioned-off part of the God Plain. They can become invisible.

**Higher beings not of the Pantheon:**

**Aerora** *(āy-ROAR-a):* The mother of gods, she was often referred to as "Mother Earth" in Ventris and Coterie cultures. Aerora has not been seen since she destroyed El at the end of the Crimson Era.

**Consorts, the**: In mythical times of the Ecru and Magenta Eras, five consorts came to Uos to carry on relations with Aerora. The consorts are the other parents of both Metacors and gods.

**Metacors** *(MEH-ta-cōrz)*: The elder children of Aerora, Metacors were giant creatures; intensely intelligent carnivores who considered humans tasty treats.

**The Pantheon:**

**Aiena** *(eye-EHN-ah)*: Youngest sister of Foex and Survjug, foster mother of Pelin and Elac. Aiena's affiliates are Shadow Dancers.

**Acia** *(AH-see-ah)*: Daughter of Survjug and Philapo, her affiliates are Nuns.

**Castasy** *(CAST-ih-see)*: Sister of Genis and Tarro, the wife of Resoan, mother to Elocu, Cencci and Tecnol.

**Cencci** *(sen-SEE)*: Daughter of Resoan and Castasy, twin sister of Tecnol.

**Elac** *(EH-lack)*: Twin brother to Pelin and adoptive father to Syche, his affiliates are the Phoe.

**Elocu** *(eh-lō-KŪ)*: Son of Resoan and Castasy.

**Foex** *(foyks)*: The oldest god, Foex managed to drink himself to death at the end of the Cobalt Era. His younger siblings are Survjug and

Aiena. His affiliates were the Magicians, who died shortly after their god.

**Genis** *(JEEN-is)*: The oldest of four—his younger siblings are Tarro, Castasy and Philapo—Genis is the ex-husband of Pelin and biological father of Syche. His affiliates are Merchants.

**Gundi** *(GUN-di)*: Son of Survjug and Philapo, older brother of Acia.

**Juste** *(joost)*: Currently in a threesome with Philapo and Survjug. She has a twin brother, Resoan, and a daughter, Kaja.

**Kaja** *(KAH-jah)*: Currently the youngest member of the Pantheon, she is a babe in arms, daughter of Juste and Philapo.

**Pelin** *(PEH-leen)*: Twin sister to Elac and mother of Syche, Pelin is a sensitive, nurturing goddess. Pursued by many gods, it was Genis who finally managed to woo and wed her; their subsequent fallout and divorce had major impact on human societies. Her affiliates are the Flame.

**Philapo** *(FIL-ah-pō)*: Philapo and his wife Survjug have recently entered into a threeway with Juste. He has three children: Gundi and Acia with Survjug, and Kaja with Juste. His affiliates are the Literati.

**Resoan** *(rih-ZŌ-an)*: Twin of Juste, husband of Castasy, and father of Elocu, Cencci and Tecnol.

**Survjug** *(SERV-judge)*: The oldest goddess, she is sister to Foex and Aiena, wife of Philapo, mother of Gundi and Acia.

**Syche** *(SĪGH-key)*: Daughter of Pelin. Her birth was severely affected by the advent of slavery.

**Tecnol** *(tek-NŌL)*: Son of Resoan and Castasy, twin brother of Cencci.

# Author's Notes

When I was younger, I wanted to be an archeologist. While I didn't think it was anything like Indiana Jones, one of my favorite cousins did underwater archeology in Scotland, Israel and China. She was so energetic. The jet setting, hours working on digs and even the cataloguing sounded fascinating to me.

Then, when I grew up, I took an introduction to archeology class at UC Santa Cruz. It was potshards. Weeks and weeks of potshards, endless slideshows of them. Archeology was tossed onto the growing pile of discarded career ideas; I received a passing grade in the class and moved on.

Many years later, my early dreams evolved a story about finding a real, live person in an archeology dig, holding onto... something. Something vital. That spark became "The Artifact of Foex." Better than potshards any day.

Another notable idea in these pages are the Flame. As a teenager, living in the suburbs within a nuclear family, I didn't know I was transgender. I just knew things weren't quite real, except inside my head. Back in the 1990s, there were no trans figures—role models or otherwise—in the media, or anywhere else near my radar. I had to make something up to get by.

Doyen was my first Flame character, emerging from a dream about an ancient, Sumerian-style orgy. She opened up a brand-new world to me. The ability to change gender whenever I wanted to? Sounded good to me.

Around the time when I took that ill-fated archeology course, I stumbled into the self knowledge that these feelings I had weren't just fiction, yet the idea of transitioning was utterly terrifying. What would people say? How do you even do these sorts of thing? My private fantasy life, having blow up to epic proportions, was soothing when matters grew too rough in the real world. Doyen, Journey, Knife and all the others kept me sane—a narrative that spanned thousands of years.

I eventually found gender transition to be tough but not impossible. Halfway through transition, I reached the end of Doyen's narrative inside my head. She had stopped running away, solving her long-term emotional problems. And so had I.

Learning to write these stories has been a journey unto itself. This is one of the results—I hope you like it. Big thank you's to Lon Sarver, D.M. Atkins and my aunt Lolly for the original inspiration.

—James L. Wolf

# About the Author

James L. Wolf is a Story Editor and author at Forbidden Fiction. He has often wished he could change from one gender to another on a daily basis, depending on his mood. As it is, he chose to change his pronoun only once, transitioning from female-to-male. James lives in the San Francisco Bay Area.

## Works by James L. Wolf

**Flame Cycle**

Chaining Flame
The Artifact of Foex

**Other Works**

Sacrifices to Ecstasy
Whisk Together
Divine Momentum
Consoling Psyche

# The Flame Cycle

The Flame Cycle tells the story of the Flame—shape-shifting sexual mystics chosen by the goddess Pelin—throughout the history of Uos. The Flame have been, at times, advisors to royalty, sex slaves, and the targets of genocide. The lives of the Flame are woven through more than four thousand years of history on the world of Uos. The Flame reincarnate eternally, recovering the memories of all their past incarnations in each new life.

James L. Wolf creates a vivid portrait of the history of this world as seen through the eyes of the Flame. They've seen Uos in all its glory and shame, through conflicts between gods and kings, revolutions in politics, culture, and science, and the most intimate details of human lives.

**Works in this series:**

Chaining Flame
The Artifact of Foex

# About the Publisher

*ForbiddenFiction.com* is a publisher devoted to writing that breaks the boundaries of original erotic fiction. Our stories combine intense sexuality with quality writing. Stories at ForbiddenFiction.com not only arouse readers through sensations, but also engage them emotionally and mentally through storytelling as well-crafted as the sex is hot.

ForbiddenFiction.com is also designed to be a social reading environment. You'll have fun even if just reading the latest post each day, yet you will have the chance for so much more. Readers and authors can be part of ongoing discussions of specific works and individual authors as well as more general topics.

Sign up for a FREE Membership today at ForbiddenFiction.com.

www.ingramcontent.com/pod-product-compliance
Lightning Source LLC
Chambersburg PA
CBHW061540170626
46811CB00001B/34

* 9 7 8 1 6 2 2 3 4 2 8 1 5 *